SEISHI YOKOMIZO (1902–81) was one of Japan's most famous and best-loved mystery writers. He was born in Kobe and spent his childhood reading detective stories, before beginning to write stories of his own, the first of which was published in 1921. He went on to become an extremely prolific and popular author, best known for his Kosuke Kindaichi series, which ran to 77 books, many of which were adapted for stage and television in Japan. *The Honjin Murders*, *The Inugami Curse*, *The Village of Eight Graves* and *Death on Gokumon Island* are also available from Pushkin Vertigo.

JIM RION is an American translator and writer living in the beautiful western Japan prefecture of Yamaguchi with his wife, son, and cats of unusual size.

THE DEVIL'S FLUTE MURDERS

PUSHKIN
VERTIGO

Seishi Yokomizo

Translated from the Japanese by Jim Rion

Pushkin Press
Somerset House, Strand
London WC2R 1LA

AKUMA GA KITARITE FUE O FUKU

Original text © Seishi Yokomizo, 1973, 1996
English translation © Jim Rion 2023

First published in Japan in 1973 by KADOKAWA CORPORATION, Tokyo.

English translation rights arranged with KADOKAWA CORPORATION,
Tokyo through JAPAN UNI AGENCY, INC., Tokyo.

First published by Pushkin Press in 2023

1 3 5 7 9 8 6 4 2

ISBN 13: 978-1-78227-884-9

Designed and typeset by Tetragon, London
Printed and bound by Clays Ltd, Elcograf S.p.A.

www.pushkinpress.com

CONTENTS

CHARACTERS

THE INVESTIGATORS

Kosuke Kindaichi	a private detective
Chief Inspector Daishi Todoroki	an officer with the Tokyo Metropolitan Police Department
Detective Degawa	a young, inexperienced detective
Chief Inspector Tsunejiro Isokawa	an old friend of Kindaichi's, based in Okayama

THE TSUBAKI HOUSEHOLD

Hidesuke Tsubaki	a former viscount, flautist and composer
Akiko Tsubaki née Shingu	Hidesuke's wife, Toshihiko Shingu's sister and Kimimaru Tamamushi's niece
Mineko Tsubaki	daughter of Hidesuke and Akiko
Shino	Akiko's lady's maid
Totaro Mishima	Hidesuke's ward and assistant
Otane	a housemaid
Doctor Jusuke Mega	a professor and medical practitioner

THE SHINGU HOUSEHOLD

Toshihiko Shingu — head of the family, Akiko Tsubaki's brother and Kimimaru Tamamushi's nephew

Hanako Shingu — Toshihiko's wife

Kazuhiko Shingu — son of Toshihiko and Hanako

THE TAMAMUSHI HOUSEHOLD

Kimimaru Tamamushi — a former count, uncle to Akiko Tsubaki and Toshihiko Shingu

Kikue — a former geisha and Tamamushi's lover

THE KAWAMURA HOUSEHOLD

Tatsugoro Kawamura — known as Uetatsu, father of Komako Horii and Haruo Kawamura, head gardener at Tamamushi's villa

Otama — Uetatsu's mistress

Haruo Kawamura — Uetatsu's son

Komako Horii née Kawamura — Uetatsu's daughter

Sayoko Horii — Komako's daughter

Gensuke Horii — Komako's husband and Uetatsu's former apprentice

The story you will read over the next thirty chapters is fiction. Some who read it may well be reminded of certain, similar incidents. I would like to assure everyone that those incidents have nothing at all to do with this story.

THE AUTHOR

CHAPTER 1

The Devil Comes and Plays His Flute

As I take up my pen to begin recording this miserable tale, I cannot help but feel some pangs of conscience.

To tell the truth, I do not want to write it. I have no pleasure in putting down in words all the misery it holds. The events I am about to describe are filled with such darkness and sadness, are so cursed and hate-filled, that not a word I write can possibly offer the faintest glimmer of hope or relief.

Even as the author, I cannot predict what the final sentence will be, but I fear that the relentless dread and darkness that precede it may end up overcoming the readers and crush their very spirits in its grasp. By their nature, stories of crime and mystery leave little enough good feeling in their wake, but this case in particular is so foul that even I feel it is perhaps too extreme. On that point, it seems that Kosuke Kindaichi and I are in agreement. When I asked him to provide me with his case files, he was hesitant about agreeing.

In truth, I should have written about this case before two or three other Kindaichi adventures I have published in the last few years. The reason it comes so late is that Kindaichi was reluctant to reveal its secrets to me, and that was mostly likely because he was afraid that unveiling the unrelenting darkness, twisted human relationships and bottomless hatred and resentment within might discomfit readers.

However, as the booksellers grow louder in their demands, I have resolved to offer up—with Kindaichi's full agreement—the whole story. Naturally, despite my protests over its writing, and the fact that it gives me no pleasure to do so, now that I have taken up the task I will give this case everything it deserves.

As I write this now, my desk is covered with all the various materials Kosuke Kindaichi provided me, but among them the two objects that stir my heart most are a photograph and a single-sided vinyl record.

The photograph is roughly postcard size. It features the half-length portrait of a gentleman in his middle years. When it was taken, the subject was forty-two years of age. (As an aside, all the ages given in this story are *kazudoshi* in the traditional way of counting—meaning the child is born one year old, and a year is added on every New Year's Day. The reason being, when this incident occurred, Japan had not yet adopted the Western style of figuring age.) Forty-two is, as they say, an unfortunate age for men. Perhaps it is the influence of that superstition, or thoughts of the horrific incident I am about to recount, but as I look on the picture, I sense a heavy shadow lying over the man's countenance.

His complexion is perhaps somewhat dark. His forehead is broad, and his hair parted neatly on the left. He has a proud nose, a furrowed brow and dark eyes that look as if they are troubled by some internal turmoil, a discord hidden forever within. His mouth is small, with lips on the thin side, though they do not give any impression of harshness. Rather, there is a femininity or weakness about them. Even so, his jaw is quite prominent, hinting that beneath the apparent fragility exists a powerful will that could burst forth with sudden violence if pressed. He wears a plain suit, but the bolo tie hanging down his chest reveals a certain artistic sensibility. So, the impression of the picture as a whole is that of an aristocratic, relatively handsome man, but who could he be? He is, in fact, a key figure in this horrific incident, the former viscount Hidesuke Tsubaki. It was just six months after this picture was taken that Tsubaki made his fateful disappearance.

The other item that draws my attention so powerfully is a ten-inch vinyl record published after the war by the G— record company, of a flute solo entitled "The Devil Comes and Plays His Flute".

The composer and flautist both are that same Hidesuke Tsubaki. In fact, the composition was completed, and the performance recorded just one month before his disappearance.

I do not know how many times I played this record before I began to draft this story. And no matter how many times I listen to it, I cannot help but be struck by the creeping dread that fills it. That is not solely due to any associations with the story I am about to recount. The melody itself is somehow eerie, with an unfamiliar distortion in the key. It transforms the basic melody, which is itself full of darkness, into something deranged and terrifying.

I am no kind of musical expert, but there is something about this piece that reminds me of Doppler's flute song "Fantaisie Pastorale Hongroise". However, while Doppler's work is rather merry, Tsubaki's "The Devil Comes and Plays His Flute" is filled with misery and heartbreak from start to finish. And the crescendo section is so frenzied that even an utterly tone-deaf listener like me cannot not help but feel my skin crawl, as if I were listening to the enraged, wretched shrieks of dead souls sounding out across the midnight sky. "The Devil Comes and Plays His Flute"…

The name is clearly a reference to the line "The blind man comes and plays his flute" from Mokutaro Kinoshita's poem, "Harimaya". However, this piece contains not a hint of the sentimentality that Kinoshita's poem does. Its sound is the shriek of the devil's flute, as the name so aptly indicates. It is a melody of bitter hatred, as if it were drenched in foul blood.

If even someone as unfamiliar with the music as I can feel that unnaturalness, I can only imagine the shock and horror that must have filled those connected to the incident each time they heard this piece begin playing out of nowhere after Tsubaki's disappearance. Given the eerie melody and the events I am about to recount, it is indeed quite easy to imagine.

"The Devil Comes and Plays His Flute"... Looking back, this piece of twisted music always held the key to unlocking the mysteries central to the horrors I am about to recount.

The year of these incidents, 1947, was one that kept the newspapers busy. I can recall at least three major events that caught the public's attention that year. The connections between two of them are already commonly known, but the strange thing is that the third, which everyone assumed to be totally unrelated, was actually deeply connected, if less openly.

I am referring here to the horrific Tengindo Incident, a crime which sent shockwaves throughout Japan.

Tengindo! I am sure that even just seeing the name written sends chills down the reader's spine. What happened was so shocking that surely everyone can recall it, even today.

There is likely no need to go into the details, which even the foreign press called "unprecedented in the history of crime", but I will still give a brief outline. It was 15th January of that year, at around ten o'clock in the morning. A lone man showed up at Tengindo, a jewellery shop famous even for luxurious Ginza. The man was around forty years old, his complexion somewhat dark. He gave the impression of an aristocratic, relatively handsome man, but on his arm was a city health officer band, and in his hand a bag like that a doctor would carry.

14

He went to speak to the manager in his office at the back of the shop and showed a business card from the Tokyo Department of Health, bearing the name Ichiro Iguchi. He claimed that someone in the area had been spreading an infectious disease, and that he would need all staff who had been in contact with customers to take some preventive medicine.

Later, some would argue that the manager and his staff had been too eager, in ways reminiscent of the war, to blindly obey a government official, but this man calling himself Ichiro Iguchi presented such a calm, reassuring demeanour and respectable character, that no one saw any cause for suspicion.

The manager immediately called his staff into the office. Since it was still too early to expect customers, and the staff were already done arranging the showcases, every member rushed in when called. The cleaning crew from the back even came too, and in the end thirteen people all told, including the manager, crowded into the room together.

When he saw that everyone was present, the monster calling himself Ichiro Iguchi took two bottles from his bag and mixed some of the contents from both into enough teacups for everyone. He then told them to drink. Totally unaware of the horrible fate that was only seconds away, those good folk did as they were instructed and drank the mixture. Within moments, they were afflicted with all the miseries of hell.

The cups had contained potassium cyanide. The staff fell like dominoes, collapsing where they stood. Some stopped breathing as soon as they did, while others lingered on, moaning and gasping in despair.

The monster Iguchi looked on his work, then gathered up his things. He fled the manager's office and grabbed a handful of the jewels on display, then disappeared into the bustling Ginza streets. The intense investigation that followed revealed that his theft was shockingly small, amounting to only some 300,000 yen in value.

The gruesome crime was discovered just ten minutes after the murderer fled, when a customer happened to come into the shop and, hearing unusual sounds and cries for help from behind a door in the back, looked inside. The discovery sparked an unprecedented commotion.

Of the thirteen victims, only three were saved. The other ten, I regret to say, passed away before the police or doctors could arrive. And so, that is what became known as the Tengindo Incident. The planning of this crime was so simple and effective that it could have gone down in the annals of crime history as a work of genius. However, the brutal, cold-blooded viciousness of it shocked the public like none other, even in those wicked days after the war's end.

And although the extreme nature of the crime at first suggested it would be a simple matter to find the murderer, this proved to be untrue. The police were unable to track him down, and so the incident took on an even greater power over the public mind.

Naturally, the police held nothing back. They followed every lead in trying to find the criminal, tracing his flight after the murder and even uncovering where the Ichiro Iguchi business card had come from. They were able to create a photo composite, based on interviews with the three surviving victims and two or three witnesses who saw him burst out of Tengindo, and used it to enlist the help of the public at large. The appearance of that composite during the manhunt helped put this case I write about in motion. It was edited and improved five times, and each time every newspaper in the country published it anew. All the various little tragedies that resulted are likely still fresh in the public mind.

The composite triggered a flood of letters and anonymous tip-offs to police. The sheer volume sent the police into chaos as they followed up on every letter that came in saying that "so-and-so in such-and-such village looks just like the picture". Even though they knew most leads would end up a bust, the detectives had to approach each one as if it were a real chance. They contacted all of the identified people to come in for questioning.

There were also quite a few cases where police officers on the street grabbed someone because he resembled the picture, which caused its own sort of trouble. This was not just in Tokyo, either. It was a nationwide frenzy.

This is where we will find the connection to the story I am going to relate in these pages.

As I wrote before, the Tengindo Incident took place on 15th January, and some fifty days later, on 5th March, the morning paper featured another story that caught the eye. It was a prelude to all the horrific things that followed.

This was all before Osamu Dazai wrote his work *Setting Sun*, about the decline of the aristocratic class after the war, so we did not yet have ready terms like "the sunset clan" or "sunset class" to describe these people, newly bereft of their noble privilege and falling into ruin. But, if we had, then I think it likely that this case would have been the first to see the term used.

The 5th March morning edition reported that Viscount Hidesuke Tsubaki had apparently vanished. This affair was the first public glimpse into the aristocratic class's sad fall, so of course the world was fascinated. Viscount Tsubaki had actually disappeared four days previously, on 1st March. At ten o'clock in the morning, the viscount wandered out of his house without a word of explanation to his family, and never returned. When he left, he wore a plain grey overcoat over an equally plain grey suit, and an old fedora on his head.

The family at first did not believe he had actually vanished. Or rather, they did not wish to believe it, so they waited for two days, then three. Of course, during that time they did try contacting various friends and family to try and track down his whereabouts, but they learned nothing. Finally, on the afternoon of the fourth day they filed a missing person's report with the police, and that was the first public hint of the tragedy to come.

There was no note, but from the viscount's reported attitude around the time in question, everyone felt the most likely explanation was suicide, so the police department issued a nationwide alert and had his picture published in the morning papers the next day. The picture they used is the same one that now rests on my desk.

Given the lack of a note, even if his disappearance was due to suicide, there was no hint as to his reasons. However, it was not difficult for people to imagine one.

The viscount had apparently lacked the vitality necessary to deal with all the changes and turmoil rocking Japanese society at the time. He was a gentle, somewhat delicate and polite gentleman, to such an extent that he seemed almost completely unequipped for daily life. He had held a middling position with the Ministry of the Imperial Household until the end of the war, but lost it when the ministry was scaled down and replaced with the Imperial Household Agency.

Some also said that the situation at his home was the reason for the disappearance.

The viscount's mansion in Azabu Roppongi survived the firebombing of Tokyo, but that fact ended up bringing him no end of misery. After the war, his wife's brother the Viscount

Shingu had moved onto the estate with his family after his own house burnt down, as did his wife's uncle Count Tamamushi and his mistress. Those around Tsubaki said that this situation was simply too much for the sensitive viscount's nerves.

The estate in Azabu Roppongi was Viscount Tsubaki's home; however, in point of fact the property remained in his wife Akiko's name.

The Tsubaki family was a noble one, and one of the most prominent of the old aristocratic lines, but it had produced no notable members since the Meiji Restoration of 1868, and although the family had received titles from the Imperial family, their yearly stipend had dwindled. In Hidesuke's youth they had been reduced to poverty, and he himself had struggled to maintain the basic appearance necessary for a man of his station. He had been saved by his marriage to a member of the Shingu family.

Akiko's family, the Shingus, were peers of the old feudal daimyo lineage rather than of the ancient court nobility, and even among the aristocracy, were famous for their wealth. And what is more, the Shingu family were backed by the even greater personage of Count Tamamushi. He was Akiko's maternal uncle and had been a leader of the House of Peers and a guiding force of the influential Kenkyukai parliamentary faction. He had never taken a ministerial role himself but had always remained a powerful political force in the shadows.

Hidesuke Tsubaki had often wondered why Count Tamamushi would assent to letting his darling niece marry a man such as him, and there were rumours that the count eventually came to regret the marriage, accusing the viscount of being an incompetent, impotent weakling who spent all his time blowing on a flute.

To a forceful, obstinate man like the count, someone like Tsubaki with no concerns for social influence or ambitions at all, must have seemed utterly ineffectual indeed. Yet when that same man looked on his nephew Toshihiko Shingu, who filled his life with liquor, women and golf, the count praised him as being a true figure of nobility. That should indicate just what kind of man Count Tamamushi was.

The wilful count and dissolute brother-in-law came into Viscount Tsubaki's house and began denigrating him as an incompetent almost immediately. Those who knew him spoke of how even the mild-mannered Tsubaki was pushed beyond the limits of his tolerance.

Putting all of that aside, when Viscount Tsubaki's whereabouts were still unknown and the newspapers still filled with the news, his record company saw the opportunity and attempted to cash in by releasing the recording of "The Devil Comes and Plays His Flute". As I have mentioned, that work was actually filled with great meaning, but no one at the time recognized the fact. What's more, as a particularly sombre flute solo, rather than a more accessible popular song, it was simply not very well received.

No one learned what had become of Hidesuke Tsubaki for nearly two months, although many were already certain of his suicide. After the war ended he had spoken often about death, and said that if he had to die, it would be best to do so quietly alone somewhere in the mountains, where no one would find his remains. Which, it seems, is what he tried to do.

On 14th April, forty-five days after Tsubaki left his family home, his body was discovered in the woods covering Mount Kirigamine in Nagano Prefecture. The police had made a preliminary identification based on his clothing and belongings, and a message was sent immediately to the house in Roppongi.

When word arrived, there was some dispute within the household over who would go to claim the body. The shock of his disappearance had weakened the viscount's wife Akiko terribly, and indeed she was not by nature particularly well suited to such things, so everyone decided that their daughter Mineko would go instead, and her cousin Kazuhiko said he would accompany her. He was Hidesuke's nephew, but on top of that he had also been the man's flute student.

Still, it would not do to send the pair alone, as they were much too young. Kazuhiko was twenty-one years old, while Mineko was only nineteen. They would need someone with more experience of the world to go with them. The family agreed that Kazuhiko's father Toshihiko would be best suited, but he himself was reluctant. He mocked his younger sister, saying that he would rather find a high-class prostitute or someone to play golf with, than go to claim his brother-in-law's body.

In the end, though, Akiko's insistence and the promise of a decent bit of pocket money for a night on the town convinced him to go. The three were also joined by young Totaro Mishima, the orphaned son of Hidesuke's friend, whom he had taken in after the war. In fact, it was he who dealt with all of the red tape when they arrived on the site, and did so very efficiently.

The body was autopsied and then taken for cremation in the town of Kamisuwa, near where it had been found, but what shocked everyone was that even though the surroundings and the inquest both suggested that Hidesuke had gone to his place of death and taken cyanide directly after leaving his home on 1st March, the body had barely begun to decompose. Naturally, his appearance was not quite what it had been when he was alive, but his daughter, nephew and ward were all three able to identify the corpse at a single glance. Presumably, that unusual preservation had something to do with the cold local climate where he was found.

CHAPTER 2

Viscount Tsubaki's Parting Note

Kosuke Kindaichi's lifestyle in 1947, the twenty-second year of the reign of the Showa Emperor, was a strange one.

He had been discharged from the army only the previous autumn, and without a home to return to had settled at the Pine Moon Inn, a *kappo ryokan*—a traditional lodging specialized in dining—in the Yamanote area of Omori, Tokyo. An old friend of Kindaichi's, Shunroku Kazama, had become a successful general contractor in Yokohama after the war, and he put his mistress in charge of the *ryokan*. Kindaichi ended up staying in a room there and settled down like he'd grown roots.

Luckily, his friend's mistress was a kind woman, and she took to looking after him like he was her own younger brother—though, in fact, she was the younger of the two. Kosuke Kindaichi was an energetic man of action when he was on a case, but the rest of the time he was as indolent as a cat. That meant he required quite a lot of care as a tenant, but the mistress never made a single complaint, and even went so far as to offer him a bit of pocket money. Kindaichi took full advantage of this and settled in like a stone in mud. As comfortable as he was, though, there were occasional difficulties.

One of these was that, as his reputation spread, more and more clients came to ask for help, both men and women. Even the men were often hesitant to visit him in his private rooms, but for older women in particular, it took quite a lot of courage to step alone through the door of that out-of-the-way *ryokan*.

Then, having mustered that bit of courage and gone through the gate, they found themselves in a small room in an isolated annexe building only about four and a half tatami mats in size, squeezed in with Kosuke Kindaichi. It was not a comfortable situation.

The visit that began this case was on 28th September 1947.

Kosuke Kindaichi sat across from a discomfited woman in that same small annexe room. She looked to be around twenty years old. She wore a pink cardigan sweater over a crêpe de Chine blouse with a black skirt. Her hair was cut short, and overall she was quite plainly dressed for a modern young woman.

It would have been hard to call her a beauty, with her prominent forehead over too-large eyes, and cheekbones and chin that were too small. On balance, her whole face seemed out of proportion. It made her look almost foolish, yet at the same time she gave off an aura of great pride. Her air of irritation was not unusual for Kindaichi's clients, who were often unhappy at being forced into such a position, but that didn't explain the dark shadow that seemed to envelop her whole body. They sat in silence.

He observed the woman closely, but from his guest's perspective it likely seemed he was just sitting there calmly puffing on his cigarette. She, on the other hand, sat uncomfortably. She seemed at a loss as to how best to break the silence, and occasionally fussed at her knees. After their initial exchange of greetings, Kindaichi waited for his guest to open up, while she seemed to be waiting for him to draw her into conversation. He was, sadly, not at his best at times like this.

Suddenly, the ash from his cigarette, grown long in the silence, fell from the tip. The woman stared at the fallen ash on the tabletop, her eyes wide in surprise.

"Um—" she started, just as Kindaichi let out a breath, and the ash puffed into the air.

"Oh!" she cried out, and pressed her handkerchief to one eye.

"Oh, no, I-I'm so sorry. Did it get in your eye?" Kindaichi hurriedly bent forward across the table.

"No, no…" The woman rubbed strongly at her eye once or twice, then quickly pulled her handkerchief away and gave him a small, chiding smile. The smile revealed charmingly discoloured teeth. For that moment, at least, the dark shadow wrapped around her seemed to lighten just a little.

Kindaichi rubbed at his shaggy head and said, "I-I beg your pardon. How clumsy of me. Is your eye all right?"

"Yes, it's quite fine, thank you," the woman said, her original pride restored. She was clearly straining to maintain a diplomatic tone, but at last they had found room to speak.

"So, you talked to Chief Inspector Todoroki at the police station, I hear?" Kindaichi asked.

"I did, yes."

"And he said you should come to me?"

"That's right."

"Well then, what can I do for you?"

"Oh, well…" The woman hesitated a moment. "My name is Mineko Tsubaki."

"Yes, you said that earlier."

"I'm sorry, of course you wouldn't realize from just my name. My father was Hidesuke Tsubaki. The Tsubaki who disappeared last spring?"

"A disappearance last spring…" Kindaichi muttered to himself for a moment, then his eyes widened. "You mean Viscount Tsubaki?"

"Yes, though he would no longer be a viscount, or anything else…" Mineko said, her voice cold, almost self-mocking, and she stared squarely at Kindaichi with wide eyes. He scratched furiously again at his tousled hair.

"Well, well, well… That's really something." Kindaichi frowned as he looked closely at the woman's face. "But what brings you to me now?"

"Yes, of course, that's… Well…" The dark shadow enveloping Mineko's body seemed to grow more intense, as did her aura of frustration. She twisted her handkerchief between her fingers in irritation and said, "I know that this story may sound silly, but for us, it's deadly serious."

She looked sharply at Kindaichi, and it was as if her over-large eyes were drawing him in. "I wonder if my father truly is dead."

Kindaichi gaped in surprise and jerked as if an intense shock had run through his body. He gripped the sides of the table as if to steady himself and asked, "Wh-why do you say that?!"

Mineko folded her hands primly on her knees and stared at him in silence. The shadow wrapped around her seemed to swell and billow like dark flames. Kindaichi took up his cup and sipped at the tea, long gone cold, to calm himself.

"From what I read about that case in the papers, they found your father's body in the mountains somewhere in Nagano, didn't they?"

"Yes, on Mount Kirigamine."

"How many days was that after he left your house, again?"

"It was the forty-fifth day."

"I see, so then the body must have been quite badly decomposed and hard to identify. But I thought the newspapers said he was clearly recognized as the Viscount Tsubaki."

"Oh, no, the body had barely decomposed at all. It was almost disturbing, how little it had."

"Then you viewed the body yourself?"

"Yes, I claimed his remains. My mother didn't wish to."

There was a hint of darkness in her tone when she said the word "mother" that made Kindaichi peer more closely at her face. Mineko seemed to notice that and lowered her gaze, her ears reddening, but soon looked up again. The blush receded, and the quiet shadow wrapped itself around her more tightly.

"At the time, then, you were certain the body was your father's?"

"Yes, I was," Mineko said, nodding. "I believe it even now."

Kindaichi narrowed his eyes at her in consternation. He started to say something, then had second thoughts, and said instead, "Were you alone at the time? Did no one else go with you?"

"My uncle and cousin were with me. And Mishima-san."

"Did those people know your father well?"

"Yes, of course."

"And did they also confirm that the body was your father's?"

"They did."

"So, after all of that," Kindaichi said eventually, his brow furrowed, "why has this doubt about your father still being alive come out now?"

"Kindaichi-san!" Mineko's voice grew suddenly emphatic. "I believed that body was my father's, and I still believe it to this day. But, even without any decay, the shape of his face was so different from when he was alive. Maybe it was all of the anguish and misery he endured before his suicide, or the pain after he took the poison, but I remember in that instant someone whispering that he was like a different person. I even felt it myself. So, later, when people started pushing me, saying perhaps the body wasn't my father's, even though I am absolutely convinced that it was, I couldn't help but feel shaken. And now, as his daughter, and the person who most closely examined his remains, when others see my uncertainty, of course they start to feel it, too. My uncle was so uncomfortable that he barely looked at Father's face."

Her tone grew dark again when she mentioned her uncle.

"Your uncle, that's…?"

"My mother's older brother. Toshihiko Shingu. He was also a viscount, before."

"So, then, your cousin would be his child?"

"Yes, his only son."

"I see. Now, did your father have any distinguishing marks on his body?"

"If he had, then there would have been no room for doubt."

Kindaichi nodded and went on. "Yes, I can see that. But who is it that started bringing all this up in the first place? Saying that the corpse wasn't your father's?"

"My mother." There was a coldness in her voice at this. It was so sharp, and so hard, that Kindaichi could not help the surprise showing on his face.

"Why would she do that?"

"Mother never believed that he killed himself. When we still had no idea if he was alive or dead, Mother never once thought it possible. She insisted that he was alive somewhere, in hiding. She seemed to be convinced he was dead for a time after his body was found, but before too long she stopped believing. She said we were all being fooled, and that the body wasn't his. She even started saying that he had used someone as a body-double and was still in hiding."

Kindaichi sat looking at her. Some unnameable emotion began to seethe deep in his gut, but he kept the unease to himself. "Surely, though, that's just your mother's love speaking?"

"No, no, not at all." Mineko spoke as if the words tore at her throat. "My mother is afraid of him. Afraid that he is alive, and that he'll come back someday to get his revenge…"

Kindaichi's eyes narrowed in disbelief. She seemed to feel she had said too much. The blood drained from her face, but she did not turn away or avert her eyes. She stared straight at him, as if defying his unbelieving gaze. The shadowy flames wrapping around her billowed higher.

Since the question had touched on marital issues, Kindaichi would not ask any more unless Mineko offered more on her own. Naturally, she hesitated to do so.

Kindaichi decided to change the subject. "I understand that your father left no note behind. So, your mother must have—"

"No, actually, there was a note," Mineko interrupted him.

Kindaichi was taken aback. "I'm sure that the newspapers all said there was no note!"

"It showed up much later. At the time, the fuss around my father's disappearance had settled, so when I found it, I kept it within the family. We didn't make it public out of worry it would set off more rumours and gossip."

Mineko took an envelope out of her handbag and handed it to Kindaichi. He saw that the front read "To Mineko", and the back "Hidesuke Tsubaki". The characters were written in a clean, delicate hand. It was, of course, already open.

"Where was it hidden?"

"It was in the pages of one of my books. I had no idea about it. Last spring, I rearranged my shelves and moved unneeded books or ones that I'd already read into storage. Then, in summer, I went to air them out and check for insects, and it fell out."

"May I read it?"

"Of course."

The letter said:

Dear Mineko,

Please, do not hold this act against me. I can bear no more humiliation and disgrace. If this story comes to light, the good name of the Tsubaki family will be cast into the mud. Oh, the devil will indeed come and play his flute. I cannot bear to live to see that day come.

My Mineko, forgive me.

There was no signature.

"I suppose there is no doubt that this is your father's handwriting?"

"None."

"But what does he mean by this 'humiliation and disgrace' he says can't bear? If he was talking about the loss of his title, then I can't see how that that would reflect on his house, since it affects the entire class of peers."

"No, that isn't it…" Her tone was biting. "Father was indeed concerned about such things, but that's not what he meant."

"Then, what…?"

"Father… my father…" Sweat began to bead unpleasantly on Mineko's forehead. Her breath grew heavy and fierce, as if she were possessed. "In spring, the police came and questioned my father as a suspect in the Tengindo murders."

Kindaichi once more gripped the edge of the table in shock. It was like someone had hit him with a hammer. He gasped and cleared his throat, struggling to find something to say.

However, before he could, Mineko spoke on in a sharp, haunted tone.

"In truth, the photo composite that they kept revising and publishing in the newspapers looked exactly like my father. It was… unfortunate. However… That is not what drew the police's attention to him. Someone sent them a letter tipping them off. I do not know who it was. But whoever it was, it is without a doubt someone in our household. Someone living at the estate, and within the Tsubaki, Shingu or Tamamushi families, I'm certain."

In that instant, Mineko's face appeared to Kindaichi like that of a terrible witch, and the dark shadow that lay across her seemed to burst into raging black flames.

CHAPTER 3

The Viscount's Mysterious Trip

As a suspect in the Tengindo murders, Viscount Tsubaki had been put through intense, repeated interrogations by the police. That fact came as no surprise to Kosuke Kindaichi. But who would ever have dreamed that a member of the aristocracy would be marked a suspect in such a terrible case!

Kindaichi felt a heavy weight settle deep in his stomach like a ball of lead when he thought about the cruel fate of that class in such painful decline.

"Th-this…" Kindaichi swallowed loudly. "This is the first I've heard of it. I remember that case very well, but the newspapers never mentioned… that."

"Yes, well, my father's position was still such that we were able to keep it secret. He was taken in for questioning over and over, though. And as a suspect, he was also shown to the surviving Tengindo victims for identification. That wasn't all. We in the family were also questioned about my father's whereabouts on 15th January, the day of the Tengindo Incident," said Mineko.

"I see, they wanted to check his alibi. But when was all of this?"

"Father's first interrogation was on 20th February."

"So, that would put it about ten days before his disappearance. Of course, you must have been able to prove his alibi right away?"

"Actually, no, we couldn't. We had no idea where Father was or what he was doing on 15th January. We still don't."

Kindaichi gaped in shock at that. Mineko's voice shook with emotion.

"I checked my diary entry for that day the moment the Tokyo police asked. I had written that Father had left on a trip to Ashi no Yu, a hot spring inn in Hakone, on 15th January. At the time he was working on a flute composition but had run into a block, so he said he was going to stay at Ashi no Yu for two or three days to work through it. He came home on the evening of the 17th, but of course we all just thought he had been exactly where he said. The police, though, said that they had contacted the inn and the staff found no record of his stay."

She twisted her handkerchief in her hands. "From there, it seems that Father refused to talk any more about what he had been doing during that period. Which, of course, upset the police even further and for a time my father was in terrible trouble."

"But in the end, they let him go, of course."

"They did. Their suspicion began to approach certainty, which apparently frightened Father so much that he finally revealed where he had been on the 14th and the 15th. It seems they were able to confirm his alibi, but it took almost a whole week."

"Where had your father been?!"

"I don't know. He refused to tell anyone in the family."

Kindaichi felt a flutter of nervous suspicion in his breast. What possible reason could a man have to hesitate in offering an alibi when under suspicion of a crime as serious as the Tengindo murders?

"Were there any special circumstances that would require such secrecy?"

"I simply can't imagine what they could be," Mineko said. Her voice was indignant. "Father was a frail-minded, or rather, a timid person. He was such a weak little man that even I found it irritating when I was a child. His only pleasure in life was playing the flute. I can't imagine a man like that could ever have a secret that terrible. But most of all…" Mineko's voice suddenly thickened with emotion. "From the middle of January, right around the time of that trip, he was acting… strangely."

"Strangely how?"

"He seemed deeply distressed, and whenever anything out of the ordinary happened, he would get so frightened."

"Frightened? Really?"

"Yes, but he'd been like that to some extent since the end of the war. I thought perhaps he had simply grown worse, but when I think about it now, it really was strange."

"It seems to hint at something happening to disturb him around the new year. Do you have any idea what that might have been?"

"Not really, it's just…"

"Just…? Just what?"

"Well, it's just that great-uncle Tamamushi came to live at the estate at the end of last year."

"Who is this great-uncle Tamamushi?"

"He's my mother's uncle, on her mother's side. His name is Kimimaru Tamamushi. He was a count until this spring."

"I see." Kindaichi readied a memo pad and fountain pen on the table and looked back up at Mineko's face. "You just said that whoever tipped off the police about your father must have lived at the estate. Why is that?"

"Because…" she began, before trailing off. The shadow wrapped around Mineko seemed once more to blaze up into pitch-black flames. "That's what Father told me. I can remember it clearly even now. It was 26th February, the day after he came home from being cleared of those terrible suspicions. Even after the police accepted his innocence, everyone at home was still frightened around him, and no one but I would even come close. I was the only one who comforted him. That evening, Father was in his study on the first floor. The sun had gone down, but he had no lights on. He was just sitting in his chair, staring blankly into space. The sight of him, so lonely there, is still vivid in my mind. I could find no words to comfort him. I went to his knee, and all I could do was weep."

Mineko's face twisted strangely, and she seemed about to break into tears. She did not, though. Instead, she spoke on, her eyes wide, "Father stroked my hair, and said to me, 'Mineko, there is a devil in this house. That is who wrote to the police about me.' Those were his exact words."

The shadow on her grew darker still. Kindaichi, though, was no longer surprised or confused by it. The secret to why she was shrouded in such darkness was becoming clearer by the moment.

"I was surprised, and looked up at him, asking him what he meant. He did not speak long, and his words were broken, hesitant. But basically, he said that the anonymous letter sent to the police included details about my father's comings and goings around the time the Tengindo Incident occurred. It also had, in detail, things that he had said, things that only someone who lived with us could have known."

Kindaichi felt a chill in his belly, as if something cold and clammy was crawling up his body from the floor. "Did your father say who it was?"

Mineko shook her head, her eyes shrouded.

"Was this simply something he suspected, or did he know clearly who had written the letter?"

"I think my father knew it clearly."

35

"And what about you? Can you think of anyone would do such a cruel thing?"

Mineko's lips twisted strangely. Her eyes flashed with anger.

"I am not certain. But, if you are looking for suspects, there are plenty I could offer. Starting with my mother…"

"Your mother?!"

Kindaichi gasped and stared at Mineko's face. The creeping cold brought another unpleasant shiver. She simply stared back at him.

He took up his pen and said, "I see. Then, let me just confirm everyone who lives at the estate with you. There are three families, correct?"

"That's right."

"Let's start with yours, then. So, your father was Tsubaki Hidesuke. How old was he?"

"Forty-three."

"Who else is there?"

"My mother Akiko, forty. But…"

"But what?"

Her face tightened in irritation.

"If you end up meeting my mother, I imagine you'll think I'm lying to you since she looks so young and beautiful. When she was very young, people said she was one of the most beautiful women in all the peerage, and even now she looks no older than thirty. For her, having a daughter as ugly as me must be unbearable. I wish it wasn't so."

Kindaichi looked at her, and started to speak, but immediately thought better of it. She did not seem the type to welcome empty compliments. He went on with his questions instead. "Then there is you. How old are you?"

"I am nineteen."

"Do you have any brothers or sisters?"

"No, none."

"Then it's a family of three. Do you have a butler or other household staff?"

"We used to, but those days are all over. Oh, but there are still three other members of the household."

"Who are they?"

"One is Shino. She is an old woman, maybe around sixty-two or sixty-three, who accompanied my mother from the Shingus when she married and has been with her for her whole life. She manages the household."

"She must be a very strong person."

"Yes, extremely. She still thinks of my mother as a child and refuses to refer to her as a lady now. She calls her 'child' or 'young mistress', and it seems to make my mother very happy."

Kindaichi thought he heard a note of sarcasm behind the words but ignored it.

"And the other two?"

"One is Totaro Mishima. I'd say he's about twenty-three or so. It seems that my father and his were friends in their school days. After he was discharged last autumn, he didn't have anywhere to go, and Father took him in. He has become very valuable to the house."

"Valuable in what way?"

Mineko blushed a bit, "Kindaichi-san, do you know how we survive now? We have to sell our things just to eat. But we don't know anything about that kind of business. Dishonest merchants would take such advantage of us. But when Mishima-san started visiting us, all of that went much more smoothly. He is quite good at that sort of thing. That and procuring food. He grew to be so useful that Father asked him to come live with us."

"He sounds admirable for such a young man, indeed. And the last one?"

"Our housemaid Otane. She's around twenty-four, and also much prettier than I."

Kindaichi once more ignored the bitter sarcasm in her voice, saying, "So, those are the six people in the Tsubaki household. What of the other two families?"

"The Shingus live in an annexe on the grounds. Their house burnt down in a bombing raid during the war, and they've been with us ever since. Uncle Toshihiko is forty-three, like my father. The family also includes aunt Hanako and their only son Kazuhiko. I don't know how old she is, but Kazuhiko is twenty-one."

"It's just the three of them? No housemaid or anyone else?"

"They don't have any servants." Mineko let out a sarcastic laugh at that, but immediately blushed, as if she'd realized how disrespectful it must sound. But when she raised her face again, her gaze was defiant.

"Kindaichi-san, I think it's probably better to get everything in the open in a situation like this. My uncle had been struggling financially long before his house burnt down, and he finally turned to my mother for help. The man has clearly never had to work or otherwise earn his own way in his life. He's shiftless and lazy, and determined to maintain his same old dissolute lifestyle. The way he sees the world is that everyone owes him what he wants, and it is only right that he should live a life of ease without having to work for it."

Kindaichi smiled and said, "Wasn't that a common way of thinking among the aristocracy?"

"I suppose that might have been true. My uncle is certainly a prime example. But it was no accident that he came to my mother for help. Mother's father died when she was fifteen years old. He had doted on her and left her far more in his will than he did my uncle. Mother also inherited quite a fortune from her own maternal grandfather, so she is quite wealthy. Everyone has been very generous to her, you see, because of her beauty. Mother brought all of that wealth with her when she married into the Tsubaki family, but from my uncle's perspective that is unfair. When he'd used up all of his own money, naturally he turned his gaze to Mother's. That is one more reason my father hesitated to protest when my uncle's family and great-uncle Tamamushi showed up. Father was always so weak and isolated. They treated him like he had come begging to join their family, rather than Akiko marrying into his."

Her tone grew angry as she spoke. Kindaichi ignored this as well and asked, "And is the former count Tamamushi alone?"

"No. He has a very pretty assistant named Kikue-san. I think she's around twenty-three. Of course, she is more than just an assistant."

Kindaichi understood immediately. "How old is your great-uncle?"

"I think he's turning seventy soon."

"And did he not have any other family to go to, either?"

"Oh, no, the Tamamushi family has a very respectable heir. There are also lots of other children in the family, but great-uncle is so arrogant and selfish that no one wants anything to do with him. And yet, Mother respects him very much."

Kindaichi looked down at the list of the ten people discussed, which read:

Hidesuke Tsubaki	43
Wife Akiko	40
Daughter Mineko	19
Lady's Maid Shino	62 or so
Totaro Mishima	23 or so
Housemaid Otane	23 or so

Toshihiko Shingu	*43*
Wife Hanako	*40?*
Son Kazuhiko	*21*
Kimimaru Tamamushi	*70*
Mistress Kikue	*23 or so*

He showed it to Mineko, and asked, "So, do you believe that any of these people could have sent that letter to the police?"

She looked over the list. "No, not all of them. I don't see what reason Mishima-san, Otane the maid or Kikue-san would have to do so, and I can't believe that aunt Hanako or Kazuhiko would. Aunt Hanako is so kind. But as for the other four—my mother, Shino, uncle Shingu or great-uncle Tamamushi—any one of them could have done it."

"In other words, those people all disliked your father."

"No, they didn't dislike him. It was worse than that. Those people despised my father."

Mineko was almost gnashing her teeth in suppressed rage.

"Uncle Shingu and great-uncle Tamamushi considered him a complete incompetent. And my father, quiet man that he was, never said a word against them, no matter what they did to him. Their greatest pleasure became to taunt and bully him, to cause him all kind of trouble. They made a toy of him. Especially uncle Shingu because he is a man of no character himself." Mineko spoke sharply, her tone so harsh Kindaichi almost expected blood to start pouring from between her teeth.

He stared closer, his expression full of interest, and asked, "And did your mother join in?"

"No, she was not quite so bad."

Now, Mineko's tone grew sombre.

"Mother's not a malicious person. She's in many ways like a child, really, and great-uncle Tamamushi has a lot of influence over her. She's instantly swayed by the things he says and does. And because he treated Father like nothing more than a dog or cat, Mother soon took to ignoring him as well. And now, she regrets it. No, I think it's more fear than regret. She's as frightened as a toddler, worrying that Father will return to get revenge on her."

"I see, and that's why she's so immersed in this fantasy that your father is still alive."

"Yes, exactly, but things would be better if it were still just a fantasy. Kindaichi-san… Mother saw my father only recently."

"She did? When, where?!" Kindaichi stared in shock at the girl. Her face once more took on a witchy look.

"It was just three days ago, on the 25th. Mother went to Togeki theatre with Kikue-san and Otane-san. Their seats were near the stage. During the interval, they were looking around the theatre, and there, sitting in the front row of the balcony, was my father. Ever since, it's like my mother has lost her reason. Kikue-san and Otane-san were terrified, too…"

"So, the other two both agree that is was your father?"

"Yes, in fact, Kikue-san was the first to notice. She's the one who told Mother and Otane-san."

"Did they do anything to check and make certain that it was your father?"

"They were far too unsettled. Kikue-san and Otane-san both said they just didn't have the courage at the time. They said when the man noticed them looking, he slid down in his seat, and when they finally did work up the courage to go see, he had vanished."

When she finished this sentence, Mineko looked into Kindaichi's eyes as if gauging his reaction. Anxiety spread through the depths of his spirit like a cloud of black ink. "What happened then?"

41

"Now, they've decided to hold a divination tomorrow evening at our house."

"A divination, you say?" Kindaichi's eyes widened at this sudden turn in the conversation. However, Mineko went on, her expression unchanged.

"That's right, we are going to try to find out if Father is truly alive or dead through a divination. Oh, that's right, I almost forgot! Kindaichi-san, could you please add one more name to your list?"

"Whose?"

"Jusuke Mega. He is around fifty-two years old. He's a professor and practitioner of medicine and has been caring for my mother since before she married my father. And no, there's nothing particularly wrong with my mother, she just tends to think there is. And so, Doctor Mega is always coming out to the house and has become like a member of the household. He's going to be performing the divination."

That caused Kindaichi's eyes to widen even further. However, Mineko did not seem to notice anything odd in what she was saying.

"It really is all the rage these days. A few local ladies get together at our house fairly often for sessions with the doctor. To be honest, the reason I came here today is, I was hoping you would come and join us tomorrow evening."

When the conversation came back around to the matter at hand, Kindaichi looked harder into Mineko's eyes. He leaned forward a little, and asked, "So, you think something might happen tomorrow?"

"No, not particularly. I've never really thought much of divination and such. It's just, if you come tomorrow, then you'll get a chance to see all the people on that list in one place and really observe them. Please, Kindaichi-san," Mineko's voice grew suddenly emphatic. "I've been feeling so anxious lately. When it was only my mother believing that Father might be alive, I could deal with it. She's always been somewhat irrational like that. But, if she actually did see someone who looks just like Father, that changes things. It's possible for people to resemble each other, I know, so it might just have been a coincidence. But, thinking of it another way, I began to wonder if it was too much of a coincidence. I mean, with Mother convinced that he's still alive, isn't it too much of a coincidence for her to see someone who looks just like him? I'm starting to worry that someone has a hidden plan at work. And when I think of it that way, then it also strikes me that there's something odd about how my mother's fantasy about Father still being alive started. My mother is very sensitive. She's very suggestible. I'm starting to think that someone could have been manipulating her into thinking that way. And if so, then why is whoever it is doing this? That is what frightens me."

Mineko looked at Kindaichi with haunted eyes, and said, "That's why I went to consult Chief Inspector Todoroki, who had been in charge back when my father was a suspect in the Tengindo murders, and he told me that you would be more qualified to help me. And so…"

And so, that is what brought Mineko to Kosuke Kindaichi.

CHAPTER 4

Divination

The estate of former viscount Hidesuke Tsubaki was in the upscale district of Azabu Roppongi, on the right going up the slope from the Roppongi intersection towards Kasumi district. It spread out over 1,200 *tsubo*, or around 4,300 square feet of land. The area had suffered terrible damage during the war, but the Tsubaki residence was strangely untouched. In 1947, when reconstruction was still just getting started, the huge *hinoki* cypress and oak trees on the grounds stood out nakedly in the surroundings.

Before the bombing, the grand old houses of grand old families, home to Viscount So-and-so or Count Such-and-such, had filled this area as if they had sprouted from the soil, and Hidesuke Tsubaki's house was a perfect example. The estate had originally belonged to Akiko's maternal grandfather and had been passed down to her after his passing. The buildings included a two-storey house in the Western style popular in Japan's Meiji Period, or the late nineteenth century, with an attached traditional Japanese one-storey house, and another one-storey Japanese-style house set apart but attached by a walkway. This last was built new as a home for her mother on Akiko's marriage.

When Hidesuke Tsubaki married her, both of his parents were still alive but they weren't allowed to live on the estate. Akiko brought her own mother with her. Even though Akiko was officially a part of the Tsubaki family on the family register, in truth Hidesuke was essentially treated like an adoptee into the Shingus. Akiko's mother passed away before the war, and now her place had been taken by the former count Tamamushi and his lover Kikue.

There was one more building on the Tsubaki family estate, an uneven blend of Japanese and Western architecture found in a distant corner of the grounds. This annexe had once been the home of a servant couple and had also served as an office for Akiko, the house's official owner and manager, but now it had been taken over by former viscount Shingu and his family.

The story picks up at around 8 o'clock on the evening of 29th September 1947, the day after Mineko's visit to Kindaichi.

Kindaichi sat in the spacious, old-fashioned drawing room of the Tsubaki manor opposite a rather peculiar character.

The man looked to be in his early fifties and was shabbily dressed in a tattered morning coat and a crooked tie. His face, wide and flat as the back of one of the Heike crabs of the inland sea, was half hidden behind a great unruly beard, but rather than having the aura of a tired old man, he seemed bursting with terrible energy. And despite his apparent age, his rounded body was still firm, while his skin fairly glistened with oil. His physical appearance was overall quite unpleasant. This was the central figure of the evening's proceedings, Doctor Jusuke Mega.

Kindaichi was answering the man's questions.

"Oh, I wouldn't call myself an aficionado of these sorts of things, but I do have some interest, yes. But this is the first I've ever heard of sand divination, I think you called it?" Kindaichi said. He was dressed in the same worn-out kimono gown over worn-out *hakama* trousers as ever and held his crumpled, shapeless hat in his hands. He had forgotten to hang up the hat at the door and so was forced to carry it around with him.

"Oh, ho, well, this is not exactly what I'd call my own discovery, of course. Rather, it's an ancient form of divination used from days of old in China that I have, you see, improved in my own way. You'd be surprised how accurate it is!"

"You must have done a lot of research."

"Oh, yes, yes, for over ten years now. I spent a bit over a year in Peking around the start of the second war with China. That's when I first learned it, but then, you know, after that I studied this and that."

"Do they just call it sand divination over there?"

"Oh, no, over there it has names like *keiboku* or *fukei*. I reckon you could say it's a lot like *kokkuri-san* table-turning in Japan, but it's much deeper, indeed. Anyway, boy, did you really go to the same school as Kazuhiko-san?"

Doctor Mega's great glistening eyes stared at Kindaichi, who stuttered out in reply, "Y-yes, I-I did, that's right!" He hurriedly changed the topic. "Anyway, when does the divination get started?"

"When the blackout hits," said Mega, his eyes now filled with cold mirth.

"I beg your pardon?"

"That's right. Akiko-san's a true mystic. She feels it works best when the whole house is dark. Of course, I can't read the signs in the dark, so I'm having them put in a rechargeable lantern. The half-hour emergency blackout's scheduled for half past eight, so it won't be long now."

Anyone who was in Tokyo in 1947 likely remembers well the strained power supplies and the frustration of dealing with the scheduled blackouts that went district by district to help ease the load on the power plants. It seemed that the evening's ceremony would take advantage of the district's planned blackout.

46

Just as Doctor Mega took out a large pocket watch to check the time, a young man poked his head in from the hallway and said, "Doctor, we've finished most of the preparations, but could you come and check?"

"Oh, sure, sure, I can do that."

The doctor stood up with a grin, but suddenly seemed to recall the guest. "If you don't mind, Kindaichi-san, I'll go on ahead."

"Oh, of course, please do."

"Mishima-san, did you remember to prepare the lanterns?"

"Yes, I asked Otane-san to take care of both."

When Kindaichi heard the name Mishima, he took a closer look at the young man. He was tall and well built, with pale features. He was not particularly handsome but had a cheerful demeanour and seemed overall quite a charming young man. He gave Kindaichi a short bow of greeting and followed Mega out. As Kindaichi watched them leave, he noticed that the doctor shuffled along on terribly bowed legs.

Kindaichi took out his own watch, and saw it was exactly twenty past eight.

The blackout would be starting soon, but where was Mineko? When Kindaichi had arrived, she'd rushed to the entryway and shown him into the drawing room, where she'd introduced him to Doctor Mega. Then, she had hurried off again, saying she had to inform her mother of their guest and had never returned.

Kindaichi took out his handkerchief and mopped his brow and fanned himself with his crumpled hat. It was a terribly hot, muggy evening, one to raise a sweat even when you were just sitting quietly. It would likely rain soon. He sat in silence, vaguely pondering the weather. He heard a light tread in the hall, then a middle-aged man entered the room. He came to an abrupt halt when he saw Kindaichi.

47

This must be Toshihiko Shingu, Kindaichi thought. The man was fairly tall, but his skin had an unhealthy sallow look. He seemed somehow both terribly arrogant and terribly timid at the same time. The wide expanse between his nose and slack lips gave him a dull, vacant look. Shingu stared at Kindaichi with suspicion for a moment, but when Kindaichi stood to greet him, he jerked back in fright, then rushed from the room.

Well, well, sir, it seems you're a shy one, Kindaichi thought.

As he sat in bemused silence, he could hear Shingu speaking somewhere in the house, "Hey, Mineko, who the hell's that weirdo in the drawing room?"

His voice was thick and harsh. Kindaichi couldn't hear her response, but after a moment Shingu went on, "What, Kazuhiko, he went to your school? That guy?! You shouldn't just bring any old creep home like that. You've got to be more careful!"

It seems he doesn't trust me at all. What an impression I must have made! Kindaichi smirked in self-mockery, and just then Mineko came in, accompanied by a young man of about the same age. The young woman's expression was indignant.

"I do beg your pardon. Kindaichi-san, here is Kazuhiko-san," she said curtly.

Kindaichi was immediately struck by how little Kazuhiko looked like his father.

"Kindaichi-san, I hope my father didn't say anything too rude," the boy said, his expression one of aristocratic chagrin.

Kindaichi amended his assessment, thinking how lucky it was how little Kazuhiko resembled his father. He wasn't as tall as the older man, but was well proportioned, and had much more refined features. However, a dark shadow seemed to lie over his youthful spirit, most likely cast by all the tragedy that had befallen this family since the Viscount Tsubaki's disappearance.

"Oh, no!" Kindaichi said, smiling. "Not at all. It seems I startled him before I could offer a proper greeting, though, and he left. I suppose he must think me quite odd, ha!"

Kazuhiko's cheeks flushed in shame. Mineko frowned and shrugged her shoulders.

"Uncle is always like that. A big man when no one's around, but even at his age he's too shy to so much as speak to strangers."

Just then, the sound of rustling silk came from beyond the door, and Mineko jerked.

"Oh, here's Mother!" she gasped.

However, all warmth was gone from her voice, and Kindaichi remained seated, frowning, as he turned towards the door.

And so it was that he caught first sight of the widow of Viscount Hidesuke Tsubaki. There was such strangeness in that first impression that Kindaichi could not shake it off for the longest time. Nothing that Mineko had told him about her mother had been an exaggeration. The woman standing there, her whole face alight with a smile, seemed far too young, too delicately beautiful, to have a grown-up daughter like Mineko. She was full figured in proportions perfectly matched to her beauty, shaped like that of a porcelain *Ichima* doll. Her rounded cheeks held childlike dimples, and she was dressed in a vibrantly coloured *komayori* silk kimono with an *obi* sash worked in thick thread of gold. If he hadn't known better, he would have assumed she was another daughter of the family. Even as this vision of elegant beauty dazzled the eye though, Kindaichi could not help feeling a creeping, unhealthy sensation work across his body at the first sight of her.

Akiko was certainly beautiful. However, it was the beauty of an artificial flower. She seemed as hollow as a woman in a painting. Akiko's smile filled her whole face. It was a dazzling, beautiful smile. However, it was one that someone had taught her to make, not one of genuine feeling. Her eyes were pointed at Kindaichi, but they seemed to actually be looking somewhere else, somewhere far away.

"Mineko-san," Akiko said, cocking her head to one side coquettishly. When he heard her voice, Kindaichi once more felt that dreadful crawling sensation. It was a saccharine voice, sweeter and higher than a child's. "Is this the guest you and Kazuhiko-san invited? Why didn't you introduce him to your mother?"

"If you'll excuse me," Kazuhiko said, and slid past Akiko out of the room, as if he couldn't stand to be there any longer. Mineko watched him go with dark, angry eyes, but immediately stepped next to her mother, took her hand and led her over to Kindaichi. He shot up from his seat.

"Mother, allow me to introduce you. This is Kosuke Kindaichi. He studied at the same school as Kazuhiko and is very interested in divination. So, we invited him to join us tonight. Kindaichi-san, this is my mother Akiko. Oh, I am so sorry, but I have something I need to do in the other room. If you'll excuse me, Mother," Mineko said in a rush, then lowered her eyes, and nearly ran from the room.

"Oh, that child!" Akiko said, furrowing her brow in a purely artificial manner. "She stomps about like a boy. Girls these days are so ill mannered. No matter how often I tell her so, she simply refuses to listen!"

Then she turned back to the guest, her movements full of practised grace, and said, "Kindaichi-san, please won't you sit down?"

He could not help but feel perplexed by her offer. The hands of the clock were nearly at half past eight, when all the lights were scheduled to go out. Then, he would be trapped in the pitch-dark with this woman… The very thought made Kindaichi break out in a cold sweat.

"Yes, well, I think I prefer to stand. Don't you think, Lady Akiko, that it's about time for us to head for the divination?"

"I'm sorry, the what? Oh, yes, of course, that's why you're here, isn't it? Please, Kindaichi-san," said Akiko, her face suddenly darkening, "tell me, what do you think? Is my husband truly dead? No, no, it's all a lie. I'm certain he is still alive somewhere. After all, I saw him just recently. Please, Kindaichi-san…"

Here, Akiko shivered with her whole body, like a child might. "I'm so frightened! What shall I do? I know that he is out there, waiting for his chance to get revenge on us all!" Akiko's fear was clearly not an act, nor even exaggerated. She truly did believe what she said, and it terrified her.

At the same time, even as she talked about fear and revenge, her whole body radiated an unspeakable aura of sensuality. It was so far beyond ordinary experience that it became incomprehensible, grotesque, even horrifying.

As Kindaichi grew accustomed to the powerful aura rolling off her like the bewitching scent of some elfin blossom, he found himself feeling more pity than desire.

"Lady Akiko, can you tell me why you think that to be true? What could your husband want with revenge?"

"It is because I was so bad. My husband was so quiet and good that I found myself treating him poorly. Kindaichi-san, isn't it just the scariest thing of all when quiet, good people finally do something? I wonder if maybe he really was behind the Tengindo murders…"

"Oh!" Kindaichi was so taken by surprise he gasped.

"Lady Akiko, is this where you've been?" A beautiful young woman came in just then, dressed in a scarlet evening gown and pearls. She was thin, tall and graceful.

"Yes, Kikue-san, did you need something?" Akiko seemed unhappy at the interruption.

"We're about to get started. Could you please come along?"

"Yes, I'll be right there. Kikue-san, I was just asking Kindaichi-san about my husband. I was wondering if he might actually have been the Tengindo murderer."

Kikue glanced at him before answering, "I'm sure you were, but you'll have time to talk all about that later. Right now, it's time for the divination. Come along, we should be going now, right?" She placed a hand gently on Akiko's back, then turned to Kindaichi. "Kindaichi-san, this way, please."

"Oh, yes, after you." Kindaichi wanted to take a closer look at this Kikue, but just then, the lights went out.

"Oh, dear. I should have brought a torch."

"Kikue-san! Kikue-san, I'm frightened!"

"It's all right, Akiko-san. I'm right here with you. And so is Kindaichi-san."

"Don't leave me, Kindaichi-san... Stay with me! I... I..."

"It's all right. I'm right here. I'm not leaving."

Standing stock-still in darkness so complete he couldn't see his own nose, Kindaichi was overcome with foreboding.

Mineko had been right to be afraid. Someone could easily take advantage of the fantasy that had taken hold of this delicate soul to plan any kind of terrible crime. And there in that darkness, the hidden plan was moving inevitably forward.

"What was that?!" Akiko suddenly cried out, and the rustle of her clothing filled the darkness.

"What's the matter?"

"Someone... Someone is walking on the first floor! In my husband's study!"

Kikue stood quietly for a moment, then said, "Akiko-san, you're hearing things. Who would be on the first floor now? Did you hear anything, Kindaichi-san?"

"No, nothing at all."

"No, no, someone just left his study. I heard the door close. And then footsteps!"

But then, finally, Otane brought a torch, and Kindaichi forgot all about the possible footsteps. "Forgive me. The blackout caught me by surprise, and it slowed me down. Our clock seems to be running late."

Akiko seemed to calm down with the arrival of light. Kikue immediately took the lead, saying, "Thank you, Otane-san. Now then, my lady, let us go. Kindaichi-san, if you will?"

Kikue led them through the hallways. It was too dark to get a look at the state of the house, but it seemed the divination room was deep in the back. On the way, Mineko caught up with them with another torch.

"What a shock it was, the lights going out all of a sudden. Our clock must be five minutes slow."

Soon, the group reached the divination room.

"After you, Kindaichi-san…"

"Thank you…" He hesitated a moment. He realized that he was still holding his crumpled, sweat-stained hat.

"Ahem. After you, Kindaichi-san?" Kikue said again, and he gave up. He tossed his hat towards a table next to the door, half hidden in the gloom, and stepped into the dim room.

CHAPTER 5

Kaendaiko—The Flaming Drum

That evening, the room where Doctor Mega oversaw his eerie divination would become the scene of a bloody locked-room murder. As a place of such import, I will spare a few words here to describe it in detail.

The Western-style room was large, covering about eighteen tatami mats, or thirty-nine square yards. It was long and narrow, with a thick oak double-door opening onto the hallway that could be barred from the inside. Just above that door was a long ventilation window, or *ranma*, extending the width of the door and fitted with four panes of glass, two of which could be slid left and right to open it. The window was only about six inches high, so even if the glass were removed, no one could fit their head through, much less their whole body. The entire front opposite the entrance was made up of windows, all double-paned, with the outer windows secured behind metal shutters.

This room had been the vanished Viscount Tsubaki's studio. He came here to compose and perform whenever he had a free moment. Thus, he had chosen this room because it was set away from the drawing room and the bedrooms, and the walls were soundproofed enough that even if, say, someone were to have a minor fight inside, it would be no surprise if everyone else in the house remained unaware.

However, that evening when Kikue guided Kosuke Kindaichi into the room, the interior was vastly different. He never would have known just how big it was if the crime hadn't brought him back inside. The reason was that heavy black curtains hanging from the ceiling concealed its depth in three directions, giving no hint at what lay behind.

Inside the curtains was the space of about eight mats, or seventeen square yards, in size. A rechargeable battery-powered emergency lantern hung from the ceiling, and the dim, narrow circle of light spilling from beneath its shade fell on a large round table. Members of the three families, the Tsubakis, Shingus and Tamamushis, sat gathered around it in silence.

Before Kindaichi could observe the people in detail, though, his attention was drawn to a bizarre arrangement of items on the round table.

The table was topped with what looked to be a shallow circular ceramic plate about four feet across, which was covered in fine white sand carefully smoothed over. Above that was a nearly indescribable contraption. It consisted of another shallow round plate some four inches across, with five delicate sticks of bamboo radiating outward. The five sticks protruded regularly like the points of the star, projecting another four inches from the edge of the ceramic plate. About six inches in from the ends of the bamboo sticks, five more thin bamboo sticks pointed down to serve as legs, holding the plate about a foot above the surface of the sand. The five legs created the points of a perfect pentagon as they held the plate steady.

From the centre of the upper plate hung a metal cone about an inch and a half long, point down, just touching the sand. The cone dangled from rails fixed to the bottom of the bamboo radials and the plate so that even the subtlest of vibration on the sticks would set it to moving, where it would draw upon the surface of the sand. So, this must have been the divination, what Doctor Mega said was called *fukei* or *keiboku*. The plates, bamboo radials and bamboo legs were all painted a shade of crimson often seen in Chinese decorations.

And so, enough of the unusual contraption, let me now turn my pen to describe the people around the sand divination table that evening.

Seated facing the door was the man leading the ceremony, Doctor Mega. On the curtain behind him was an ink drawing on Chinese paper that appeared to be of a Daoist immortal, or *sennin*. Later, Kindaichi learned that this *sennin* was called Kasen, and the doctor called upon her power when performing his divination. With that mystical picture hanging behind him and his own coarse visage, Doctor Mega himself took on the look of Gama Sennin, the legendary immortal hermit who worked magic through a toad familiar.

From this toad wizard sitting in the middle, to the right as Kindaichi saw it sat Akiko while to the left sat an old man with a face as white as bleached cotton. Kindaichi knew at first glance that this must be Kimimaru Tamamushi, former count, leader of the House of Peers and a guiding force of the powerful Kenkyukai parliamentary faction. All the many disappointments during and following the war must have dampened the former count's once formidable vitality, but even so his eyes held a gimlet sharpness and cold ruthlessness that seemed entirely inhuman. His skin, far too smooth for his age, was a dull eggshell white, although a large dark age-spot on his right temple spoke to his advanced years. Even so, he was well groomed with cleanly trimmed beard, and as he sat comfortably in a kimono of glittering fabric with a black scarf around his neck, he gave off the aura of a true aristocrat.

Next to the former count Tamamushi was Toshihiko Shingu, and next to him sat a quiet-seeming woman of around forty in a black dress, who must have been his wife Hanako.

Hanako Shingu gave an impression the very opposite of Akiko's. The two women were roughly the same age, but compared to Akiko, Hanako seemed at least ten years older. She was neither as beautiful as Akiko, nor as peculiar, but was the perfect image of a woman in her middle years, with a calm, reserved manner, a full figure and intelligent, clear eyes. And yet, it took only a glance to get the impression that her life was one filled with inexorable weariness. When Kindaichi compared her to Toshihiko, dulled by his profligate lifestyle, sitting next to her, he could not help but feel a touch of pity.

Now, next to Hanako was their son Kazuhiko, and then came Totaro Mishima. Those were the five people sitting to the left in a line extending from Kindaichi to Doctor Mega himself.

As for the right side, as I said before, Akiko was directly beside the doctor. Next to her sat an old woman who was as ugly as any in the world. This must have been Shino, the senior lady-in-waiting who had accompanied Akiko here when she left the Shingu household.

Ugliness of such purity and extent is actually not unpleasant. Indeed, it becomes a kind of art at that point. The corrosion of age seemed to have washed all marks of shyness or vanity from her expression, and she stood unabashed in front of guests as if having forgotten her own ugliness, even putting it on display, making it an object of awe. In a way, this woman seemed to have left some elements of human weakness behind.

Next to Shino sat Mineko, and then came Kikue, making up the four people to Kindaichi's right. Otane, the maid, did not join them.

However, these people were not all present at the moment

Kindaichi entered the room. The slow clock meant that the blackout had come earlier than expected, and it ended up taking everyone quite some time to get situated.

When Kindaichi arrived with Kikue, Akiko, and then Mineko coming after them, the former count, the lady-in-waiting Shino and Toshihiko's wife Hanako were already waiting in the room, looking bored and impatient.

Doctor Mega came in soon after Kindaichi's group arrived, rudely buttoning up his trousers and shuffling along on those bowed legs of his.

"Good, good, we're about ready. Welcome. I thought we had some more time, so I visited the toilet, but then the lights went out. That was a shock, I tell you. Outrageous!"

The doctor muttered as he shuffled to his seat, but no one offered a laugh or even a nod in reaction. They all sat as stone-faced as the sphinx.

Just a step behind him, Kazuhiko and Totaro Mishima came in together. Kazuhiko went to his mother's side without a word, while Totaro set another emergency lantern on the floor, muttering about the clock. It seemed he had brought a spare in case the lit lantern ran out of battery.

"Doctor, Otane-san said she forgot which lantern she had charged today. So, this one," he said, looking up at the lantern hanging from the ceiling, "might go off in the middle of things. What should we do?"

"Oh, that's fine. If it goes out, it goes out. We'll deal with it then. So, then, is this everyone?"

"No, I'm sorry, my husband..." said Hanako, trailing off.

"Oh, right, Shingu-san still isn't here. That one's always late. Just like a true lord, never in a hurry. Ga hahaha!"

As this Gama Sennin sat laughing like a toad himself, Toshihiko Shingu came in with a dark, unhappy look on his face. He sat between Tamamushi and Hanako. Gama Sennin settled down and ran a hand up his face.

Finally, everyone was gathered.

With the eleven people packed into the room, there was a bit of confusion as everyone settled into position. When they were ready, Mishima stood up, closed the double doors and drew a black curtain across the entrance from the inside.

With that, the party was completely enclosed in a box of black curtains. Soon, that dark space would play host to a truly unusual act of divination. I will attempt to describe it in as simple a way as possible.

First, the old toad, or rather Doctor Mega, stood, bowed to the image of Kasen on the wall and in a low voice, began chanting something like a Shinto invocation. It sounded like some mysterious sutra, though it was not the usual Sanskrit or Chinese. From the frequent use of the name Kasen, it was likely a kind of spell to invoke the immortal's spirit to attend the rite. The doctor's voice was not particularly good, but something in it was so intimate, so powerful, that it naturally worked its way into the spirit. Its primary role seemed mostly to be to focus the attention of the attendees.

As he chanted, the others seated around the table folded their hands together, half-closed their eyes and stared straight ahead. Kindaichi followed their lead.

The old toad wizard's low, droning voice filled the small space like the buzz of a flying insect, going on and on and on... Listening to it, Kindaichi found himself drifting into a dreamlike trance.

Oh, no, Kindaichi cried out silently to himself. *If I don't take care, I'll hypnotize myself!*

He looked furtively around to help wake himself up, and when he did so he noticed something odd.

Totaro Mishima was sitting to his left, his hands together in front of him, and appeared to be entering a trance himself. What struck Kindaichi as odd, though, was that Mishima wore a cotton glove on his right hand, but not the left.

Kindaichi was bemused. As he stared, though, he started to get an idea of why Mishima did so. As he fell deeper into the trance, Mishima's fingers twitched ever so slightly—all of his fingers except the middle and ring fingers of his right hand, which remained totally motionless. Kindaichi realized those fingers must be missing. He didn't know if they were cut off at the base or halfway up, but his habit of keeping one hand gloved was likely forgiven in this rather strict social class as it helped hide the unsightliness.

Kindaichi snapped back to himself when he realized the rudeness of his staring, so he looked instead to the right. When he did so, he got another bit of a shock.

Kikue was sitting there. She also had her hands together at the edge of the round table, and he saw that the pinkie finger of her left hand was half missing. Kindaichi could not help staring at this until Kikue herself gave him a little bump on the leg with her knee. She gestured forward with her chin. When he looked, he saw the toad-faced doctor glaring angrily at him.

Kindaichi flushed like a schoolboy caught mid-prank in class and scratched at the bird-nest of hair atop his head. He caught himself again and hurried to return his hands to the edge of the round table. He half-closed his eyes as befitting someone half in a trance.

To his right, Kikue smirked as she surreptitiously pulled out a handkerchief and placed it over her left hand, then also half-closed her eyes as if in a trance. This little show revealed that Kikue, at least, was not much of a believer in

Doctor Mega's mysticism and remained in full control of herself.

The old toad's incantation suddenly ramped up. As it grew in intensity, Akiko stood, swaying. Kindaichi looked up in shock. She seemed to be completely hypnotized. That beautiful face, as perfect as a porcelain doll's, was completely devoid of even the faint trace of ego it had held before, and her eyes stared entranced into the distance.

Kindaichi thought about what Mineko had said the day before.

My mother is very sensitive… She's very suggestible.

Looking at Akiko's state, he could not help but see just how right Mineko had been. He also saw how dangerous that fact was. It made him deeply afraid.

Akiko, still staring into the distance, reached out her trembling right hand. She extended the index, middle and ring fingers and gently placed them on the nearest of the five sticks radiating from the dish above the sand.

The doctor's chanting grew ever more fervent. Next, Mineko stood. Kazuhiko abruptly did as well when he saw her. They both copied Akiko and reached out three fingers of their right hands to touch one of the radial sticks.

With that, three of the sticks had been taken and two were left. Those two stuck out in front of Mishima and Kikue. They stood at the same time and did as the other three, extending the middle fingers of their right hands and placing them on the radiating sticks.

Kindaichi was somewhat surprised. Apart from Akiko and Mishima—and he really didn't know enough about Mishima to tell—he did not think that Mineko, Kazuhiko or the smirking Kikue were caught up in the old toad wizard's spell. Even so, they stood and put their fingers obediently on their radials, their eyes half-closed.

When all five were standing, Doctor Mega's chanting voice suddenly grew gentle and sweet. It seemed now as if he was trying to sing a baby to sleep with a quiet lullaby.

Kindaichi snuck a look at the faces of the other four people around the table. He saw that they were all directing their gazes towards the centre of the radials, focusing on the metal cone hanging below the crimson dish. He did not know if they all believed in the divination or not. But in that instant, at the very least, he could see a kind of intense nervousness in all their expressions.

The thick tension filling the curtained room felt so strange and otherworldly that Kindaichi was reminded of stories he'd read about the witches' sabbats of medieval Europe.

Then, someone drew a breath with a sound like a sob. As he watched, the hanging cone started to move, leaving tiny tracks in the sand as it did. It stopped and started fitfully as if a thing alive, and slowly drew a semicircle in the sand.

Kindaichi realized as he watched that the system shared certain aspects with Japan's *kokkuri-san* divination. The radiating bamboo sticks transmitted the subtle tremors of the five people's fingers to the central disk, which then caused the hanging cone to move. As described, the rails covering the bottom of the dish and radials allowed it to move freely anywhere within that area, leaving traces on the sand. When all was finished, Gama Sennin the toad wizard, or rather Doctor Mega, would read the marks that the cone had left and judge their meaning. This time, the group was hoping they would reveal if Viscount Tsubaki was alive or dead.

The cone grew gradually more active. It drew two semicircles in the sand, then a third, but as it finished the last one, the lantern above their heads flickered, then faded and left the room in pitch-darkness.

There was a stirring for an instant, someone gave a low cry, and there was a sense of movement in the dark. How stressful it was for Kindaichi, sitting in that unbroken blackness, straining his ears to catch any sounds. The palms of his clenched hands grew damp with sweat, but the motion quickly ceased.

Doctor Mega croaked a gruff, scolding sound, then began his chanting again. With that, the bizarre divination continued in the darkness, until after a few minutes the room was filled with light again. It was not the spare lantern. The blackout had ended, and the electricity had returned on its own.

Kindaichi quickly glanced around the room. No one seemed out of place. Everyone was in the same position they had had before the lantern went out. He took out a handkerchief and wiped his sweaty palms.

Almost as soon as the lights had come on, Doctor Mega had stopped his chant. When he did, Akiko slumped back into her chair, as if she had awakened from her trance. The maid Shino embraced her, gently rubbing her back as if soothing an infant. The other four also took their seats, their faces haggard and dripping with sweat.

Doctor Mega muttered the final three syllables of his incantation inside his closed mouth, then stood and looked at the sand to make his judgement. Kindaichi sat up and turned his own gaze to the centre of the dish.

The cone had come to a complete stop, and around it was a peculiar shape. It was mostly rounded, with lines like a halo of flame surrounding it and extending out from one end. It reminded Kindaichi of a *kaendaiko*, a decorated drum used in ancient *gagaku* music. The thought unconsciously escaped his lips.

"Huh, that looks just like a *kaendaiko*," he said.

When he did, Doctor Mega—who had been staring in confusion at the surface of the sand—turned his gaze to Kindaichi

63

almost unwillingly. There was a strange kind of surprise in his eyes.

The doctor dropped his eyes to the sand once more and looked at the *kaendaiko* as if enthralled. He then looked nervously at Akiko and Shino, and then glanced at Tamamushi and Toshihiko Shingu.

It was only then that Kindaichi realized Tamamushi, Shingu and Shino were every bit as shocked as Doctor Mega. They too were staring at the mysterious mark in the sand, faces twisted in something like fear. They were not the only ones to show surprise. Mineko and Kazuhiko, and Kazuhiko's mother Hanako were also staring wide-eyed at the sand.

Mishima and Kikue were the only ones who betrayed no trace of similar feeling. They seemed more confused by the others' extreme reactions, in fact, blinking as they looked around the table.

The former count Tamamushi leapt up from his seat. His eyes were filled with rage as he looked from person to person. "Wh-who was it? Who did this?!" he demanded.

However, before anyone had the chance to answer, someone began knocking loudly at the double doors. Mishima stood, drew the curtain slightly aside and opened the door a crack to speak to whoever it was. It was the maid Otane, and she must have been in a state of near panic from the rushed way she was speaking to him. He seemed ever more shocked by whatever it was she said and leaned out as if listening to something. Then, he pulled back the curtain and threw the door open.

Soon, a mass of people rushed from the room following the terrible melody they heard.

CHAPTER 6

The Silenced Flute

"The Devil Comes and Plays His Flute"…

Kosuke Kindaichi would hear that song repeatedly before this case came to its end, but the very first time was then, the moment that Mishima opened those double doors.

The quavering melody drifted from some far-off place, flowing gently through the quiet house. It had a bizarre, twisted quality to it. And yet, that still seemed insufficient to explain the fearful reactions of the others in the room.

Kindaichi looked around at them, a stunned expression on his face. Even Akiko, who had reacted to the mark of the *kaendaiko* earlier with only a kind of bafflement, now seemed overcome with true terror. She was clinging to Shino and trembling like a child. As the flute melody grew louder and more frenzied, she pressed her hands over her ears.

"No, my husband has returned! That's him, playing his flute! Someone! Someone, please, make him stop!" Akiko screamed like a child in a tantrum, and it seemed to break the spell on everyone else.

Mineko put on a hard, determined expression and rushed from the room, pushing people out of her way. Kazuhiko followed on her heels. Kindaichi also went after them, still unsure what was going on.

The blackout was over, so the hallway was blazing with light. Mineko led the way down the hall followed by Kazuhiko, who was in turn followed by Kindaichi running after. Behind him came

Mishima and Kikue. As they raced down the hall, the sound of the flute grew louder. It seemed to be coming from the drawing room. Mineko was the first to reach the door. It was still open, as Kindaichi and the others had left it in the dark, and the lights inside were all on. There was no sign of anyone there. Yet the mad flute melody went on.

"Oh, Mineko! The first floor!" Kazuhiko said and took off running. Mineko, Kindaichi, Mishima and Kikue followed. As he ran, Kindaichi sensed someone else trailing along behind them.

The stairs to the first floor were around a bend in the hallway after the drawing room. They all rushed to the foot of the stairs, but then stopped as one. Looking up, they saw that the floor above remained in total darkness. Yet, sure enough, the sound of the flute came from there.

"Who are you? Who's up there?" Mineko's voice shook as she called out. There was no answer from above, only the flute melody filling the air like the sound of weeping.

"Who's there?" she asked again and flipped the wall switch. The lights above flickered on, but still no answer came, and the flute played on.

"Let's go and see, Mineko-san," Kazuhiko said and went up half a dozen steps. She hesitated a moment, then followed. Kindaichi and Mishima went up the stairs too, but Kikue stayed below with Toshihiko and Hanako Shingu, who had joined them.

There were two or three rooms on the left side of the hallway, and the flute music was coming from the furthest one. When the group realized this, they all came to a stop at the top of the stairs.

"Kindaichi-san…" Mineko gasped and clutched at his arm. "That's Father's study. It's coming from Father's study!"

The study door stood open a crack from which leaked a glimmer of light, faint as a firefly. Kindaichi left the stunned group behind and moved to the door. He opened it a little further and peeked inside. The lights were off, but there was one faint source of illumination. Kindaichi quickly noted what it was.

"Is someone in there, Kindaichi-san?"

He slowly shook his head, then asked, "Mineko-san, is there an electric phonograph in this room?"

"A phonograph? Oh, you mean a record player? Yes!"

She leapt to Kindaichi's side like a shot and flipped the switch by the door. The study lights came on.

It revealed a tidy room that seemed to speak of the vanished Viscount Tsubaki's character. In one corner was a large electric record player. That eerie flute melody was flowing from its speaker.

"Who? Who would play such a terrible prank?!"

When she realized it was only a record, Mineko slumped with relief. She stumbled over to the gramophone and lifted its lid. As she did, the needle reached the end of the track and the automatic stop engaged, halting the record's spin.

And so ended the devil's first performance of that terrible piece of music.

The group stood in silence looking at each other for a moment, until finally Mineko said, as if she had just realized something, "I must go see to Mother. I have to let her know there's no need to worry."

She once more had that determined look on her face, but when she turned to leave, Kindaichi took her arm and stopped her.

"I'm sorry, Mineko-san, but I'd like you to stay here for a moment. I have some questions to ask you."

Then, he turned to Kazuhiko and Mishima by the door, and said, "You two, go down to the ground floor and let everyone know what happened. Tell them it was just a prank and that there's nothing to worry about."

Kazuhiko hesitated a moment, then nodded silently and left his spot by the door. Mishima went after him.

Kindaichi walked over to the record player and very carefully removed the record. He held it to the light and read the label. "Oh, your father wrote this piece," he said, surprise in his voice. He had not heard it before, so he had been unable to name the melody.

Mineko nodded wordlessly.

"And it looks like he was also the performer on this record."

Again, she only nodded.

Kindaichi placed the record with that same great care back on the turntable, and then turned to her, "Why don't you take a seat, Mineko-san? We can't talk with you standing there like that."

She glanced at Kindaichi's face, hesitated a moment, then demurely sat down. Her previously pale cheeks were flushed, and the skin around her eyes was dark and sunken from stress and fatigue. The overall effect was to make her stern expression look even harder and somehow pitiable.

Kindaichi sat on one end of a desk a little way away.

"Mineko-san." She did not respond.

"There are lots of things I'd like to ask you, but first of all is this. When everyone first heard the flute music just now, why did they all react with such fear? I suppose, of course, anyone would be surprised to suddenly hear music playing in a supposedly empty house, but the way everyone reacted just now… It was more than that. Why was everyone so frightened?"

"That song…" Mineko started hesitantly. "It was Father's last composition. Just after he wrote and recorded it, he was caught up in the Tengindo Incident, and then… then… he vanished."

Mineko's voice was thick with choked sobs.

"In a way, that piece is like his parting gift. And yet, the name of it, and as you just heard, Kindaichi-san, the melody… It seems so full of darkness and spite that my mother is terrified by the mere sound of it. She's convinced that he put all of his hate into it when he played it. That's why, after he disappeared, my mother smashed all the copies, five or six, we had in the house."

Kindaichi raised his eyebrows in surprise. "All of them? So, there wasn't a single one left here?"

"That's right."

"So, where did this one come from?"

"I can't imagine. That's what frightens me." Mineko shrugged in misery. "Who could have brought and played it? And why?"

Kindaichi slid off the desk and started pacing slowly around the room.

"'The Devil Comes and Plays His Flute' certainly is a peculiar title. I wonder what it could mean?"

"I don't really know myself, but perhaps Father intended it to refer to the times we live in. These terrible times after the war… Perhaps to Father, these truly are the days when the devil has come to play us all to hell."

"I see."

"But my mother takes it to mean something else. She believes that it refers to my father himself. Someday, he will return as the devil and play his flute. That might also be because, after he disappeared, no matter how we searched we could never find his golden flute."

"A golden flute?"

"Yes, it was his favourite. Flutes are usually made of silver or wood, but Father had a golden one specially made to order. He said that it was because gold makes for a gentler sound. That's the flute he played for the record, in fact."

"And it's been missing since your father's disappearance?"

"Yes, that's right. And so, my mother thinks that he will someday come back as a devil, playing his golden flute as he gets revenge. Of course, I don't agree, but… When that music suddenly played in the dark, I thought, for just a moment… Mother was right, Father has come back, playing his flute."

Mineko's cheeks broke out in fine goosebumps. Clearly, that moment when she heard the flute playing in the dark had brought great terror to this house.

"Your father must have been a very skilled player."

Mineko raised her eyebrows and said, "The Tsubaki family were formal *gagaku* musicians for the Imperial court for generations. I don't know if such things run in the blood, but my father was certainly a first-rate player. He only composed occasionally, though. His great dream was to one day go to France and study with Marcel Moyse, the greatest flautist in the world. It breaks my heart to imagine how much happier he would have been if he hadn't been surrounded by such people, and he could have gone out into the world with his flute. My father was not an incompetent. Not like great-uncle Tamamushi and uncle Shingu always said."

When she choked out that last sentence, Mineko began shaking with rage and hate. It made Kindaichi pity her even more. However, he took pains to ignore his feelings and continued pacing the room.

"But, Mineko-san, that could mean the playing of this record tonight holds some very important message for us. 'The Devil Comes and Plays His Flute'… Who is it that is coming to play, and why?"

Mineko shuddered and said, "Please don't talk like that, Kindaichi-san. It frightens me too much. I can't stand all this."

Kindaichi stood over the trembling girl and looked kindly down at her.

"Mineko-san, you can't let yourself be so afraid. You're all that keeps this house together. You have to be strong. Now, as to whoever put this record on, do you have any guesses?"

She stared down at the rug on the floor for a while, then finally shook her head. "I don't know. But, if we look at who had the opportunity, it really only could have been Otane-san. Everyone else was there at the divination. Unless someone snuck in from outside."

"Do you think that Otane-san is capable of such a nasty trick?"

"Oh, no, not at all. It's unimaginable. More than anything, she truly cared for my father. Apart from me, she was the only person here who did. And my father doted on her. His attentions were always proper, of course. But why would someone with such attachment to him do such a thing?"

Kindaichi continued to look gently into her eyes.

"Mineko-san, I think you're making one mistake. It's certainly possible for Otane-san to have played the record. But she wasn't the only one with the opportunity to do so. In fact, most of those attending the divination could have."

She stared at Kindaichi's face in shock. "H-how is that possible?!"

"Because it's an electric record player. The person who set it up had to have known about the blackout coming at half past eight. Or, to put it another way, they knew that the electricity would come back on when it ended at nine o'clock. So, when the power went out, they came up here, set the record, put the needle on the track and turned on the switch. Without power, the turntable wouldn't turn, and the record wouldn't play. Then, whoever it was could go to the divination like they knew nothing at all. When nine o'clock came and the power company turned the electricity back on, it would also go to the record player,

71

and since the switch was already on, the tubes would heat up and the table would turn. The record would play all by itself."

Mineko had listened to Kindaichi in wonder. When he finished, she shook herself, and asked, "But why do such a thing?"

"I can think of all kinds of reasons. First of all, they wanted to force everyone to hear the song and be afraid. But they also would have wanted an alibi for the timing. And then…"

"Then… What?"

"Well, I'm just guessing, but I feel like they wanted to distract everyone's attention from the divination itself."

"What for?"

"I don't know that myself, yet. I actually wanted to ask you about something related to it. That strange shape that appeared at the divination just now. What was that? Why did everyone react with such shock and fear when it showed up?"

Mineko's expression twisted, and she said, "I don't know what it was, either. And I can't imagine why everyone reacted like that. But I think I have seen a similar shape before."

She was now speaking in a low whisper, and her breath was coming in ragged gasps.

"When? Where?"

"I told you that I went to claim my father's remains after he was discovered on Mount Kirigamine. I found a small journal in the pocket of his suit. I thought we might find a suicide note or such in it, so I glanced through it. When I did, on one page, I noticed a shape just like that one, and above it…" Mineko took a deep breath, shivering.

"What? What was above it?"

"He had written 'the devil's mark'. And it was clearly my father's handwriting."

"The devil's mark?!" Kindaichi had to stop and catch his breath.

"Yes, but at the time I didn't think too deeply about it, or pay it much attention at all, really. Since it was written just before his terrible death, I just thought it was part of all whatever it was going through his mind at the time. I had nearly forgotten it, in fact. But then when it showed up like that this evening…"

"Who else knows about that? About your father putting that sign in his journal?"

"I'm not sure, to be honest. I did show Kazuhiko, who came with me to claim my father's remains. But since the journal was with his belongings, it came home with his remains, so anyone could have seen it since. I believe Mother has it now."

Kindaichi thought once more about the shock that he had seen on those faces, Doctor Mega, former count Tamamushi, Toshihiko Shingu, and even the old maid Shino. It had not been simple surprise. He was certain that they knew something else about that peculiar *kaendaiko* shape.

But what could it be? What meaning did the devil's mark hold?

"One other thing, Mineko-san," Kindaichi said, looking down at the young woman sitting so quietly. "When the lights went out earlier, where were you?"

At first, she did not seem to understand the question, but after staring blankly up at Kindaichi for a moment, her face went scarlet, and she answered in a rage, "Kindaichi-san! Could you honestly believe that I could have—"

"Wait a minute, now, Mineko-san, don't get so upset. I'm just asking the question." Kindaichi looked around the room. "All that about someone coming in here to set up the record just after the blackout is still just a guess of mine. But a little after the lights went out, your mother heard someone leave this room."

"She did?"

"Yes, that's right. I was with her in the drawing room at the time. Kikue-san had come to escort us to the divination when the lights went out. We stood there in the dark for a moment, and then it happened. Your mother said someone was in this room. That someone was walking in her husband's study."

"Oh, my!"

"She seemed very frightened. But we, that is, Kikue-san and I, didn't hear anything. And then Otane-san came with a torch, so we left it at that. But now, looking back, I believe your mother was right. I think that was when someone came here to set the record."

Mineko shuddered slightly, and said, "Mother has excellent hearing. Almost shockingly so."

Her expression softened, then, and she looked up at Kindaichi with teary eyes.

"I'm sorry, Kindaichi-san. I shouldn't have let your question upset me. I suppose everyone has an equal duty to make their statements at times like this. I can't expect any special treatment, of course."

"No, Mineko-san, it's not like that—"

"I was in my room crying when it happened. I was weeping so hard that I didn't even realize the lights had gone out. Kindaichi-san, I ought not be ashamed of Mother, ought I? I do my best not to be, I really do. But she always acts like that whenever she meets someone new, and I just hate it. I know I'm such an ungrateful daughter."

She shrugged her shoulders and lowered her eyes. She was a picture of bleak despair. Mineko, as mentioned, was no great beauty. And, perhaps due to her mother's condition, she had been forced to mature beyond her years emotionally, which gave her face an even harder look. Now, though, looking down as her slumped shoulders told of such deep sorrow, Kindaichi could see the charming girl beneath that hard facade.

He thought about trying to say something comforting, but as he struggled to find the words, Mineko suddenly looked up and said, "Should we go downstairs and ask them all now, Kindaichi-san? Ask them where they were when the lights went out?"

"Well, we could, but I think it might be a waste of time. Since it all happened in the dark, we'd have no way of telling who was lying. But anyway, yes, I suppose we should go downstairs."

Mineko's eyes flashed when she looked at Kindaichi now, but she merely bit her lip. She said nothing.

They went downstairs and found Kikue in the drawing room on the sofa, reading a book. Kazuhiko stood nearby staring vaguely at an oil painting above the mantelpiece. When Kikue saw the two enter, she put down her book and stood up.

"Mineko-san, was it really a record just now?"

"That's right, just a record." Mineko offered no more details and tried not to look at Kikue. It seemed she wanted as little to do with the woman as possible.

Kikue, though, seemed to pay that little mind.

"Then, do you know who put it on?"

"Not yet, no."

"Well, at the very least, it wasn't me," Kikue said, and turned her bright eyes on Kindaichi before going on, "Right, Kindaichi-san? You can vouch for me, can't you? I don't know who did it, but it must have been right after the blackout started. Remember? Lady Akiko was frightened by someone walking around on the first floor. It must have been then. And if it was, then I was right here with you and her."

Mineko looked now at Kikue with shock, then turned to Kindaichi.

He just smiled and said, laughing, "You're a clever one, Kikue-san! You figured out exactly when the record must have been set!"

"Anyone could have done that, though. When the record started playing, everyone here except for Otane-san was sitting around the divination table. She would never play such a nasty trick, though, and who would sneak in here? Which means it must have been one of us, and then when could we have done it? If you think of it that way, then it's obvious. Whoever it was must have used the blackout for their little trick."

"But then, why do you think it must have been someone at the divination who did it?"

At that, Kikue turned mischievous eyes to Mineko and Kazuhiko, saying, "As for that, Kindaichi-san, I think you'll work it out after you spend a bit more time around here. Everyone here is a bit twisted somehow. All they feel for each other is suspicion, resentment and fear. I couldn't tell you why that is. It's as if they're all just waiting for their chance to stick the knife in. As if they think that if they don't, then they'll be on the other end of the blade. Oh, dear, do forgive me, Mineko-san. Look what I've gone and said!"

Mineko's face went scarlet with rage. And yet, the fact that she was unable to say a word in response was likely because Kikue was speaking only the truth.

Kindaichi looked at Kikue with deep interest. As mentioned before, she was a slender, attractive woman. Her beauty was the opposite of full fleshed; indeed, you would almost call her bony. The explanation for the almost irresistible allure she gave off was likely due to her masterful body language. In contrast to Mineko's constant harsh expression, Kikue always had a mischievous, mocking grin. Her eyes were wide, her cheekbones sharp, and her lipstick dark.

I wonder if this is what they mean when they talk about the modern "après guerre" woman, Kindaichi mused.

Mineko glared for a moment at Kikue, still shaking in rage, then suddenly turned to Kazuhiko.

"Kazuhiko-san, where is everyone?" she asked.

It was Kikue, though, who answered.

"They said they're giving up on the divination. After all, your mother's hysterics got quite out of hand. So, Kazuhiko-san's mother and Shino-san took her back to her room. Then Doctor Mega gave her a shot which finally calmed her down. I'm sure he'll be staying the night. To watch over her, of course." Her tone held, if not exactly malice, at the very least a note of biting sarcasm. Mineko flushed bright red with humiliation at it.

Kikue, still smirking, went on. "Kazuhiko-san's father went stumbling back to his house, and My Lord started calling out for a drink, as he does. Even though the doctor told him to stop because of his blood pressure... But he's such a pain when he gets like that, so I'm leaving him to it. Anyway, I just don't get it at all. Why was everyone so scared? Huh, Mineko-san?"

It was an excellent point, and once more exactly what Kindaichi had been thinking. What had frightened everyone so much?

Mineko only looked at the woman with indignation in her expression, shrugged and turned to leave. However, just as she reached the door, she turned back as if she'd just recalled something.

"I beg your pardon, Kindaichi-san. I have to go tend to Mother. I'm sorry, but I think you should perhaps return home now."

"Right, of course." His voice was light, but inside he felt a pang of disappointment. He'd wanted to stay on and observe this fascinating family for a while longer.

However, as he was leaving, an odd little occurrence held him back. Looking at it later, he came to see this fracas actually held great significance. Noticing him glancing around the drawing room, Kikue asked, "What's the matter, Kindaichi-san, have you misplaced some great treasure?" Her tone was teasing.

"M-m-my hat. H-h-h… hat… Where is it?" Kindaichi stammered.

"Oh, right, your hat. It was sitting just outside the divination room. I'll go and get it for you."

"No, no. I can get it."

The four of them all walked to the divination room together, and there they found his hat.

Earlier, Kindaichi had tossed it aside in the darkness, and he hadn't realized it had ended up in an odd spot. A heavy black table stood to the left of the door, on top of which was a bronze vase. The vase, by coincidence, stood just about at Kindaichi's ear height, and when he'd flung his hat aside, it had slipped over the mouth of the vase like a lid.

"Oh, look at that! Ha ha ha, what an odd place for it to end up," Kikue said, laughing. She reached up to take the hat, but the vase began to tip over.

"W-watch out!" Kazuhiko and Mineko came from either side and caught the vase between them. At the noise, Totaro Mishima came running out of the room.

"Is everything all right?" he asked.

"Oh, yes, it's fine. It's just, Kindaichi-san's hat is caught on the lip of this vase, and it won't come off. Mishima-san, get it for him, would you?"

"Let me see," Mishima said as he took her place, but the hat still wouldn't budge. It appeared the mouth was almost exactly the same size as the hat, and part of the dragon or whatever it was that was engraved around the edge had snagged the lining.

78

When Mishima tried to force it off, it shifted with a ripping sound from one of the seams.

"Oh, no, how awful! Don't damage Kindaichi-san's pristine hat!"

"Hahaha, Kikue-san, you tease too much!"

Kindaichi's laughter seemed to set something off. A voice, full of violent rage, bellowed from within the room.

"Who's that?! Who's out there messing about?!"

Kindaichi jumped in surprise, but the others all remained surprisingly calm. So, he snuck a look into the room, and saw it was the former count Tamamushi.

The old man was now sitting in the chair Doctor Mega had used, with a square whisky bottle on the table in front of him. He glared back with bloodshot, drunken eyes.

The round table with its sand and crimson spirit-writing tool was still there, unmoved, but Kindaichi then noticed something odd in the room.

It was a statue, about fifteen inches tall or so, on a pedestal about three and a half inches across, standing on a high-legged table on the left side of the room, just in front of the dark curtains.

Wait, was that there before? Kindaichi cocked his head to one side, wondering, but then realized that it would have been outside the circle of dim light the lantern had cast.

So that's why I didn't notice it… he thought. He stood there absently, pondering the statue, until old man Tamamushi burst out again.

"Who are you?! Who do you think you are, standing there staring like that?!"

Kindaichi jumped back in surprise when a handful of sand hit the floor at his feet.

"Hee hee!"

Kikue bobbed her head in apology. "He's just cross that I went off without him. Well, Kindaichi-san, all apologies and such. Goodbye," she said absently, walking into the room with a tug at the hem of her evening gown.

Soon Mishima safely freed Kindaichi's hat.

"I'm sorry, Kindaichi-san, I'm afraid I ripped the lining a little."

"Oh, that's fine, that's just fine."

"Kazuhiko-san, please show Kindaichi-san to the door. I really must go and see to Mother now," Mineko said. She had likely had enough for the evening. She spun on her heel and stomped off with a shrug of her shoulders. Kindaichi watched her go.

Then he heard Kikue's fawning voice oozing out of the open door. "Enough of that, now. What are you doing, drinking so much? Don't come crying to me when the doctor is cross with you. What? No! Oh, what a bad boy you are! Are you jealous? Of that vagabond-looking thing?"

It seemed that "vagabond-looking thing" meant him, Kindaichi. He followed Kazuhiko to the door, the skin of his back crawling, and hurried out of that house.

It was well after midnight by the time he returned to his lodgings in Omori.

As soon as he did, he tried telephoning Chief Inspector Todoroki at the Tokyo Metropolitan Police. It took ages for anyone to answer, and when someone finally did, they said that the chief inspector was out.

Kindaichi was disappointed. He'd rung the chief inspector countless times since the day before hoping to ask about the connection between the Tengindo murders and Viscount Tsubaki before he inspected the Tsubaki household.

Kindaichi retired to his room in a kind of mania. Even after he crawled into bed, he couldn't sleep. In his mind, he kept seeing suspicious face after face spinning around the Lady Tsubaki as she was overcome with hysteria, with that eerie flute melody playing as the strange *kaendaiko* mark faded in and out…

Kindaichi rolled around in his bedding, until just as he was finally nodding off with dawn starting to break outside his window, one of the Pine Moon Inn housekeepers woke him with a knock.

"Kindaichi-san, there's a telephone call for you."

"Huh? Who is it?" He sat up in his bed and looked at the watch lying by his pillow. It read half past six.

"Someone called Tsubaki-san. It was a woman's voice."

Kindaichi leapt from the bed, and rushed to the main hall in his pyjamas, his heart pounding. He burst into the telephone booth and picked up the receiver.

"Hello, Kindaichi here! Yes, this is Kosuke Kindaichi. Is that you, Mineko-san?"

The voice at the other end was thin and distant, buzzing like a mosquito.

"This is Mineko. Mineko Tsubaki. Kindaichi-san, please come at once! Something has happened… Last night, finally… finally…"

"What happened? Hello? Hello, hello, Mineko-san, what happened?!"

"Please, hurry! There's been a murder… In our house… Oh, Kindaichi-san, I'm so frightened! So very frightened! Come at once…"

Her voice was drowned out by other voices and noise, and he could make out nothing more. Kindaichi slammed the phone down and rushed out of the booth.

The devil was finally playing his flute, and the curtain had fallen on the first bloody act of the tragedy of the Tsubaki family.

CHAPTER 7

Blood and Sand

30th September, 1947.

It was a leaden grey morning of the kind so common as summer moves into autumn, which seem to weigh on the spirit, when that first blood-drenched tragedy was discovered in the Azabu Roppongi estate of the former viscount Hidesuke Tsubaki.

It was half past eight when Kosuke Kindaichi alighted from the crowded train at Roppongi. As he walked towards the Tsubaki estate gate, he noticed that the neighbourhood was quite busy, perhaps due to the morning rush hour.

As the reader may recall, the whole quarter had been burnt down in the bombing raids, leaving only the Tsubaki house still standing. It was exposed and lonely, jutting out from the desolate wastes all around. As he approached, he found the house surrounded by thronging rubberneckers, swarming like ants around a sweet. Their expressions spoke of suppressed excitement, yet they also seemed strangely heavy, like the morning weather. The air hummed with a note of confusion.

The Tsubaki house had not been spared completely by the fires. Some buildings within the estate had burnt, and the incendiary bombs had left many of the garden trees only charred trunks. The wall around the grounds was in a particularly bad state due to the intense heat of the surrounding fires. The family's finances after the war were such that they could not afford proper repairs, so they tried to fill in the gaps with rough logs.

From time to time, one of the swarm of gawkers would slip through the remaining holes in the wall, and one of the police officers stationed around the house would chase them off with a yell. And that morning, the policemen were in a near panic. They were in constant motion, running here and there, chasing off onlookers and arguing with reporters. It was like they were trying to quash a riot.

The commuters stuffed in the endless passing trains stared out at the chaotic scene with curious eyes. Thus, news of the Tsubaki murder spread like wildfire through Tokyo, even before it hit the newspapers. Looking back now, it's clear there were several reasons for the particularly intense sensation surrounding the Tsubaki murders in the city.

The first was that this murder happened among the then very prominent "sunset clan" of the declining former nobility. The second was, of course, the inevitable associations made with the recent disappearance of Viscount Tsubaki. The third, although at the time it was not yet known, was the perhaps subconscious connection to that unprecedented crime, the Tengindo murders. All of these together seemed to make the prosecutor's investigation team extremely tense.

Yet, at the same time, this first murder at the Tsubaki house was more than unusual enough on its own to excite the investigators.

Kosuke Kindaichi had rushed to the scene at Mineko's plea, but now he had to wend his way past barrier after barrier simply to get onto the estate grounds and within touching distance of the case itself.

For of course, none of the nerve-wracked police could believe that this vagabond-looking man, with his shabby kimono and even shabbier *hakama* trousers, his crumpled and shapeless sack of a hat atop a great shock of unkempt hair, would possess investigative genius. Which is why, if Chief Inspector Todoroki himself had not been in charge of the investigation, the police officers on watch would have run Kindaichi out the gate in a rage like a rubbernecker or reporter, no matter how much he protested in Mineko's name.

"Ha ha ha, this is quite the hubbub, Chief Inspector! What's got everyone so worked up?"

Todoroki's intervention had finally got Kindaichi in the front door, and now he stood there, wiping the sweat from his brow and laughing like an idiot. The chief inspector, though, was in no mood for jokes.

"Kindaichi-san, there's nothing to laugh about. This is a bad one. It's so bad, I don't even know what to say." His voice was so oddly choked that it shocked Kindaichi into silence.

The two men were long-time acquaintances. Around 1937 or so, Kindaichi had butted into a case the chief inspector was working and wrapped it up quite neatly. Ever since, Todoroki had been oddly attached to the shaggy little wanderer. Not only did he not mind Kindaichi's involvement in cases, he openly welcomed it. Kindaichi, for his part, respected the chief inspector's frank and clear-cut character. All of which is a way to say, the two had long since become something of a team. And yet, Kindaichi had never seen the senior policeman so worked up before.

"What's happened, then, Chief Inspector? I heard there's been a murder. Who's the victim?"

Todoroki gaped at Kindaichi. "You mean you don't know?"

"I don't. Mineko-san rang me earlier, but we got cut off."

"Well then, you just come right along. They're photographing the crime scene."

Detectives and uniformed police were wandering to and fro around the drawing room and the long hallway. They were all nervous and solemn-faced. Kindaichi knew a few of them and bowed in greeting as they passed by. He did not see any of the household.

Todoroki led Kindaichi to the room which had hosted the mysterious ceremony of the night before. Two detectives stood in front of the door, and Kindaichi stopped short.

"Chief Inspector, are you saying this is where the murder happened?" he asked.

Todoroki nodded. "I heard you were here last night."

Kindaichi followed him silently into the room, which was repeatedly illuminated by the investigation team's camera flashes. Kindaichi quickly looked around him, avoiding the blinding camera flashes as he did, and the first thing he noticed was Doctor Mega and Totaro Mishima standing silently in one corner. Both seemed surprised to see him walk in with the chief inspector. Kindaichi found their presence strange as well, but then he noticed the chaotic state of the rest of the room.

The room was still blocked off in three directions by the black curtains, and the round table stood in the middle just as it had. The chairs around the table were still lined up as they had been, but two or three to the right of the door were overturned. Lying among them was the corpse of the former count Tamamushi.

"Ah. So, Count Tamamushi is our victim?"

"That's right. Who'd you think it was?"

In truth, the first face that had sprung to Kindaichi's mind when he got the call from Mineko was that of Lady Akiko.

The photographers clustered around the body, and the flashes grew more frequent. Kindaichi backed into a corner to get out of their way but managed to get a clear view of the body.

He saw a large wound on the back of the former count's head, and his cotton-white hair was stained crimson. The blood had run down and soaked into the rug. A statue lay on the floor about a yard away, covered in reddish-black stains.

At first glance it seemed that the former count had been beaten to death with the statue, but on closer inspection there was room for doubt, due to the scarf around the corpse's neck. The black silk scarf was pulled so tight that it had dug into the flesh, and was tied in a reef knot. It looked as if Tamamushi had been strangled.

As Kindaichi looked down on the corpse's face, an indescribable chill ran down his spine. What had the count seen just before his death? The wide-open eyes and twisted lips spoke of unspeakable horror in those final moments. What could have so deeply frightened this cunning politician, once a power in the national parliament and a towering member of the house of peers?

Kindaichi examined the rest of the body. Tamamushi had clearly put up a considerable fight before his murder. His *obi* sash was loosened so the front of his robe gaped open, and the right leg of his long underwear was pulled up all the way to the thigh. Blood dotted the kimono front from chest to belly, and though he still wore thin summer *tabi* stockings on his feet, both slippers had been kicked far from the body.

"Chief Inspector, is that enough?"

"Yes, that'll do. Now, make sure you get close-ups of the table and wide shots of the room in general."

"Understood."

The photographers were finished with the body, so Kindaichi moved in for a closer look. He saw that the floor around the corpse was covered in sand, which was spattered with drops of blood.

Kindaichi looked more closely at the face, and said, "Chief Inspector, it looks like the victim was struck in the face first."

"It would appear so, yes. We assume the bloodstains on the kimono, chest and belly are from his nose."

There was a large bruise on the man's face, right around the bridge of the nose.

"But then, it's odd that there's no blood on his face," mused Kindaichi.

"Seems somebody wiped it off. Here, take a look. There's a handkerchief on the floor there."

Kindaichi looked to where Todoroki was pointing and saw a scarlet-stained handkerchief balled up and tossed under an overturned chair.

Kindaichi's eyes widened.

"But who would have done that?"

"Who knows? I can't imagine why the murderer would, but at any rate, somebody clearly wiped the blood off his face. See? There are marks like someone tried to wipe the spots off his kimono, too."

It was just as he said.

"What were they trying to do by wiping off the blood?" said Kindaichi, puzzled. "With the room in a state like this?"

"Like I said, we don't know. There are just too many question marks." Todoroki clucked his tongue in exasperation.

Kindaichi looked up from the body and examined the round table where the photographers were now clustered. It was still covered in sand, just as the night before, but the divination contraption with its five radiating sticks had been shattered and overturned, leaving great tracks across the sand, and everything was splattered with blood.

Kindaichi held his breath as he took in the vivid red stains on the white sand. Then his eyes widened. It had been smoothed over in one spot, and there, stamped in red-black blood as if by a seal, was that mysterious *kaendaiko* shape, the devil's mark.

He gaped at it, then turned to Doctor Mega, who must have noticed it, too. When his gaze met Kindaichi's, he turned his head away with an exaggerated cough. Totaro Mishima still stood nearby, a confused expression on his face, looking back and forth between the mark and the others' faces.

Kindaichi moved over to the table and leaned in very close to the devil's mark. It was between two and three inches high and not quite two inches wide, and appeared to be much the same size and shape as the one that had appeared the night before. Unfortunately, the sand had been disturbed, erasing the previous night's mark without a trace, so there was no way to compare the two.

He turned to the senior policeman. "Chief Inspector, please make sure to get pictures of this… This devil's mark."

"What's that? Devil's mark, you say?"

"Right, exactly. Look, see, this kind of rounded teardrop shape drawn in blood? Please get some pictures so we have a record of it."

Eventually, the photographers finished with the room, and Chief Inspector Todoroki gave a signal. At that, the two detectives who had been waiting in the hall came in and closed the double doors. That was when Kindaichi first realized that there was a large hole in one door, as if it had been hacked through with an axe.

The detectives set the bar across the closed door and bolted it, before pulling the door curtain across, which Kindaichi saw was stained with blood too. It was smeared and smudged, showing clearly that the curtain had been closed when blood was splattered around the room, but that someone had drawn it aside while the blood was still wet.

"So, Doctor Mega, is this right?" Todoroki asked.

"No, the *ranma*…" Doctor Mega started, then turned to Mishima. "Right, Mishima-san? It was closed too, wasn't it?"

"Yes, that's right. It was. I opened it from outside."

"Okay, then, close the windows in the *ranma*, would you?" The chief inspector gestured to a detective, who brought a chair over and put it next to the door. He stood on the chair and closed the glass in the long, narrow vent over the door. When the detective had closed it, Todoroki looked over the room once more, then turned to Mega and Mishima.

"Doctor Mega," he said, with an odd note in his voice, "is the room now exactly like you found it at three o'clock this morning, when the incident was discovered?"

"Yes, it is," he confirmed, his toadish face filled with anxiety. "Right, Mishima-san? It was like this, right?"

"Yes… Well, of course, there was no hole in the door yet. That was me. I brought the wood axe and broke it open so we could reach in through the hole and unbar the door, then draw the bolt." Mishima looked around the room nervously. He was still wearing that cheap cotton glove on his right hand.

The chief inspector stared at the two men, his eyes blazing.

"So, then, apart from that, it's the same? And when you showed up, no one else was in the room besides the victim, right? And the windows on the other side of the curtains were all locked from the inside, as you say?"

Kindaichi, who had been watching the detectives and the chief inspector in great confusion, suddenly started scratching fiercely at his great mop of hair.

"Y-y-you can't mean, Chief Inspector, th-th-that this is a locked room murder?!"

"A locked room murder? What is that?!" Todoroki spun towards Kindaichi. He looked angry enough to take a bite out of him.

"It has a name, does it? Well, don't ask me if that's what it is, but just look at this! How is this possible? We've got clear signs of a struggle. The victim was struck with that statue, resulting in two or three wounds on the back of his head before a massive, final blow. On top of that, he was strangled with his own scarf. We won't know if the actual cause of death was the head wounds or strangulation until we get the autopsy results, but this sure wasn't any suicide. And yet, there was no one else besides the victim in the room when Kikue-san looked in through the *ranma*, or when these two, Mineko-san, and the victim's mistress Kikue, broke open the door to get in. And all the windows were locked from the inside, too. How is this possible?!"

Chief Inspector Todoroki's voice grew louder and louder as he spoke, his cheeks flushing scarlet.

Kindaichi, though, just went on happily scratching at the sparrow's nest atop his head.

CHAPTER 8

Gods of Wind and Lightning

After the photographers were finished and the body taken away for autopsy, the room was left in a shambles, as if a storm had swept through it. The forensics team's white fingerprint dust covered the furniture, creating an eerie contrast to the crimson bloodstains.

Kindaichi followed the chief inspector through the curtains that cut the space off from the rest of the room. Beyond them, he saw there were two windows facing the garden. They were double-paned for soundproofing and also covered with a thin iron mesh for security. Kindaichi tugged at the mesh to see if it was loose anywhere.

"I see. Even if the windows weren't closed, we wouldn't have to worry about anyone getting out through here."

He examined the room once more, then he turned to Doctor Mega and Totaro Mishima and asked, "So, this is how you found the doors and windows when you came rushing up. Then, when you broke through the door and got in, there was no one in the room but the victim, is that right?"

The two men nodded. Their eyes looked troubled. Mishima wore a doubtful expression on his downcast face as he glanced back and forth between Kindaichi and the chief inspector.

"So, it's like this… The murderer made this enormous mess, then just vanished like smoke. But common sense tells us that's impossible, so, we have to think about what kind of trick was used to escape the locked room, or what trick was used to lock the room after they left. Chief Inspector Todoroki, what about the *ranma* above the door? Did you try it out?"

The chief inspector gestured to one of the detectives, who tried to get out through the glassed vent. The impossibility of the task became clear immediately. The vent was more than wide enough side to side to accommodate a full-grown man, but it was so tight top to bottom that he could only get his arm in the gap. Not even the smallest man could have got out that way.

"Thanks, that'll do. So, that eliminates anyone escaping through the *ranma* after the act. Of course," Kindaichi said and grinned, "if anyone wanted to get out, there's a door right there, so there would be no need to try squeezing yourself through that tiny space. So if the *ranma* is out, that leaves the door. The question now is, how did someone bar and bolt the door and close the door curtain from the outside?"

"Wait a moment," Doctor Mega interjected and cleared his throat. "I'm sorry to interrupt, but that curtain must have been closed during the attack. At least, I think that's what the blood spatter shows."

"Right, right." Kindaichi nodded, and went on. "So, the murderer would simply have had to be careful opening and closing the curtain when they left, which means they only had two things to do once outside. Bar the door, then set the bolt. Of course, I wouldn't call those impossible tasks."

He tapped the glass of the *ranma*. "If there were no openings at all, it might be another story, but this *ranma* is in the perfect spot, narrow as it is."

"Meaning?" Todoroki frowned at him doubtfully.

"Well, for example… Let's say the murderer tied a string to the bar and bolt before they left, then ran the string out of the *ranma*. They could then have climbed up on that table in the hallway and used the string like a fishing line to lower the bar and set the bolt. Then, with a little more skilful manipulation, they could have worked the string off the ends of the bar and bolt too. If so, they would have had to set it up like that before they left the room. But once the string was loose, then *voila*, just pull it out and close the window. One locked room murder!"

Just then, an angry outburst interrupted Kindaichi's lecture on the perfect murder.

"Th-that's nonsense! C-complete and utter nonsense!"

Everyone turned in shock to see Doctor Mega sputtering in rage. He had swollen up like an angry toad, and his eyes were fairly shooting sparks.

"Why would anyone go to all that trouble?! Locking everything up like that, it doesn't change anything about the murder! Using a string to lower the bar? To set the bolt?! This isn't some damned child's game! Sure, sure, you can come up with all kinds of theories and whatnot, but look here. All that trouble and trickery, it's… Listen, Kindaichi-san, the murderer must have been in a hurry to get out of here. Someone could have come by at any time, and they surely knew that. 'Once the string was loose, then *voila*!'… What kind of nonsense is that?!" Mega, unable to contain himself, started waddling around the room on his bandy legs, nearly spitting with rage at Kindaichi, who just grinned.

Mega's rage grew even greater at that. "What? What's so funny?!" he bellowed. "Are you grinning at what I'm saying? Or maybe it's my legs that amuse you? Is that it?!"

Kindaichi finally burst out into laughter.

"Ha ha ha, oh, I'm sorry, Doctor. You're right, I totally agree!"

"What?!"

"Forgive me. I'm saying, I agree with everything you just said. It's just, the chief inspector here was so confused by the situation that I thought I'd have some fun and show off a bit by imagining how it could be done. In other words, it's a mere possibility. Possible, yes, but, I must admit, not very probable."

"Oh, enough! Stop playing with semantics to try and confuse people!"

"I'm just saying that such a thing could be done, but it's doubtful that it happened in this case."

"Of course, it's doubtful!"

Kindaichi paid no mind to the doctor's grumbled interruption.

"First of all, there's no reason at all to lock up the murder scene. A murderer might do it if they wanted to hide their crime by making it look like suicide. You know, if the death itself wasn't so obviously caused by someone else. But we can rule out suicide at first glance. There was no motivation at all for the murderer to go to all that trouble and risk discovery just to lock up the room."

"Still, Kindaichi-san," the chief inspector broke in. "That might be true, but the fact remains that the room really was locked up tight. Unless these two clow— um, beg pardon, unless these gentlemen are lying."

"Oh, now you're accusing me of lying?!" That seemed to be the final straw for the old doctor. He went into a towering rage, frothing at the mouth like a rabid toad. "Why would I need to lie to you lot?! I have been trying to tell you, it doesn't matter if the room was locked or not! A man was murdered here! What good would it do anyone to try and lie about that?!"

The words he spat at Chief Inspector Todoroki echoed in the closed room. Kindaichi patted the doctor on the back, saying, "Now, now, Doctor, the chief inspector was only talking theoretically. He's just being thorough, you know. No one actually thinks you're lying. By the way, Mishima-san?"

"Oh, um, yes?" Mishima, who had been staring vacantly into space with a confused look, spun around at the unexpected sound of his name.

"I've still not heard who it was who first discovered the murder."

"That was Kikue-san."

"Why would she—no, never mind, I'll ask her myself later. So, then, Kikue-san came and told you after she discovered the crime. Is that right?"

"Yes, that's right, she looked into the room through the *ranma*, then came running to wake me up. As you know, I'm the only man living in the house now. Shingu-san and his family are in the far house. It was quite a surprise for me, as you can imagine. I jumped out of bed and hurried here, and of course the door wouldn't open. So, like Kikue-san, I climbed up on the table and looked in through the vent," Mishima said.

"So, the lights in the room were on?"

"Yes, that's right. I suppose that's why Kikue-san could see, as well."

"Ah, of course. Did you immediately realize there had been a murder?"

"Not at all! I think you must have noticed when you looked through it yourself, but the *ranma* is too narrow to even fit your head through. You can only see a small part of the room. All I could see were his lordship Tamamushi's legs as he lay there on the floor. I couldn't see his head. Then Kikue-san asked me to look at the sand, and that's when I saw what looked like blood."

"Did you notice that peculiar mark at the time?"

"Hmmm, let's see…" Mishima thought back for a moment, then went on. "No, I didn't notice anything. You can only see a small section of the table through that window. And, of course, I was quite upset."

"What did Kikue-san say about what had happened?"

"She was sure that he had drunk too much and had a stroke. I agreed. Then, we woke Otane-san and asked her to call Doctor Mega."

"And where was the doctor spending that night?" Kindaichi had asked this last question innocently, but Mishima's face crumpled in shame and misery when he heard it. He flushed bright crimson and his features twitched in discomfort. Kindaichi was wondering why his question had disturbed the young man so when a harsh, venomous laugh behind him cut off that line of thought. It was Doctor Mega.

"Oh, Mishima my boy!" The doctor's eyes glinted maliciously. "Why don't you answer the man? Why don't you just say it? Doctor Mega was spending the night in the good lady's room! Ha ha ha!"

Kindaichi and Todoroki both stared at Mega wide-eyed. He wore an ugly, mocking smile. Kindaichi stared at those glinting eyes and the glistening, oily skin, and hot and cold flashes ran over him, as if the old wizard's spectral toad were crawling over his skin.

"Th-that's…" Kindaichi cleared his throat. "That's right. He is the lady's attending physician, so naturally he had to be on hand. She could have another of her episodes at any time, after all."

"Hah! Well, I suppose you could put it that way. Quite the attending physician I am! Ha ha ha!" Doctor Mega croaked out another laugh.

Kindaichi wondered how Mineko would have reacted if she had been there. His belly twisted with rage at the shameless old toad. "Yes, yes, I see," he went on swiftly. "So, then, the doctor woke up and came as well. And what of Lady Akiko?"

"Oh, well, you see… The lady…" Now even the old toad seemed embarrassed. He broke off, mopping his face, before going on. "Well, I left her to Shino-san when I came. Luckily, that Otane is a cautious one and kept the details to herself when she came to get me, so the lady didn't know anything. Mineko-san woke up when she heard all the ruckus. So, when she showed up at the room more or less everyone in the house was mixed up in the business."

"Did you look in through the vent as well?"

"Of course I did. How could I not?"

"Did you notice the mark on the table?"

"I didn't notice anything. I don't suppose you can see it from there."

"Right, well then, please, go on."

"Kikue-san and Mishima-san both reckoned it was a stroke, but it didn't look right to me. You can't tell a dead body just by looking at the legs, but with all that blood sprayed around like that, I didn't think it could be just a little nosebleed. So, I told Otane to call Shingu-san, but…"

"You sent Otane-san?" Kindaichi said and glanced over at Mishima.

He looked embarrassed again.

"Thinking back on it now, I should have gone myself. If I had, then we might have a better idea about what actually happened out there."

"Out where? What do you mean?"

"When Otane-san ran off to get Shingu-san, well, she says she saw Viscount Tsubaki. She was just seeing things, though, I'm sure. All the fuss must have overexcited her."

Kindaichi looked at Todoroki. A darkly ominous feeling spread up from the bottom of his belly like a cloud of ink through water. This case was quickly leaving the bounds of any normal murder investigation.

"V-Viscount Tsubaki?" Kindaichi said in a low voice.

Doctor Mega, though, just scoffed.

"A dream. A fantasy. A hysterical illusion. Otane had taken a fancy to the viscount. If you ask me it was just a hallucination brought on by some kind of longing for him."

"But… But Otane-san says she's certain of what she saw," Mishima said angrily, glaring at the side of the old toad's head. "And it wasn't only Otane-san. Lady Akiko and Shino-san saw him, too. I know you're trying to keep it quiet, Doctor, but Otane-san told me."

"Wait. Lady Akiko and Shino-san also saw the viscount, or someone who looked like him?" Kindaichi's heart was starting to pound. Todoroki glared back and forth between Mega and Mishima.

Mishima nodded, his eyes dark. "And it set off another one of Lady Akiko's episodes. That was another bit of commotion we had to deal with last night."

Doctor Mega had nothing to say to that.

Kindaichi tried to suppress the turmoil in his chest. "I see. I'll leave that to ask Otane-san and Shino-san later. So, then Shingu-san showed up. Is that right, Doctor Mega?"

"Yes, that's right, and I told him something was off about it all. So, I said we should call the police, but Shingu-san wouldn't allow it. We still didn't know for sure Tamamushi was dead, and if he was still breathing we had to get the door open as quickly as possible, he said. He was pretty insistent, which isn't really like him. And of course, no one here wants to have any more to do with the police than necessary, so I agreed we should break down the door. We had Mishima-san run out to the shed and bring the wood axe."

"So, then you chopped through the door panel, and reached in through the hole to raise the bar and pull the bolt?"

"I tried to reach in first, but the hole was too narrow. I got stuck. Mineko-san noticed and took pity on me, so she said she'd try. She couldn't reach through, either. So, Mishima-san widened the hole a bit more with the axe, then reached in and opened the door himself. Isn't that right, Mishima-san?"

Mishima nodded silently.

"So, you all rushed in. Did you move the chairs at all?"

"Come now, Kindaichi-san, be serious. Even I know you shouldn't touch anything at a crime scene. But, of course everyone was in a state, so there were some accidents. I opened the curtain and was the first one in, and right off I tripped over a chair and fell on my arse. So, the way things were, who could say who touched what? Even the person doing the touching probably couldn't be sure," Mega said.

"So, who exactly entered the room?"

"Everyone did!"

"Who exactly is everyone?"

"Well, me and Mishima-san, Kikue-san, Mineko-san. Then the three Shingus, the maid Otane… And then Akiko-san and Shino peeked in, too. I ran them off when I noticed that, though."

"And when did someone notice the mark?"

"Let's see… Oh, yes, that's right. I noticed Shingu-san and Mishima-san fiddling about with something, and when I went over to see what it was, that's when I saw it," Mega continued.

Kindaichi turned to Mishima. "And what was it you and Shingu-san were, ahem, fiddling with?"

"Well, you see… It was like this," Mishima went on, hesitantly, "I don't know why, but I saw Shingu-san trying to… Well, I suppose he was trying to erase the mark, for some reason. And I stopped him."

"So, Shingu-san had already noticed the mark… And you had, too?"

"No… That is, not exactly. I just felt that Shingu-san was acting strangely, fussing with the sand on the table the whole time. I walked over, trying not to attract any attention you know, to stop him because I knew that the police would want to examine everything when they arrived, and suddenly he grabbed a handful of sand to throw over it. I jumped over to snatch his hand and stop him, and that's when I saw the mark."

"I see. I suppose that Shingu-san made some kind of excuse. What happened then?"

"Oh, well, right then I heard Lady Akiko screaming. I suppose that must have been when… when whoever it was that looked like Viscount Tsubaki appeared, and she had her episode. Doctor Mega and Shingu-san rushed over to help."

"I assume everyone else did, too?"

"No. That is, Kikue-san, Kazuhiko-san, Otane-san and I stayed behind. Mineko-san came in a little later and asked me to call the police. So, let's see, it was around three o'clock when Kikue-san woke me up, but it must have been after four when we finally notified the police."

Kindaichi couldn't think of anything else he needed to ask, so he picked up the statue that had bothered him earlier. It was carved from wood, and although it was covered in blood, he immediately recognized it as an image of Raijin, the Shinto god of lightning and storms.

"Is this always in here? I didn't see it last night during the divination, but when I peeked in on my way home, I noticed it on that table over there."

"Yes, it's always kept in this room," Mishima answered.

"But unless I'm mistaken this is Raijin. That means there must be a matching Fujin wind-god statue, but I don't see it anywhere."

"Actually, as far as I know, that's the only one. Do you know anything about this, Doctor?"

"Huh, no, I don't know anything about it. Does it really have a twin?"

"Yes, it's always Fujin and Raijin as a pair, the gods of wind and lightning together."

Kindaichi gripped the statue by the neck and hefted it. As described before, it was about fifteen inches or so tall with a pedestal about three and a half inches across. The size and weight made it an ideal weapon. He put it down and wiped his hands. "Chief Inspector, I think we're done in here," he said. "Let's talk to the others in the drawing room. We can't bring the ladies in here."

As they left, Kindaichi pulled over the hall table and climbed up on it. It was the same one that had held the vase that gave his hat so much trouble the evening before. He looked through the window and saw it only revealed a small part of the interior, but craning his neck revealed that the devil's mark on the white sand was clear to see.

CHAPTER 9

The Golden Flute

"Can you imagine my surprise? I mean, you're a famous detective and I, without having any idea at all, was inexcusably rude all evening. I'm so sorry! I do hope you'll forgive me, Kindaichi-san."

Those were Kikue's first words on sitting down when Kosuke Kindaichi and Chief Inspector Todoroki called her into the drawing room.

She was dressed in a dark kimono and seemed to be wearing little make-up, as would befit her being in mourning for the deceased Tamamushi, but her expression and demeanour were as bright and brazen as ever, without a hint of sadness.

Kindaichi frowned and said, "Oh, come now, Kikue-san, this is no time for jokes. Please, just answer the chief inspector's questions as best you can."

She cocked her head and stuck out her tongue at his tone, like a naughty schoolchild caught mid-prank by a teacher. And yet, she quickly answered when the chief inspector asked for her family name and age. When he got to her relationship with the victim, though, she rolled her eyes and muttered, "How rude." But eventually, she did answer.

"If you must know, I was his mistress. His woman, you see," she answered coldly. Now it was the chief inspector's turn to feel uncomfortable.

"Ah, yes, I see, of course. So, um, when did that, uh, relationship begin?"

Kikue rolled her eyes again, but answered without a hint of shame, "Well, I've been with him since I was sixteen, so nine years, I suppose. I was an apprentice geisha in the Shinbashi entertainment district when we met. It was he who made a woman out of me."

There was a chuckle from the detectives in the drawing room. She didn't even give them a glance. The laughter quickly stopped.

The chief inspector saw that this woman was a formidable character indeed, so he left that line of questioning behind and turned to the events of the previous night.

This is what she said: "Right, so, after Kindaichi-san left, I really pushed at the old man—I mean his lordship—to leave off drinking and go to bed. But the old man—I'm sorry, I mean his lordship—was quite irritated about something. He refused to listen. Not only that, he flat out told me to get out and go on to bed myself if I wanted. Which was quite a relief... I'm sorry, I mean, I had no choice but do to what his lordship demanded. So, I headed back to our rooms and went to bed."

"Around what time was that?" Kindaichi butted in.

"I think it must have been some time after eleven. I didn't really pay much attention."

"And where were Mishima-san and Otane-san?"

"I asked them to go to bed earlier. I didn't want them seeing the old man sulk."

"So, after you left, the elderly gentleman stayed behind alone."

"Sure enough. Oh, I mean, yes, that is correct." Kikue poked her tongue out at him again.

"And how was the gentleman's demeanour then?"

"I think I just told you he was sulking like a spoiled child. He kept muttering under his breath."

"Had he been like that all evening?"

"No, I wouldn't say all evening. I think it started after the divination. I suppose it must have been that odd mark thing that did it. That's right, you said it looked like a *kaendaiko*, didn't you, Kindaichi-san? And then there was that business with the flute music, of course. But really, I feel like the *kaendaiko* was the bigger shock. He seemed to be terribly fascinated by it, and all twitchy."

"Twitchy? Like he was afraid?"

"Yes, that's right. It was very odd for the old man—I mean, his lordship. He wasn't usually like that."

"Hmmm… So, then, you went off to your rooms sometime after eleven o'clock. What did you do then?"

"I went straight to bed. Well, at first, I thought his lordship would be along soon, so I stayed awake waiting. But I just kept waiting and waiting, and he showed no sign of coming, so eventually I nodded off. With the lights on and everything."

"And you woke up again around three?"

"That's right, and I didn't know what to think. I mean, the lights were still on, and his lordship's bed was empty, even though the clock showed three. I thought to myself, that's a bit much even for a sulky old man, so I went to check on him. I found the lights on, and the door locked up tight, and no matter how I yelled he didn't answer. So, I climbed up on that table and looked in through the *ranma*. And, well, I saw him lying there."

"What was your first thought at that moment?"

"I thought he'd had a brain haemorrhage, of course. I'd warned him he was drinking too much, and the doctor had told him to cut down, too."

"By the way, did you happen to look at the sand dish, or notice that mark when you did?"

"No, I didn't notice anything. I don't suppose it's visible from the vent."

"Well, you can see it from certain angles. Quite clearly, in fact."

"Oh, dear, well, I didn't notice it myself."

"Do you know what that mark means?"

"I don't, no. Why would the old man—oh, dear, do forgive me, it's just a habit of mine. Why would his lordship be so shocked by it? I can't figure that out at all. But I'd say there are plenty of other people who know."

Kikue frowned, and she finally started to seem serious.

Kindaichi thought for a moment, then said, "So then, you called for Mishima-san. We've already heard from him and Doctor Mega what happened after that, but is there anything else you can think of, something they might not have noticed?"

Kikue sat in thought for a while, then said, "Oh, yes, that's right. I suppose you've heard that Otane-san and Lady Akiko saw the late viscount?"

Kindaichi, his voice tense, replied, "Yes, I have. What are your thoughts on that?"

"I'm not a superstitious person by nature, you know. So, if it weren't for what happened the other day at the theatre, I'd be the first in line to tease them about it. But it's so strange. That man at the theatre looked just like the viscount. It gave me such chills. It felt like someone had dumped ice water over me. Otherwise, I'd have run right over and found out who he really was."

"So, do you think that man came here last night?"

"Who else could it be? I mean, it's not like the viscount had doppelgängers running around all over the place. Ugh, perish the thought!"

"So, what do you think? Do you believe the man actually was the viscount? Or just a stranger that looks like him?"

Kikue stared at him with wide eyes, then her whole body shuddered. "I-I don't know—is all I can say. Kindaichi-san, you'll have to forgive me. I was just so frightened. I don't consider myself a coward, but…"

"No, no, I'm sorry for asking. All right then, you're free to go. If you would, please ask Otane-san to come in."

They had a long wait. In the meantime, the chief inspector and the detectives had a heated conversation about Kikue's demeanour, but in the end, they could only come to the conclusion that her true feelings were a mystery.

"All that's sure is the woman isn't the slightest bit sad about the old man's death. More than that, I reckon, there's a part of her that's positively relieved. And she's not even trying to hide it," someone offered up to general agreement.

Otane arrived soon after.

Watching the maid coming in after Kikue was like watching a thin shroud of clouds sweep in to hide a blazing sunlit sky. Her shoulders were hunched unhappily, and in general she gave off the impression of a frightened little bird trapped in someone's palm. The result was that it was much harder to get any answers than it had been with Kikue. She answered easily when asked for her family name, age and the length of time she had served the family, but when it came to questions about her having seen the viscount, or at least someone who looked like him, she tensed up terribly, and her responses became slow and uncertain.

So, I will just offer a summary of her comments here.

When Doctor Mega ordered Otane to call Toshihiko Shingu, she rushed out of the back door. She was in such a hurry she forgot to pick up a torch. However, although there was some cloud cover, the moon was bright, so the garden was fairly well lit. And as large as it is, she is quite familiar with the estate grounds. So, Otane hurried through it without much trouble.

As has been mentioned, the grounds were filled with large *hinoki* cypress and oak trees. Although most were scorched and withered from the firebombing, some trees still stood, and they cast a thick shadow as she passed through.

Otane rushed between the trees, but suddenly stopped short. She had heard a sound. It was low and faint, and it cut out suddenly, but she recognized the high-pitched sound. She felt she must have been imagining things, but still her knees began shaking.

Then, she heard it again. It could not be called a melody, just a few notes, but there was no mistaking it. It was a sound she had heard for years: a flute.

A shock ran through her whole body like ice water, but she gathered up her courage, and cried out, "Who's that? Who's out there?" Her voice trembled.

Then, someone stood up from the underbrush some ten yards away. Otane's heart almost stopped on the spot. She tried to cry out, but her tongue was frozen in her mouth. She stared with unshaking focus, or rather, her whole body had gone numb so she couldn't avert her eyes. It was too dark for her to see clearly, but it was a man of medium build and height, dressed in a Western-style suit. He stood facing Otane, and she saw him hold something up to his mouth. A short sound came forth.

She saw it clearly. It was a flute. And just then, a break in the clouds let a beam of moonlight through to illuminate the man.

"S-s-so, O-O-Otane-san, d-d-did you s-s-see his f-f-face? C-c-clearly?"

Kindaichi struggled to get the words out through his stutter. Todoroki was so worked up that he looked like he was about to bite through the end of the pencil in his mouth.

The tension filling that drawing room was beyond the power of words. Everyone present was staring at Otane hard enough to bore holes through her. If gazes could set fires, then Otane and everything around her would have been burnt to a crisp.

"No, no." Otane's face crumpled in misery, and she drew a deep breath. "The moon was behind him so I couldn't see his face. But… but…" She took another deep breath. It put a tremble in the ends of her words.

"But, what?"

"When the moonlight fell on the flute he was playing, it shone. It sparkled. It… it was… a golden flute. It was the golden flute that the master played every day, the flute he loved… And… and the flute that disappeared along with him…"

Otane covered her face with her hands and began weeping. As her shoulders shook with her sobs, large pearl-like tears oozed from between her fingers.

For an instant, the room was filled with an icy silence. It was as if a chill swept through everyone's bodies. They all had to resist the urge to turn around and check behind them to see if anyone was lurking there.

"Otane-san," Kindaichi said after a moment, his voice thick and hoarse, "do you think that person was Viscount Tsubaki, or do you think it was someone pretending to be the viscount to frighten you?"

"No, no, I don't know!" She shook her head wildly back and forth. "But I'm sure that was the master's flute. And… and… I didn't see his face clearly, but the line of his jaw, and that sad posture… They were just… just like the master's. And then, mistress Akiko and Shino also…"

"That's all right, we can ask them what they saw. Now, tell us what you did next."

Otane sobbed and wiped her face with her sleeves, but went on, "I was so stupid. When I knew it was the master, I should have gone to him. He was always so kind, and so good to me. But... but I—"

She shook herself as if in anger before she continued, "The fear got too much for me, and I ran away towards Shingu-san's house."

"And I suppose you told someone there what had happened? That you saw someone who looked like Viscount Tsubaki?"

"Yes, yes, I did. But no one believed me. And of course, they were very worried about his lordship Tamamushi. However, on the way back to the main house, I passed by the spot where he had been, and when I mentioned it to Kazuhiko-san, he took a look around. Whoever it was had already gone, though, and he didn't find anything."

From the way Otane spoke, it was obvious that she believed the man in the trees had been Viscount Tsubaki. This murder case was growing ever more eerie. Everyone in the room exchanged nervous looks.

"I would like to ask you one more thing, Otane-san," Kindaichi said, struggling to keep his voice as casual as possible and not reveal the great excitement he felt. "It's about the room where his lordship was murdered. Did you look in through the *ranma*?"

Otane shook her head. "No, I was too frightened."

"Well then, do you know who did look? We already know that Doctor Mega, Mishima-san and Kikue-san all did."

"Yes, and young mistress Mineko and Kazuhiko-san did, as well."

"What about Shingu-san? Did he look?"

"That gentleman is… a fearful person. He's more fearful even than I am."

It seemed that Otane was of a similar opinion to Mineko, at least as far as the former viscount Shingu was concerned. When she spoke his name, the frightened woman's cheeks trembled in disgust.

"Thank you, that'll do. You may go."

"Thank you, sir." Otane turned her dull eyes on Kindaichi as she stood up and said, "Um, who should I call next?"

"Oh, no, thank you, I think we need to talk here for a bit. We'll have someone else go when we want to call anyone else in."

"Very well."

Otane bowed politely then turned to leave but stopped at the drawing room doorway as if nailed in place. She was frozen by the sight of an object in the hands of a detective who had come rushing in. As he passed, she took two or three steps after him, as if drawn in his wake.

The detective called out, "Chief Inspector, we found this in the bomb shelter in the back of the garden. I'm not sure if it has anything to do with the murder, though."

It was a battered leather case, about a foot long and three inches wide. Todoroki took it and opened it. It was empty.

"Kindaichi-san, what do you think this is?"

"Well, now…" He reached out to take it, but was interrupted.

"M-may I see that?" It was Otane. She was breathing heavily. Her hands quivered strangely as she reached out and touched it. Then, lips trembling, she said, "This… this is a flute case. I think that perhaps if you asked Mistress Mineko or Kazuhiko-san to look they could say more certainly, but I think this… is the case for the master's golden flute."

"A f-flute case? But a flute is much longer and thinner…"

"Oh, it can be broken down into three pieces. Then you store the pieces in this case."

"Then, this must surely be Viscount Tsubaki's flute case."

Chief Inspector Todoroki snatched it back and once more opened it up to look. He fiddled around with the interior, then his eyes opened wide. The veins at his temples swelled and the muscles in his cheek twitched wildly. He stood stock-still, looking into it for a moment, then he suddenly slammed the lid shut and took a deep, calming breath and turned towards Otane.

"O-oh, well, thank you, Otane-san, y-you can go now."

"Should I call mistress Mineko or Kazuhiko-san?"

"No, no, that's fine, just fine. We'll be talking to them later anyway, so you just head on out."

When she had vanished down the hall, Kindaichi stumbled over to his side and reached out a hand. "What is it, Chief Inspector? What did you find?"

Todoroki took another deep breath and opened the case.

"This fell out from behind the fabric lining the back of the case."

He held out a single golden earring sparkling with diamonds. Kindaichi's eyes bulged. He had no idea what it meant, but then the chief inspector turned to the detective who'd discovered the case and said, "Sawamura-san, take this earring to Tengindo in Ginza and ask if this is one of the pieces stolen in the robbery on 15th January. Make sure you don't tell them where it showed up, though!"

When Kindaichi heard that, the shock was like a hot poker running through his brain.

CHAPTER 10

Typewriter

"Ch-Chief Inspector!" Kosuke Kindaichi stared in amazement at Detective Sawamura's back as he took the earring and ran out of the room, and then he spun towards his friend. "Do you really think that earring was one stolen during the Tengindo murders?" His knees were shaking in excitement, and his tongue was thick in his mouth. Todoroki stared intently into Kindaichi's eyes, his gaze burning.

"I wo—" He cleared his throat, then tried again to speak. "I won't know for sure until Sawamura comes back with his report, but there were two sets of diamond earrings on the stolen goods list from the Tengindo Incident, but it seems the murderer was in a bit of a rush, as he only got half of one set."

"So, the other earring is still at Tengindo?"

"That's right; they're keeping it safe. So, if this earring matches the one stolen, they'll be able to tell immediately."

An eerie shiver ran up Kindaichi's spine.

"Chief Inspector..."

"Yes?"

"I've been trying to ring you over and over since the day before yesterday. There's something I need to ask you."

"Oh, sorry about that. I meant to contact you, too, but it's been so busy."

"Never mind. So, it seems that you were the one who sent Mineko-san my way."

"Yes, that's right. I felt like the story was just a bit too weird for us, but if I'd known anything like this was going to happen, I'd have paid closer attention."

"No, that's fine, but she told me that Viscount Tsubaki was considered a suspect in the Tengindo murders."

The chief inspector nodded silently.

"It also seems that the informant who set you on him was someone living here at the estate. Is that true?"

"Well, we can't be sure, but the letter did include details that only someone close to him would have known."

"What exactly was in that letter?"

Todoroki cocked his head, and said, "I don't remember all the details, but it did say that the viscount closely resembled the photo composite that was published. Also, he went on a trip around the time the Tengindo murders happened. He had told everyone here that he was staying at Ashi no Yu inn in Hakone, but he never checked in there. Then, just after his mysterious trip, the viscount consulted Totaro Mishima about selling some jewellery. That's about all I remember it saying."

Kindaichi paced the room thinking for a moment, then eventually stopped short. "So, did you look into the informant?"

"No, we never really thought about it. We don't much care who sends us information. We were only concerned with finding whoever was behind the Tengindo murders. And from the start, the viscount was behaving so suspiciously that we were really hot on him. But in the end, he coughed up an alibi. When we checked it out, we found that it was solid, and we had to let him go, free and clear. At which point, the information and informant were no longer important. So, we didn't investigate them any further."

Kindaichi started pacing the room once more. "So where did the viscount go on his trip?"

"Seems he went out west, to the Kansai region. He stayed at a *ryokan* inn in the Suma district of Kobe in Hyogo Prefecture from the night of the 14th through the 15th, the day of the murders. We checked it out, and it was rock solid. Or at least, that's what I thought, but now… Damn it all. If that earring was stolen from Tengindo, then…"

He clicked his tongue in irritation, pulled out a handkerchief and wiped the sweat from his thick bulldog neck.

It was no wonder that the man was so worked up. If the earring did turn out to be from the Tengindo Incident, then everything in the case would be turned on its head. It could be that Viscount Tsubaki had pulled the wool over the Metropolitan Police's eyes with a trumped-up alibi. In which case, the viscount's suicide would also come into question. Would that also turn out to be another masterful trick that Tsubaki had pulled? It could be that he was still alive somewhere after faking his own death.

Kindaichi felt a cold chill run up his spine. If all of that were true, then this case would go against all common sense and judgement, and all the strange suspicions and illusions of that bewitching flower Akiko could turn out to be the truth.

"But, then," he said, "why did the viscount wait so long to offer up an alibi? What would he be trying to hide that was more important than being a murder suspect in the awful Tengindo Incident?"

"Exactly! That's what made us all so suspicious! But from what the viscount said, it had to do with some complicated family issues. He said he needed us to keep his trip to Kansai and his stay in Suma a secret from his household. In fact, he only told us about it on the condition that we would keep it a secret."

"But what kind of family issues could they be?"

"I know. Thinking about it now, it is odd. Damn, so what was he playing at?" The chief inspector was still angrily wiping at his sweaty neck.

Kindaichi didn't answer, just kept pacing the room. Finally, he said, "By the way, do you still have the informant's tip-off letter at the department?"

"Of course we do."

"Well, if the informant really was a member of the household, couldn't we use that letter to track them down? Through the handwriting, for example?"

"No, that won't work. I mean, it wasn't handwritten. It was typed."

"Oh, really?" Kindaichi's eyes popped. "You don't mean it was written in English?"

"Not English, no, it was Japanese written in roman letters."

"Chief Inspector, I'd love to have a look at that. Could I?"

"Of course. You can see it anytime you drop by department headquarters."

Just then, hurried footsteps approached, and both men stopped talking to turn to the door.

Mineko came bursting in. She was as pale as wax, and her eyes were sharp and fierce. She had obviously talked to Otane. "Kindaichi-san!" Her teeth were audibly chattering as she forced out the words, "Did you find Father's flute case?!"

Then her eyes fell on the table, and she cried out, "There it is!"

She rushed over, snatched up the case and examined it with trembling hands. Finally she said, "Yes! Oh, it's true!" She groaned, and it was as if the sound was being wrung out of her whole body. Then she collapsed into a chair with a thump, both hands covering her face.

"Mineko-san," said Kindaichi, resting a hand on her shoulder, "are you sure it's your father's case?"

She nodded weakly, her face still in her hands. She finally pulled them away and looked at the leather case with misery in her eyes. "Kindaichi-san, Chief Inspector, what could it mean? Could it be that my mother was right all along? Did my father truly come back here last night?"

They had no answer for her questions.

Mineko went on, her voice an agonized moan, "How can I believe what anyone says? No matter how many times Otane says she saw my father, or Mother or Shino either, I can't believe them. Because... because, if he truly had returned home, he would have come to me before anyone else, wouldn't he? But that case... Oh, this terrible case... Kindaichi-san, did my father truly return here last night?"

Mineko put her face in her hands again.

"A policeman reported the case was found in the garden bomb shelter," said Kindaichi gently. "It could have been there for ages."

Mineko shook her head fiercely and said, "No, it couldn't have. I went to the bomb shelter two or three days ago. Whenever I want to get away from everyone or to think quietly, that's where I always go. I go sit in the quiet for a couple of hours."

Living in this peculiar home with three families all together, insulted by her mother and ignored by her relatives, that cold bomb shelter must have become a cherished sanctuary for the hard young woman. Kindaichi could not help but feel a pang of empathy at the thought of her longing for solace.

"There, there, Mineko-san," he said, patting her shoulder. "No more crying. This is not the time for tears. There are still lots of things I need to ask you."

She wiped her tears as she nodded and raised a face as white as parchment.

"Forgive me. I know that, but the thought of my father is just so sad. Even now he's dead, he's still being used by someone, some terrible person. But I won't cry any more. Ask me whatever you want." Mineko bravely sat up straight.

"All right then, first off, I want to ask about what happened last night. The others have already given us their stories, but I'd still like to hear it in your words."

Mineko nodded and started to speak. Akiko's episode had quieted down not long after Kindaichi went home, so Mineko had retired to her room. However, she was too worked up to get to sleep. She never even dreamed that the former count Tamamushi had remained alone in the divination room. Eventually, she started to nod off, until she was woken at around three o'clock by the sound of Otane's voice when she came for Doctor Mega. At that point she had gone down to the room with everyone else. Mineko told her story calmly and reasonably, but it held nothing new for them.

"Did you look in through the vent then?"

"I did."

"And what was your first thought?"

"I thought he had been murdered before Doctor Mega said anything, although Kikue-san and Mishima-san were talking about a brain haemorrhage."

"Why were you so sure?"

"I just had a feeling. I'm sure you can understand that, Kindaichi-san. And there was so much blood on the sand."

"That's right, what about that strange mark printed in the sand? Did you see it when you looked through the *ranma* vent?"

"No, I didn't notice it."

Kindaichi began scratching his head.

"When did you finally see it?"

"It was when Mishima-san and my uncle were standing next to it, arguing over something. That was after we'd been told to go back out into the hallway, but I peeked in just before and saw that mark."

"According to Mishima-san, Shingu-san was trying to throw sand over it to erase it."

"Yes, I'd say that sounds likely," she snapped.

The two men exchanged a look, then Kindaichi went on, "By the way, about the Raijin statue used as the murder weapon. I understand it's always kept in that room?"

"Yes, that's its usual spot."

"But, it's Raijin, right? That means it should be in a pair with a Fujin statue, but Doctor Mega and Mishima-san both claim not to have ever seen anything like that. Is there no Fujin statue?"

Mineko sat and looked Kindaichi in the face for a moment. She seemed confused by the question. "I suppose there's no reason they would know," she said eventually.

She sat and thought for a moment, then went on, "It must have been last summer, before Mishima-san came to stay with us. One evening, a thief broke into that room and stole the standing clock and the Fujin and Raijin statues we had there. Two or three days later, though, we found the Raijin statue lying in one corner of the garden. So now we have only the one left."

Kindaichi frowned at that.

"But why would the thief leave just the one statue?"

"I guess it ended up being too heavy, and they decided it wasn't worth the trouble."

"That's just it, though. If they thought Raijin wasn't worth the trouble, why would they think Fujin was worth carrying off? I mean, any proper thief would know they were a matched set."

"I'm sorry, Kindaichi-san, I have no idea how thieves think." Her voice sounded angry now.

Kindaichi looked somewhat abashed and said quickly, "Oh, dear, I'm sorry, I'm sorry, of course you don't. Well then, let's leave that for a moment, and move on. Did your father hold Mishima-san in particular trust?"

Mineko hesitated before answering. "What do you mean by trust, exactly?"

"Well, for example, let's say he wanted to sell some jewellery. Would he consult with Mishima-san in secret?"

Mineko nodded. "If that's what you mean by trust, then yes. However, Father didn't have any jewellery. Mother, of course, has more than she could ever need."

Kindaichi turned towards the chief inspector in shock. The informant's letter had clearly said that Viscount Tsubaki had consulted with Mishima in private about selling jewellery. And he did it right after the Tengindo Incident.

"But hypothetically, what if he got your mother's approval first? Might he have sold some then?"

"No, it's out of the question." Mineko's face took on its usual dark sadness when she talked about her mother. "You could pass a camel through the eye of a needle before you could convince my mother to sell her jewellery. She would give up the house before she gave up any jewels. She's completely obsessed with them. She's almost maniacal about it."

The other two exchanged meaningful looks again. If the claims in that letter were true, then whose jewellery had Tsubaki been trying to sell? Kindaichi's heart grew heavier by the moment. With a sombre face, he said, "I see. Well then, we'll leave that aside as well. I have one more thing I'd like to ask about. Is there a typewriter in this house?"

Mineko looked at him in surprise. She stared intently at him, as if trying to unearth some deeper meaning to the question, then eventually answered, "Yes, there is."

Kindaichi and Todoroki shared another look. Kindaichi went on, breathing more quickly, "There is? Who uses it?"

"I do. And why do you look so surprised by that, Kindaichi-san? Is there something wrong with me typing? After the war, Father recommended I learn, so I asked Mother for a typewriter and took lessons. I studied for five months. After I graduated last spring, I found a position with a certain company's public relations department. However, after everything that's happened, Mother began insisting that it wasn't respectable and won't allow me to work. I still want to, though. If it weren't for all this…" Mineko's eyes teared up again. However, Kindaichi was in no mood to offer any more comfort.

"Where is that typewriter? Could you show it to me, now?" He turned to leave, but she stopped him, saying, "Wait, I'll bring it here. It's quite light."

Mineko wiped her tears again and left the room.

"Todoroki-san, do you remember anything about the type in that informant's letter?"

"Well, now… I can't say one hundred per cent, but if there's a typewriter in this house, it has to be the same one."

Mineko soon returned with a small piece of equipment that looked like it would fit in a handbag.

"What a charming little thing. What's the brand?"

"It's called a Rocket. It's made by a Swiss company called Hermes. It isn't officially available in Japan yet. Would you like to watch me type?"

"If you don't mind!"

Mineko placed the typewriter on a table, opened the top and adjusted the machinery inside. She rolled a sheet of paper into it and propped up an English reading text to copy from. She set to typing with a clatter, and had soon filled the sheet with text. She seemed quite skilled.

"Is this enough?"

Kindaichi accepted the sheet of paper from her, took a look, then handed it to the chief inspector.

He stared at the typed words with wide eyes for a moment, and finally gave Kindaichi a nod. Kindaichi gasped audibly, then said, "Could you tell us, Mineko-san, if anyone else here can type besides you?"

"Yes, Kazuhiko-san and Kikue-san can. Kikue-san in particular is quite skilled. She can do it with her eyes closed. Her fingers remember the position."

"Kikue-san is really that good?"

"Yes, I taught her at first. She's really quite deft and dedicated. I'm not very fond of her, but I must admit I admire that quality in her."

Just then, Otane came to announce that lunch was ready and ask if they would be joining the family. It had passed noon without their realizing it.

CHAPTER 11

The Devil's Mark in the Flesh

Tokyo still struggled with food shortages in 1947, so lunch was a very modest affair, but it managed to satisfy.

"Let's keep moving, Chief Inspector Todoroki. We still have to talk to Lady Akiko and Shino-san, and then the Shingu family. Although I somehow doubt Lady Akiko will be of much help."

Todoroki looked at his watch and said, "Sawamura should be back with his report any time now. Kindaichi-san, why don't we go take a look at that bomb shelter before we get into any more interviews, what do you say?"

"That sounds fine to me!"

In fact, Kindaichi was tired out by the ever-growing tension from the morning's repeated revelations. The two men walked out into the garden, and a detective there guided them to the bomb shelter.

It was in a corner of the grounds far from the other buildings and completely surrounded by trees. A closed-top concrete structure, about four and a half tatami mats in area, it was so well appointed that it seemed more like an underground room than a bunker. It even had a simple but comfortable chair and table set. The only drawback was that it was dark, without any light fixtures.

The chief inspector looked around the gloomy shelter.

"So then, this is where Viscount Tsubaki, or someone pretending to be him, hid out last night?" he said.

Kindaichi ignored him, seemingly lost in thought, until he finally took to muttering under his breath. "I see, yes. This is the perfect spot. There's even a table and chair…"

Todoroki heard that and stopped short.

"Eh? Perfect for what? Perfect for that girl Mineko to come and meditate or whatever?"

"No, Chief Inspector, I was thinking about the typewriter. The type in that informant's letter matched the one in the house, right?"

"Yes, more or less. We'll have to have an official comparison done to know for sure, though."

"Please do. But for now, let's assume it was typed on the same machine. If it wasn't Mineko-san, who was it, and how did they manage it? That's what I was thinking about just now. Her room is the old-fashioned style that's closed off by *fusuma*, sliding screens rather than doors, so anyone could get in. But it would be much too risky to type in there, so they would have snuck the typewriter out, used it, then snuck it back in. But where did they do the typing? As you know, a typewriter is as loud as firing a machine gun. You could never do it in secret inside the house. So, whoever it was must have done it outside the house, but they didn't have a lot of time. And so, I was thinking that this bomb shelter would make the perfect spot. It even has a table and chair."

Todoroki took another look around, and said, "But what about the lack of light? You couldn't see the letters on the keys."

"You're forgetting what Mineko-san just said. Remember? She said Kikue-san can type with her eyes closed. Her fingers remember."

The chief inspector gaped in shock.

"Kindaichi-san, a-are you saying you think it was that Kikue woman?"

123

"No, no, that's not what I mean. What I'm trying to say is, with training people can type with their eyes closed. So, it stands to reason they could also type in the dark. Anyway, I think it's time to go. I doubt there's much more we can learn here."

The shelter had doors at both ends. The two left from the far one. After the gloom inside, even the leaden sky was almost blinding.

"Oh, that's right, Chief Inspector," Kindaichi said quietly, glancing around, "there was something I wanted you to have your men search for."

"What's that?"

"The Fujin statue that matches the Raijin."

Todoroki looked at him in surprise. "But, Kindaichi-san, wasn't it stolen last summer?"

"To me there's something not quite right about that story. If the thief had dropped Raijin, why would they have kept Fujin? No, no, if they dropped one, then they most definitely dropped the other. Anyway, I can't help thinking that the Fujin was here until recently, too. In fact, until last night."

Todoroki looked expectantly at Kindaichi, waiting for an explanation, but he had clearly finished talking. After a moment, the chief inspector frowned and said, "All right then. I suppose we can take a look around."

"Thank you! Just, please don't let anyone in the household know what you're looking for."

However, the Fujin statue was not found until much later, and when it turned up it was already too late to do any good.

On the way back to the drawing room, they passed a glass hothouse, which was set half underground, and although the section protruding above ground wasn't that high, the building looked quite spacious. It was long and narrow, about three yards wide and nine or ten yards long. As they passed, they saw a table covered in small pots inside, and more red earthenware pots hanging from the roof. A figure in work clothes was standing on the other side of the table. Whoever it was saw them walking by, they opened a small door and leaned out to take a look.

"Do you need something?" It was Totaro Mishima. The pruning shears he held hinted that he had been tending the plants.

"Oh, no, we were just walking by. Those look like some pretty rare flowers." Kindaichi bent down and looked through the door over Mishima's shoulder. The hot air that wafted across his face was heavy with the green smell of growing things.

"Yes, orchids, pitcher plants and alpine plants. The pitcher plants are quite rare. They eat insects. Would you like to take a look?"

"No, sorry, we're busy at the moment. Next time, though! They all sound fascinating."

"They are, like. The late viscount collected them, but now Kazuhiko-san has inherited them and is taking care of everything. I help out sometimes and all. I was just feeding a spider to one of the pitcher plants. Et's a little creepy, I suppose."

Kindaichi frowned a bit at him, then said, "By the way, Mishima-san, there was something I wanted to ask you."

"I see. Wait there a moment." Mishima washed his hands at a water jar by the door, quickly put his right glove back on, and then climbed up onto the ground.

"What is it?"

"It's about something that happened back in January. Viscount Tsubaki went on a trip, I believe. When he got back, is it true that he consulted you about selling some jewellery?"

Mishima's expression darkened, but he answered, "I have already told the police about that. But, yes, he did. He never did sell anything, though. In the end, his wife refused."

Kindaichi glanced at Todoroki, then looked back to Mishima.

"You mean to say that the viscount was hoping to sell some of his wife's jewellery?"

"That's right. He didn't tell me that at the time, but that's what he said when he called off the deal."

The three men walked silently towards the main house. After a moment, though, Kindaichi reopened the questioning.

"Mishima-san, I understand that your father and the late viscount were friends at school. Is that right?"

"Yes, at middle school."

"So, were you born in Tokyo?"

"No, I was born in the Chugoku region, out west, in Hiroshima Prefecture. I don't know if the city was Kure or Onomichi, but somewhere around there."

"Ha, you don't know where you were born?"

"Well, my father was a schoolteacher, and the school board sent him around to different places. My first memories are of Okayama Prefecture, next to Hiroshima."

"Ah, I see. I thought I noticed a western accent. Did you ever live around Kobe?"

"Not that I know of, no. I only remember Okayama and Hiroshima. I couldn't say where else my father lived, though."

"So, what brought you to this house?"

"That's quite a story. When I was discharged, I came home to find my mother had died. My father had already been dead for a while, and since I didn't have any other relatives, I came to Tokyo more or less out of desperation. I ended up as a broker for all kinds of black-market goods, and I started dealing with items coming out of these old estates. And that reminded me of the viscount. I'd heard his name from my father, and I remembered they had exchanged some letters back when they were both still alive. So, I thought he was probably having the same troubles as everyone else. Last autumn I came to see if he had anything he wanted to sell. Et ended up being the perfect timing. From that point on, I'd come calling every now and again, and eventually he asked me to just live here. I got the feeling that was the lady's decision, and not the viscount's. As for why I stayed on after his death, well, to tell the truth, they wouldn't last a day without me."

Just then, the three men came to an old, dried-up pond. Kindaichi started to walk around it, but Mishima stopped him, saying in his western accent, "There's a bredge here, let's use et. Don't worry, et's fine."

Kindaichi followed him across the precariously dilapidated bridge, but he had a curious gleam in his eye.

Mishima left them soon after, and Kindaichi and the chief inspector went on to the drawing room. They found an agitated Detective Sawamura waiting. His expression brought Kindaichi up short, and he immediately thought of the Tengindo murders.

"Chief Inspector!" Sawamura made as if to speak, but he stopped at a gesture from Todoroki, who quietly closed the door and walked over close to the detective, before asking, "So? What did you find out?"

Detective Sawamura didn't say anything. He simply took two envelopes out of his pocket. The name Tengindo was printed on the front of each, and the back was hand-labelled in fountain pen. The detective read the labels as he said, "This is the earring that you found earlier in the flute case, and this is the one left at Tengindo. See for yourself."

Kindaichi looked at the two earrings that had come rolling out of the envelopes, then squeezed his eyes closed. The thought of the terrible fate inexorably twining itself around this household filled his belly with lead.

Todoroki leaned back and gave a deep sigh. "That seals it. The man who was here last night, regardless of whether he was Viscount Tsubaki or someone else, is connected to the Tengindo murderer."

"But, Chief Inspector," protested Kindaichi, shaking his head fiercely, as if to trying throw off the emotions gripping at him. "Couldn't it just be that there are lots of these earrings out there?"

"No, it couldn't. These were part of a certain noblewoman's collection, and she had them made to order. There are no others like this set. Sawamura, come here a minute."

Todoroki whispered something into the detective's ear, who then quickly gathered the earrings back into their envelopes, stuffed them into his pocket and blew out of the room like a hard wind. He was most likely headed back to headquarters to make his report. Kindaichi could only imagine the chaos that would cause. He swallowed audibly, like he was gulping down something hot, and closed his eyes.

The chief inspector returned to his pacing. "Well, with that over, what do we do next?"

"I suppose we should interview Shino-san. She apparently also saw the viscount, or his twin, last night."

"Right!"

Todoroki immediately had one of his men summon her.

After some small trouble, the detective led the old woman into the room. She stopped at the door and simply looked from Kosuke Kindaichi to Chief Inspector Todoroki for a moment, then came in without a word. She sat down unbidden and looked again at the two men.

"I do not know what you have called me for, but I would appreciate it if we finished this as quickly as possible. I must return to Akiko-san right away." Her tone was thorny with irritation.

As has been described, perhaps no other woman in the world was as ugly as she, but at the same time, no other woman could have been as dignified. She had a broad forehead, protruding eyes and a snub nose over a wide mouth. Her whole face was as wrinkled as an old, worn-out dishrag. And yet, her hair was immaculately coiffed in a small bun at the back, her austere *yukata* robe was arranged perfectly, and her hands were folded demurely on her knees. The haughty aura she gave off as she stared sharply at the two men was strong enough to quell a rampaging army.

"Oh, sorry, we'll try not to trouble you for long. We just wanted to ask about last night," said Kindaichi.

Todoroki leaned forward. "We understand that last night you saw someone who strongly resembled Viscount Tsubaki. Could you tell us about that?"

Shino's gaze sharpened.

"Is that all? Then, I shall tell you," she said, her tone harsh.

"After everyone had gone to the studio, Akiko-san asked me to take her to the lavatory. And, before you ask, as much as she depends on me, that is not normal. However, last night was filled with such unpleasantness, and she was so frightened... No, we did not yet know about the murder. At any rate, she would not go by herself. So, I accompanied her, and as I was waiting outside for her to finish, I heard her scream. So, as indelicate as it might sound, I went inside as well. Akiko-san was pointing out of the window, saying that the viscount was standing there. She seemed to be losing control of herself even then. I looked outside to check, and about five yards from the window..."

"You saw Viscount Tsubaki, or someone appearing to be him?"

"Yes, holding a golden flute."

"Did you see his face clearly?"

"I did. The moonlight was falling directly on his face."

"Was it actually Viscount Tsubaki?"

Shino stared at the chief inspector with eyes as sharp as a bald eagle's. "How could I possibly know that? I only glimpsed him for a moment. But the resemblance was striking."

"What happened next?"

"Naturally, I rushed outside. It was right around then that Doctor Mega and Toshihiko—I'm sorry, Shingu-san—heard the screams and came running, so I told them what happened."

"Did the two men search for him?"

"No. Doctor Mega is elderly, and Shingu-san, well, he is not a particularly courageous man."

When she said this last, Shino's voice took a hateful tone, as thick and dark as ink.

Kindaichi and Todoroki exchanged startled glances. It was clear that nearly everyone in the household held Toshihiko Shingu in similar low opinion. There had to be more to it than simple dislike of his laziness and libertine lifestyle.

"What happened then?"

"That is really all I have to say. We called the police soon after, and I simply waited until all of you appeared. And of course... I was concerned about Akiko-san."

Shino began to stand, but Kindaichi rushed to stop her.

"Oh, one moment. I have one more question."

"What is it?"

"It's about the strange mark that appeared last night at the divination. The one that looks like a *kaendaiko*. What does it mean?"

"I do not know," Shino answered emphatically.

"But, at the time, I saw how surprised you were."

"Naturally. Anyone would be surprised, with that odd shape appearing in the dark as if it had been stamped there... And now, if you will excuse me."

She stood up from her seat and quietly left the room. Once more, she gave off that almost unbearable air of dignity.

But before Shino's figure had even disappeared from the doorway, a muffled voice and heavy footsteps filled the hall, coming closer. The voice was Toshihiko Shingu's. Shino came to a sudden stop and looked towards him, then hurried off down the hall.

Shingu burst into the room after her. He appeared to be quite drunk. His hair was standing up wildly and there was a dazed glint in his eye. On top of that, he was dressed only in his undershirt and trousers, without a dress shirt or jacket.

He stood with his beady eyes on Kindaichi and Todoroki for a moment, then a leering grin rose on his face as he started to pull off his shirt.

"Darling, please, there's no need for that! You can just explain—" His wife Hanako followed him into the room and struggled to stop him, but he brutally threw her off.

"Enough! Be quiet! You know the old bag already told them!" he said, and finally got his shirt off. He wavered on his feet as he went on, saying, "Right, so, I suppose you already heard from old Shino. Well, go ahead, take a good look at your devil's mark!"

Shingu turned his back to the two stunned men, revealing a pink birthmark in the same *kaendaiko* shape as had been on the sand, clear to see on his bony left shoulder.

CHAPTER 12

Y and Z

The *kaendaiko*…

Could this be the true meaning behind that devil's mark, the bizarre shape that had appeared to everyone not once, but twice since the previous evening, with such apparent significance?

Kindaichi was, for just a moment, almost thrown off balance by the revelation. But he quickly regained his composure enough to stare intently at Shingu's shoulder. As he did, he felt a strange shuddering rise up from the depths of his belly, like poisonous bile boiling up from the devil himself.

There was something grotesque about the pale pink *kaendaiko* standing out sharply against Shingu's sallow skin, stretched over emaciated flesh and patched with matted hair, as if standing testament to his decadent lifestyle. The room was filled for a moment with a crystalline silence. Everyone was petrified by the sight. They broke out in a cold sweat, to a man.

It was a long moment later that Chief Inspector Todoroki cleared his throat and spoke at last. "That's enough, Shingu-san. Please, get dressed."

His face still twisted in a scowl, he allowed his wife to help him put on his shirt, and took the seat that Todoroki offered him.

"That is quite an unusual mark. Were you born with it?" Kindaichi asked.

With the excitement of the moment past, Shingu's wild expression faded, and he nodded his head dully.

"It is unusual, I suppose. You can't usually see it at all. It looks like just a pale tracing under my skin, most of the time, and you can't even spot it unless you really try. But when I have a few drinks or a hot bath… I mean, when the blood really gets going, it shows up like that. Clear."

"Ah, so you've been drinking, have you?" asked Kindaichi, looking closely at Shingu's face.

"Yes, I suppose. A bit. But I'm not a drunk or anything. With all that's going on, well, a man can't get on without a drink or two. And then, I reckoned it would be easiest to just… Get it out of the way. Quickly as possible."

Kindaichi felt there might be something more to the drinking, as he recalled what Mineko had said about him.

"A big man when no one's around, but even at his age he's too shy to so much as speak to strangers."

Shingu probably wouldn't have been able to get through this interview without a few drinks in him.

"Did you know about this mark, ma'am?" Kindaichi asked Hanako Shingu, who started with surprise.

"Oh, well—"

"Of course she does!" Shingu cut her off. "We're married, after all. How could I keep something like that from my wife? What's got you so anxious anyway?" he snarled this last sentence at Hanako.

Something about her hesitation seemed to have irritated him.

"I see, I see. So then, who else knows about it?" asked Kindaichi.

"I suppose almost everyone in the household. I was born with it after all. I couldn't really say about the kids, though…"

"And Shino-san, too?"

"Of course she does. Didn't she tell…?" He trailed off, then looking back and forth between Kindaichi and Todoroki, seemed to realize something. "You mean to say, she didn't tell you about it? She didn't say anything?"

"She didn't, no. In fact, she more or less refused to tell us anything at all. I asked her what that *kaendaiko* shape meant, and she said she had no idea."

This time, Toshihiko turned his shocked gaze on his wife. His pale, dull face grew angrier by the moment.

"Hey, Chief Inspector, Kindaichi…" Shingu grumbled, twisting his hands in irritation, "I can't understand that. I don't get it. It's like everyone's trying to hide it. I mean, it's not like it's anything to boast about, but it's not some secret to keep hidden away, either. I don't go showing it off, but I'm not bothered by it or anything. So, then, why is everyone… Kindaichi-san…"

Shingu's eyes were full of anger as they turned to him.

"You remember the ceremony last night, right? The way everyone was so shocked when that shape appeared in the sand… I suppose I was, too. And so was Hanako. I mean, when something looking like your own birthmark appears out of the blue like that, right? But it feels like there was something different about everyone else. I know a strange shape appearing like that would be enough to surprise anyone. But they all know about my birthmark. So, why didn't anyone mention it? Why didn't they say, you know, without any bad feeling or anything, hey, look, that's the same shape as on Toshihiko's shoulder, or something?"

Kindaichi nodded without a word. That was exactly what he had been wondering.

Shingu kept his bleary, drunken eyes on the two men.

"It really got to me, last night. I was waiting for someone to say something. I was ready for someone to bring it up. I would have agreed with them. But no one did. Everyone seemed too scared to open their mouths. It was like, some kind of nasty curse or something. Why the hell was everyone so scared by my birthmark? Why are they trying to hide it? That's what I don't get. All my relatives already know about it."

Kindaichi stared probingly into the man's eyes and said, "And why didn't you say anything yourself, last night?"

"I wasn't trying to hide it or anything. I don't have any reason to hide it."

Shingu's sickly dark eyes flashed in irritation. His usual throaty voice had been replaced by a toneless squeak. "I was just taken by surprise. Not just by the mark appearing like that, but everyone's reaction to it. More than surprised, to be honest, I was taken off guard. And before I could say anything, that record started playing."

Kindaichi nodded again and asked, "Then I assume that was the reason you tried to get rid of the bloody mark after the murder?"

"Of course. To be honest, at the time I was kind of in a panic. There we were at the scene of a murder, and there was that birthmark drawn in blood. I couldn't see any reason for it. I still can't. But I couldn't help but think some kind of disaster was coming for me, after what had already happened. So, I just tried to erase it. Almost on instinct… Looking back, I suppose it was a stupid thing to do."

Kindaichi silently stood up, put his hands on his hips and took to pacing the room.

Finally, he said, "By the way, when Viscount Tsubaki's corpse, or rather, what we believed was his corpse, was found, he had a notebook in his pocket. One page had a drawing of a shape just like your birthmark, and it was labelled 'the devil's mark'. Did you know that?"

The hate and anger in Shingu's eyes grew as he stared at Kindaichi, and he nodded grudgingly.

"What do you think about that?"

"I just… I just can't figure that out, no matter how I look at it." Shingu was overcome with a fit of coughing, as if struggling to cut through thick phlegm filling his throat. He went on, "The only explanation I can think of is, that bas— that Hidesuke was crazy. Or did he actually think I was some kind of devil?"

A harsh laugh burst from Shingu's throat, but in fact it almost had the sound of a sob.

Kindaichi glanced quickly at Todoroki, then said, "Can you think of anything that would have made Viscount Tsubaki feel that way about you?"

Shingu's face darkened further as his rage burned hotter.

"I bet you lot know all about that, don't you? If you've talked to anyone around here, they'll have told you how things were between me and Hidesuke. He and I never got on. I hated him, that bastard."

"Why was that?"

"What reason did I need? I've hated him ever since he married Akiko. We were never able to talk like brothers. I suppose I just don't like pests like that." His squeaky voice had a strangely hysterical note, like the squeals of a child throwing a tantrum over sweets, or someone grinding their teeth in rage.

"Darling, please…" Hanako tried to calm her husband, but he once more pushed her away, saying, "Leave me be! If I tried to hide it, you know the others would tell it all. But none of that's reason for him to label me a devil. Me! When he's the one who robbed me of everything, all my money!"

"The Viscount Tsubaki robbed you?"

"What else can you call it? Akiko got everything that should have been mine. And then, when he married her, it went to him. What is that if not stealing?"

"Darling, please, don't say such nasty things…"

"Nasty? What's nasty? I'm just telling the truth. That's all. But that Hidesuke was just too weak. He never got to use it the way he wanted, ha ha ha!"

With the cruel laughter ringing in his ears, Kindaichi looked at Shingu's face afresh, realizing for the first time the true source of his hatred for Hidesuke Tsubaki. Their conflict had never been about a clash of character or values. Shingu would have hated any man that married Akiko, and he would have harassed that man just the same.

"I see, I see. And yet, I don't think that would quite have been reason enough for Viscount Tsubaki to call you the devil. Do you?" asked Kindaichi.

"Of course not. Like I just said, I think the man had lost his head."

"Maybe he had, or maybe that *kaendaiko* shape points to something other than your birthmark."

Shingu and his wife both looked at Kindaichi in surprise. Todoroki also threw him a quizzical glance.

Kindaichi kept slowly pacing the room as he went on.

"Otherwise, there really isn't any way to explain how the late Tamamushi and the others reacted when it appeared at the divination. Shingu-san has an unusual birthmark on his shoulder. That same shape appeared unexpectedly in the sand. Why would that surprise everyone so much? And not just surprise them. As Shingu-san just said, they were frightened. Very frightened of something, or someone. There must be a reason for that, but if it isn't Shingu-san himself—who actually bears the mark—then I can only assume it's something else. So, that means the shape in Viscount Tsubaki's notebook could also be pointing to something other than the birthmark, something that Shingu-san himself isn't aware of."

The room fell silent. Kindaichi kept pacing, hands still on his hips. Toshihiko Shingu looked frightened and anxious as he watched him.

"Um…" It was Hanako who broke the silence, with a strained voice. Her face, pale with anxiety, was contorted painfully, as she said, "I… I actually spoke with my husband about that this morning."

"I see. Go on, please."

"I was thinking that, perhaps someone drew that shape in blood in the sand to frame my husband. To make everyone think that he did that to his own uncle, and then left his mark there afterward."

"Oh, I see. Yes, I thought of that, too. And if that were the case, the *kaendaiko* stamped on the sand would have no hidden meaning but simply point to the mark on your husband's shoulder, making the case that much easier to solve. But that still doesn't satisfy me about everyone's reaction at the divination. There hadn't been a murder at that point, but they were still very unsettled by it. I really can't help but think that it has some other meaning. Or maybe…" He smiled gently. "… maybe there's some reason for all those people to be afraid of Shingu-san that he and his wife aren't aware of."

"What could that possibly be?" asked Hanako.

"Well, for example," Kindaichi said, a mischievous glint in his eyes, "they might be afraid that one day Shingu-san could end up killing someone in a fit of sleepwalking!"

"That's ridiculous!" Hanako's pale face twitched as she vehemently rejected the idea.

"Ha ha ha, of course it is, of course. I really do think that there must be some other meaning to the *kaendaiko* that you two don't know."

"Truly? Well, that would be a relief. But if it was some kind of attempt to frame my husband, then I can offer a perfect alibi. Last night, my husband was with me the entire night, in the other house."

Hanako had likely been wanting to say that the whole time.

"Thank you, yes, I'm sure he was. Right, seeing that birthmark was very helpful. Please, feel free to go now. Oh, and if you see Kazuhiko-san, would you ask him to come here? There's no need to worry, we just have a few simple questions."

And their questions really were quite simple. The night before, Kazuhiko had been one of those to view the murder scene through the *ranma* vent above the door.

"The bloody mark must have been there on the sand. When you were looking in, did you notice it?" Kindaichi asked, and the answer was an equally simple no.

"I see. Thank you very much. That's all it was. Oh, sorry, one more thing…"

"Yes?"

"I understand you were studying the flute under Viscount Tsubaki. Are you very good at it?"

"Oh, I wouldn't say I play that well, but I suppose I'm competent."

"Do you think you'd be able to play his last composition, 'The Devil Comes and Plays His Flute'?"

"Yes, I think I could. With the score."

"Is that so! I'd love to hear you play it sometime. All right. Thank you! That will be all."

Later, Kindaichi would look back and think that if he had only asked Kazuhiko to play the piece in question right then, he probably would have stumbled on the real murderer much earlier.

He didn't, though, and so, soon after the questioning was over, he and Chief Inspector Todoroki returned to the Tokyo

Metropolitan Police Department Headquarters, where they immediately examined the informant's letter.

As Todoroki had said, it was typed, but even an amateur could see that it had come from Mineko's typewriter.

"I don't see much room for doubt," Kindaichi said.

"Hmph. I'll send it to forensics for a thorough examination, but it seems clear enough to me."

"Right, and just like Mineko-san said, that machine—a Rocket, I think she called it—is not yet officially available in Japan, so it's not going to be something you can just find anywhere. But…" As he read the letter, Kindaichi frowned and cocked his head to one side.

"Is everything all right?" Todoroki asked.

"Well, it's just… There's something quite strange about this. Look, Todoroki-san, all the Ys and Zs are switched."

The text of the letter itself didn't offer up anything particularly useful. As the chief inspector had said, it described how the viscount had taken a trip somewhere around the time of the Tengindo murders, and although he told his family that he was going to Ashi no Yu in Hakone, he actually hadn't. It also described how some time after that unknown journey, he had asked about selling jewellery.

However, words including "Ashi no Yu" were actually written "Ashi no Zu", or "unfortunately" was "unfortunatelz", while, for example, "amazed" was typed "amayed". Afterward, someone had gone back and corrected those letters with a purple editing pencil.

CHAPTER 13

Kosuke Kindaichi Goes West

2 October.

The evening of the third day after former count Tamamushi's murder. Kosuke Kindaichi found himself pressed into one corner of a second-class car headed west on a semi-express bound for Kobe, feeling half-crushed to death.

Most people would dress in simpler Western garb for such a trip, but he was determined to remain in his usual traditional outfit. However, the already shabby *hakama* and kimono were now in even greater disarray, with the latter falling apart at the seams, and his *tabi* stockings covered in mud. The state of his clothing spoke of the great difficulties he had faced in reaching this cramped corner seat.

Travelling was a still a hardship in the autumn of 1947. Even getting a train ticket was no mean feat. Luckily, Kindaichi's connections with the police simplified that issue, but since the trains tended to be packed with black marketeers and their buyers, they were not places where public displays of police presence were welcome, and his connections did not go as far as securing him a proper seat. So now, Kindaichi found himself squeezed into this sardine-can of a train car looking like a crumpled handkerchief and gasping for breath.

He was not travelling on his own, though. A young detective named Degawa was supposed to be in the same car, but there was no way to fit him in among the other sardines. In any case, they would have chosen to sit separately. Given their destination on this particular journey, they felt it would be best to avoid attracting attention.

And their destination?

It should go without saying that the police were following up once more on the alibi that Viscount Tsubaki had offered when he was accused of being the Tengindo murderer.

When the news broke that a man resembling the late viscount had appeared like a phantom on the night of former count Tamamushi's murder, there was enormous public uproar and fear. The newspapers ran articles day after day, and every one of the major publishers had posted the majority of their reporters on the case. If it somehow came out that this crime might be connected to the terrible Tengindo murders, then the journalistic feeding frenzy would likely overwhelm the police.

So, Detective Degawa's dispatch had to be kept as quiet as possible. With the police also checking into the viscount's trip to Nagano Prefecture, where his body was found—naturally, they had sent another detective there—who knew what the press corps bloodhounds would sniff out if they noticed police were once more looking into the viscount's activities around the time of the Tengindo murders?

Kindaichi, however, had a somewhat different goal in mind when he asked to join the investigation. For one thing, no one could now be sure if the alibi Viscount Tsubaki had offered for the Tengindo murders was true or cleverly cooked up, despite the police's earlier confirmation. If it turned out to be staged, then it would be a masterful trick without precedent. However, if the previous investigation had been right and he truly had taken his secret trip west, then it must have held some extraordinary secret. Solving all the mysterious tragedies that had befallen the late viscount's family would likely require getting to the heart of that secret. Or so Kindaichi believed.

In fact, Kosuke Kindaichi had another particularly strong motive for taking the viscount's journey so seriously.

As mentioned previously, on 30th September, the day of Tamamushi's murder, Kindaichi visited the Tokyo Metropolitan Police Department, where he discovered a strange typing mistake in the informant's letter. He immediately rang Mineko and asked her what could explain it. She, however, did not know.

"The Y and Z are switched? Whatever does that mean?" she said, her voice full of confusion.

"Well, I was wondering if when you type, you sometimes accidentally switch a Y for a Z, and vice versa."

"Well, when you're still getting used to it, there are all kinds of mistakes you can make, but switching Y and Z like that… I don't really understand what you're getting at."

"You see, all of the other letters are correct, it's only those two. They're all switched. I was just wondering if there might be some kind of mechanical error, or perhaps a typist's habit, that would explain a mistake like that."

"I've never heard of such a thing. Switching only the Y and Z… How odd. But what could it mean? Is there something wrong with our typewriter, do you think?"

"No, no, please don't worry. I just wanted to see if you knew. It's fine that you don't."

Kindaichi hung up the phone, hopeless about finding any answer. But he was unable to stop thinking about it. It wasn't just one or two instances, but every single Y and Z were switched. He couldn't help but think that meant something.

Then, a day later, he got his answer. This time, it was Mineko who rang him.

"Kindaichi-san, it's about that Y and Z problem you called me about yesterday. I found something that might help…"

"You know how that kind of mistake might happen?"

"Yes. It kept bothering me, so this morning I called and asked my typing teacher. She told me what it might be."

"Well, what did she say?"

"I'd prefer not to discuss it over the phone, if you don't mind. Could I come to visit you? To tell the truth, there is something else I think you should hear. I've discovered something dreadful. I'm afraid that I have made a terrible mistake."

Mineko's voice was shaking so much that Kindaichi's heart skipped a beat.

"Oh, I see. That's fine, of course. I'll be waiting for you."

An hour later, she sat across from him in his annexe room at the Pine Moon Inn in Omori.

"So, about the typewriter..." Mineko's bleak face was pale, and her eyes shone with agitation, but she struggled to control the quiver in her voice as she spoke.

"Yes, you said you found something."

"That's right. I asked my teacher at the typing school, so this isn't something I've experienced myself. Kindaichi-san, I'm not sure if you know this, but the keys on a typewriter are not arranged in alphabetical order."

"Yes, I'm aware. I saw that yesterday at your house."

Mineko nodded and went on, "The letter keys are arranged according to how frequently they're used. In other words, the most commonly used letters are placed so that they are most convenient to the fingers needed. So, when typing, you can use all ten fingers, and each finger has its own letters. That's also how a highly trained typist can type with their eyes closed. Because the fingers remember."

"I see, so, wait a moment. If you could type with your eyes closed, that must also mean you could type in the dark, right?"

"Yes, of course."

"Now, what does that have to with the Y and Z?"

"Well, the letter arrangement is the same on any machine. That means if you learn to type on a Remington, you can type on a Rocket, even with your eyes closed. However, there is one exception. The keys are arranged differently on typewriters made for the German market."

"Different how?"

"The Y and Z are reversed compared to other typewriters."

Kindaichi's eyes snapped open wide. He reached up and started scratching at the great sparrow's nest atop his head with all five fingers, so fiercely that the dandruff began to fly like goose down.

"Oh, my!" Mineko slapped her handkerchief over her mouth and rocked back on her bum. She stared at Kindaichi with stunned eyes and choked out, "Kindaichi-san!"

"Ahahah, s-s-sorry, sorry, y-you're s-saying th-that G-G-German t-t-typewriters h-h-have r-r-reversed Ys and Zs?" Kindaichi stuttered out, then gasped as he gulped down the tea sitting on the table. He then pressed one hand to his abdomen, just below his navel, which seemed to help him stop stuttering and scratching at his head. Mineko patted at her chest to calm herself.

"Yes. Exactly. I don't speak German, though. I can only assume that the frequency of Y and Z in German is the opposite of English. So, a typewriter being exported to Germany would have the machinery adjusted to reverse those keys."

"Yes, I see. So, then, are any of those typewriters found in Japan?"

"Yes, trading companies dealing with Germany would probably have some."

"So, then, it's like this… A person who learned to type on a German-market typewriter well enough to type even with their eyes closed would accidentally switch Y and Z if they used your typewriter to type in the dark or something."

"My typewriter? Kindaichi-san, what was that about my typewriter?"

"Oh, no, that was just an example."

Kindaichi's mind wandered back to that dark bomb shelter in the garden of the Tsubaki estate. As he imagined some unknown person sitting in the gloom, typing without realizing their reversal of Ys and Zs, a nameless emotion seemed to well up from the depths of his belly. At the very least, they had made one serious mistake.

"Thank you so much. That is extraordinarily helpful. So, then, what was the other thing you wanted to tell me?"

"Yes, about that…"

Mineko, who had up to then been staring directly into Kindaichi's eyes, suddenly started trembling, as if she were on the verge of weeping.

"I… I made a huge mistake. But now having realized that, I'm more confused than ever."

She then took an envelope out of her handbag. "Kindaichi-san, you already saw this, but I think you should read it again."

The Viscount Tsubaki's final note to Mineko, the same one that Kindaichi had seen when she first came to him. The text has already been reprinted in this book, but for reference, here it is again.

Dear Mineko,

Please, do not hold this act against me. I can bear no more humiliation and disgrace. If this story comes to light, the good name of the Tsubaki family will be cast into the mud. Oh, the devil will indeed come and play his flute. I cannot bear to live to see that day come.

My Mineko, forgive me.

"So, what about it?"

Kindaichi looked up at the young woman in confusion then suddenly blurted, "Wait, is this a fake?!"

"No, no, not at all. That is definitely my father's handwriting. But, Kindaichi-san, you see that there's no date on the note. That is why I made the mistake."

"Which is?"

"As I told you before, I found this letter long after my father's disappearance. It was in summer, when I went to air out my books in storage and it fell from inside one of them."

"Yes, I remember you saying so."

"This is the book."

This time, the handbag produced the second volume of Goethe's *Wilhelm Meister's Apprenticeship*, in a pre-war translation.

"I see. And what is it about this book?"

"I had this book on my desk last spring. I put it into storage without realizing it, but I don't think my father would have chosen some book at random from the storehouse. With all the books in there, he would never know when or if I would see his note. So, he must have put his note in this one while it was still on my desk, don't you think? And it was even his recommendation that got me to start reading it in the first place."

"I see, I see. So…?"

"So, the problem is, when did I put this book into storage? I never thought about it, but yesterday, after what happened, I looked through my diary entries from around the time of his disappearance, hoping they might help me remember something about what had happened. And then I found…"

She took another book from her handbag. It was a woman's diary with a red cover.

"Please, look at this."

Kindaichi followed her trembling finger, and saw under the date 20th February:

Morning. Finished Wilhelm Meister.
Afternoon, decided to clean up around my desk. Put finished books into storage.

She had written it in purple ink.

"I see, that means you put this book into storage on 20th February, so your father must have hidden his note in it before then."

"That's right. But, Kindaichi-san, 20th February was the day that the police took my father for interrogation as a suspect in the Tengindo murders."

He had been staring into Mineko's burning eyes. Now he instinctively leaned forward across the low table. "Wh-wh-what?! Th-th-that must mean he had decided to kill himself b-b-before he was a Tengindo suspect?"

"Oh, Kindaichi-san!"

"And s-s-so, your f-f-father didn't kill himself because he was a suspect in the murders."

"No, he didn't! In fact, his interrogation in relation to the murders most likely delayed his suicide by ten days."

Mineko's eyes filled with tears, but she kept talking without wiping them away.

"According to my diary, I finished reading this book that morning. So, he had to have placed the letter in it that afternoon before I put it into storage. He must have planned to set off on his final trip right after that. But then the police came and took him away, and he had to put it off until 1st March. I suppose he must not have wanted to die under such terrible suspicion. He wanted to wait to be cleared."

Kindaichi's chest was heaving like a boat in a storm. This discovery must have been an enormous shock for Mineko, just as it was for him. "So, if the Tengindo case didn't drive your father to suicide, it must have been something else."

"Exactly. He could have had any number of reasons, but what I can't understand is the note itself. He said he could bear no more humiliation and disgrace. That if the story came to light, the good name of the Tsubaki family would be cast into the mud. What was that humiliation, the secret that could drag my family's name into the mud? I was sure it was his being under suspicion in the Tengindo murders. But this note was written before he was ever accused, so it must be something else. What kind of truth could lead to such humiliation that my father would kill himself over it?"

Sitting in that sardine tin of a train car, Kindaichi thought back on Mineko's twisted, tear-stained witch's face. The cold demonic energy that had wavered around her like a dark flame seemed to have seeped into him and taken root somewhere in his body.

That was one reason he had decided to take this journey.

Viscount Tsubaki had taken a mysterious trip from 14th to 17th January—if in fact it had been Viscount Tsubaki. He felt that the key to all these enigmas was hidden in that journey.

The train rolled on through the dark, heading ever westward.

The bustling black marketeers and their customers seemed to have all settled down and drifted off to sleep. Kindaichi and Detective Degawa, surrounded by those dubious characters, tried to get some sleep themselves, their vital mission weighing on their minds. But never in Kindaichi's wildest dreams did he imagine that someone else with an intimate connection to their case was on that same train.

CHAPTER 14

The Outskirts of Kobe

Kosuke Kindaichi's Tokaido Line train pulled into the main station at Kobe two hours late. From there, he and Detective Degawa took a government line to Kobe's Hyogo station, and then transferred to the Sanyo Electric Railway to Suma Station. It was after one in the afternoon on 3rd October before they were finally settled in at a *ryokan* called the Three Spring Garden Inn, near the pond at Sumadera temple. They had planned to stay there, and even though they were unfamiliar with the area, they had little trouble finding it. However, rain had started pouring as soon as they reached the city, and Kindaichi immediately had the feeling that their investigation would not be easy.

The one saving grace, he found, was that the Three Spring Garden Inn was not one of the shady new-built inns, aimed at couples looking for some brief privacy, that had proliferated after the war—the ones with the fake *onsen*, hot spring signs. Rather, it was a grand old lodge with a long history—as well as wide gables to keep the rain off—and a calm atmosphere.

Kobe had been heavily bombed in the war, and the district of Suma itself was mostly burnt out, but the area around Sumadera temple had been largely spared. These few old, miraculously surviving buildings standing in that heavy autumn rain served as faint reminders of better days long gone. The Three Spring Garden Inn was itself a serene testament to those days, as well.

That also meant, though, that it was stiffly formal, and Kindaichi and Detective Degawa had to go through quite lengthy negotiations before they even managed to get through the door.

They had refrained from sending word ahead to the local police since they were trying to keep the details of the renewed investigation quiet, so Degawa had to convince the innkeeper that their work was on the up and up. Then once he had succeeded, Kindaichi could not help but sense a certain heightened tension filling the stately old inn.

"Degawa-san, I get the feeling this is going to be a tricky bit of investigation, so we should try not to rush things. For now, what do you say to starting with a hot bath and a meal?"

The maid who had shown them to their tatami-mat room was visibly nervous, and as he watched her slink out of their presence, he nodded his agreement with Kindaichi's caution, saying, "Yes, let's not get ahead of ourselves." Despite his words, though, the young detective was excited about this important work.

Degawa was a couple of years younger than Kindaichi, and what he lacked in experience was more than made up for by a zealous spirit that seemed to actually radiate from his short, stocky frame. The detective who had checked Viscount Tsubaki's alibi originally had another assignment now, so young Degawa had been chosen to take his place. The honour of such an important task was reason enough for his enthusiasm.

Still, he agreed calmly to Kindaichi's suggestion of a bath and a late lunch. He casually probed the maids who came to serve them with a few questions, to see if any of them would open up, but none offered even a single word in response. Clearly, the innkeeper had warned them to keep quiet.

"Damn, their mouths are all sealed up tight."

Degawa smirked as he watched the maids scurry out of sight. Just then an authoritative-looking woman of around forty appeared. She was as round as a small hill. Here, finally, was the inn's *okami*—the woman running things.

"Welcome. I imagine you're well tired after that long trip. I do hope everything's to your liking."

The *okami* greeted them with impeccable manners, befitting someone so experienced in her business, but the two men could sense a note of caution in her tone.

"Oh, actually—" Detective Degawa broke off, searching for the right words.

"Is there a problem?" she asked, shooting him a sharp stare. "I spoke to our head clerk. He says you're here looking into Tsubaki-san again?"

Her expression betrayed her annoyance at this. While most people these days were happy to get their names in the press no matter the reason, clearly this innkeeper was not. Kindaichi was starting to get the feeling their opponent here was a formidable character indeed, and Degawa seemed to have noticed as well.

"Yes, that's right. We're so sorry to be bothering you again with this," Degawa resumed.

"No, no bother, really, it's just… Well, we thought that was all finished up and everything."

"So did we, to be honest, but there's been another incident. I'm sure you've heard about it. A few days ago, in Tokyo?"

"Oh, dear, do you mean the one that was in the papers? That sure gave us all quite a shock."

"I can imagine. But it means we need to look into everything again."

"Like I said, I thought you looked into everything properly the last time. There's nothing I can tell you now that I didn't then."

The woman showed no signs of lowering her guard, so Kindaichi decided to get involved. "I hope you don't mind my interrupting, Okami-san."

"Not at all."

"We're not out here to check up on you and your place."

"You're not? Then, what are you here for?"

"The d-detective who came here last time was only trying to verify if Viscount Tsubaki had been here around 15th January, and that was all. Wh-when that was established, we all thought that line of investigation was closed, until this new murder happened. They didn't send us out here to reopen the question of whether the viscount really stayed here, but to investigate what he did during his stay. To find out why he came here in the first place. The earlier investigators didn't look into any of that because they didn't know they needed to."

"Ah, I see. Yes, I think I understand." She finally seemed convinced they were sincere. "Then, we're not directly involved in your investigation?"

"Exactly so. Nothing w-w-we do is going affect you or your inn. We actually could have stayed anywhere, but since we're focusing on the area around Sumadera t-temple because that was where the viscount spent his time during his trip, I thought if we stayed here it would make things more convenient for us."

Kindaichi, as rough and tumble as he might appear, has an unusual charm that seems to draw in and persuade people. As he scratched away at his great shock of hair throughout his stammered explanation, the *okami* seemed to relax.

"Well, that makes some sense. If that's the case, then I'm sure I have no objection. I confess, I was worried you had started to doubt what I said the last time."

"N-no, not at all!"

"I also think it's just so sad that a quiet, charming fellow like that would ever be suspected of something so terrible as those Tengindo murders. I admit, we felt a bit put out over the whole thing."

Kindaichi instinctively glanced at Degawa.

"So, that means you were aware that the last investigation was connected with the Tengindo murders?"

"Well, of course! I mean, the police never mentioned anything about it, but there was that picture of the murderer en the papers, and well, with the date and all... But of course, if that kind of news got out, you know, et would cause all kinds of trouble around here, so I told all our people to keep their mouths nice and shut, like. But then we got that other business, and then thes new murder and all, and well, we got to talking about things, like."

Her Kobe dialect grew stronger by the word, which was evidence that she was finally letting her guard down in truth. Kindaichi cleverly picked up on that and pushed a bit harder.

"So, do you think that was the reason Viscount Tsubaki killed himself?"

"What else could it be? Et was just after that, and everything. Et seems the newspapers didn't know much, though, and they said all kinds of things and all," she said and gave a little shake of her head. "And, when he stayed here, you know, I ded think he seemed a bit odd. He had the spirit of death on him, like."

"Odd? How so?"

"Oh, now, et wasn't anything bad, really, but he just seemed so dark and quiet, like. To be true, we all were a bet worried he was actually here to kill himself. You know, thes es a place people like to do that and all. And you know, in our business, we do get guests like that now and then, like."

"Thank you, Okami-san. I was also hoping you could tell us what the viscount did when he came here. We're trying to work out a timeline, so the order is important. To begin with, did he have a reference from another guest when he came?"

"No, nothing like that. You know, things have gotten so bad these days that many a place won't let lone guests stay at all, like. A gentleman on his own will often refuse to stay without a promise that the *ryokan* will bring en a woman for him, you know. Such a dirty business, that es. But, you know, he came stumbling en after all the other *ryokan* around turned him away and all. We don't have a policy against men on their own, as such, but I do tend to turn away guests we haven't seen before. You know how it is. We ded say no at first, actually. But, well, him being a gentleman and all, and he just seemed to be en such a sorry state that I felt sorry for him and offered him a room."

"And that was January…?"

"The 14th, et was. No mistake. He was en the ledger and all, and what with the police coming to check just a month later, we remember clear as day, like. Et was ten en the evening on 14th January, meaning the day before the Tengindo murders, and I showed him into this very room myself."

At that last bit of information, Kindaichi and Detective Degawa both started looking around the room in wonder. Kindaichi had noticed that despite the initial reluctance to even let them in, they had ended up in a much nicer room than he had expected. Now, he realized that the innkeeper had a hidden motive for that.

They were in a large eight-mat room with an adjoining six-mat room, and the *shoji* screens opened onto a well-tended garden visible through the autumn rain. It was a deeply calm, reserved space, and the man in question had been sitting in this very room at the time in question. The thought generated a certain tension in both men's bodies.

The detective, his face now tight with nerves, asked, "How long did the viscount stay here?"

155

"He stayed for three nights, the 14th, 15th and 16th. He left early on the morning of the 17th, like."

"And was he here that whole time?"

"Oh, no, of course not. He went off somewhere on the 15th and the 16th, but you can't think he could leave at nine en the morning on the 15th and show up around ten at Tengindo in Ginza, do you? Not hardly!"

Kindaichi could see her expression darkening and hastened to calm her down. "No, ma'am, that's not at all what he's getting at. We're just trying to establish the order of events, like I said. By the way, apart from that, there's something else I'd like to ask. Are you absolutely certain the man who stayed here was Viscount Tsubaki?"

"Oh, now, you... Here, just a moment, Detective, could you ring that bell for me? Thank you."

He rang as asked, and one of the maids who had brought their lunch appeared.

"Osumi-chan, be a dear and go ask the head clerk to bring the ledger, would you? And you come along with him, thank you, pet."

Osumi returned right away with the clerk in tow. He was a fair-skinned man of about thirty-five, dressed in a striped kimono and heavy apron in a style perfectly suited to this traditional old inn. It was he who had confronted the visitors at the front door. The *okami* opened the ledger and slid it over in front of the two men.

"The guest wrote thes entry himself, and I do believe the handwriting analyst confirmed et was Tsubaki-san's writing, like. Esn't that so?" she asked the head clerk.

He nodded mute agreement.

As one would expect from such a fine inn, the ledger was made from thick *washi* paper, and the names were all written with brush and ink. There, on the open page, was the Tsubaki estate's Azabu-Roppongi address, and the name Hidesuke Tsubaki, written in what even Kindaichi could see was the man's own handwriting. The date box was filled in with 14th January.

"Now, surely you wouldn't think we would do anything tricky with the date en the ledger for the sake of some stranger we've no connection weth at all, would you? And the clerk and Osumi-chan here even went all the way to Tokyo to make witness statements. They ded one of those, what do you call them, a line-up? They confirmed et, they did, there was no mistake. The man who came to stay here from the 14th until the 17th was Tsubaki-san. Esn't that so?" she asked Osumi, who also nodded mute agreement.

The head clerk fidgeted anxiously at his knees, and asked, "Okami-san, es there some kind of problem?"

Kindaichi answered in her stead. "No, no, not at all. We came down here to investigate some other things. But just to clarify what happened and in what order, you see, we want to make sure one more time that the person who stayed here from the 14th actually was Viscount Tsubaki. Degawa-san, I think we can put that down as confirmed, don't you?"

"Yes, I suppose so," the detective said with a grimace. The ambitious young man must have been thinking he could make a name for himself by discovering a flaw in the alibi, but the staff had put an end to that. It was also becoming clear that they were unlikely to learn anything new from these people that wasn't already in their testimony.

But Kindaichi, betraying not a hint of disappointment, went on, "So, clerk, as we were just explaining to Okami-san here, our goal this time is actually rather different. We'd really appreciate your help in our real investigation."

He explained again what they had told the proprietor, and

the clerk and Osumi exchanged thoughtful glances, but they had no new information to offer.

"He really was just a very quiet man. I don't know that I heard him say more than a few words. Yes, he did go out on the 15th and 16th, but I don't know any more about where he went than you do," said the clerk.

After he said this, bowing a little in apology, Osumi spoke up, "He went out the morning of the 15th and all, but he came back just after noon. He had lunch, then he went out again, and came back en the evening, like. I reckon that means he dedn't go very far, at least on that day, you know."

"Oh, that es right," the *okami* said and nodded thoughtfully. "She's got that right. I still remember talking about that during the Tengindo investigation. And then on the 16th, he said that he would be getting back late, so he wanted us to fex him up a *bento* lunch to take."

"Oh, right, right, and I made him up a rice ball and all. What time did he get back, was it?"

Osumi thought for a moment, then said, "Et had to be around five in the evening, I reckon. Et was winter and all, so it was already dark, like. I can't rightly say why, but he was so thin and… Frayed, like. He had the look of a man with no life left en him. Okami-san had been saying that she reckoned he was here to kill himself and all, and I was well worried, like. Then he came back like that, and I thought he'd gone and done et, and come back anyway. From the dead, like."

Kindaichi and Degawa exchanged a quick glance.

If something had happened to Viscount Tsubaki on this trip, then it was almost certainly during this outing on 16th January. And that is what had driven him to suicide.

"Did he give you any idea about where he was going or where he'd been?"

"Not a word, no. First off, et felt so eerie, like, when I was serving dinner, that I couldn't bear to talk to him. His face looked such a state and all."

The clerk interrupted, "You know, he must have gone to Akashi. That's what I think."

Detective Degawa perked up at that. "You do? Why?"

"I can't rightly recall ef et was that day or the day before, but he asked me ef et would be better to take the government line or the Sanyo line to Akashi. And so I said, that would depend on where en Akashi he was going to. After that, he just went quiet and walked off."

"Listen, Okami-san, Osumi-chan, can you think of anything, anything at all, that he might have said? Even in passing? Like the clerk remembered, just now. It doesn't matter how small it might be, we want to hear it," said Kindaichi.

The three fell silent and looked at each other for a moment, then Okami-san smoothed her kimono over her mountainous thighs and said, "So, you mean to say, you came to find out why Tsubaki-san came out and all, but you've got nary a clue what et could be yourselves, like? You don't have even the slightest idea what kind of thing et might be, even?"

She glared at Kindaichi as she said this.

"No, I wouldn't say that," he replied. "I think that there was something about his family, something that he didn't know but had heard rumours about recently, and he came here to look into it."

Okami-san started fidgeting nervously when she heard that. She mopped her brow with the end of her sleeve, then turned to the clerk and Osumi, and said, "You two can run along now, thank you. I'll call for you ef I need you, like. Oh, and bring us en some tea, would you, pet?"

Kindaichi and Degawa exchanged looks once again.

She knew something.

CHAPTER 15

Count Tamamushi's Villa

"You know, the other day I read the newspaper and didn't I get half a shock? That story, about his lordship Tamamushi's murder, like."

The *okami* continued fidgeting as she offered them the tea that Osumi brought, as if she was still hesitating over whether to speak up, but it seemed she might be ready.

"His lordship Tamamushi," began Degawa, glancing over nervously at Kindaichi. "Did you know him?"

She nodded slowly, and said, "I did, yes, but that can wait until later." She picked up her teacup and looked down at it as she caressed its warm sides, then went on. "I never would have dreamed that Tsubaki-san had any connection to his lordship Tamamushi until I read et en the newspaper. I mean, I had no idea that Tsubaki-san was even a viscount and all when he came here, like. He didn't put et en the ledger, you know. I didn't find that out until the business with the Tengindo murders. Even then, I never would have dreamed he'd married his lordship's niece and all. His niece, now, I knew her, too. A long time ago, like."

The two men looked at each other again. Degawa opened his mouth to say something, but Kindaichi stopped him. The innkeeper was in the mood to talk. It was best not to interrupt.

"So. Akiko was her name. Et was the newspaper that reminded me of her. She was so lovely, she was. Plump and darling as a little doll, you know. But, the nobility, well, they have their ways, not like we common folk. She came by time to time, you know, and would deign to have a chat, like. I reckon she must have been right about my age."

Kindaichi noticed Degawa opening his mouth again and glared him into silence.

The woman took a slow sip of tea and put her teacup on the table, then looked back and forth between the men.

"But, what I've got to tell you, et's not to do with all that, you mind. I only knew that Tsubaki-san had married young Miss Akiko when I saw et en the papers and all. And, well, I was just thinking, ef only we'd treated him a bit more proper, like, when he was here, you know. And then you said all that, just now, well… Et made me think, et did. When Tsubaki-san was staying here, he mentioned his lordship Tamamushi's name. Just the one time, mind you, just the one time."

Kindaichi and Degawa both froze. Okami-san went on, still looking back and forth between them.

"Et must have been the morning of the 15th, I reckon. Like I said afore, the man was just so quiet and dark, like, that I was afraid he was here to do himself harm. And then, the girl who did his breakfast came and said he had just the queerest look on his face, so I came to see to him myself. I reckon I was here ten or twenty minutes, talking about thes or that, you know. I don't rightly recall what we were chatting about, but I do know there was some talk of all the grand old houses and villas that used to be about, but they were all burnt down in the war and all. Et must have been that what made him say that he'd heard that Count Tamamushi once had a villa en these parts."

"Count Tamamushi had a villa here?" Kindaichi blurted out, forgetting how he'd been keeping Detective Degawa from speaking this whole time. "Is that true?"

The *okami* nodded, her great double chin wobbling.

"Oh, yes, indeed. Now even the foundations are all burnt away, though. En truth, he left it before the fires. He sold it off long ago, you know."

"Do you recall just how long ago?"

"Well, let me see… I don't rightly recall when it were, but there's a hill called Tsukimiyama over yonder, you know. There's where Count Tamamushi had his villa, and that would have been when I was but a girl, like."

"So, when you talk about knowing Count Tamamushi and Akiko-san, that's when it was?"

"Just so. Back then, when someone came to visit at the villa, they used to come here for dinner. I do hate to brag and all, but there's no better place for dinner in these parts, you know. Course, there are all kind of places to eat over Kobe city way, like."

"And that was back when you were a girl. That must mean that this inn is your family's?" said Kindaichi.

"Yes, I was born to this place, me. I had me a husband, and he married into the family here, but he was sickly, like, and passed a few years back."

A strange little smile played across her face, but her serious expression returned immediately.

"Now, I don't recall his lordship visiting after I married, so he must have sold the villa by then, I reckon."

"I hope you'll forgive me, but how old are you? In your forties?"

"Only just, like."

"Forty years old, then. The same as the Lady Tsubaki…"

"Yes, ef I remember her age right, like."

"And when did you marry?"

"When I was nineteen. My folks waited for me to leave school, like, then rushed me right into et."

"So, that means that Count Tamamushi must have sold off his villa more than twenty or twenty-one years ago."

162

"I s'pose so. And so, the last time I saw Miss Akiko must have been when I was sixteen or seventeen, I reckon."

"And Akiko-san came from time to time?"

"Well, now... I don't rightly recall, you know, but et seems that some young men and women relations would come out en turn each summer. The newspaper the other day also reminded me that I saw young Toshihiko-san from time to time, and he came out to his lordship's villa with Miss Akiko. I saw them together at times, you know. We were all so young, those days."

Her eyes misted over, and she seemed to be taken away from the room into the past for a moment. Detective Degawa, though, had no time for her nostalgia.

"Okami-san, could we get back to what you were just saying? Viscount Tsubaki was asking about Count Tamamushi's villa?"

"Right, about that," she said, then sat and tried to recollect for a moment. "When I think on it, I likely shouldn't have said anything, you know. His lordship's name came up, and of course I mentioned that I'd known him way back, like. When I did, though, Tsubaki-san seemed to go on his guard, like. He changed the subject quick as. And that was the end of et. If I hadn't read the newspaper, like, and you all hadn't come by, I suppose I'd have forgot all about et, like."

The *okami* fell silent and sat staring down at her knees for a moment. Degawa sat up on his knees. "It sounds like Count Tamamushi's old villa could have something to do with Viscount Tsubaki's reason for coming here," he said excitedly.

"I'm sure I wouldn't know. Any rate, that was the only time his lordship came up."

She sat quietly smoothing her knees, but it was evident that she knew something else, and was struggling over whether to say it or not.

Kindaichi glanced briefly at Degawa, then leaned forward on his knees. "Listen, Okami-san. This man came all this way to see if he could turn up something that the earlier detective missed in his investigation. You can see he's still young. He's got a long career in front of him, and he's got to make a name for himself. But for him to do that, he's going to need the help of kind people like you. So, if there's something else you can think of about Count Tamamushi, it would be really helpful."

She smoothed her kimono again, then said, "That's as might be and all, but et's not really up to me."

"Listen, Okami-san, did something happen when Viscount Tsubaki's wife, Akiko-san, was here?"

At that, she looked up at Kindaichi in astonishment.

"Ah, now I see. That's what her husband, the viscount came here to check into, then. Some old family scandal, like. But I don't know anything like that. What I do know might well be a scandal, but et's not to do weth Akiko. And that's why I wasn't sure if I should say anything or not, you know."

The men exchanged glances again. She truly did know something. Something about a scandal involving the Tamamushi family or other relatives.

"Okami-san, anything at all. If you know something connected to those people, whatever it might be, please tell us."

She hesitated for a short while, then finally opened her mouth. "Ef you insist so, then I reckon I ought to say. But… This story stays here between us, ef you please. That's why I sent the clerk and Osumi out, now."

The *okami* poured a cup of tea and took a quiet sip, as if to calm herself. She looked at the two men and spoke, "As you know, we have a garden here, modest as et es. We have landscapers come en and see to et, like. But back then, back when his lordship owned the villa, that landscapers' business was run by a man named Tatsugoro Kawamura. Everyone just called him Uetatsu. He must have been around forty-two, no, forty-five or so. He had a handful of men under him, but Uetatsu himself saw to the garden at his lordship's villa."

"I see, and so?"

"That Uetatsu had him a daughter, like. Name of Komako. She must have been, oh, two years younger than me? A lovely, pale thing, she was. You know, that villa his lordship had was most seasons so quiet you could hear a cuckoo cry on the mountain, so they don't need many around to look after the place, but en summer relations come wandering en one after t'other. Now, the girl Komako, like I said, was a good girl, and was taught proper manners and etiquette and such, so every summer they took her on as a servant at the villa, like. A temporary maid. Then, Komako went and got herself en a way, ef you catch my meaning."

Kindaichi's eyes widened. "With someone at the villa?"

"Indeed."

"Who was the father?"

"That, I'm afraid I don't know. No, I reckon I should say et all. First off, I heard all thes quite after the fact, like. But, as you say, you want to know the order of events and all. When Komako turned up en a way, someone—I reckon his lordship Tamamushi—sent her back to Uetatsu with a bit of money. Et must have been quite a bit, too, for Uetatsu came off well from et. After that, you see, he started to live high. Now, as for the girl, they couldn't just leave her on her own, not en her state. So then, Uetatsu married her off to one of his landscapers, name of Gensuke Horii. Genyan, we called him."

"I see, I see. And then?"

"Like I said, I heard all this long after the fact, but it seems Komako had a baby girl, a darling little thing, name of Sayoko-chan. Komako herself was a beauty, and knew how to behave.

She was a good girl. But that Genyan she was weth, though, he was seven years older than her, and a man of no character at all, like. That Genyan should have treasured a kind, beautiful girl like Komako, but oh, how he abused her. He'd punch her and kick her and even drag her around by the hair, like. I simply couldn't feature it, you know, how a man could behave like that. I asked my pa, rest his soul, about it, and he said to me, 'There's naught for it, her bringing in that other man's child and all,' he said. That Genyan knew when he married her, but I reckon over time et wore on him, like. That's when I found out that Komako had got her child, or rather, someone had gotten her with child, at Tamamushi's villa."

"So, did your father know who Sayoko's father was?"

"Well, I wonder about that. I reckon my pa must have had an idea. But you know, he stopped himself up short even just telling me that little bet, so ef he did know he'd no way tell me about it, like. But, whoever the girl's pa may be, you can be sure the servants weren't pairing up and all. Ef they were, his lordship wouldn't have no need to pay Uetatsu off. I reckon it must have been one of his lordship's relatives."

"What about Toshihiko Shingu, Akiko-san's older brother? You said he used to come visit, too. Do you remember meeting him?"

Okami-san furrowed her brow, and said, "You know, I can't rightly recall at all. I know that Miss Akiko's brother came to visit with her, but I've been trying to remember more about him ever since I read that article. Try as I might, I just can't recall. At that age, you know, I would have been keener on talking with a boy than a girl... And even just the idea of a little viscount roundabouts, you'd think I'd have hunted him down. But I just don't recall. He must not have made much of an impression, like."

Okami-san likely had no idea just how apt that comment was. Even knowing nothing of Shingu's character, a casual glimpse of him would certainly not leave much of an impression. It was like Mineko had said, he was only a big man when no one was around.

"What do you think, is it possible that Shingu-san was the father?"

She considered a moment before answering. "He certainly could be, I reckon. But ef that were the case, then why would Tsubaki-san sneak down here to look into that? I can't make sense of it. What would be the great shame in it coming out? Et's not such a rarity, like."

"What about this, then?" Degawa offered. "What if we imagine that his lordship Tamamushi was the father?"

Okami-san, though, put that idea to rest immediately.

"Well, of course, his lordship Tamamushi was only around fefty in those days, and I hear he did have an eye for the younger ladies. So, I can't say it's out of the question, like. But ef he had gotten the girl en a family way, don't you think he'd have done it a bit more proper, like? Seen the baby born safe and put her en foster care? But, no, he put them both out like unwanted cats. That to me sounds like the father was still too young to have his own household, a person of rank, you know, and ef the whole thing came out, then it might cause more problems down the road, like."

"Well, what became of Komako-san and her child afterward?"

"I'm sure I don't know. I only know up to around when Sayoko-chan was four or five. I heard that Genyan ended up a complete good-for-nothing, and he quit his job with the gardeners and went off to Kobe or Osaka to be a day labourer, or some such. That's some ten years ago, now."

"If Sayoko were still alive, how old would she be now?"

"Well, let's see…" Okami-san counted on her plump toddler fingers. "Twenty-two, twenty-three… Must be around twenty-four, I reckon. If she's still alive, she must be quite a beauty."

"And what about Uetatsu? What happened to him?" Degawa asked.

"That's right, I ought to tell you about that. I reckon Uetatsu must have been blackmailing his lordship Tamamushi or some such. He always seemed to have money to spare, and even passed his whole landscaping business on to an apprentice. He picked up with some young woman, and I hear he spent all his time gambling, like. He'd already been something of a gambler, playing in penny ante games and the like, but then he went and became something like a professional. Then, I hear he had a child with that woman of his. Now, weth all of that business, he couldn't go and stay around here, so he went off to Itayado. Et's just one station up from Tsukimiyama. When my pa was still with us, rest him, he still came en to tend our garden, but after everything, we lost all connection."

Okami-san finished by saying, if they wanted to learn what eventually became of Uetatsu, then they should ask his successor Uematsu. Detective Degawa wrote his address in his notebook. Kindaichi looked on absently, then stood up and went out onto the *engawa* walkway around the garden.

The rain had faded to a sprinkle, and the sky was lightening. In the distance, the mountainous silhouette of Awaji Island stood like a smear of ink across the expanse of the Seto Inland Sea. He stared at it, his mind wandering, trying to connect Viscount Tsubaki's letter to the *okami*'s story. However, nothing she'd said could help him unravel the meaning of that note.

Like the woman had said, whether the girl Sayoko's father was Toshihiko Shingu or Count Tamamushi, there was nothing unusual in the story. It was just another wealthy noble fathering a child on a servant. Neither would add up to a secret of unbearable humiliation and disgrace. It had to be something else. Something else, something much graver, must have happened when Count Tamamushi had his villa at Tsukimiyama. And Viscount Tsubaki had caught wind of that, and it had driven him to suicide. But what could it have been?

Kosuke Kindaichi looked out at the falling rain and gave himself a little shake. He still had no idea, not in his wildest dreams, that the distant shadow of Awaji Island floating in the smooth sea would have any connection to this horrific business.

CHAPTER 16

The Devil's Birthplace

After Detective Degawa left to find Uematsu, Kosuke Kindaichi had a maid make up his futon, and was now stretched out on it thinking.

Kindaichi had survived the distant wilds of New Guinea during the war, and he was not nearly as frail as he seemed, but neither was he as full of vim and vigour as young Degawa. The long steam locomotive journey had tired him out.

He listened to the sound of the soft autumn rain filtering through his pillow and lay dozing for about an hour. When his eyes opened around four o'clock, Degawa still hadn't returned. He got out of bed and opened the *shoji* screens onto the *engawa* around the garden. The rain had let up, and the garden was far brighter than before he'd settled in for his nap.

Kindaichi folded up his futon mat and bedclothes, and then Okami-san came in with tea and some light snacks.

"You just leave all that the way it was, now. The girl'll come en to clear it up and all," she said, as she put the tray down and poured tea. "Did you get a bet of rest en?"

"I had a lovely nap, thank you. It's so quiet here. I feel completely refreshed, honestly. So, is the detective still not back yet?"

"Not yet, no."

"Is Uematsu's house so far, then?"

"No, not at all. I reckon he's gone off someplace else after, like."

Kindaichi recalled that Degawa had mentioned that he might pop in at the local police station if he got the chance.

"Or could be that Uematsu wasn't at home, you know. I know I said they were gardeners, but times being what they are, there's not much call for such. I hear he's turned to shadier business, like."

But Kindaichi, munching on a rice cracker, was already thinking of something else. "By the way, that place where Count Tamamushi had his villa. Is it far from here?"

"Not at all, no, maybe ten or fifteen minutes afoot. Why d'you ask?"

"Well, if I'm just going to be sitting around here, I thought I might as well go take a look."

"Not a whole lot to take a look at, though. The war dedn't leave much more than an old stone garden lantern."

"That's plenty for me. The rain's even let up. I think I'll go for a walk and see. Which way is it?"

"Well, ef you insist on going, I reckon Osumi'll be able to show you, like. She's just headed out that way, ef I recall, so it's no bother."

She rang the bell, and Osumi—who it appeared had just been stepping out—came around the outside of the room and looked in through the *shoji*.

"Osumi-chan, if you're headed out to your sister's, could you be a dear and take our guest here? He's going that way too."

"'Course, but, where's he off to?"

"You know the old villa that Katsuragi-san, out of Osaka, used to have? Just this side of Murasamedo Hall? This gentleman says he wants to see where the villa was."

Osumi gave Kindaichi a confused look and said, "But there's naught left of Katsuragi-san's villa, not even ruins, like."

"Yes, and that's fine. I just want to get a look at where it was."

"All right, then, please come round to the front. I'll just step out through the back gate and come round to you."

Soon Osumi came hurrying up to him. "Sorry for the wait. Right, et's just this way. Ef you'll follow me, then, sir?"

Though the rain had just lifted, the soil was sandy and rocky, so although there were puddles, there was no thick mud to speak of. At the same time, the soft damp soil made for pleasant walking under his wooden *geta* sandals. The western sky was growing red, hinting at the next day's weather.

"It looks like it's going to clear up tomorrow," commented Kindaichi.

"Well, et'd better. We can't be having with all thes rain, like. I'm well done with it."

They chatted like that as they walked along. Not far from the Three Spring Garden Inn, their path took them up a slope which offered a clear view all the way to the seaside. Kindaichi could easily see just how deeply the war had devastated the area. There were piles of broken roof tiles and scorched earth, and weeds were growing up unchecked between the heaps. But there were also signs of renewed activity, with those ubiquitous temporary buildings people had taken to calling "barracks" lining the Sanyo Main Line and Dentetsu tracks. The path Kindaichi walked, though, was still essentially untouched since the war.

"This is terrible. It looks like they really hit this area hard."

"Didn't they just?"

For the next short while, they talked about the war. Osumi recalled the terror of the air raids, how they turned the whole area into a sea of flame, and then how the crowds of fleeing people were raked by machine-gun fire. The kind of stories almost anyone who had lived through those times could share.

"The business and shopping streets are already picking back up, you know, even ef et's all barracks now," Osumi went glibly on. "But this area was all full of estates and villas, and those rich folks aren't so keen on barracks, you know, so now they're just tied up paying the property taxes on burnt wrecks, like."

Osumi went on to recount what had become of the local estate and villa owners since the end of the war. She'd gone through about a third of them, when she suddenly remembered their original goal.

"Oh, I do beg your pardon, sir, but why were you wanting to look at the old Katsuragi villa?"

Kindaichi shook his head and said, "Oh, you know, I just wanted a look around. I know there won't be much to see, really."

"I reckon it's got something to do weth your investigation and all, right?"

"Well, it does, and it doesn't, I suppose."

Osumi glanced surreptitiously at him after this evasive answer.

"Um, listen, sir, I think I might have thought of something. Et's to do with that Tsubaki-san you were asking about afore."

"You did? What is it?" Kindaichi finally caught on to her meaningful looks. "Osumi-chan, if you have anything at all to say about Tsubaki-san, then let's hear it. No matter how small, no matter how meaningless it might appear. I want to hear anything you might remember!"

"Yes, I reckon I understand, but I had forgot about it. Then, when Okami-san asked me to guide you to the old Katsuragi villa, et must have jogged my memory, like. That's when I thought of it."

"Thought of what?"

"Last January, when Tsubaki-san came up thes way, I remembered that I saw him around the old villa grounds."

Kindaichi squeezed his eyes shut tight. He felt like his heart had skipped a beat.

"Viscount Tsubaki was there? Do you remember when that was? The 15th, or the 16th?"

"I don't remember it that well, but I reckon it must have been the 15th, right? Cause, like I said, he went out with a *bento* box on the 16th, so he wouldn't have been sticking around here, like."

"I see. And what was he doing?"

"I'm sure I don't know. My sister lives just to the other side of the old Katsuragi villa. Happy to say, her house made et through the war. Okami-san gave me the day off, so I went off to see her. Oh, right, that means et was the 15th! I went to see her the 15th day of the new year. So, et was on my way home from there. When I passed the edge of Katsuragi-san's old place, I saw a man standing there. Et seemed a bit creepy, like, to be honest. I mean, et was right around sundown, so everything was so gloomy and dark. So, I rushed past as quick as I could, and then that man turned to look. That's when I saw it was Tsubaki-san. I was right surprised, I was. Just as I was thinking ef I should give him a bow or something, he turned away and walked towards the road to the other side of the ruins, and then went along on back."

"Did you say anything to him about it later?"

"No, et seemed like he didn't know it was me that had seen him, like. He didn't say anything about et, so I reckoned I shouldn't, either. And, well, et was dark and all. I couldn't be dead certain et was Tsubaki-san, really. Could turn out to be someone else and all."

Kindaichi walked on in silent thought for a while.

He was sure the man Osumi had seen was Viscount Tsubaki, who'd come all this way west to look into something that had happened at Count Tamamushi's villa. So, even now that all that remained of it was a burnt-out ruin, he would naturally have been interested in coming to see it.

174

Viscount Tsubaki had known that something had happened here, had known about some terrible deed done on these grounds. What had he felt, standing next to those scorched ruins? Was it resentment? Grief? Indignation? If this had helped him make his decision to commit suicide, then he must have been in incredible emotional turmoil.

"And there was one more thing, sir."

Kindaichi's silent reverie shattered like glass at Osumi's sudden words.

"Huh? What? What was it, Osumi-chan?"

"I think I might know where Tsubaki-san went on the 16th, like. Course, thes es just a guess and all, so I could be wrong."

Kindaichi stared at Osumi's face, silently. She had a broad face and flat nose, and her clear complexion was really her only attractive feature, but there was still something charming in her small, clever eyes that spoke of a good heart. And as someone in her business, dealing with guests every day, she had to have a keen eye for observation.

"Osumi-chan," Kindaichi said, putting force into his words, "a guess is fine. Surely, you've heard the saying about a drowning man clutching at straws? I'm drowning right now. I've got nothing to clutch at. Now, you're saying you just have a guess, but I'd be stupid indeed to ignore the observations of a clever girl like you."

"Oh, now, don't go calling me clever, like." Her denial, though, held a distinct note of happiness.

"None of that. I can tell what a sharp mind you've got by the way you talk. And you wouldn't be so good at your job without it. You've got to notice things that most people don't. So, tell me about the 16th of January. Where do you think Tsubaki-san went?"

Osumi fidgeted at his charming words, but answered, "Well, I'm sure I don't know how to take all that, like. But, ef you're asking and all, I'll tell you. Just, don't blame me ef I'm wrong, right?"

Osumi swallowed nervously, then said, "You know how the clerk said Tsubaki-san had asked the best way to get to Akashi, right? That's what got me thinking. The evening of the 16th, when Tsubaki-san came back, he went right en to the bath. I took up his suit and cloak for cleaning, and I noticed they reeked of the sea."

"Did they, now?"

"They did, and of course we're not far from the sea here all around, so that's not so strange. But that smell from his clothes was something more. Like he'd rolled around en the tide. And even apart from that reek, I found two or three fish scales around the hem of his trousers and cloak."

"Fish scales?" Kindaichi stared into her eyes, then said, "And what do you think about that?"

"I reckon that Tsubaki-san must have taken a fishing boat from Akashi. Not that he went fishing, mind you, but he must have crossed over to Awaji on it."

"A fishing boat to Awaji…?" Kindaichi spun around.

The peak of the hill hid it from view, but he knew that the inkblot of the island was there, across the darkening sea. Kindaichi felt a suspicious flutter in his chest.

"But, Osumi-chan, if he wanted to go to Awaji, aren't there better ways? There must be a ferry."

"Oh, sure, there is. There are five or six proper sheps a day, grand ones, going back and forth between Akashi and the port of Iwaya on Awaji. But, sir, wasn't that Tsubaki-san trying to keep his trip a secret, like?"

"That is true. When the Tokyo police checked his alibi, he told them he'd stayed at the Three Spring Garden Inn, but he refused to say anything more than that. Actually, he only told them about the inn on condition that they wouldn't investigate any further."

"Then that explains it," Osumi said, beaming, and went on, "The fishing boats would be a safer choice than the ferry. I don't know if you knew, but Awaji has become a real black-market centre, with buyers coming out from Kobe and Osaka all the time. I mean, you could buy eggs en Iwaya, bring them back to Akashi and get three times the price for them, like. And all those black-market folks cross over on fishermen's boats. Even the fishermen don't come back to port with their catches any more. They meet up with customers from Kobe and Osaka out on the ocean and finish their deals on board their boats. Which means that these fishermen are all half a part of the black market themselves, so even ef the police come sniffing around, they wouldn't talk none. So, ef Tsubaki-san didn't want anyone to know about him going over to Awaji, then I reckon the fishermen would be a safer choice than the ferry, like."

Kindaichi took another look at Osumi's face. Her logic was clear and ordered, and he admired how deeply she understood the local business world, despite her relative youth.

"Now, look at that, Osumi-chan, it's just like I said. That's as sharp as it gets."

"Oh, now, come right on." Osumi's *bunraku* puppet-like face flushed pink. "Never mind all that, now, sir. Now, whether or not Tsubaki-san actually crossed to Awaji, I reckon there's no mistake that he got on one of them fishing boats."

"Why are you so convinced?"

"That's because my old pa was always going out fishing, and he used to go out Akashi way to fish when things were going well during the war. He'd hitch a ride on a fishing boat out to sea for it. They say you can catch the best fish in Japan out there, like. When he came back from those trips, he always smelled just like Tsubaki-san's clothes did. Course, Pa passed en the war."

Osumi's voice lost its cheer at that, but she quickly came back around. "Oh, now, look at that, I got so caught up talking that I lost track of where we were and near to went right past. This is where the old Katsuragi villa was, sir."

At this, Kindaichi shook his head and looked around like he was waking from a dream.

He saw a stretch of about two and a half acres of scorched land spread out in front of him. It looked like a brick wall or something similar had been up on the hillside where they stood, but it was completely burnt away, and now all that was left was bare land. No buildings, no trees; nothing was left. Nothing, except for the stone lamp that Okami-san had mentioned. It, too, had been scorched white by the flames, and now it stood forlorn in the autumn dusk.

"There really is nothing left," Kindaichi said, regret in his voice. "So, where was Tsubaki-san standing when you saw him?"

"Over there, by the stone lamp on the banks of the old pond. He was standing right beside et. And when he noticed me, he rushed off through the old gate to the other side. Why not go look for yourself, sir?"

Kindaichi followed her gaze and saw a few stone steps, hinting at what once must have been a gate.

"Okay then, Osumi-chan. You go on. You'll be late to your sister's."

"No, et's fine. Her house is just right there, like." Osumi tromped down the scorched, crumbling stone steps, and Kindaichi followed after.

At the bottom, they stepped out into an overgrown field piled with charred tiles and other rubble. The red heads of knotweed, damp from the rain, danced like waves in the breeze on their

178

long stalks. Osumi and Kindaichi trudged through them, the hems of their kimonos soaking up the damp, heading towards the lantern.

Once, this garden must have been a wonderful place. The layout of the land, with the pond and hill, and the remaining garden stones, gave a hint of its past glory, though now it was nothing more than a dismal ruin.

"Et's a shame, et es. We never ded get to come inside, but you could see from outside the wall that the old house was grand as any palace."

That building, "grand as any palace" as it might have been, was now nothing more than a few scraps of foundation overgrown with weeds and scrub, whispering reminders of lost days of glory.

A single dragonfly came and alighted on the lantern shade. Osumi reacted with the glee of a child and raced over almost on instinct to try and catch it. It naturally refused to wait for her grasping fingers and flew off into the dusk sky.

Osumi, though, stopped and stood stock-still, staring intently at the stone lantern, until she suddenly turned to Kindaichi and called out, "Sir, sir, over here!"

Her voice was shaking with wonder.

"What is it, Osumi-chan?"

"Come over here, there's something odd written here! Here, 'the devil'... What's that word, then?"

"Devil?" Kindaichi stumbled in shock, then rushed up.

"Here, right here. Under the lantern shade."

There, on the front of the flame space of the stone lantern, were letters written in blue pencil. They had darkened from the rain. The writing resembled that of Hidesuke Tsubaki, and the words read:

Here, the devil's birthplace.

179

CHAPTER 17

Myokai, the Nun

It was after nine that evening when Detective Degawa finally returned to the inn. As zealous as he was, between the previous day's journey and his hard work since that morning, Kosuke Kindaichi could see he was exhausted.

"You've been working so hard! You must be worn out."

Kindaichi could not very well go to bed before the detective returned, so he had sat up chatting with the *okami*. When he saw Degawa's drawn face, he couldn't help but feel a pang of sympathy.

"You can say that again," Degawa groaned. "It really is tough to get around when you don't know the lie of the land."

"That's certainly true. You gents certainly are working hard, I see," the *okami* said kindly. "Will you be needing any dinner, then?"

"No, thanks, I already ate."

"Well then, why don't I run a bath for you, then perhaps a drink before you turn en?"

"You don't mind? I'd appreciate that, thank you."

While the detective soaked in the tub, the *okami* had a maid prepare him some sake as a nightcap. Okami-san seemed the type of woman who enjoyed having someone to look after, and now that they'd got in her good graces, she was eager to reward the young man for all his hard work.

"That was a great bath, thank you. I finally feel myself again." Degawa, face aglow, was apparently back to his normal high spirits.

"Sounds like you're ready for that drink. And a bite to eat won't hurt. Go on, Okami-san insists," Kindaichi prompted him.

"Well, if she insists. I thank you for your gracious hospitality, Okami-san!"

"Oh, now, enough of that, like. Course, this bream came direct from a fishing boat out to Akashi. I had the man bring it special, like."

Kindaichi turned to her as soon as he heard the words "fishing boat" and "Akashi". He started to speak, but immediately thought better of it.

"Anyway, Degawa-san, it seems you put in a lot of work out there. Did you learn anything?"

"Oh, well, let's see. I kept running into leads that seemed promising but ended up falling through. But, as it's just the first day, I suppose I'd call it a success."

"Ah. Ef you're talking about your work, I reckon I'll excuse myself, like." Okami-san started to shift her great body to rise, but Kindaichi hurried to stop her.

"No, no, please stay right here, Okami-san. I'm sure we'll have need of your wisdom. Well, Degawa-san? She can stay, can't she?"

"I suppose so. We still don't know our way around these parts at all. And I have to admit, I'd prefer not to ask too much of the local police. I think you could be a big help, Okami-san."

She seemed happy with the attention. She settled her heavy hips back down and said, "Well, if I can be of any help at all, course, I suppose I can stay. But I won't go sharing anything what I shouldn't, like. So then, did you find whatever happened to old Uetatsu-san?"

"I did. About that…"

Kindaichi himself was not a big drinker, but Degawa clearly was, and he gladly held out his cup for Okami-san to refill. He watched her with relish while he spoke.

"It seems old man Uetatsu is dead."

"Oh, dear, es that so? And he always seemed like such a strong sort," said the *okami*.

"Yes, well, it was an air raid that got him. Over around Itayado, I think the town is called? One evening, old Uetatsu got drunk and ran outside during an air raid, wearing nothing but a loincloth, I hear. He was hollering up at the planes, saying 'Come on, come on, drop away!', and wouldn't you know it, he took a direct hit. Died on the spot, I heard."

"And I had no idea! None at all! O'course, I was evacuated at the time, so wasn't around these parts. But I reckon that was a fitting end for the old man, like."

"Ha, that's exactly what Uematsu said! He was laughing out loud by the end of that story."

"So then, was that all you learned about Uetatsu?" asked Kindaichi.

"No, not quite. When he died, it seems Uetatsu had a young woman living with him, name of Otama. And Uematsu also said that this Otama wasn't someone that Okami-san over here would know. It seems old Uetatsu kept going through girl-friends, and this Otama living with him at the end was about thirty-five or so, and she used to be a waitress or some such. I was wondering if you had ever heard anything about her from Uetatsu?"

"Not a word. Wait, what about Komako-san or little Sayoko-chan?"

"Yes, I learned some things about them, too."

Degawa spoke between bites of sea bream sashimi.

"When Uetatsu kicked the bucket, that woman of his took refuge with Uematsu. Because he's known for helping people in trouble, I suppose. He says when he heard her story, he couldn't just toss her out. So, he took her in and saw to recovering

Uetatsu's remains. The way it was, though, there wasn't much to be done, so he held the simplest funeral. At that time, the closest relatives Uetatsu had were his daughter, Komako, and a son by another woman, Haruo. Now, the son was apparently off to war, so Uematsu thought he really should track down Komako-san. But he hadn't had any contact with her for years, so he had no idea where she was or what she was doing. At which point, that woman Otama said she knew and would go and bring her back for the funeral. Which, of course, was a surprise for Uematsu. When she came back, it was their first meeting in ten years or so, but he said she was in a terrible way, and not a shadow of her old self."

"Oh, the poor dear," said Okami-san. "And she was such a sweet thing. She must have been through so much, like. And what of the man Genyan, or little Sayoko-chan?"

"That's where things ran dry. The man Gensuke, like you said, went off to Kobe city to work as a day labourer. He took ill, I understand, lost his mind and died. It seems likely that he gave his illness to Komako-san, too. Or at least, that's what it looked like from her face, Uematsu said."

"That's what it was? Poor, poor thing. And the girl? She must be almost grown by now."

"It seems she has passed, as well."

"No, not little Sayoko-chan, too?"

"That's what I heard. But Uematsu said there was something odd about that. When he asked Komako-san about the girl, she just said she was dead, and nothing else. She refused to say when, where or how it happened. Uematsu felt like there had to be something more going on with that."

Kindaichi sat and thought for a moment, then asked, "By the way, when did old man Uematsu last see little Sayoko?"

"Around when she was eleven or twelve. He said she was

cute as a button, and everyone was sure she would end up a real beauty."

At that, Degawa, still holding his cup, looked meaningfully at Kindaichi.

Kindaichi immediately understood. Degawa was convinced that someone linked to this case was the girl Sayoko, now all grown up. If she was alive, she'd be around twenty-three or so. And she must be a great beauty… The facts immediately called to mind a certain figure for both. But Kindaichi cut off that line of thought as quickly as he could. He couldn't let himself jump to any conclusions. He would wait until they had more solid facts about what had become of Sayoko, like whether she was actually alive.

"So, what was Komako-san doing then? Unmarried, her daughter dead…?"

"Seems she took on as a kind of housesitter over around Ashiya or Sumiyoshi after all the rich folks evacuated. Unfortunately, Uematsu didn't know exactly what house it was. He had asked Komako, but she didn't want to say. She was a single mother on her own and didn't seem to want anything to do with anyone from her past who might know her history. Uematsu respected that, so he didn't push too hard, and once the funeral was over, she left and that was that. So, he said he doesn't know if she's still watching some rich person's house, or if she got killed in an air raid, or if she ran off somewhere else entirely."

"Et's all just so sad, like," Okami-san put in. "Ef it weren't for that damned war, people wouldn't be scattered all over like thes."

It was an excellent point. There was no telling how much the war and its ongoing aftereffects would slow down their investigation.

"Now, what about Otama, the girlfriend? It sounds like she knew where Komako was living."

"Right, on to her. So, Otama stayed with Uematsu for two or three days, then it seems she went off to some relatives over in Tottori Prefecture. He doesn't know what happened to her after that."

"So, is that another dead end?"

"I wouldn't say that. That was about all I could learn from Uematsu, but then I went to Itayado to look around where Uetatsu's house had been. Luckily, things have recovered pretty well over that way, and most of the people who used to live there have come back and put up barrack housing. There were lots of folks who knew Uetatsu and Otama. I talked to each and every one trying to find out about Komako, and Sayoko, and that boy Haruo who went off to war. I asked about Otama, too, but not too many knew much about the others."

Kindaichi frowned at that. "That makes it sound like Haruo didn't live with his father."

"Indeed, it does. That's what Uematsu said, too. It seems old Uetatsu bounced from one woman to the next, so it was hard to keep Haruo around. Once he left primary school, he moved off to the city to work on his own, and hardly ever came home to visit the old man. And for Komako, it likely wasn't much fun for her to come around either, what with younger and younger women being in the house. So, she stopped visiting, too. Which is all to say I didn't end up learning anything new about Komako and Sayoko, or about Haruo. Luckily, though, I did meet someone who ran into Otama recently. In fact, just about a year ago."

"Oh, so then she came back this way from Tottori?"

"Yes. That woman, the one who met Otama, she said that last autumn she was over at the Shinkaichi entertainment district in central Kobe and happened to run into her. They just stopped and chatted for a bit, but from the way she talked, she was at a couples-only *ryokan* inn. Meaning, one of these dodgy new places with the fake *onsen* sign. Anyway, she's apparently a live-in maid at one. So, I rushed over to Shinkaichi to take a look around."

"My, you have been busy, Detective! Did you find out where Otama-san ended up, then?"

"Well, the thing is, that woman said she didn't know the name of the inn. She said Otama-san might have told her, but she forgot if she did. So, I didn't have much choice but to go where she said she ran into her, and check them, one by one."

"Are there really so many of them? Is Shinkaichi that kind of place?"

"Ah, I suppose you might not be aware, Kindaichi-san, but Kobe's Shinkaichi is every bit as big an entertainment district as Asakusa's Sixth ward. And Fukuhara is right next door, which is every bit as big a red-light district as Yoshiwara up in Tokyo. At any rate, it's quite a place. So, anyway, there are lots of inns like that, but luckily, I only had to check six or seven before I found the one where she'd been."

"Had been? So, then, she wasn't there any more?"

"I'm afraid not. She was there until March of this year, but she's gone now."

"And they don't know where she is."

"Exactly. And it's no wonder. It seems she just up and ran off in the middle of the night and took some valuables with her. She likely made sure they could never find her."

"What bad luck!" Okami-san said, letting out a deep sigh. "After you went to all that trouble and got so far, like."

Degawa didn't seem discouraged, though.

"Don't worry, Okami-san, it's all part of the job. I could hardly call it work if everything went easy the first time. I'd actually say that today went fairly well, all told."

"Well, ef you say so. I can sure enough tell et's hard work, like. Any rate, here's something hot from the kitchen for you, then."

"Oh, thank you kindly!"

"Did you learn anything else there, Degawa-san? About any friends of hers or such?" asked Okami-san.

"I asked, of course. Otama said she had lost all her relatives in the war, so she never had a single visitor the whole time she was working there. Then, just recently—in fact, the day before yesterday, someone came asking if someone named Otama-san lived there."

"That recently? What kind of person?" asked Kindaichi.

"Apparently, it was an *ama*, a nun from a Buddhist temple. The staff at the inn told her that there was no one by that name living there now, and no one knew where she had gone. The *ama* went home terribly disappointed, and as she left, she said that if they ever learned where Otama-san was, to let her know that Myokai, the *ama* from Awaji Island, was looking for her."

"Awaji?" Kindaichi jerked in shock and leaned forward across the table. "D-D-Detective Degawa, did you f-f-find out who th-th-that *ama* was?"

Kindaichi's reaction was so intense that the detective and Okami-san both leaned back to stare at him. Degawa put his sake cup down and asked, "Kindaichi-san, why are you so interested in some nun?"

"I'll tell you l-l-later. Now, can you tell me about how old she was? What kind of woman was she? Anything at all?"

"Well, I asked the usual, just the basics. But I didn't realize she was important, or I'd have tried to find out more. Anyway, it seems she was in her mid-fifties, petite and pretty, if sickly. Oh, and she had a small mole at the corner of her right eye."

"Oh, do you say so? That sounds just like Komako-san! She had a little mole by her right eye, just like that. But she's not en her fefties. I reckon she'd just be about forty-two or so."

"Of course! That's it, Okami-san!" Kindaichi's voice was trembling in excitement. "Don't you remember what Uematsu said? She was in a terrible way, and not a shadow of her old self. All her suffering, and her illness, must have aged her before her time. And listen, Degawa-san..."

"What?"

"I'm certain that on 16th January, Viscount Tsubaki crossed over to Awaji Island to visit her."

Degawa's eyes widened in shock. "How do you know that?"

Kindaichi told them both about Osumi's speculation.

"I was impressed by how sharp her eye was at the time, but I never imagined we'd find evidence so soon. But if what Degawa-san just told us is true, then don't we have another clear connection to Awaji? I think we have to go over and see for ourselves."

"Ded Osumi-chan really say all that?"

"Okami-san, that girl's sharp as a tack. I could tell how clever she was just from the way she talked. Oh, by the way, Degawa-san."

"Yes?"

"You said she came looking for Otama just the day before yesterday?"

"Yes, that's right."

"That was 1st October, right? The first newspaper articles about the murder came out on the 1st. I imagine that *ama* Myokai must have read about it and thought of some connection. So, she crossed over from Awaji to talk to Otama."

Degawa's shock was obvious. His eyes dropped from Kindaichi's face, and finally, he said in a trembling voice, "Now

188

that you mention it, Kindaichi-san, from what the inn staff said, the *ama* was really worked up."

The room fell silent for a moment. The three of them looked at each other, an odd glint in all their eyes, until finally Kindaichi cleared his throat with a thick cough.

"I think we have to get to Awaji and find this *ama* as soon as we can, but we really don't know much about the island."

"Yes, I asked about that too, but all she said was she was *ama* Myokai on Awaji. I suppose that would have been enough for Otama."

Kindaichi turned to Okami-san with a grin. "Okami-san, I knew we'd be glad you were around. I think we've got no choice but to ask for your help."

"Oh, what could I possibly do? I'd be more than happy to help ef I can, 'course."

"It's about what you just said earlier, that you had a fisherman from Akashi bring you a sea bream. That means the local fishermen know you, right?"

"Oh, sure, we've had dealings with them since my pa's day. So, even during the war, we never wanted for fish round here, at least."

"That's it! We need your connections. One of those fishermen must have taken Viscount Tsubaki across to Awaji on 16th January. But, like Osumi-chan said, they're not likely to admit to anything when the police get involved. So, could we borrow you to help find out who it was? Of course, it might not be the best idea if you told them why or what exactly we're looking into. But we can also promise that we won't poke around into any other shady business they might be involved in."

"That makes good sense. En that case, then I'm glad to help and all. Leave et to me, right? I'll find out for you by noon tomorrow, you wait and see," Okami-san said, patting her bulging chest with one pudgy toddler hand.

And so Kosuke Kindaichi and Detective Degawa's investigation turned for the first time towards Awaji.

CHAPTER 18

Digging up a Scandal

That night, Kosuke Kindaichi and Detective Degawa stayed up late talking, so the next morning Kindaichi ended up sleeping well past nine thirty. When he woke, the shutters were still closed, but he saw that the room next to his was empty, and the detective gone.

Kindaichi leapt out of bed when he saw the time on the watch by his pillow. Degawa's cast-off *yukata* robe was in the laundry basket, and his suit was missing from the hanger. Worried that the detective had already left him behind, Kindaichi threw open the *amado* rain shutters in a panic to discover that the weather had turned during the night and it was pouring down outside.

"Oh, dear…" he groaned. He stepped out onto the covered *engawa* walkway and closed the screen behind him, staring forlornly at the rain. Out in the garden, raindrops threw up clouds of mist when they struck the stones, and the trees were obscured by the heavy downpour. Naturally, Awaji Island was hidden from view.

He was thinking that the day was certainly off to a bad start when Osumi, who had been absent all the night before, came in.

"Good morning, sir. I came to open all the shutters."

"Morning. Seems the weather's changed again."

"Sure enough. But Okami-san says that et's just as well."

"How so?"

"Those fishermen won't be going out en this, like."

"Oh, no, I suppose not."

Kindaichi realized that the day might actually be off to a better start than he'd feared and looked out at the rain once more.

"And the man on the radio said et would slow down and clear up en the afternoon and all."

"Better and better! And what about heading to Akashi?"

"Head clerk's already gone off."

"That's a bit of a pity for him in all this rain. Did Degawa-san go with him?"

"No, he went off somewhere else, I reckon. You get washed up, now, sir."

Kindaichi washed, then sat down to a late breakfast. When he did, the *okami-san* came in to say hello.

"Ah, Okami-san, my apologies. I understand you had the head clerk go off to Akashi while I was asleep."

"Never you mind that, like. He set out early this morning. I reckoned et would be a good chance and all, with this rain. All the fishermen'll still be en port, you know."

"I hope he's lucky and finds the man we're looking for."

"If Osumi's right and one of them really ded take Tsubaki-san across, he'll find him, sure enough. That clerk may be young, but he's a sharp one."

"I am sorry for all the trouble we're putting you to."

"Now, never you mind all that."

"And what of Degawa-san?"

"He's off back to the city. He said he was going to visit that place from yesterday and see if he couldn't learn anything else about Otama-san or where that *ama*-san might be."

"All that while I was asleep…"

"You must have been all tired out. And you two were up late talking, too. You eat up, now, and rest until the clerk and Degawa-san get back."

"Thanks, but I'm fine."

192

When she had left, Kindaichi went to the desk and wrote two letters. One was to Ginzo Kubo, and the other was for Chief Inspector Isokawa.

If you have read *The Honjin Murders* and *Death on Gokumon Island*, then you should already be familiar with these two. Ginzo Kubo is a fruit farmer in Okayama Prefecture and has long served as a kind of patron for Kindaichi. Chief Inspector Isokawa works at the Okayama Prefectural Police headquarters and has been a friend of his since the Honjin murder case.

Kindaichi had been hoping to see them on this trip, since Okayama was not far to the west, but the investigation was starting to look like it wouldn't allow for much free time, so he settled for letters.

He asked Osumi to post them both. Then he lit up a cigarette and tried to piece together all that he had learned the day before as he watched the rain falling on the garden.

After discovering Viscount Tsubaki's handwriting on the stone lantern on the burnt-out grounds of the former count Tamamushi's villa, he felt he'd found some clue to the reason behind the viscount's journey west. He must have come to investigate something about the Tamamushis or the Shingus, his wife's family.

But "The devil's birthplace"? What could that eerie phrase mean? Degawa seemed convinced it had to do with the child Sayoko, but she hadn't been born there. Komako might have conceived her there, but the baby had been born after Komako married Uematsu's apprentice Gensuke Horii. In any case, why would Tsubaki call Sayoko a devil? Did he even know her?

Degawa was trying to find someone connected to this case who could be Sayoko living under another name. Kikue and Otane were the only women of around the right age, but even assuming one of them was really Sayoko, and Degawa seemed

193

convinced it was Kikue, why would Viscount Tsubaki call her a devil?

Wherever or whoever Sayoko was now, there were the two men who could have been her father: Toshihiko Shingu or Count Tamamushi.

Kindaichi and Degawa had discussed it at length the night before.

Kindaichi was taken aback by both the possible options. "If Kikue is actually Sayoko, then Tamamushi's mistress is either his own daughter, or his nephew's daughter. Either way, that would certainly be scandalous!"

But the detective had not been so sure about that. "Oh, come on. If Shingu were the father, it wouldn't be that big a scandal at all. I mean, those high-born folk aren't like us commoners. They play pretty loose with those kinds of things. Just look at a history book. Stuff like that happened all the time. Uncles and nieces getting together, aunts marrying their nephews or fathers going after their sons' wives."

"But his own daughter? I mean, I've heard of that happening in other countries. I even read about one noblewoman who took her brother as a lover, with her father's blessing! But I can't imagine Count Tamamushi would ever…"

"Well then, what if Kikue isn't really his mistress? They just put on like she is in public, but in fact he's setting up a way to take care of his illegitimate daughter."

But Kindaichi found that hard to believe too. Why go to all that trouble? Count Tamamushi hadn't seemed the kind of man to care much for a daughter, but if he did actually love her enough to take her in, he surely would not have wanted to paint her with the stigma of being his young lover.

"So, what if Count Tamamushi hadn't known that Kikue was his daughter?" Degawa offered.

"Meaning that Kikue did?"

"Yes, if she knew it and hid it to get close to him. Like, she knew she was his daughter, and that he'd discarded her, and was looking to get her revenge."

"That would mean that Kikue knowingly entered into a physical relationship with her real father?"

"Well, yes. Which could be a reason for Viscount Tsubaki to call her devil."

If Degawa was right, that would certainly be a truly monstrous trick, and something well deserving of the name "devil". But would it drag the good name of the Tsubaki family into the mud, as the viscount had written in his final note? Naturally, the Tamamushi family was now connected to the Tsubakis, so any disgrace to the former might well reflect poorly on the latter. However, as delicate as Viscount Tsubaki might have been, and whatever disgrace might come to Count Tamamushi, it hardly seemed enough to drive the viscount to suicide.

This problem remained no matter who Sayoko really was. If Otane were the illegitimate child, either of Viscount Shingu or Count Tamamushi, that could not possibly have any bearing on the Tsubaki family name. Everyone said that Otane had been devoted to Viscount Tsubaki, and he had been quite kind to her, but even if that indicated some deeper relationship between the two—highly unlikely, given the viscount's evident propriety—and even if he had discovered Otane's true identity after they began their affair, that would surely have been no motive for suicide.

If Otane were Viscount Shingu's child, that would make her Tsubaki's wife's niece, while if she were Tamamushi's child she would be his wife's cousin. That might make for some scandal, but surely nothing that would shock Viscount Tsubaki to such an extent, nor drag his family name into the mud. Besides while

195

Otane was a lovely young woman, she certainly wasn't the great beauty that everyone seemed to expect Sayoko to become.

"But listen, Kindaichi-san," Degawa had said, "Okami-san says that this *ama* Myokai is actually Komako. And what with the viscount going out to visit her, it seems likely that she's right. If so, then what could Komako have told him? She wasn't even a full-time maid at the villa; she only went out there to help in summer. I doubt she knew any big secrets about either family. Apart from Sayoko, that is. Which means she must have told him about Sayoko. What if she was in a position to be a real danger to the viscount?"

Kindaichi had his own opinion about that.

"All of that might be true, but Uematsu said that the last time he saw Sayoko was when she was around twelve. That means she must have been in Kobe up to that point. Even if she'd left for Tokyo right after that, she would certainly have some traces of her Kobe accent, even now. But neither Kikue nor Otane have a hint of one."

"You're bound to lose your accent, though, living in Tokyo that long. I mean, maybe if you move when you're an adult it might not work that way, but if you move when you're twelve, you're going to end up a Tokyoite to the bone."

"Some things don't change that easily. Things like how the stress accents around Kobe are reversed from Tokyo, and out here, you might notice how sometimes short 'i's get flattened to 'e's. Like, 'bridge' becomes 'bredge', or 'it' becomes 'et'. The only person around the Tsubaki estate with even a touch of an accent like that is Totaro Mishima."

"Yes, well, he did grow up in Okayama, after all. But if you spend long enough in Tokyo, even that's sure to change. And Kikue came out of the geisha world, so they could have trained the accent out of her."

Degawa was clearly set on the idea that Kikue was Sayoko, but Kindaichi still had his doubts.

On reflection, Degawa's hypothesis went that when Komako ended up pregnant, her father Uetatsu got a huge pay-out from his lordship Tamamushi, and lived the high life for years afterward. That in itself was not unusual. No matter whether it was Viscount Shingu or Count Tamamushi, someone in that house had tarnished his daughter's honour and future, and Tamamushi had taken responsibility and agreed to compensate him for it. However, it seems that Uetatsu went on to blackmail the count and continue his lavish lifestyle for years, and that made no sense.

There had to be more to it. If the money had been meant for Sayoko's care, Tamamushi would most certainly have made sure that it actually got to Komako and was used to support her. A man of his acumen and power would not have allowed Uetatsu to intercept it. In fact, if he had felt enough responsibility to pay for the girl's upbringing, he could have just taken Komako in and looked after her himself. It would have been an easy thing for Tamamushi to find her a husband.

"The real sticking point for me is how Uetatsu could have been blackmailing Count Tamamushi," said Kindaichi. "The count was not the kind of man to allow a gardener to shake him down. For any kind of blackmail to succeed, the count's secret would have had to be really bad—much worse than an illegitimate child."

"There is that," Degawa muttered. He couldn't seem to find any objection. "The whole business with Sayoko is nothing unheard of for the upper classes. It doesn't seem enough to use for blackmail."

"You're right. Especially if Count Tamamushi was the father. But can we be certain that Uetatsu really was blackmailing him? Okami-san's story was all second-hand anyway, so it might not be accurate. I think we'd better look into it a little more closely."

"Agreed," Degawa said. "So, tomorrow I'll head back out to Uematsu's place, then on to Itayado to ask a few more questions."

As Osumi had predicted, the rain lessened as noon approached, and the sky began to brighten. The trees in the garden, which had been obscured by the dark rain, appeared now as if a veil had been lifted, and birds came out of hiding to begin chirping from the branches. At the same time, the temperature seemed to drop, and Kindaichi found that the inn's light *yukata* robe and padded *dotera* jacket left him a little chilly, so he put on a shirt and changed into his usual kimono and *hakama* trousers.

Detective Degawa returned around half past eleven, soaked to the bone.

"Oh, welcome back! You must have had a terrible journey in the rain. I'm afraid I overslept."

"Don't worry. It looks like the clerk isn't back yet, either."

"Yes, he must be having a hard time with the search. So, how did things go with you?"

"Well, Kindaichi-san, I have something strange to tell you about."

Degawa hung his wet jacket and socks up to dry, then came over to sit cross-legged opposite Kindaichi. His expression was uneasy.

"What happened?" Kindaichi asked, concerned.

"Well, first thing this morning I went off to Uematsu's place, like we discussed last night. After I talked to him, I went to Itayado. I asked around about the blackmail business, and it seems pretty clear. No one knows for sure that it was blackmail exactly, but Uetatsu clearly had money coming in. Uematsu and all the Itayado locals were in agreement on that. He was always losing at the gambling houses, but he'd just tell his creditors not to worry, that he had a money tree planted up in Tokyo. Then, he'd disappear for a few days, come back with his pockets bulging and pay off his gambling debts. The locals were all pretty envious, but no one knew who was giving him the money, or where they were. But still, Uematsu said he had a feeling that it must have been Count Tamamushi."

"Why was that?"

"Because of the girl, Sayoko-chan, of course. Or at least, Uematsu didn't know of any other reason that Uetatsu could have for getting money from his lordship."

Kindaichi thought for a moment, then said, "So, did Uematsu have anything to say about who Sayoko's father might be? Viscount Shingu or Count Tamamushi?"

"No, he's got no idea. All he knew was that someone had his way with the girl one summer while she was helping out at the count's villa, and that's what got her pregnant with Sayoko, but neither Uetatsu nor Komako would ever say who had done it. Even with Gensuke dragging her around by her hair and beating her, Komako never said a word about who the girl's real father was. She kept that secret tight, whether out of hard-headedness or shame, no one knows."

That set Kindaichi thinking silently again. Finally, he said, "So, what was this strange thing you mentioned?"

"Right, that." Degawa fidgeted at his knees a bit, and said, "While I was going from Uematsu's to Itayado, I went to see the old Tamamushi villa, since it's on the way. I thought I'd check out that stone lantern you mentioned. And the writing had been erased."

"Erased?!" Kindaichi's eyes widened in shock.

"That's right. Someone scraped it off. There was a place scratched clean, right on the front of the flame space, where you said it had been."

Kindaichi was unable to speak for a moment. He could only stare at the detective's face. When his voice returned, he said, "So, then, last night, after Osumi and I left the ruins, someone came just to scratch those letters out?"

"That's the only explanation I can think of. And I find it hard to believe it was just some local kid's prank."

"Which means that someone mixed up in all this is here, right now…"

Degawa nodded grimly. "I can't imagine that the murderer himself came all this way, so he likely sent someone to do his work for him. Then, there was something else…"

"There's more?!"

"When I had finished asking around at Itayado, I went on over to Shinkaichi, in Kobe. The inn where Otama had worked is called Minato House. I went by one more time to ask about the nun Myokai. I didn't learn anything new about her, but they said that not an hour before I got there, another man had come around asking about Otama."

Kindaichi once again could only stare wordlessly at him. A sense of unspeakable unease rode from the depths of his belly.

"He got really pushy about her, apparently, but in the end, they sent him home without telling him anything. I normally wouldn't have thought anything of it. But what with the stone lantern and all, it bothered me, so I asked them about him."

"And?"

"I was getting a really bad feeling about the whole thing, so… I brought this out."

Detective Degawa stood up and took something out of the pocket of his jacket where it hung drying. It was a photograph of Viscount Tsubaki.

"I asked them if the man asking could have been the man in the picture..." Degawa stared intently at Kindaichi's eyes as he spoke, his voice hoarse. "They said the man who came had glasses and a beard, but still looked just like the one in the photo."

They stared at each other in shock. Did this mean that Viscount Tsubaki truly was alive?

It wasn't long before the head clerk returned with the fisherman they had been seeking, and the rain had finally cleared completely.

CHAPTER 19

The Mountains of Awaji Island

The rain had lifted, but clouds still hung low and dark in the sky, and the waves on the leaden sea at Akashi Port were running high.

The port was shaped like a coin purse with its mouth facing south. At its back were two piers, each about thirty feet long and seemingly made of old ship parts, jutting out over the filthy, debris-covered seawater. The Bantan Line steamships bound for Iwaya used one pier, and the other was for Marusei Line ships sailing around the Awaji route.

Rain-battered fishing boats were clustered around the roots of the piers, rocking like cradles on the heavy swells. One rather elegant lighthouse still stood at the mouth of the port. Awaji Island rose beyond it like an ink painting.

The eastern half of Akashi and Kobe city had survived relatively untouched through the war and still had some old houses, but the western half looked to have been completely lost to the fires. Now it was covered with the same slapdash temporary buildings that had spread across most of Japan. None of the beauty that the Suma and Akashi districts had once been famous for was left to be seen.

The passenger hall shared by the ship lines was just such a building: a rickety wooden shed standing between the two piers and reeking of pitch. Right now, around twenty bored and blank-faced passengers were gathered in and around it, waiting for their ferry to dock.

Kosuke Kindaichi didn't go inside. He stayed on the pier, deep in thought. Meanwhile Detective Degawa pretended to inspect the ship-line posters and timetables pasted to the walls of the passenger hall.

The fisherman that the head clerk had brought was named Sakuzo Yoshimura. He was around fifty, with short salt-and-pepper hair.

He said that while he couldn't remember the exact date, he did recall taking a well-dressed middle-aged man from the beach at their fishing village of Niihama, to the west of Akashi port, across to Nagahama beach on Awaji Island back in January. The gentleman had seemed deeply depressed, and barely spoke a word at first, but opened up a bit after asking the best way to get to a village called Kamaguchi.

"Kamaguchi… Are you certain that was the name?"

When Kindaichi pressed him on that, the fisherman nodded.

"Aye, no doubt. Reason I'm so sure, like, es my niece moved over to Kamaguchi after she married. I go by to see her, like, time and again."

Kindaichi glanced at Degawa before turning back to Yoshimura. "What did you answer, then?"

"Well, I told him to walk from Nagahama to Iwaya, then take the bus towards Sumoto and get off't a place name of Oi. That'll lead right ento Kamaguchi."

"Did he mention what business he had in the village?" Degawa asked.

"No, dedn't ask."

"Yoshimura-san, this might be an odd question, but does Kamaguchi have a nun's temple or the like?"

"Aye, et does. More of a shack than a temple, like, and half fallen down t'boot. Was empty for years and all, but then a nun came to live last year or the year afore. Name of Myokai, I hear."

Kindaichi stole another glance at his colleague. That was it: Viscount Tsubaki must have gone to visit Myokai.

"Yoshimura-san, can you remember anything else that man might have said?"

"Well, after I told 'em the way to Kamaguchi, he asked about how long the trep to Oi might take. So, I told 'em, et's about a twenty-minute walk from Nagayama to Iwaya, then you should fegure another twenty to wait for the bus, then forty minutes on the bus from Iwaya to Oi. So, altogether, about an hour and a half or so. He sat quiet for a while, then asked, pretty as you please, ef I could come get him at Nagahama. He reckoned he'd be back there around four o'clock. Then—"

"I see, so, wait a moment. What time did you take him across?"

"Just after ten, I reckon."

"And what time did you arrive?"

"Just before eleven. We had good luck and a calm sea. The trep from our village across to Nagahama takes right around a half hour, like."

If he arrived at Nagahama around eleven, then figuring an hour and a half to Oi, and probably another half hour or so to find the temple, then he would have met up with Myokai at around one in the afternoon. Figuring another two hours for the return trip would give him about an hour to talk. That'd be plenty of time to discuss all kinds of things.

"And did you go pick him up around four?"

"I ded. After all, the man had paid hes way and all."

"And was he there when you did?"

"Aye, I got to Nagahama around half past three, and he showed up earlier 'n I thought. Then, he had me take 'em to

Akashi Port and drop 'em off at the Bantan Line pier. Reckon that was around half past four."

With the ten-minute walk from the port to Akashi Station, then thirty minutes by train from there to Sumadera, and a ten-minute walk from there to the inn, he could well have been back around five o'clock, just like Osumi had said.

Finally, Degawa showed his picture of Viscount Tsubaki, and Yoshimura immediately confirmed that was his passenger.

This cleared up all doubt that Tsubaki had crossed to Awaji and met the nun Myokai, but what did he learn there? For, as Yoshimura put it, when he went to pick the man up after his talk, "He looked pale as ef he'd seen a vision of death etself."

Whatever it was must have been truly terrible.

The weather finally seemed to be clearing and the dark clouds breaking up, allowing blue sky to show through here and there. The leaden sea also began to brighten with the sky.

Before too long a ferry came cutting through the waves, white foam trailing from the prow. The passengers clustered around the passenger hall began shuffling towards the pier.

The ship was the *Chidorimaru*, weighing in at around seventy tonnes, and once inside the harbour it turned to come to a smooth, clean stop at the pier. About thirty passengers from Iwaya disembarked, and after they were done, those waiting slowly filed on board. Kindaichi and Degawa were the last.

They both stayed on deck rather than heading down into the cabin. There they leaned on the iron railing and watched the waves. A handful of stragglers came rushing up the pier after the crowd had boarded, and once they made it on, the *Chidorimaru* set out. Degawa looked back at the pier, then suddenly nudged Kindaichi with one elbow.

"Kindaichi-san, something's up."

"What's that?"

"Look over at the passenger hall. Those three men standing in front of it? They're plain-clothes police."

Kindaichi looked back at the landing and saw three men, all dressed in suits, questioning one of the passengers who'd just left the ferry—a middle-aged man, also wearing a suit, and carrying a suitcase.

"Ha ha ha, can you tell that from here?"

"Of course. They have the look. I knew they weren't passengers even before the ship docked. They've got a net up, for sure, but who are they trying to snag?"

"Don't you think they're just after black marketeers?"

"Nah, if they were, they'd be checking bags. That's the second man in a suit they've questioned. And they're not looking at his bags at all."

As they watched, the man produced something from his pocket. The policemen looked it over, then let him go without going through his suitcase. The man rushed past the shipping company offices and headed into town, but the three detectives ducked back into the empty passenger hall. They appeared to be sticking around for the next ship to dock.

"I see. That is odd."

"Very. Something must have happened on Awaji. That's an emergency cordon, that is."

The men traded uneasy glances and fell into silence for a time. The shiver that raced through both of their bodies was not due to the chill sea breeze.

"You don't think…"

"I was just going to say…" Degawa cut himself off and looked out to sea again, but then he shook his head as if to clear it and looked down at his watch. It read a few minutes past two.

"I think we might end up spending the night on Awaji tonight, Kindaichi-san."

"Do you think so?"

"If we get to Iwaya at half past two and have that forty-minute bus ride and thirty-minute walk to the temple at Kamaguchi, it's going to be almost four by the time we get there. Then, it looks like the last bus from Sumoto to Iwaya leaves at six, and it stops at Oi around ten to seven. If we make it, we can get the last ferry back, but if we miss that bus, we're stuck."

"I see. So, if we get to the temple around four, then we'd have to leave by around twenty past six if we want to walk back to Oi in time to make that last bus. That only gives us two hours and twenty minutes to find out everything we can."

"Yes. That might work out if Myokai is there at the temple. But if she's out gathering alms or something, we might not make it. It looks like Tsubaki finished his business in an hour or so, but we can't assume it'll go so well for us."

"Well, if we miss the last bus, then we'll just stay in Kamaguchi. Let's hope someone will have room for us," Kindaichi said. He found himself feeling somehow discouraged.

"I can't say anything about Kamaguchi, but Itaya, the next town over is a bit bigger. It's just a couple of miles from Oi and won't take an hour to walk. If we make it there, I hear they have lodging for travellers."

"Well then, shall we play at being pilgrims and stop there for the evening?" Kindaichi laughed quietly, but just then the ship gave a great roll and both men had to grab for the railing to keep their feet. A large steamer headed south to Kyushu was ploughing through the strait. The *Chidorimaru* headed straight into its wake and pitched up and down. Soon, though, it recovered and returned to its calm journey with the monotonous thrumming of the engines.

Before they realized it, the ship had passed the strait's halfway point, and the great mountains of Awaji Island stood right before their eyes. The gaps between the clouds widened, and the island now stood against an almost blindingly bright blue autumn sky. The surface of the sea took on a beautiful patterning like agate stripes, perhaps due to the currents in the strait. With the rain lifted, fishing boats now dotted the horizon. Above, flocks of seagulls wheeled.

But none of this scenery made any impression on Kindaichi. The uneasiness that he and Degawa had earlier shared continued to loom over his head. What they were both thinking but hesitated to say out loud was that someone had erased that message from the stone lantern, and a man had come to Minato House to ask about Otama.

The rubbing out of the writing could have been a simple prank, and the man could simply have been a friend of Otama's looking to track her down. And of course, the detectives on the lookout around Akashi port might not have had anything at all to do with their case. It could all have been simple coincidence. They did their best to keep all of that in mind, but they could not suppress a growing feeling of foreboding.

Kindaichi tore his hat from his head and began scratching at his dishevelled mop. His tousled hair, the sleeves of his kimono, and the hem of his *hakama* all fluttered in the sea breeze. Degawa rested one cheek on the tall metal railing and started chewing his fingernails. Awaji Island spread out above them now.

The *Chidorimaru* soon slowed as it approached the breakwaters around Iwaya port. The town wrapped around a low hill like a thin belt, and its narrow sandy beach was lined with fishing boats. Iwaya port had only one pier, and Kindaichi could see the silhouettes of a handful of people standing along it.

The *Chidorimaru* would stop there for thirty minutes, then set sail back to Akashi.

When they alighted they found the bus for Sumoto waiting with five or six people already on board. Once more, two men with the air of plain-clothes detectives stood in front of the nearby passenger hall. They eyed Kindaichi suspiciously.

Most of the ferry passengers got on the bus. Kindaichi and Degawa had hurried to be the first and managed to get seats in the back. When they sat down, they noticed a building to the right of the pier with a sign reading Hyogo Prefectural Police: Iwaya Station. Just as the driver was closing the door, three men rushed out of it and leapt on board. A uniformed officer, a plain-clothes detective, and the third looked like a doctor. The bus departed immediately.

Kindaichi and Degawa exchanged looks.

The doctor found an empty seat and sat down, but the two police officers stood next to the driver's seat, talking quietly.

After the bus left Iwaya's town centre, it headed south along the shoreline. The beach came right up to the left side of the road, and the sea was not far away at all. The houses of fishermen and farmers lined the road to the right, with the hillside of terraced fields coming right up behind. Everywhere they saw the broad leaves of sweet potato vines.

Degawa suddenly stood up.

"This is getting to me, Kindaichi-san. I'm going to go ask what's going on."

He pushed his way through the standing passengers to the driver, removed his hat and talked to the officer in uniform. Kindaichi couldn't hear what they said, but saw Degawa pull something out of his pocket and show the other man. It must have been his badge and ID. The policeman looked surprised, then the plain-clothes officer joined them in heated discussion.

Kindaichi watched with interest as they talked and saw that Degawa's face was growing pale and grave. Kindaichi's belly grew heavy, like a lead ball of anxiety was sitting there.

None of it had been coincidence.

After a short conversation, Degawa turned to Kindaichi and beckoned him over with a jerk of his head. The look on his face reminded Kindaichi of what Yoshimura had said. He was as pale as if he'd seen a vision of death.

He approached the three men, and Degawa said in a hoarse, trembling voice, "It's no good, Kindaichi-san. We were right. He got here ahead of us."

"Then... she's dead?" His voice was every bit as hoarse and unsteady as Degawa's.

"Yes, it seems she was strangled."

Kindaichi squeezed his eyes shut. A surreal dread washed over him. For some reason, he heard the crescendo of "The Devil Comes and Plays His Flute" echoing in his ears like the wailing of dead souls.

Detective Degawa introduced him to the two policemen, and the uniformed officer explained what had happened, despite his obvious confusion at Kindaichi's presence.

The Iwaya Police Station received a report around noon that the nun Myokai was dead. Her body had been discovered rather late because of the storm that morning. When the rain subsided around eleven, a village girl had gone to the temple to take the nun some vegetables. Myokai had been teaching the local girls sewing and knitting, so they helped her out as best they could.

The temple *amado* shutters were all closed, but when the girl tried the front door, she found it unlocked. She went inside, but the nun didn't answer her calls. She thought it odd, though, because the woman's sandals were still on the doorstep inside, so she opened the bed closet, and saw Myokai's foot sticking out from her futon.

"That set off a panic, as you could well imagine. We pieced together that last evening around six, someone got off the bus from Sumoto and asked the way to the temple at the tobacconist's next to the bus stop. Right now, that man is our only suspect, so we set up a cordon at the ports and such. But I reckon it's too late. If he came over from the mainland, then he's probably long gone off the island."

Kindaichi was surprised at his forthrightness. "Do you have any reason to think he did come from the mainland?"

"Yes, the bus he took would have been the five o'clock from Sumoto, which is just in time for passengers from the ferry that leaves Kobe at half past two."

"Do you have a description?"

"Just that he was around forty, wearing a suit. Nothing more detailed, but we're just now asking the bus driver and conductor for more."

"By the way, about this nun. I heard you call her Myokai, but do you know her real name?"

The officer took out his notebook to check. "Komako Horii, aged forty years or so. We don't know much else about her, I'm afraid."

Kindaichi squeezed his eyes shut in despair and shook his head slowly to clear it. He was feeling like he might pass out.

Komako Horii. When Komako was pregnant with Sayoko, her father had married her off to his apprentice, Gensuke Horii. It was, of course, the same woman.

CHAPTER 20

Assassin

They arrived at Oi around twenty past three.

Looking out the windows of the crowded bus, Kindaichi saw frantic-looking police racing around on bicycles. The air seemed full of tension. When they pulled into the bus stop, one bicyclist got off to talk quietly with the uniformed policeman standing by the driver.

Oi was a small village of farmers and fishers, with not even ten houses lining the road. Those few standing on the seaward side had nets drying in the sun behind them. The houses on the other side of the road stood right up against the steep hillside that climbed towards the mountain beyond.

That was Mount Asagiri. The nun's temple was nestled in its foothills.

This area was in the very southern reaches of the Iwaya Police Station's jurisdiction.

As they alighted from the bus, some locals came out of their houses and gathered in the shade to watch the proceedings. A policeman approached and led the other officers and Kindaichi past them.

Their target was a house with a tobacconist's sign hanging from the eaves, but since tobacco was still technically under rationing, the display shelves were now lined with household sundries and odds and ends, all coated with a fine layer of dust thrown up by the passing buses. The men entered the shop, and a curly-haired proprietor came out of the back. She wore a frightened expression and was massaging her breast as if she'd just been nursing a baby.

"This woman's in charge of the shop. The bus passenger from last evening asked her about the nun," a local policeman said.

She seemed as nervous as if she herself was responsible for Myokai's death, but she did her best to answer their questions. This is what she had to say: The evening before, at around ten minutes to six, a man in a suit had come to her door not long after the bus had left. He was alone and burst inside and asked where he could find the nun Myokai. She told him the way, and he left without even a word of thanks. He seemed to be in a great hurry.

"So, ma'am, did you not see him again?" the same uniformed officer asked.

"I ded, actually," she answered. "About an hour later, he came back to the shop. He asked ef the bus from Sumoto had already passed. I looked at the time, like, and saw et was ten past seven. The last bus from Sumoto should have been long gone, but last evening I reckon et was running late or such. Et showed up as we were talking, like. He got on, and off he went."

"Did he mention whether or not he had actually gone to see Myokai?"

"Oh, I asked 'em myself, I ded. He said he'd gone to the temple but she hadn't been home, so he planned to try again en the morning."

"Can you tell us how long it takes to get to the *ama* temple and back?" Degawa interrupted with his own question.

"An hour's more 'n enough, like. Even ef you had trouble finding your way."

If he'd left at ten to six and come back at ten past seven, that would have given him plenty of time to make it to the temple, do his foul business and get back.

"Now, ma'am, could you tell us about this man's accent? Was he from this area?" asked Detective Degawa.

Her answer to his question was quick and firm, "No, no, he was from back east. He was talking low, like, but he spoke pretty as you please."

"I see, I see. Could you tell us, did he look anything like this man in the picture?"

The local police had all widened their eyes in surprise when Degawa pulled out the photograph.

She took a close look at it, then said, "Well, the man last night had a hat and glasses on, and a beard and all, so I can't be fully sure, but I reckon he looked quite a bet like thes man."

Degawa glanced at Kindaichi. Glasses and a beard, but still that resemblance... It had to be the same man who had gone to Minato House.

Kindaichi felt a chill run up his spine.

Detective Degawa turned to the local policemen, who were staring back and forth between the photograph and the man holding it.

"I'll fill you all in on this later. For now, we should go and see the crime scene," he said.

Their path took them off the main road and onto a side road leading up the steep slope, which seemed to go on forever. The farmers in the fields stopped to watch them pass. A few even trailed along after. While murders might not be that rare in the city, out here in the quiet countryside, it was a major event. A kind of panic was spreading through this area.

They walked for around twenty-five minutes before they finally reached the temple. It stood about halfway up the hill, far from the town, and the hillside next to it was lined with pale gravestones. There was a small reservoir pond just behind the temple that collected the water from a stream as it ran down into the valley. Dreary shadow concealed its surface.

The temple itself barely seemed worthy of the name. It was a small thatch-roofed house with no wall or fence, close up against the graveyard. It was no wonder that no one had moved in during or after the war, even with the housing shortage.

The crowd of locals who had been following the policemen gathered around the temple.

The local officer in the lead told the onlookers to stand back and opened the rickety old *shoji* sliding door. Inside was a narrow dirt-floored entryway, and beyond that was a small, raised room of just four and a half tatami mats. The body was laid out there, with the head pointing north as tradition dictated. Three men were sitting around the corpse. The doctor from Iwaya had hurried up there as soon as he got off the bus and was talking in a low voice with the village doctor. An older priest sat stiffly, a little apart from them.

"How does it look, Doctor?" The officer had removed his shoes at the entryway and climbed up into the room.

"Well, we won't know any details until the autopsy, but there's no doubt about strangulation being the cause."

"What about the time of death?"

"That will have to wait for the autopsy, too. But, from what the local doctor says, it couldn't have been today. It must have been last night, or maybe early evening. Sorry, I can't be more specific."

The room grew cramped as more men shuffled in. The priest withdrew, opening a *shoji* and stepping out onto the rain-damp deck to make room.

Kindaichi stood at the back and peeked nervously at the dead woman's face from behind the others.

The nun's small, clean-shaven head seemed somewhat out of proportion, but her gently closed eyes and nose were as

215

shapely as a porcelain doll's. She must have been quite lovely in her younger days. But she looked older than forty. She was petite, and such women tend to age quickly, but even so the burden of her painful fate must have worn her down and aged her prematurely. He could certainly understand why the women at Minato House had put her in her mid-fifties.

The smoke rising from incense burning by her head tickled Kindaichi's nose. Something about its scent mixed with the damp autumn air in this narrow valley to invoke a wave of sentimentality in his breast. If she had never gone to help at Count Tamamushi's villa that fateful summer, she might have led a very different existence. Those events had scarred her life like the talons of a devil.

There, in that villa, she had been tormented, raped and impregnated. Later, she had given birth to Sayoko... That time had not only shrouded her whole life in darkness, but had now taken her life completely.

The thought inspired intense frustration and anger in Kindaichi. But could that be the only reason this woman had died? No, it couldn't be. She must have known some other, greater secret connected to the case which had marked her for death. But what could it be?

Kindaichi's rage grew as he gazed down at the woman's delicate face.

The secret must have been truly important, to drive the murderer to take the great risk of coming out here to silence her. What terrible knowledge did that little head hold?

"Well, I think that's it for me. What should we do with the body?" the lead officer asked.

The doctor from Iwaya packed up his bag and got to his feet.

"The ambulance should be on its way. It'll take her to town for the autopsy."

"All right. Until then."

"What about crime scene photos?" Degawa asked.

"They finished them earlier."

"So, is it all right if I take a look around, then?"

"Go right ahead."

The local police watched Degawa with open curiosity. The first thing he inspected was a stack of neatly folded newspapers in front of the closet. The newspapers were folded precisely in four and arranged by date, hinting at Myokai's careful nature. Degawa flipped through them in order, and then turned to a local policeman.

"Do you know which newspapers she subscribed to?" he asked.

The policeman slid the door open and spoke to the crowd of local residents milling outside, then shut it again.

"Just the *K*—, apparently."

"I thought so. That's what most of these are. But look, Kindaichi-san," he said, "she has seven different papers from Osaka and Kobe from 1st October, and three papers each from the 2nd and 3rd."

The two men stood silently for a moment.

1st October was when the papers had broken the news of the murder at the Tsubaki estate, and that was also the day Myokai had gone to Minato House to ask about Otama. She must have bought every newspaper she could find when she was in Kobe. Then, on the 2nd and 3rd, she had not been satisfied with just one paper either, so she had bought all she could find locally. It showed just how intent she was on getting the latest news around that time, most likely due to the murder.

Once again, Kindaichi felt a surge of frustration at being one step behind the murderer.

"By the way, wasn't there a priest here a moment ago? Who was that, exactly?" he asked as he looked around the room.

"That's Jido-san, the head priest at Hojo temple in the next village over. He looked after Myokai and got her to live here."

Kindaichi glanced at Degawa, then said, "I see. Could someone call him in for a moment?"

Jido-san, who had only stepped out to make room, returned immediately when called. With the doctors gone, there was now just enough room around the dead woman's resting place for the priest, Kindaichi and Degawa to sit down together. The local police had climbed down to the earthen floor and stood looking with great interest.

"I'm sorry we are forced to talk under these circumstances, sir..." Kindaichi sputtered, scratching away at his mop of hair. "The fact is, though, this woman... The departed is connected to a case that brought us out from Tokyo. We apparently were only a day or so behind the murderer. It's such a terrible tragedy. But, if it's all right, there are some things we'd like to ask you."

"You came all the way from Tokyo?" Jido-san raised his white eyebrows. He must have been well over sixty years old, but was still a plump and healthy-looking man. "Then, you must know all about Myokai."

"Actually, we don't, but there's a very difficult problem that we were hoping she would be able to help us solve."

"What might that be?"

Kindaichi paused for a moment before continuing. "It's a murder investigation. I believe that Myokai might have known a secret connected to it."

That caused a stir in the crowd gathered around the doorway.

Jido-san frowned. "I see... Sorry, and you are? I didn't catch your name?"

"My name is Kosuke Kindaichi. This is Detective Degawa on assignment from the Metropolitan Police Department."

Jido-san stared wide-eyed at him before replying, "Kindaichi-san, can I assume you men think Myokai might have known who was behind the murder at Viscount Tsubaki's house? And that's what got her killed?"

His mention of the Tsubaki estate murder set the crowd murmuring louder. Meanwhile, the policemen stared with bated breath at the three men. Kindaichi straightened himself up on his knees.

"I see you're familiar with what happened. So, yes. That is exactly what I think. It would be too great a coincidence, otherwise. The murderer must have known we were coming here to investigate, so either he or an assassin sent by him got here ahead of us and made sure Myokai-san couldn't talk."

The tension emanating from the watching policemen was palpable. The occasional sad sighs and dry coughs from the crowd only served to accentuate the quiet in the temple.

Kindaichi leaned forward to break the silence. "But how did you guess that this had to do with the Tsubaki murder, sir? Did Myokai-san mention anything to you?"

Jido-san nodded. "That's right. It was the day before yesterday, or maybe the day before that. Around noon. Myokai came out to visit with a stack of newspapers. She showed me some articles about that murder, and said she had an idea about what happened there. The day afore, she'd gone out to Kobe to talk to some acquaintance about it, but she said they weren't there, like. So, she came out to talk to me."

"D-did Myokai-san tell you anything? About the murderer?"

"Well, now, Kindaichi-san, now's I think about it, I'm sorry to say she didn't. Poor Myokai didn't open up about anything important at all. Not a word."

Kindaichi gave a groan. The glimmer of hope vanished just as it seemed in reach.

The priest went on, "I'm partly to blame, I fear. It all seemed so far-fetched that I half doubted her, and I didn't really listen as close as I should have. And Myokai herself was all worked up, and her story wandered all over. I reckon she hadn't quite made up her mind to open up about the real story. So, I told her to come back when she'd settled down… I truly regret that now. I should have asked her more." He sighed deeply. Then, he seemed to recall something. "She did tell me something unusual, though. I doubt it'll be of too much help, but I reckon it's got to do with the connection between her and Tsubaki."

"Yes?"

Kindaichi and Degawa both leaned forward.

"This was the first time I'd heard it, now, and it gave me quite a surprise. It seems Myokai had a daughter back when she was still called Komako. The girl's name was Sayoko."

"Yes, we know."

"You do? Then, do you know who her father was?"

"No, sadly, we haven't been able to find that out. Who is it?"

"That Shingu-san, you know. His name was in the newspapers. He's the one who fathered Sayoko on Komako."

Kindaichi and Degawa looked at each other in shock. So, Viscount Shingu had raped Komako and fathered her child.

"And that's what put Myokai into such a fright. She thought that the murders in the Tsubaki house weren't over. She was sure that Shingu-san would be next…"

Kindaichi gaped at Degawa. And his head began to buzz, as if an angry bee were flying around in his brain.

"Why would Shingu-san being the girl's father get him murdered?"

"That, I don't know. Like I said, Myokai's story wandered all over the place. Now's I think on it, she must have been afraid to get to the real heart of it all."

220

"Do you know Sayoko yourself?" Degawa asked.

"Yes, I met her once."

"When? Where?"

"It would have been September 1943, I reckon. Over at Saru's house in Sumiyoshi... Not that you'd understand that. I suppose I'd better tell you how I came to know Myokai."

This is the story Jido-san told.

He had been the head priest of a large Shingon sect temple at Sumiyoshi, in southern Hyogo Prefecture. However, he passed responsibility to a disciple in 1942 and retired to his home town in Awaji. But he still went to Sumiyoshi from time to time to visit a family called Mizoguchi, who were great patrons of the temple. The old head of the family was a great admirer of the priest, and whenever Jido-san visited he would end up staying for a night or two. Komako was a maid at the Mizoguchi estate.

"Whenever I stayed, she would come talk to me, saying she was carrying a great sin. In other words, she was trying to find a way to live her life through the teachings of the Buddha. She seemed so sincere and was such a conscientious woman, that I found myself looking at her a bit more seriously. At the time, she was single, with just her daughter as family, who I understood was also a servant somewhere. One day, when I was staying at the house, the girl came to visit. She was lovely. She must have been around twenty."

"Do you know what became of her after that?" Degawa said. His voice was trembling with emotion. His fists were clenched painfully on his knees.

"She died, poor thing. Suicide, I hear."

"Suicide! Wh-when w-was that?" burst out Kindaichi.

"I don't really know for sure. She was someplace far away from Awaji and Sumiyoshi, so I don't know the details. Oh, wait, that's right. Her memorial tablet should be around here somewhere."

Jido-san opened up a small cabinet by the departed's head and took out a black-lacquered wooden tablet. "Name in death Jiunmyosei Daishi... Yes, this must be it. Living name Sayoko Horii, deceased 27 August 1944."

Degawa snatched the tablet and glared at the words inscribed there.

"So... Sayoko really is dead, then..." His voice was filled with despair. It was understandable. His pet theory that she had grown up to be Kikue had been shattered in a single blow.

"Do you know why she did it?"

"Well, about that," Jido-san said, with a hard glint in his eye. "I couldn't say exactly as to what happened at the time. I didn't even know she'd died until long after the fact. But, just the other day, when Myokai was here talking about all this business, it did seem that the girl's suicide had something to do with this murder at the Tsubaki house. At the time, I really couldn't make head nor tail of it, though."

"Jido-san, are you absolutely certain that Sayoko is dead?" Degawa was still holding the tablet, but he clearly hadn't given up his theory completely. Jido-san raised his white eyebrows.

"You're holding her memorial tablet in your hands. Those don't lie. If you still don't believe it, go to Sumiyoshi and ask the Mizoguchi family. They might have more to tell you. After all, the girl was the main reason Myokai decided to become a nun."

Degawa got directions to the house in Sumiyoshi from the priest and decided to do just that.

"By the way, Jido-san, there's something else I was wondering. Did Myokai-san say anything about Viscount Tsubaki coming to visit her last spring?"

"Oh, yes, I did hear about that. She mentioned it the other day. That was something else she refused to open up about, but she did seem very worried about it."

The bee in Kindaichi's head buzzed ever louder. Now it was not just one, but dozens. A swarm. What was it that Myokai had told the viscount? What did she know that got her killed?

Kindaichi and Degawa had more questions, but the priest had told them all he knew, and they learned nothing else. Degawa asked Jido-san if there were anyone else Myokai-san might have confided in, but he only said if there were something she didn't want to tell him, then there was surely no one else she would have revealed it to.

Just to be sure, the detective asked around the village, but no one could tell him anything more than the priest had.

That day saw Kindaichi and Degawa return to Iwaya long after eight o'clock in the evening, so of course they had no way to get to Akashi. They were forced to stay overnight in town, but it turned out that they were able to learn something more as a result.

The man who had asked about the nun Myokai at Oi had certainly arrived on the ferry from Kobe. The reason he had made it in time to catch the last bus back to Iwaya was that the bus had broken down soon after leaving Sumoto and was delayed by twenty minutes. The delay meant that he had not been able to catch the last ferry, and had also been forced to spend the night in Iwaya as well—and it turned out he had stayed at the same guest house as Kindaichi and Degawa, before checking out of his room at six in the morning and taking the ferry to Akashi. He had entered a Tokyo address and name in the ledger, but of course both would turn out to be fake, so Kindaichi didn't pay much attention.

"The problem is this, Degawa-san," Kindaichi said gloomily, "this man was on the two thirty ferry from Kobe to Sumoto yesterday. From the steamer timetable, it looks like there's an earlier one: the ten o'clock. That one would have fitted his plans much better. He'd have been able to do his business without the danger of having to stay overnight on Awaji. Much less risky. And yet, he didn't take the ten o'clock. Don't you think that has to mean something?"

"What are you getting at?"

"It must mean that he wasn't in Kobe at ten. His train got there later. Which almost certainly means he must have been on the same train from Tokyo that we took, don't you think?"

Degawa's eyes opened wide. "The same train?"

"He must have been. He knew what our investigation would find and that we would end up talking to Myokai. So, he took the same train out west as us, and while we were wandering around Sumadera, he came straight to Awaji and killed Myokai. Then, he left the island early this morning, went by Tsukimiyama to erase the message on the stone lantern, then on to Minato House in Kobe."

"So, why did he go to Minato House last?"

"It must be for the same reason he sought out Myokai. If Otama had been there, he'd have taken her somewhere, and then…"

"Kindaichi-san!" Degawa broke off and took a deep breath, before going on. "If that's true, we can't be sitting around here waiting! Otama's in danger!"

"Yes, she is. That's why I can't stand being stuck here. But, well, now it looks like Otama disappearing from Minato House was good luck for us. He couldn't track her down in just one day. Now it's a race to see who can find her first… I think that's going to be what settles this case once and for all."

"Right. Then, I'm catching the first ferry to Akashi in the morning."

———

However, things did not work out that way. The pair had to talk to the local police at Iwaya station, so they couldn't catch the ferry until after ten.

Detective Degawa was heading straight to Kobe, so Kindaichi parted ways with him at Sumadera station and went back to the Three Spring Garden Inn.

Just as he stepped in the front door, the *okami* came running from the back.

"Oh, Kindaichi-san, there you are. You've got a visitor. He's been waiting."

"A visitor for me? Who is it?"

"He says he's from the prefectural police, like."

"What on earth…?" He rushed to his room, where he found a man of around forty.

"You must be Kindaichi-san? Is Detective Degawa not with you?"

"Degawa-san has gone on to Kobe. And you are?"

The man held out a business card from the Hyogo Prefectural Police. He was a chief inspector.

"We got a call from the Tokyo Metropolitan Police Department this morning, asking us to contact you here as quickly as possible."

"From Tokyo? What about?"

The officer took a look around before going on in a low voice, "There's been another murder at the Tsubaki estate in Tokyo."

Kindaichi sat silent and wide-eyed for a moment. When he tried to speak, it felt like his throat was on fire. "And who was… the victim?"

"Man name of Toshihiko Shingu, they said. So, the word is that you're to leave the rest of the investigation here to Degawa-san, with our help of course, and rush back as quickly as you can."

The bees buzzed angrily in Kindaichi's head once more. Toshihiko Shingu, murdered… Just as Myokai had predicted. But how had she known?

The bees grew from the dozens to the hundreds, the thousands, until the roar in his head was like rolling thunder. The whole world spun like he was drunk on bad liquor.

CHAPTER 21

Fujin Appears

On the evening of 4th October, the sixth day after the late Tamamushi's murder, the great Tsubaki estate in Azabu Roppongi was oddly empty. Most of the residents were out according to their own plans. Or so it seemed, though it soon turned out that certain of those plans were not what they thought. Rather, if their stories were to be believed, they had been tricked out of the house by an unknown party.

That evening at dinner, Toshihiko Shingu looked around the spacious family living room from his spot at the low table.

"It's awful quiet around here this evening. Where is everyone?" he asked in his thick, dull voice.

Akiko had been wracked by fear ever since Count Tamamushi's murder, so she had demanded that everyone gather together in the family room every day for dinner, apart from Totaro Mishima and the two servants, Otane and Shino. That evening, though, Akiko's old nursemaid Shino, Akiko's ostensible physician Doctor Mega and Count Tamamushi's mistress Kikue were nowhere to be seen.

"They're all out," Mineko said. Her voice held more than its usual note of anger. It frayed the girl's nerves every time she heard her uncle's slow drawl.

"Out? All together?"

"Not at all. Don't you know?"

"Know what?"

"Kikue-san is at the theatre. She sat right here at this table last night, saying she was glad she'd got tickets for tonight rather than tomorrow."

"Oh, right, right. I forgot. But why would she be so happy about that?" Shingu's vacant, idiot eyes lingered on Mineko's face. His face was as sickly pale as ever. The sight of his gaping, slack-lipped mouth fed her aggravation.

"Have you forgotten even that much? Tomorrow is great-uncle Tamamushi's first week memorial service. No matter how flippant Kikue-san might be, she certainly couldn't skip that for a night at the theatre."

"Oh, yes, I suppose you're right." The sound of his drawling reply grated even more.

"You are always like this. All you ever think about is your own fun. There's no room for anything else in your head."

"Mineko-san," Akiko, sitting at the head of the table, glittering like a queen, interrupted with her saccharine child's voice. "You shouldn't speak to your uncle like that. I'm sorry, Hanako-san."

"It's fine," said Hanako.

"Do forgive her. I simply cannot imagine who she gets that from."

"Oh, no, think nothing of it," Hanako answered blandly. This was a frequent occurrence, and she'd given up even trying to act interested. "Everything Mineko-san says is true."

"Do forgive me, aunt." Mineko seemed to realize she'd over-stepped the mark. "I don't know why I get like this. I just find myself getting so irritated whenever uncle Shingu speaks."

"I'm sure it's just a clash of personalities." A look of sadness ran over Hanako's face, but her husband paid no attention.

"Akiko-san, what about old Shino?"

"She's gone to Seijo, brother dear."

Whenever Mineko heard her mother say those words, "brother dear", she could not help but hear the voice of a fawning schoolgirl. It gave her chills. That alone was enough to keep her feelings turned against the man.

"Seijo? So she must be at Aikawa's, then." He meant the household of his and Akiko's maternal grandfather, the one who had passed the estate to her.

"Yes, that's right, brother dear. Uncle Aikawa sent a telegram asking her to visit. It just came, actually. Shino went rushing off as soon as she saw it."

"He sent a telegram? What did he want with her?"

"I'm sure I don't know. But aunt Aikawa has always liked Shino. She probably has some errand for her to run."

"I hope she brings a bit of pocket money back for me! Haw!" Shingu raised his dullard voice in laughter, a nasty grin on his face. "And where's the old toad? Where's Mega?"

"Oh, how mean, brother dear. Old toad!" Akiko seemed genuinely displeased and glared at him with puffed-out cheeks.

Shingu hurried to take back his offence. "Oh, sorry, sorry, I meant, where is Doctor Mega? Did you finally kick him out of the house?"

Akiko, apparently angry over the toad comment, refused to answer, so instead Mineko did: "Doctor Mega has a meeting this evening, so he's off to Yokohama. He said he would be back by ten o'clock at the latest."

"A meeting? But I thought that was the day after tomorrow?"

"It seems someone telephoned this afternoon to tell him that it had been moved to this evening. So, he had to rush off in quite a hurry," Mineko said in a monotone, as if reciting from memory.

Shingu raised his thick eyebrows. "Hm. Everyone's running all over. Kazuhiko, aren't you and Mineko going out later, too?"

"Yes," Kazuhiko answered quietly.

"Where to, was it?"

He kept his eyes lowered and stayed silent.

His father rambled on. "Probably off to see a film or such. Ah, must be nice to be so carefree!"

His tone was so nasty that Mineko could not help but snap at him. "No, uncle. It's nothing to do with being carefree! Kazuhiko is going out this evening to talk about a job opening."

"Oh, a job is it?"

"Yes! That's right. He has been searching for quite some time, but just recently my typing teacher told me about a very promising opening. So, this evening we are going to get an introduction."

Her voice trembled in outrage.

Shingu stared blankly at her and Kazuhiko as if unsure how to respond, then turned to Hanako and asked, "Did you know about this?"

"Yes, I did. I think it's a fine thing and am all for it." She spoke calmly, but there was still a tremble at the tail of her words.

"Haw! Well then. You're going to work, are you, Kazuhiko? How much are you going to give me? Plenty and often, I hope!"

"Dear, don't be so mean."

"What's mean? You shut your mouth. Kazuhiko, when you're out there, see if there's a spot for me, too. Preferably some place that'll pay a nice big salary but not expect any work!"

"Dear, please!"

"Don't you 'dear' me! What gives you the right to talk to me like that? With a father like yours. His son-in-law in such straits and not a bit of cash to help out. I never should have married you! I bet if I'd married someone else back when I was young, I wouldn't be in such a state today."

Hanako straightened up and thrust out her chest, staring full in her husband's face. Her own was pale as a sheet, but when she sat tall like that, she had all the hauteur of a true lady. Her eyes glinted with a complex feeling, something like contempt mixed with pity.

Kazuhiko sat silently, face down and shoulders slumped. His brow was beaded with thick sweat, and he was clenching and opening his fists on the tabletop.

"Uncle!" Mineko interrupted again, her voice sharp and angry. "How dare you? You used up all of her money, and now you have the nerve to talk to her like that? How can you?"

"What was that?!" Shingu, who had started to blanch under his wife's fierce gaze, turned now to Mineko, his own eyes full of rage. "A man has the right to his wife's property, doesn't he? But let's talk about you, you little thief!"

"What did you call me?"

"Yes, that's right, you thief. Your mother got everything that should be mine! And when she dies, it's all going to be yours. It's the same as if you just reached out and stole my rightful property!"

"Dear, please!" Hanako once more tried to stop her husband. "Don't be so rude. Mineko-san, please do forgive him. Your uncle has been feeling so much stress these days. Dear, I'll figure something out this evening, there's no call for all this."

Mineko was so enraged that her whole body seemed ready to burst. But she was in no mood to keep arguing with the vile, greedy man any longer. She rose from the table after one final contemptuous glance. "Kazuhiko-san, we should be going. It's already seven o'clock."

"All right," he said, and as he started to stand, blurted out, "See you later, Mother." He gave a little bow, his hands braced on the table, then followed Mineko out. He didn't say a word to his father.

Shingu turned to his wife, smiling as if he'd already forgotten his fight with Mineko, and said, "Is that true, Hanako? You're heading out to get some money?"

"Yes, I'll work something out."

"Do you really think you can?"

"One way or another."

"That's not good enough. You have to do something!"

"I will."

"Okay then, well, hurry up and go. It's dangerous out late at night."

"Yes, of course. But…"

"But? What's the matter?" The man's voice grew harsh once more.

"I'm just worried about leaving Akiko-san on her own. Shino-san and Doctor Mega are both out, and there's no telling when Mishima-san will be back."

"I can keep an eye on Akiko, don't you worry. But where is Mishima, anyway?"

"He's out shopping for the seventh-day memorial tomorrow. Things are so scarce these days."

"Well, I bet he'll be home soon. Otane's here, anyway, so there's nothing to worry about. You hurry up and go."

Most days, her husband grumbled at the merest hint that she might go out, but now that he saw something in it for himself, he was nearly pushing her out the door. Hanako rose with a sigh. Resigned to her life as she might be, she couldn't help the occasional sigh.

So Hanako left the Tsubaki estate just after seven o'clock, leaving behind only her husband Toshihiko, his sister Akiko and the maid Otane.

There were still police stationed around the walls, but they were really only for show. They were not particularly intent on the job any more.

Mishima Totaro returned around half past eight with a full rucksack. The policeman stationed at the service gate watched him suspiciously.

Otane was clearing up the kitchen when he came through the main house's back door. "Welcome home," she said. "You must be tired after that long day."

"I'm exhausted. The buses and trains are such a nightmare."

"They really are. It's a trial dealing with anything these days. But did you manage everything?"

"More or less, yes. I don't mean to give you more work, but I'm starving. Is there anything?"

"You haven't eaten? Wait just a moment and I'll put something together."

The servants had their meals in the room next to the family room. Mishima put down his pack and sat cross-legged on the floor.

"What's going on? It's awfully quiet, isn't it? Has everyone gone to bed already?" he asked.

"Everyone's gone out! It's been just awful."

"Why's that?"

"Well, for over an hour, it's been just me, the lady and Shingu-san in this huge old place. I was so frightened, this whole time."

"Ha ha! I never took you for such a timid little mouse, Otane-san. There might have only been three people inside, but there are policemen all over outside. You were fine the whole time!"

"The policemen are still here?"

"Yep, one of them gave me a nasty look when he saw me come home with that big pack on my back. I'm not a fan of that, I tell you. But where is everyone else, anyway?"

Otane brought a tray, saying, "Here you go! Tuck in."

She then told him all about everyone's plans. She didn't forget to mention the minor storm that had struck at dinner time, either.

"Hmmm…" Mishima sat stirring his rice in broth, eyes wide. "Then Shingu-san must be really hard up right now."

"Well, of course he is. With their house completely burnt down like that. And, you know, he never lifts a finger; just puts his own fun before everything. He'd lost all his other real estate and everything even before the fires. His wife must have had a fortune once, but I hear he's gone and spent that, too. Then he complains all the time about how her family refuses to help. It's shameful. He's the very image of sloth. That man—"

Just then, almost as if to keep her from saying too much, a bell rang. Otane looked at the indicator lamp on the wall and stood. "That's the front door! Someone must have come home."

It was Shino. When Otane opened the front door, Shino had a terrible expression on her face.

"Otane, did anything happen while I was gone?" The old woman's voice was trembling, and Otane could only answer, confused, "No, nothing at all…"

"Is Lady Akiko all right, then? Nothing's happened to her?"

"No, she's perfectly fine, ma'am."

"I see." Shino seemed relieved as she stepped up into the house, then she turned and said towards the door, "I'm terribly sorry, but could you wait here for a moment? I simply can't relax until I go and see that she's all right with my own eyes."

"Understood," said a voice from outside.

"Oh, is someone there?" Otane asked.

"A policeman was waiting outside the gate, so I had him come with me. Otane-san, come along now. I'm so frightened…"

"Oh, my, ma'am, has something happened? What is it?" It was so rare for Shino to lose her composure that the mere sight of it set the maid's knees trembling in fear.

"Never you mind, just come along." Shino rushed down the hall, not even bothering to remove her coat. Otane followed after. When they reached the *shoji* sliding doors leading to Akiko's room, they heard a voice from inside.

"Who is that? Otane, is that you?" It was Akiko, her voice as childish and fawning as ever.

"Oh, my, Akiko," Shino gasped in relief, and slid the *shoji* open. Akiko was sitting at her writing desk, practising calligraphy. Despite her childish ways, she was highly skilled at it, and took whatever time she could to practise.

"Oh, it's you, Shino. You're home early. What did aunt Aikawa want?"

"Oh, Akiko-san, it was so strange. Lady Aikawa said she had no recollection of sending any telegram."

"Oh, my!" Otane gasped. Shino turned to her and said, "Ah, Otane-san. You may go. And would you let the policeman know that nothing seems to be out of the ordinary, so he's free to go, as well."

"Yes, ma'am."

"Oh, just a moment, Otane," Akiko called out, and the maid sank back to her knees. "Could you have Kikue-san come in when she gets back? I want to hear all about the play. I was going to go, you know. I had tickets and everything…"

"Yes, ma'am."

As she was closing the *shoji*, Otane's eyes fell on the two rumpled sleeping mats in the back room. The sight made her blush. Akiko and Doctor Mega were now openly living together as a couple, and that was their space now.

Otane went back to the front door and let the policeman go as instructed. As she was about to close the door, though, Kikue came walking back up the drive.

"Hey, Otane-san, what's going on? Wasn't that a policeman just now?"

"Yes, but it was nothing, really—Oh, that's right, the lady

is waiting for you, Kikue-san. She wants to hear all about the play."

"Oh, of course she does. But it was such a bore. The lead, Kikugoro, was clearly having a bad night."

As they were talking, they heard more footsteps approaching. Otane opened the door again and saw that Doctor Mega had also returned in a terrible mood. His face, so coarse and toadish at the best of times, was purple with rage.

"Oh, dear, Doctor, has something happened?" Kikue asked. "You aren't your usually sunny self!"

He glared at her as he answered, "Can't you hold your cheek for even a minute? I've had enough nonsense for one day, I tell you."

"Nonsense? What do you mean?"

"I got all the way out to Yokohama and found out the meeting is the day after tomorrow after all. I was so angry I couldn't bear it, so I went by old Tomoda's house to give him a piece of my mind, and it turns out he wasn't the one who rang."

"Oh, my!" Otane gasped, and her heart started racing. Shino had been called out by a fake telegram, and now the doctor had been tricked, as well.

Mega sensed something amiss too. "Otane, did anything happen while I was out?"

"No, not as such…"

"Well, that's good. Oh, but I'm fed up with it all."

"Now, now, Doctor, let's go inside. I'm sure a look at your lady's lovely face will put your mood to rights," said Kikue.

She took his arm and led him inside. Otane watched them go with a sigh, as she was not particularly fond of Kikue. In fact, she quite disliked the woman. But she could not deny that she had her charms. Kikue brightened up the house simply by being there.

When Otane went back to the servants' room and told Mishima about the mysterious telephone call, he responded with surprise, "Are you sure that nothing happened while everyone was out, Otane-san?"

"Yes, and that's what is so odd. It all makes me so afraid. Mishima-san, would you go and make sure all the doors and windows are locked?"

"Of course."

There proved to be nothing amiss with the doors or windows. Mineko and Kazuhiko returned after ten o'clock, and at the front door Otane told them what had occurred. Both were understandably shocked.

"And nothing else has happened?" asked Mineko.

"That's right, miss. And that makes it all feel the more eerie."

Mineko frowned in thought for a while, but soon shrugged in exasperation.

"It's no good. We'll think about it all tomorrow. It's getting late, Kazuhiko-san, so let's just turn in. Otane, everyone's home, right? So, lock up the front door, and you can retire as well. I'm going to go say goodnight to Mother and go to bed myself."

Otane checked all the doors again, then returned to her room and went to bed, but not long after a knock at the back door got her up. She went to answer it, her heart pounding.

"Who is it," she asked in a trembling voice.

"It's me, Hanako."

"Oh, mistress Hanako! What's the matter?" She hurriedly retied her *obi* sash and opened the door. Hanako stood there, her face pale and drawn.

"Otane-san, is our Toshihiko here?"

"No, ma'am, is he not at home, then?"

"I see… No, he isn't. Do you know how late he stayed here?"

"Let's see, after you left, he and the mistress spoke for about fifteen minutes in her chambers, and then I believe he went home to the annexe."

"Hm. Did he mention anything about going out?"

"Not that I heard. Shall I ask the mistress?"

"No, no, it's fine. I'm sure he'll be home any time now. I'm sorry to have bothered you. Goodnight."

"Goodnight, ma'am."

Otane's heart was pounding harder as she relocked the back door. It was clear from Hanako's expression that she had not managed to bring any money home. What kind of abuse would he heap on her now?

Otane lay down to sleep, but sleep simply would not come. She tossed and turned for a while, then something made her sit straight up in bed. From somewhere in the house there came a woman's scream, followed by a man's harsh shouting, and a series of loud thuds. Through them all, she heard the woman's sobbing.

They were coming from the mistress's room!

Otane hurried to wrap a kimono over her pyjamas. As she did so, someone rushed down the hall past her door, and she heard the sound of Akiko's door opening. It must have been Shino. The thuds had ceased, but the man's shouts and woman's crying continued.

Otane went fearfully to the *shoji* screen door of Akiko's room and saw Mishima approaching from the other side.

"What's going on?" he whispered.

"I don't know."

The two pressed their ears to the door, and heard, "This bitch! This rotten bitch!" Doctor Mega growled between ragged, gasping breaths.

"Doctor, please, Doctor! There's no need to be so rough! Please, this is all just a silly mistake!" Shino said, trying to soothe the raging man. Akiko continued to cry in her keening child's voice.

"No, there's no mistake! I know what happened! The bitch had someone in here! She tricked us both out of the house tonight! And while we were gone, she—"

"Come now, Doctor, what if the servants hear you? This is just a mistake. Please, just stop this."

Then someone crashed into Otane and Mishima from behind. Startled, they turned to look. Mineko stood over them, her face pale. She was shaking in anger. She ignored their looks and slid the *shoji* screen open.

The only light was in the back room, where the beds were. Through the half-open *fusuma* there, they could see Doctor Mega gripping Akiko's hair, holding her down on the bed. Shino was hidden in the shadows.

"What is going on here? What are you doing?" Mineko stood in the hallway. Her voice was cold as ice.

The sound brought Mega up short, and Shino's face appeared from the shadows. She rushed to whisper in his ear, and then hurried out of the back room, closing the *fusuma* behind her to conceal Mega and Akiko.

"It's nothing at all, Mineko-san. The doctor is simply out of sorts this evening. You know, what with that prank telephone call. Now, please, just go back to bed. Leave all this to me, and don't worry yourself."

Mineko stood staring at Shino with eyes blazing, then suddenly spun on her heel and rushed down the hall without a word.

Shino went to close the *shoji* but noticed Otane and Mishima there. "What are you two doing? What nonsense. There's nothing for you to do here, so hurry off and go to bed now. Go on."

"Sorry, ma'am."

Otane said goodnight to Mishima, and returned to her own room. It was already nearly midnight.

But less than an hour later everyone at the Tsubaki estate would be shaken from their dreams by that terrible melody…

"The Devil Comes and Plays His Flute"… The cursed flute…

Mineko still hadn't fallen asleep. Her mind was racing with all that had happened. That ugly argument with her uncle over dinner… Kazuhiko's job introduction, which had been turned upside down by a tiny issue… And then that terrible scene in her mother's room. Any one of those incidents would have been enough to keep her from an easy sleep. Mineko trembled with rage, groaned with despair and wept with shame.

She was nineteen, now, and old enough to understand what it meant to have a woman's body. And she had finally noticed that something in her mother's body was always burning, always giving off heat like a great fire. The only way to keep that fire under control was the influence of a man—a hard man, a carnal man, a man like Doctor Mega.

She had never been able to understand until then how someone like her great-uncle Count Tamamushi, so arrogant, so full of aristocratic pride, could let his own noble niece be subject to a brute like Mega. Likewise, she had never understood how Shino, who had doted on Akiko her whole life, could let a man like him touch her.

Now, though, she understood.

It was all because of what lurked in her mother's flesh, those flames which burned so much hotter than in others' and which she lacked the wisdom to control. Count Tamamushi and the old maid Shino both feared what terrible scandals could arise from the uncontrolled blaze without a hard, brutish man to keep it in check. The fact was that they had both decided that Mega

240

was the most effective way to calm her mother's fire without bringing any harm to the Tsubaki family name.

Shame, shame, shame. How shameful it all was.

Mineko bit her pillow to stifle her weeping. Her muffled sobs sounded through the deep darkness of midnight, but soon she heard another noise, which jolted her upright.

The sound of a flute.

There was no doubt about it. The cursed melody of "The Devil Comes and Plays His Flute" could be heard faintly in the distance.

Mineko wept no longer. The false telegram and the phone call that had lured Shino and Doctor Mega out of the house flashed through her mind. Something had happened. She knew it.

Mineko turned on the light and rushed to pull a dressing gown on over her pyjamas. She went out to the hall and found Otane already there.

"Lady Mineko, th-that flute…"

"Yes, I know, don't worry. It's fine, everything is fine. But where is it coming from?"

"I don't know! I don't know where, but I think it might be out in the garden."

At that moment, the sound of the flute rose to a high, demonic shriek, and Otane began trembling like the leaves of a tree in the wind. She desperately covered her ears.

She was right, though. The flute music was coming from the garden. Mineko went to open a shutter to see, but Otane reached out to stop her. The maid's hands were cold as ice.

"You mustn't, you mustn't! Miss, please don't open the shutters!"

"It's all right, Otane, just let me go!"

"But what if it lets the devil inside?"

As they struggled, off in the distance they head the sound of another shutter being raised, and then, Shino calling out, "Otane! Otane!"

"Otane, you should run to Mother now. I'll go and see."

She opened the shutter, and the flute music grew louder. The two women both stepped backward unconsciously, as if they had been slapped in the face.

Outside was pitch-dark. Even the stars were hidden. Mineko ran back to her room to get a torch.

When she returned, Kikue was in the hallway.

"Mineko-san, wh-what is going on? What is that flute?"

Even Kikue was looking pale, and her voice trembled slightly in the dim light. Still, she cut a coquettish figure with a *haori* coat worn over a brightly coloured singlet.

"I don't know, but something isn't right. Let's go and see."

For that instant, Mineko forgot her antipathy towards Kikue. Indeed, the other woman's vibrant aura was most welcome.

The two walked barefoot out into the garden. They heard the sounds of a window opening in the Western house, and then of someone leaping out.

"Who's there?" Mineko called out in a hoarse voice.

"It's me," Mishima answered. The three of them found each other in the dark. He was dressed in a knitted sweater and trousers, but he too was barefoot.

When they walked past Akiko's room, they saw her standing between Shino and Otane. All three were stock-still.

"Where is Doctor Mega?" Kikue asked, and Shino simply pointed vaguely out into the darkness, her mouth sealed shut. She was unable to speak.

The cursed melody grew ever more intense and frenzied.

They passed through the traditional garden, then through the folding gate in the spotted bamboo fence and saw a torch bouncing in front of the long, narrow hothouse on the other side.

As the three approached, they could make out Hanako and Kazuhiko up ahead, who looked like they had just leapt out of bed as well. They had their faces pressed up against the hothouse glass and were staring intently at something inside.

"Hanako-san, what's happened?" Kikue called out, and the face that turned to her in response was as white as a wax candle.

"I-I don't know. But the flute music is coming from inside."

The others had already realized that. The mad melody was clearly coming from the hothouse. They too looked through the glass and saw a torchlight bobbing up and down inside.

"Who's that in there?" Mineko croaked.

"Doctor Mega," Kazuhiko said, and swallowed his breath.

Doctor Mega hit the light switch, and the hothouse was lit up. That was when they saw the source of the flute music.

Two electric cables dangled from the roof. One of them was missing its usual bulb, and had a plug inserted instead. The lead led to an electrical phonograph sitting on a shelf to one side. The top was open, and the turntable was spinning, sending the terrible music out into the night.

Everyone outside stood frozen, staring at the record as it gave one last mournful moan and stopped turning.

The devil had finished playing his flute.

Freed from the music's enchantment, they turned their eyes to Doctor Mega, who had crouched down to look at something on the floor, hidden behind the overgrown pitcher plants and alpine shrubs.

"Doctor, what is it?" Mineko asked through the glass.

The doctor stood up slowly. He turned his toad face towards them.

"Shingu-san is dead," he answered. "He's been murdered. Somebody split his head open with this."

The old toad held up something clutched in the sleeve of his terrycloth dressing gown. It was a statue of Fujin, the one that had been missing since it was presumed stolen the previous summer.

Even through the glass, Mineko could see that it was covered in dark, dripping blood. She felt something like a cold wind rising from around her bare feet.

And that is what happened while Kosuke Kindaichi was off in the west.

CHAPTER 22

The Ring

"So Shingu-san must have been murdered between seven and eight o'clock on the evening of the 4th," Kosuke Kindaichi said gloomily. The Fujin statue stood on the table in front of him.

It was eleven in the morning of 6th October. He had returned to the Tsubaki estate and now sat in the drawing room.

After learning of the latest murder the previous morning at the inn in Sumadera, he had left Detective Degawa to continue his investigation out west and taken the overnight steam train from Kobe. It had arrived this morning, and he had rushed immediately to the Tsubaki house.

His journey had been a hurried one, and he had found it impossible to sleep on the train, so he was completely exhausted. His bleary eyes burned, and his unshaven cheeks were drawn and pale. It felt as if his mind was wrapped in an impenetrable membrane.

"Yes, that's right," Chief Inspector Todoroki said as he paced irritably around the table. "Between seven and eight… Or, well, we reckon it must have been around half past seven."

"Why's that?"

Todoroki explained: "Well, it's like this. On the evening of the 4th, the only ones in the house were the Lady Akiko, her maid Otane and the victim Shingu-san. The others all went out for the evening. Like I already told you, Kikue had gone to a play at Togeki theatre, and Totaro Mishima was out shopping to get ready for the count's one-week memorial. Those two had been out all day. Shino and Doctor Mega left before dinner, then Mineko and Kazuhiko both left soon after. Hanako left last at five past seven. Shingu-san saw his wife off, and then he and Akiko went back to her room. They talked for fifteen or twenty minutes, then he left and headed for his own house. That would have been around twenty or twenty-five past. Now, as you know, the Shingus are staying in the annexe at the far end of the grounds, and you have to pass the hothouse to get there. Shingu-san's body was discovered at just past one in the morning on the 5th, and he was dressed in the same clothes he had been wearing. So, there's no evidence that he ever made it to his own room. We think someone pulled Shingu-san into the hothouse as he was on his way back to the annexe, then killed him."

"The cause of death was strangulation?"

"Right. Someone hit him on the head with this Fujin, and when he was down, they strangled him with a piece of hemp rope that was laying around the hothouse." The chief inspector's frustration was visible. Kindaichi, though, betrayed no emotion when he spoke.

"But, isn't it odd?"

"Isn't what odd?" asked Todoroki.

"I mean, half seven is still early in the evening. Even if nearly everyone was out, the lady of the house and Otane-san were both still awake. You'd think they'd have heard something."

"Yes, there is that." Todoroki kept up his endless pacing. "And it wasn't just the lady and her maid. We had three policemen stationed out back. And not a single one heard anything that night. Listen, Kindaichi-san," the chief inspector stopped and looked down at Kindaichi.

"It was the same with Count Tamamushi, wasn't it? That studio was soundproofed, sure, but with all of the fighting, the

246

count must have shouted, right? But no one heard anything at all. So, that means…" He trailed off.

"Means what?"

"It means," Todoroki said, glaring down at his listener, his eyes blazing with suppressed rage, "that the murderer's appearance must have stunned Count Tamamushi and Viscount Shingu so completely they couldn't move a muscle or make a sound, like frogs mesmerized by a snake. They let the murderer have complete control. I know it sounds ridiculous, but how else can you explain it?"

Kindaichi's bleary eyes suddenly took on an excited gleam. "Oh, now I see. And so, who do you think it was that did it, Chief Inspector? Who could have had that kind of power over Tamamushi and Shingu?"

"Viscount Tsubaki!" The response was immediate and emphatic, the voice was sharp as a razor.

"Viscount Tsubaki…" Kindaichi repeated. "But didn't both of the victims hold the man in utter contempt?"

"Yes, before they thought he was dead. Which is exactly why they would be so shocked to learn he was still alive now. Can you imagine if he suddenly stepped out of the shadows in front of them? Anyway, I can't think of anyone else who could have that kind of power."

"I see." Kindaichi sat and thought in silence for a moment. When he did speak again, though, it was about something else entirely.

"By the way, did you learn anything about the fake telephone call and telegram that tricked Doctor Mega and Shino out of the house?"

"We don't have anything on the telephone. It was Otane who answered, and she said it sounded like someone at a public payphone. According to Mega, the line was full of static and noise, as they usually are lately, so he couldn't place the voice. Both of them, though, were certain it was a man on the other end."

"And Doctor Mega's meeting was originally planned for this evening. Who knew about the original date?"

"Everyone in the household. Lately they've all been dining together, Shingu-san included. Doctor Mega says he announced it at dinner on the evening of the 3rd."

"What time did the call come?"

"It was around half past four. The meeting was scheduled for six o'clock, in Yokohama, so Doctor Mega had to take off in a hurry. And then a half hour later, around five o'clock, is when the telegram for Shino came."

"And was it Otane who accepted it?"

"No, it seems Shingu-san had just come home from an outing and ran into the delivery person at the gate. So, he accepted it and passed it to Otane."

"Ah. And so, Shino-san also went rushing out, then?" Kindaichi sat and chewed his fingernails in thought, then said, "It's all wrong."

"What is?"

"All of it. Someone had to know that Kikue-san and Mishima-san would both be out all day on the 4th. They must also have known that Mineko-san and Kazuhiko-san would be going out in the evening on that job hunt. Then, since that would leave only Doctor Mega and Shino, they were tricked out of the house. That's what must have happened, right?"

"Right, exactly. But what is wrong?"

"Why would whoever it was go to all that trouble to make sure everyone was out of the house?"

The chief inspector stared at his friend in disbelief. "So they could be free to kill Shingu-san, of course."

"But that's what's so strange. If it was just to kill Shingu-san, then they had all kinds of chances to do it without going to all that trouble. Besides, if you wanted to clear the way for killing Shingu-san, then the first person you'd have to get rid of would be his wife Hanako. But, from what you just said, it was Shingu-san himself who sent her away."

Todoroki's eyes widened. "What are you getting at, Kindaichi-san? Shingu is our victim. He was the one murdered!"

"Yes, I know, that's true. I'm not thinking anything. I just find it all very odd. So, Hanako-san went out to try and raise some money, is that right?"

"Right."

"Was Shingu-san really so hard up for cash?"

"Oh, absolutely. He was heavily in debt. Most of all, he needed money to hush up a scam he'd pulled. If he waited any longer, he was headed for court, and he would certainly have lost if that happened. He was into some pretty serious business, actually. He was on the verge of complete ruin if he didn't come up with a hefty lump of cash."

Kindaichi was not surprised in the least by this revelation.

"And he was depending on his wife to drum up the funds. Did she succeed, by the way?"

"No, seems she didn't."

The chief inspector said this without thinking much about it, but then he gasped as if he had unearthed some hidden plot. "Kindaichi-san! You surely aren't trying to say that this was all because Hanako—"

"No, no, no!" Kindaichi hurried to reassure him. "That's not what I'm saying at all. Whoever the murderer might be, the motive for all this is nothing as simple as money. I'm just trying to make sense of everything. If someone was trying to kill Shingu-san, why would they lure Shino out and not Hanako? Perhaps they wanted Doctor Mega gone because he was a man and therefore might pose more of a problem, but if so, why bother with Shino? That woman is always stuck to Lady Akiko's side. She couldn't possibly get in the way of a plot to murder Shingu-san."

Todoroki knitted his thick eyebrows.

"Oh, I see what you're getting at. You're wondering about what Otane and Mishima overheard on the night of the 4th. When Doctor Mega accused Lady Akiko of tricking him and Shino out of the house so she could meet up with someone. All that abuse he piled on her."

Kindaichi nodded absently.

"That's right. That's something else strange. Why would Doctor Mega think that? And what exactly did he think she had been doing while they were gone? Did Doctor Mega offer any kind of explanation for it, Chief Inspector?"

"He says he doesn't remember saying anything of the sort, but if he did then he was simply lashing out from all the irritations of the day."

"And by 'irritations' he means…"

"Apparently he was really angry about the prank phone call business."

"But why take that out on Lady Akiko?"

Kindaichi couldn't make it fit together.

"Well, enough of that," he said, as if to clear his mood. "Let's move on to the telegram. I assume you found out the office it came from?"

"Of course. It was that Kinuta Post Office in Seijo. We even know which employee received the order, and he does remember taking it. However, he couldn't recall any details about the man who sent it. He thought it might help if he saw the man again, so yesterday afternoon we showed him that picture of Viscount Tsubaki, and brought him to see everyone in the household. It wasn't any of them, though, he said. The upshot is, for the moment, the telegram isn't offering up any clues."

"I see." Kindaichi chewed his nails in silence for a moment, eyes downcast. Eventually, though, he looked up. "Getting back to the early morning of the 5th. The flute music was coming from a record player again, I suppose. Can you give me any details about that?"

"It might be best if we go look at the scene of the crime for that. The body was taken off for autopsy yesterday morning, but we left everything else as it was."

Kindaichi nodded silently and stood up slowly. Just then, though, a car pulled into the drive in front of the building. It was an ambulance, bringing the late Toshihiko Shingu's remains home after the autopsy. Todoroki and Kindaichi walked past the family members filing one by one from the back of the house to accept the body and went out into the back garden towards the hothouse. As they drew near they saw several detectives were already inside, looking curiously at the unusual plants lining the shelves. They went down the steps, opened the door and ducked into the hothouse.

Two detectives inside saluted and moved aside to let them through. Even as they did, they stared curiously at the flower-pots hanging from the roof.

"The victim was found lying here. The rope was still wrapped around his neck."

The chief inspector indicated a patch of dirt deep inside the hothouse, then pointed at a shelf to the left of the door. A well-used electric phonograph stood on the shelf, its cord plugged into an outlet.

"There's the electric phonograph, and the light switch that powered it is over here," he said, pointing to a switch beside the door.

Todoroki continued, "So, they set up the phonograph with the power out, turned the phonograph on, and then used the door switch to send power to it. That would have set the turntable spinning and played the flute music."

"Which means the murderer must have been here when the music started playing."

"Not necessarily. The hothouse lights have a parent switch up in the Tsubaki manor house. If that one was off, the turntable wouldn't run even if this switch was on. That means all they had to do was hit the parent switch when they wanted the phonograph to play. Someone in the main house could have used it to trigger the phonograph, or like you said, someone could have turned it on from inside the hothouse."

Kindaichi's eyes widened as he slowly looked around. "I see, I see. And I don't suppose anyone knows whether the main switch was on or off?"

"Of course not. It's not like anyone would be paying attention to it. It seems they usually just leave it on, and it was on when we checked."

"Well, anyway, what about the phonograph itself?"

"No one recognizes it. It's not from the house. The murderer must have brought it in. We might be able find out where it came from, but the fact that they left it here means they must be confident it won't lead us anywhere. Wait, what now?"

One of the detectives had shouted out loud, and Kindaichi and Todoroki turned to see what the commotion was. The detective was extremely worked up.

"Chief Inspector, there's something strange over here. It looks like a ring!"

"What? Where?"

The detective pointed at a flowerpot hanging from the roof. Each pot was about six inches across and was home to the same unusual plant: a long curving vine with a sac-like leaf at the end. The sac was about an inch across and about two inches deep, and each one had a leaf that formed a kind of lid at the top. Some of them were closed, others open.

A card nearby labelled them "tropical pitcher plants" and explained that they consumed insects. The detective had been looking inside them and pointed out to the chief inspector.

Todoroki looked inside and raised his eyebrows. He reached in and pulled out a gold ring with a large diamond set at the top.

Kindaichi gasped in surprise at the sight of it. "Wait, that ring…!"

"You recognize it?"

"Yes, I do. I'm sure of it. I saw it on the night of the divination. I remember it catching the light from Lady Akiko's finger. Detective, would you mind going and asking Mineko-san to come here for a moment?"

She came right away. The ring surprised her as well. She immediately confirmed that it belonged to her mother, and that she remembered she wore it at dinner on the 4th.

"A-a-and what about your mother?" Kindaichi said, the excitement aggravating his stutter and driving him to scratch his mop of hair. "D-did she make a fuss about the ring having gone missing?"

"No, not at all."

"But I understand that she's quite fixated on her jewels. I remember you using the word 'obsessed'? If a ring went missing…"

"She would be in hysterics. Yet she hasn't said a word about it. What on earth is going on?"

Mineko looked utterly baffled, but Kindaichi was now completely overcome with excitement.

CHAPTER 23

The Finger

They confirmed that very day that Toshihiko Shingu had sent the fake telegram.

The post office employee took one look at the photograph and confirmed that Shingu was the man who sent the telegram. What's more, the delivery man who had brought the telegram to the Tsubaki estate said he had delivered it at around three o'clock, and that Toshihiko Shingu had come out of the gate to receive it.

Putting those stories together, it seemed that Shingu had gone out that morning to Seijo to send the telegram then returned straight home to wait and make sure he received it himself. The intent apparently being to keep it from reaching Shino's hands too early.

Having confirmed that Shingu was behind the telegram, it seemed only natural to suspect that he had also made the telephone call. There was no way to confirm that, of course, but given the timing it was not out of the question.

Shingu had probably intercepted the telegram he'd sent to Shino, then immediately gone out to ring up Doctor Mega. Then, after having watched the doctor rush out, he'd wandered in himself around five o'clock, and pretended he had just received the telegram.

The question then was, why had Toshihiko Shingu gone to all that trouble to get them out of the house?

"I have a theory, Chief Inspector," Kindaichi said. His eyes were still bleary and dull. "He only needed to get Doctor Mega,

Shino-san and his wife Hanako out of the house. He knew everyone else was already going out, so those three were the only real problem. As for his wife, he could send her out any time. It was Mega and Shino that he really needed to get out of the way, so he worked up that little plan."

"But, why?"

"I think if you recall what you told me earlier, you might be able to come up with an answer yourself."

"What was that again?"

"Shingu-san was desperate for money. He had to get a lot of cash, as soon as possible, and he'd run out of other options. His last chance was Akiko-san, his little sister."

Todoroki's eyes widened. "So then, he lured those two out to give himself a chance to wheedle money out of his sister. Is that what you're saying?"

"Exactly. I can't think of any other explanation for that ring being in the pitcher plant. Lady Akiko would have been in hysterics if she'd lost the ring, or it had been stolen, just like Mineko-san said."

"Right…"

"But she never even mentioned it until we recovered it from the hothouse. Her own daughter didn't know. So, she must have given it up willingly. Then, the question becomes, who did she give it to? At which point, I can only think of Shingu-san, who was so desperate to raise money. He managed to convince her to help, but since she didn't have any cash to hand, she gave him the nearest thing of value—the ring from her finger. Or perhaps he was the one who suggested it. Then, his mission successful and the ring in hand, Shingu-san headed back to his house, and that's when the murderer drew him into the hothouse and killed him. I can't say if the murderer knew about the ring from the beginning or only noticed it after the murder, but at any rate they must have tried to hide it in the pitcher plant. I really can't think of any other possible explanation for how it got there."

Todoroki clasped his hands behind his back and finally stopped his pacing around the drawing room. The autumn days were short, and the lights were now on. With Toshihiko Shingu's corpse returned, the household was preparing for the wake and people were hurrying in and out.

"But there's something else, Kindaichi-san. I can see all of what you're saying. I imagine you're absolutely right, in fact. But I still don't get why he had to go to all that trouble over Doctor Mega and Shino. I suppose it might be a little embarrassing to be seen begging for money, especially from your own little sister, but all he had to do was take Akiko aside or just ask those two to leave the room for a moment, wasn't it? All that nonsense with telegrams and phone calls…"

"Chief Inspector…" said Kindaichi with a faint grin. "I think that might be because you don't really know what kind of man Shingu-san was, or how carefully Shino-san and Doctor Mega kept watch on him. He would try to wring every last yen from Akiko-san every time he got the chance. And she, being the kind of woman she is, simply couldn't resist giving him anything he wanted. Of course, putting money in Shingu-san's hands was like trying to bail water with a sieve. No matter how fast you piled it in, it just ran right back out. It didn't matter how rich Akiko-san was, it never would have been enough. So, I think Shino-san and, more recently, Doctor Mega were always on the watch to make sure that he could never get Akiko-san alone."

Todoroki nodded but could not help but feel there was something else, something not yet sufficiently explained.

Kindaichi also felt that, and sat in silent thought for a moment, until finally looking up at the chief inspector again, he said, "Anyway, Todoroki-san, the problem now isn't who sent the telegram and why; it's who killed Shingu-san. What about everyone's alibis? Have you followed up on all those who were out that evening?"

"Well, you know, we have some fairly clear facts, and some not so clear ones." He sighed. "Anyway, everyone is pretty definite about where they went. Kikue to the theatre and Totaro Mishima shopping. Doctor Mega to Yokohama and Shino to Seijo. Hanako went to her parents' house to ask for money, and Mineko and Kazuhiko to meet her typing teacher. But, at the apparent time of the murder, we can't be sure none was here. Someone could have snuck in, then back out again without being noticed."

"Didn't you say you had policemen stationed around the house? Wouldn't they have seen anyone trying to sneak in?"

"Well, the grounds are really big, you know. And you've seen the garden wall. There are still lots of gaps that they haven't fixed since the firebombing. Anyone who wanted to could get in."

"Did you check and see? Were there any tracks showing that someone had snuck in recently?"

"That's another thing. We've had problems with reporters ever since Count Tamamushi's murder. So, there are tracks all over the place. On top of that, before we could cordon off the scene yesterday, reporters had been traipsing in and out of the grounds all morning. We really messed that up, I'm afraid."

Todoroki looked disgusted with this. Kindaichi tried to soothe him. "There, there, the investigation shouldn't be all that difficult. At any rate, we can't rule out anyone from being home at the time in question, right?"

"That's exactly it. Kikue could have left before the end of the play, and since Mishima was only out shopping, he could have come home at any time. Doctor Mega got to his meeting place a little before six o'clock, then he immediately realized he'd been tricked and left. Shino-san got to the Aikawa house in Seijo a bit after six, before she also realized the trick and rushed home worried. On the other hand, Hanako only got to her folks' house in Nakano district just after eight, while Mineko and Kazuhiko also got to the typing teacher's in Meguro around the same time. So, one of those three could have actually left *after* killing Shingu-san. It all comes down to the terrible state of transportation these days. What with trains being late or too packed to get on, it's completely normal for trips to take twenty or thirty minutes longer than they should."

He gave another exaggerated sigh.

Kindaichi thought silently for a moment before answering. "Todoroki-san, you said earlier you were sure it was Viscount Tsubaki who killed Count Tamamushi and Shingu-san. It really does seem like either he or someone who looks very much like him, is connected to everything. But, setting aside the count's murder, did he have anything to do with Shingu-san's murder on the 4th? Did anyone see him, or someone who looked like him?"

The chief inspector shook his head despondently. He clearly would have preferred the double had been reported.

Kindaichi sighed. "The way I see it," he said, "whoever this is, he wasn't in Tokyo on the night of the 4th. Because he was in Kobe that morning."

Todoroki raised his eyebrows in surprise and looked at Kindaichi, who nodded and went on,

"Yes. At around half past nine on the morning of the 4th, this 'Viscount Tsubaki' showed up in Kobe. Even if he'd hopped on a steam train that minute, what with the way trains are these days, I sincerely doubt he could have been here by half past seven in the evening. No, I think he's probably still wandering around Kobe searching for a particular woman."

"You have to tell me more, Kindaichi-san," Todoroki said fervently. "It's part of your investigation down there, right? I got a report about another murder. Does that have to do with this same man—either Viscount Tsubaki, or his stand-in?"

Kindaichi nodded. He filled the chief inspector in on what the investigation in Kobe and Awaji had uncovered. Todoroki's interest grew with each new revelation.

"That's about all I can tell you myself," Kindaichi concluded, "but I imagine Detective Degawa will send a more detailed report later. Basically, it all comes down to how once, long ago, Shingu-san raped a woman named Komako at Tamamushi's villa and got her pregnant. That one incident is at the heart of what's going on now, but I don't think it ended with that. There must be something else, some other awful shadow lying over everything, which began growing back then, but I don't know what it could be. If we could only find out, then..." He trailed off.

His eyes flashed keenly for a moment, but that soon faded. He went on, as if hoping to change the subject, "But anyway, Todoroki-san, you should forget about that and wait for Detective Degawa's report. For now, why don't we try to find out a little bit more about this ring? Let's ask Lady Akiko."

The chief inspector nodded and ordered one of his men to bring her.

Kindaichi slumped into a chair and stared absently at the table in front of him. The Fujin statue from the hothouse still stood there.

It was partner to the Raijin statue that had been used in Count Tamamushi's murder, and it was of much the same height. But for some reason this one seemed oddly unstable on its base. On inspection, Kindaichi saw that was because the bottom of the base had been cut away.

Kindaichi found himself deeply interested in that. Someone had sawed off the very bottom of the statue. Moreover, it looked like someone had actually replaced the sawed-off section once. A close examination of the fresh cut revealed traces of glue. The missing section appeared to be a disk of around three and a half inches across, and not quite five inches thick. Who on earth would have cut it off, and why? And why reattach it? And why, when it was found in the hothouse once more, was that part missing again?

Kindaichi could not help but think this was very important.

Just then, the old woman Shino arrived in Akiko's place.

"Lady Akiko is feeling unwell, so I have come in her stead," she said stiffly, staring at the two men with eyes sharp as an eagle's.

Chief Inspector Todoroki raised his eyebrows.

"No, we can't have that, Shino-san. I'm sorry, but we need to talk to the lady herself."

"Lady Akiko will not be coming. This kind of thing simply isn't proper for a lady in her position."

Shino showed no sign of budging. If they truly did want to bring Akiko in, they would probably need to raise a fuss big enough to rattle the windows. Todoroki grimaced in resignation.

"I suppose you'll have to do. So, are you aware that we discovered the lady's ring in the hothouse?"

"Yes, I heard from Mineko-san."

"And did the lady have anything to say about that? Did she lose it? Or give it to someone?"

"You are wondering if Lady Akiko gave it willingly to Shingu-san," Shino said without a moment's hesitation. "That is not contrary to fact, as I understand it."

"I see. And when was that?" Kindaichi interrupted.

She gave him a withering look. "On the evening of the 4th, after everyone had left. When Lady Akiko retired to her rooms after dinner, Shingu-san accompanied her. He was apparently quite insistent in asking for aid. I assume that since they are siblings, Lady Akiko was sympathetic to Shingu-san's plight, and so she gave him the ring."

"Did you notice that it was missing when you returned from Seijo on the evening of the 4th?"

Shino hesitated before answering.

"Well, no, I did not notice at that time. It was only on the following morning, meaning yesterday, that I did. I asked her ladyship about it, and that is when she told me that she had given it to Shingu-san."

"That was after you knew about his murder. Why didn't you mention the ring then? You must have thought it was still among his possessions."

"Because…" Her stony-faced expression wavered, betraying her nervousness, but she quickly regained her composure. "Naturally, I was still quite upset. And I must admit that it is my habit to keep family matters as quiet as possible. After all, so much has happened since last spring…"

That much was certainly true. But there must have been more to it. Why else would everyone keep silent about something of such obvious value?

"There was something else," the chief inspector butted in, "about the person behind that fake telegram that took you out of the house. We are relatively certain it was Shingu-san. What do you think about that?"

Shino sat still as a stone.

"Who else could it have been? The moment I learned that Shingu-san had tricked… I mean, convinced Lady Akiko to give him the ring, I believed he was behind the telegram."

Todoroki shot Kindaichi an interested glance.

"Why is that?" asked the chief inspector.

"Why? Because it's exactly the kind thing he would have done. He was just that kind of sneak. He took every opportunity to creep close to Lady Akiko and squeeze money out of her. We… That is, Doctor Mega and I could not take our eyes off her for a moment. If we let him have his way with her, then she could have had all the money in the world, and it still would never have been enough."

That was almost exactly as Kindaichi had imagined it, so there was no reason to believe that Shino was lying. But he still felt there was something else, something she was leaving out. The idea niggled at him, like a bit of food stuck in his back teeth or an itchy foot trapped in a heavy boot.

The woman hadn't coughed up everything. But getting her to do so would be harder than getting a rooster to lay eggs.

"Very well, then. I think that's enough for now. Would you be so kind as to ask Doctor Mega to come in for a moment?" asked Kindaichi.

Shino glared at him.

"Very well. I will say, however, that Doctor Mega also believes Shingu-san was to blame for both the telegram and the telephone call. We have discussed it and are quite certain."

Shino rose and walked with palpable dignity from the drawing room.

The long wait before Doctor Mega arrived was likely due to the two of them conferring over their stories. When he did arrive, the doctor's toad-like face was fixed in a gruff scowl.

"What's this about, then? If you want to ask about the telegram, well, I reckon Shino-san has already said what needed saying."

Kindaichi stared at him glumly. "No, that isn't what we wanted to ask you about, Doctor. We understand there was a bit of an altercation that evening when you joined the lady in bed. I believe you said something along the lines of, 'The bitch had someone in here! She tricked us both out of the house tonight! And while we were gone, she—' Now, I was wondering if you could finish that sentence. What is it you believe Lady Akiko did while you were away?"

The old toad's gruff glare flickered with a brief hint of unease. That convinced Kindaichi that his question was getting close to the heart of the issue. But his opponent was a sly one, and soon fixed his expression in a sneering grin.

"Bwa ha, so that's what you're wondering? I keep telling everyone, I don't even remember saying any of that. And if I did, it was like this: the truth is, I was trying to keep from mentioning the ring, but since it's all out in the open I noticed it was missing from her finger that evening when we went to bed. I asked her about it, naturally, but her answers just got more and more suspicious. When I figured out she'd given it to that Shingu, then I realized it must have been him who tricked us with the telegram and the telephone call. That really got to me, you know. I was angry enough about that fake telephone call in the first place."

"But I'm not sure I see why you'd have said she had 'someone'. Don't you think that's a little strange?"

Another look of unease crossed that toad-like face, only to be masked by a braying laugh.

"Well, like I said, I don't remember much about it. I was running off at the mouth, you know, just letting off some steam. You try rushing off and cramming yourself on a train these days, riding all the way to Yokohama, only to find out you've been sent on a fool's errand! See if you don't get half angry!"

"But why would you be so angry about her giving the ring to Shingu-san?" asked Kindaichi.

The man could only stare in confusion.

"I hope you'll pardon my forwardness," Kindaichi pressed on, "but what business is it of yours what she does with her own possessions?"

Mega gave a guffaw that almost sounded like relief.

"Oh, that? You're trying to figure out if I've got my eye on Akiko's fortune? Well, what kind of fool would rather be poor than rich? But to tell the truth, I'm not all that attached to money myself. That's why old Count Tamamushi gave me his blessing."

"He did?"

"That's right. I reckon you lot think I forced my way in here and now I'm just shacking up with Akiko, right? All some plot of mine? Not quite, boys. The count himself oversaw the official marriage and the whole business. It was very private, mind you. So, this is no plot. Once we pass the first anniversary of old Tsubaki's death, we're going to have a formal ceremony, make it nice and respectable."

"But when did this all happen?"

"It was the first week after they found Tsubaki-san's body. I convinced the old count that with Akiko like she is, she needs someone to keep a hand on her, keep her under control. A proper man. A man like me, not greedy, but with a good strong body. Know what I mean? Bwa ha!"

Kindaichi unconsciously gripped the edge of his chair.

Mineko had seen true when she sensed that something in her mother's body was always burning, blazing like a great fire. And that the only thing that could keep that fire under control was the will of a hard, carnal man like Mega.

Mineko had realized it, and now, Kosuke Kindaichi could see it with his own eyes.

Having said all he was going to say, Doctor Mega left. After he had gone both Kindaichi and Todoroki were lost for words.

265

Some unspeakable miasma seemed to fill every corner of the room and coat their very bodies. It was as if the old toad had left a poisonous mist in his wake.

And yet his revelation had brought them that much closer to understanding a great secret. Even if they still lacked the key to the puzzle at the heart of these murders, at the very least the conversation had shed some light on the relationship between Viscount Tsubaki and Akiko.

Count Tamamushi had mocked the viscount as impotent and weak not because of his character, but because he lacked the physical vigour to keep her satisfied. This failure had cooled Akiko's feelings towards her husband, and as the count had always had special affection for his niece, he had been displeased. In short, Viscount Tsubaki had simply been too normal a man for Lady Akiko.

Oh, poor viscount! And poor Akiko!

"Ah, you're still here!" A cheery voice interrupted their reverie, and both men jumped as if stung. Kikue stood at the drawing room doorway, a brilliant smile on her face.

"It was so quiet I wasn't sure anyone was here. I've been waiting, you know. I thought it ought to be about my turn for an interview."

"Oh, yes, of course. Please, come in," said Todoroki.

"Are you sure I'm not interrupting anything?"

"No, no, please!" The frazzled Kindaichi showed her to a seat.

He was beginning to find her presence in the household rather odd. With Count Tamamushi dead, he could see nothing at all connecting Kikue and the rest of the family. And yet, not only did the others refrain from snubbing or insulting her, which might be explained by their aristocratic manners, they actually seemed to rely on her.

Indeed, if it weren't for the glamorous aura that filled the air around her, the great weight of all that had happened might have crushed the breath out of everyone here.

Kindaichi felt it keenly himself.

"Whatever's the matter, Kindaichi-san? You look so dreadfully grave. Have you run into yet another dead end?" She deliberately ignored the chief inspector, whose twisted face spoke of a terrible mood, to tease Kindaichi.

"Ha ha, I've been at a dead end from the start! I just go from one dead end to the next!"

It seemed she had helped Kindaichi regain some of his spirit at least, if he was already back to joking around.

"Anyway, your timing is perfect. There's something I wanted to ask you about."

"Oh, and what could that be? If you're still after my alibi for the murder, I've already explained enough to give myself jaw ache…"

"No, not that. It's actually about the lady's ring."

Todoroki looked at Kindaichi in confusion. They'd already learned about that from Shino and Doctor Mega.

"Ah, the ring. I thought Shingu-san tricked—I mean, her ladyship graciously gave that to her brother."

"You did?" Kindaichi stared intently at Kikue. "Tell me, had you already noticed that it was missing?"

"Yes, I had."

"When?"

"That evening, the 4th. When I got back from the theatre, her ladyship asked me to come to her room. I told her about the play, and I noticed the ring was gone from her finger."

"I see. How very like a lady…"

"What's that supposed to mean?"

"Well, the Doctor and Shino-san say they didn't realize it until much later."

"Oh, my!" Kikue's eyes widened. "Did they say that? How strange…"

"What's strange about that?"

"Well, surely they knew it from the start. I mean, in a way they're the ones who told me. Like I said, I told her about the play. As I did, I noticed that Doctor Mega and Shino-san kept looking at her funny. I couldn't figure it out at first, but then I realized they kept glancing at her finger, and that's when I saw for myself. Oh, dear… Maybe I shouldn't have told you…"

The chief inspector showed a spark of curiosity then. He finally seemed to catch on to how cleverly Kindaichi was guiding her.

"Oh, no, don't worry about it. It's nothing important, really. By the way, when you noticed the ring was gone, did you immediately think that Shingu-san had got it off her?"

"Oh, yes. I mean, those two had just the ugliest looks on their faces, and there was that business with the telegram and such. It all just seemed so like Shingu-san."

"I suppose everyone in the house knew what kind of man he was?"

"Of course! Why do you think his lordship Tamamushi moved in here? His house had burnt down, of course, but he had plenty of other places to go. No, the reason he came here was to keep an eye on Shingu-san."

Kindaichi's eyes bulged. "Then… Shingu-san must have been truly shameless!"

"Oh, yes, he was. When he lost his house, this is the first place he came, right? His lordship used to always say that letting him anywhere near Akiko would end up with her broke on the street. So, when Tamamushi's house burnt down, he used that as an excuse to move in, too. Back then, the Shingu family was staying in our—my—rooms. When we came, they had to go to the annexe, where they're staying now."

Kindaichi's heart was pounding in his chest. Why did Count Tamamushi feel such an urgent need to keep watch over his own nephew? There was something... There had to be something else there!

"There's another thing I'd like to ask."

"Of course, ask all you want."

"Don't worry, I won't keep you much longer. It's just about Doctor Mega. He mentioned that the count oversaw his marriage to Akiko-san. Meaning, I assume, just a civil ceremony. We only have his word for it, but did you know about that?"

"I did. But I don't think Mineko-san does."

"Did his lordship Tamamushi tell you?"

"Yes, of course." Even Kikue blushed at the thought. "I mean, it was so fast, wasn't it? It wasn't even a full week after they found Tsubaki-san's remains. Doctor Mega had taken to sleeping over, you know, sleeping in Akiko-san's room... Even without that, it would have caused such a commotion. There is such a thing as decency, you know. But his lordship didn't stand in the way at all when the doctor asked for permission. He gave his blessing, and they had their private wedding. That's what he said. It left me speechless, honestly. It really showed me that common folk like me can't even begin to understand how this type think."

Kikue's tone was thick with irony and mockery. For the first time, Kindaichi felt that he was getting a glimpse behind the flirtatious veil at the surprisingly old-fashioned woman that she truly was.

"By the way, just one more thing... I know this might be too personal, but I'll ask anyway. What happened to the missing little finger on your left hand?"

269

Kikue looked at Kindaichi in surprise for a moment, then suddenly burst out laughing.

"Oh, my, Kindaichi-san! What could you possibly have been thinking about that?"

She deliberately showed off the stump of her left little finger, grinning at him.

"I cut it off myself. For a good man. No, it's true! Even a woman like me can have one or two good men in her life. Looking back, I see I was a great fool to do it, but I was all wrapped in the dream. It didn't even hurt that much. The other girls were quite angry about it, and old Tamamushi, I mean, his lordship was terribly jealous. Always going on about who I did it for, where was he, and such, hee-hee. He made such a fuss."

Kindaichi nodded. He knew of this old tradition of course, although it wasn't so common these days.

"And who did you do it for?"

"Like I said, a good man. He got drafted, and he came to see me before he shipped out. I cried all night long, and then I cut off my finger and sent it to him. Oh, my, how terribly old-fashioned, right? To suffer so for love? But, why on earth would you ask about that, Kindaichi-san? Surely you don't think he came back and killed his lordship in a fit of jealous rage, do you? If so, I fear you're in for disappointment. The poor boy shipped off and died in the war. Like he went all that way just to die. Gone with the wind."

"I do beg your pardon." Kindaichi looked at her, now uncharacteristically flushed and emotional, with deep sympathy. "That's not why I asked. It's just that there are two people in the household missing fingers. It struck me as an odd coincidence."

"Oh, yes, you mean Mishima-san." Kikue examined his face with glittering eyes. "You mustn't make him out to be like me.

I lost my finger due to foolishness, but he lost his fighting for his country."

"What exactly is he missing?"

"About half of his middle finger and two-thirds of his ring finger, I think. But why are you asking that?"

He answered matter of factly: "I was simply wondering if you or Mishima-san would still be able to type in the dark."

CHAPTER 24

If A=X and B=X, then A=B

After the murder of Toshihiko Shingu, there were a few short days of calm before the third and final Tsubaki family murder, after which all the dark secrets were brought to light and the case closed.

But though it was a quiet period, not everything was at a standstill. A few mundane, and indeed almost trivial, occurrences held within them signs of the inevitable movement towards that terrible resolution. Here, I will offer up some of these seemingly innocuous events that, in hindsight, turned out to be deeply momentous developments, and crucial in solving the case.

When they left the Tsubaki estate that same day, Kindaichi seemed deeply troubled. He turned to the chief inspector and asked, "By the way, Todoroki-san, whatever came of the Tengindo murders?"

"We've been working away at it. For a while I was off that case, but now it looks like it's all wrapped up with this one, too. So I'm working both at once, and each of them a tough one."

Todoroki's brow wrinkled in frustration.

Kindaichi thought that over for a moment, then went on, "Just after that earlier case, you had a number of suspects, right? You know, all those people who looked like the montage. Viscount Tsubaki was one of those…"

"Yes, right, we even had a couple that seemed pretty good for it, but we never got anything really solid on them, so we had to let them go."

"What's happened to those suspects? Are they still under observation?"

"That would have been ideal, but we couldn't keep it up. Not in the budget, not enough men... The usual excuses, I know."

The chief inspector was clearly unhappy about it.

"Listen, what do you think about tracking down those suspects again? You wouldn't have to go back and see what they've been doing since January, just find out where they've been since the Tsubaki murders started."

Todoroki gaped in surprise. "Kindaichi-san, what are you getting at?"

Kindaichi grimaced. "Promise you won't laugh? I can't get a certain basic algebraic theorem out of my head. Maybe you've heard of it? If A equals X, and B equals X, then A must also equal B."

"And what about it?"

"Well, it's like this. Here, X is that photo composite. Viscount Tsubaki resembled it, right? But so did some other men. So then, if Viscount Tsubaki, A, resembles the composite of the murderer, X, then the man involved in this case, our B, must resemble it too, the way I see it."

"Kindaichi-san," Todoroki was almost shouting, "Are you trying to say that this other man, the one who looks like Viscount Tsubaki, might be among the Tengindo suspects?"

"Wait, now, I can't be certain. In the first place, we're still not sure if it is the real Tsubaki or a lookalike. But, if it is a look-alike, and someone is using him to stand in for the viscount, then it's a rather pretty little puzzle. Convincing doubles are hard to find. But in Viscount Tsubaki's case, they've already got that photo composite tailor-made for tracking one down. That picture might well have served to recruit stand-ins for Tsubaki from all over Japan! Ha ha ha!"

The chief inspector clenched both his fists tight. A wave of anger even he couldn't explain welled up deep in his belly.

Kindaichi went on, "Of course, this isn't algebra, so Viscount Tsubaki doesn't actually equal X. He just resembles it. That means that whoever B is might well only resemble X, or he could actually be X, just like Tsubaki might only resemble B. Or, maybe he does equal B! At the very least they will share some similarities. If a person like that consciously made himself up to look like the viscount, then the resemblance would certainly be greater than if just any old person did so. And remember that people have only caught glimpses of him so far."

"So you're saying that whoever is behind these murders looked for someone resembling Viscount Tsubaki from among the other Tengindo murder suspects to use as a double?"

"That's correct. Every time a new suspect resembling the picture got pulled in for questioning, the newspapers printed his name and address. Ha ha, it's almost like the police and newspapers were working together to scout out a double just for this case!"

"But what about the earring? That was definitely from the Tengindo murders..."

"Like I said, Chief Inspector," Kindaichi's voice suddenly grew serious. "The way I see it, solving this case will also solve the Tengindo case. Viscount Tsubaki, our A, did not equal the Tengindo murderer, X. He just resembled him. But this stand-in B might more than resemble X. He could be X.

"Think about it—our murderer in this case would have had trouble getting anyone to shoulder part of the blame for the crime, no matter how much of an incentive he was offered. And not only was the double asked to play a role in these murders, but he was sent all the way to Awaji to murder someone himself.

That makes me think that our murderer must have proof that B is the Tengindo murderer. In other words, B does equal X, so he has no choice but to do as he's told."

Todoroki could not suppress the shivers that ran down his spine at this. The murderer in the Tengindo case and the murderer in the Tsubaki case… Either would go down in the annals of crime as a monster. Now, what if they could set these two monsters against each other?

He felt like he was walking in a thick black fog.

"Right, then. We'll look into the Tengindo suspects again."

At that, they parted ways, and the next day Kindaichi got Detective Degawa's report from police headquarters.

It stated that Komako's daughter Sayoko truly was dead. He had gone to visit the Mizoguchi family in Sumiyoshi, where Komako had once lived and served, to find out more, and they confirmed everything. Sayoko had been working at a large shipyard in Kobe, but on 27th August 1944 had taken her own life with a dose of potassium cyanide. No one knew the reason, but her post-mortem had revealed that she was pregnant. She was in her fourth month.

As Sayoko had no other relatives, the Mizoguchi family had accepted her remains and given her a small funeral out of their feelings for her absent mother. That left no room for doubt of her passing. However, since the Mizoguchis had no idea what her motivation was, or who the father of her child might be, those remained in question.

The investigation had also failed to turn up any information on the whereabouts of Uetatsu's mistress Otama, but Degawa said that if he learned anything more, then he would report it immediately.

Kindaichi could not help but find his interest deepening as he read.

Who was the father of Sayoko's baby? And why did she feel compelled to take her own life?

While it was certainly not always the case, there were generally few things stronger in this world than a pregnant mother. A mother's instinct to protect her child could put steel into even the most timid woman.

Kindaichi did not know what kind of woman Sayoko had been, but she must have had a truly powerful reason to take her unborn child with her into the darkness. What could it have been?

Later that afternoon, Todoroki rang Kindaichi at his inn. The old policeman was quite worked up.

He said that one of the suspects in the Tengindo murders had been missing for two or three days. The man's name was Toyosaburo Iio, and at the time of the original investigation had been their prime suspect.

"Anyway, right now I'm having everyone do their best to find out where he is. To tell the truth, some of my men are still convinced he's our man. He was always the most likely, but he kept slipping through our fingers. We could never get any solid evidence on him, but the biggest reason he got off was that the tip-off about Viscount Tsubaki arrived just as we were questioning him. Then, when we started looking that way, Tsubaki started to seem more and more suspicious. We were so focused on him that we let Iio slip away."

The chief inspector's voice darkened.

"And, I have to say, Iio really did look like the viscount. Of course, with the photo composite and everything, all the men we pulled in kind of did. But, when I think back, that man really did look just like the viscount. If he put on the right clothes, well…"

"I'll just keep hoping your investigation comes through. And, just to be sure, don't forget to get in touch with Degawa out west and let him know."

The next day, Kindaichi went to visit Mineko at the Tsubaki estate. There was no particular reason for it. He simply felt pity for the young woman who had been through so much and thought he might try to offer her some consolation.

Luckily, Toshihiko Shingu's funeral arrangements had settled down and the household was fairly calm.

Mineko was as gloomy as ever, but during their conversation she offered up one revelation in particular that lingered in Kindaichi's mind. Apropos of nothing, she said, "I've been thinking about Father, just before he disappeared. Looking back, there was one thing that might well have been a kind of parting message. It was very strange. It was about Kazuhiko and me."

"About your relationship?"

"Yes, that's right." She turned her face away, as if embarrassed. "Father must have misunderstood things between us. He said something in a roundabout way that I took to mean I must never marry him."

"Because you're cousins?"

"Yes, exactly. And, well..." She paused for a moment before going on. "There's actually a particularly good reason for us not to. The truth is that my mother's parents—meaning my grandmother and grandfather—were first cousins. And my grandmother's parents, my great-grandparents on that side, were also cousins. There are many such close marriages in my family, going back generations, which is why my mother... Well, that's why she is the way she is. It clearly must have worried my father, but even so, he must have known that Kazuhiko and I weren't at all like that. Why would he have been worried about it? I only see him as a cousin, nothing more. And I'm certain he feels the same. Father must have known that. So, why did he say it? And why did he say it in such a roundabout way?"

CHAPTER 25

The Accent Problem

Kosuke Kindaichi was reading in bed. Despite how slovenly it might appear, he found that if he did not do so in bed, then nothing he read actually made an impression. The book this time was Goethe's *Wilhelm Meister's Apprenticeship* which he had of course borrowed from Mineko.

The story she had told him the other day, about her father's mysterious message just before his disappearance, had set his mind humming. Mineko could not help but consider Tsubaki's words a kind of parting message, coming as they did just before his death, but they had left her with more questions than answers.

The timid viscount seemed to have been afraid to say whatever he meant outright and preferred to give only cryptic hints, hoping that people would catch the scent of meaning he intended.

Take his recording of "The Devil Comes and Plays His Flute". The deeply suggestive title and melody seemed to be hinting at something important. If so, then it was only natural to wonder what hidden meanings might also lie behind the viscount's words and behaviour just before he left.

Might the fact that he left that note to Mineko hidden in the pages of *Wilhelm Meister's Apprenticeship*, of all her books, also hint at something? In fact, Mineko had only read it on her father's recommendation in the first place. Did the viscount simply want her to appreciate the book as a work of literature? Or was there another reason?

To find out for himself, Kindaichi had borrowed the three-volume set and sat up all night reading. It had been a trying exercise. He simply felt too restless to focus on getting through the heavy text. He wasn't reading it for pleasure but trying to glean some meaning or hint that the viscount might have left, which sapped any interest the novel might otherwise have held. It was nothing more than a slog, and the words he had been stuffing into his brain since the night before were starting to sting like thorns behind his eyes.

And yet he read on, as if through pure inertia. As he lay there focused on the book, he tried to ignore the tension weighing on him like a stone in his belly.

Was all this simply a waste of time and effort, a trick he was playing on himself? While he was reading, was something much more important happening elsewhere? Ever since the murderer had stolen a march on them in Awaji, Kindaichi had felt a kind of intimidation. He was growing more frustrated with this novel, dragging on endlessly as it was.

There was also something else weighing on his nerves. Something that Kindaichi had been impatiently awaiting. The date was 10th October, and by his count it should be coming any day now. The thought irritated him more and more.

Then, around three o'clock in the afternoon, it came.

"Kindaichi-san, letters for you."

He leapt up at the sound of the maid's voice and snatched the two letters from her hand. His eyes glittered as he read through them.

One was from Detective Degawa, while the other was from Chief Inspector Isokawa with the Okayama Prefectural Police.

Kindaichi had written to Isokawa from the Three Spring Garden Inn in Suma city, as mentioned earlier, and he had been anxiously awaiting the response for days.

He hurriedly tore the envelope open and skimmed the contents. As he read, his eyes grew wide, and his breath quickened. He read and reread it over again, then opened Degawa's letter. Its contents lit another fire in his eyes. The hand holding the letter trembled in excitement, while the other dug into his wild hair and scratched ever faster.

It seemed Degawa had finally tracked down Uetatsu's mistress Otama. She had told him something incredibly important.

Kindaichi laid the two letters on his lap and looked back and forth between them, pondering, a grim look on his face. In the distance, a telephone rang, and then footsteps approached.

"Kindaichi-san, telephone for you."

"Who is it?"

"It's Chief Inspector Todoroki. He seems quite upset about something."

Kindaichi rushed to the phone, worried that there might have been another murder, but Todoroki said only to come to the Zojoji temple grounds and hung up. From his grim tone, Kindaichi knew that something sinister was afoot.

The clock read half past three.

The sky was as black as ink, and gusts of wind were blowing clouds of sand and dust. It seemed a storm was brewing. Kindaichi battled through the wind all the way to Zojoji, in the Shiba area of Minato ward, finally arriving at five o'clock. The sun was setting, casting the world into twilight colours, and the wind was growing stronger.

When he entered the temple grounds, he saw police milling around, and crowds of onlookers and newspaper reporters, all with tense expressions.

Kindaichi hurried ahead and saw Todoroki emerge from a nearby crowd of people. He gestured Kindaichi over. They were in a particularly isolated spot of the temple's vast grounds, near where a vicious murder had taken place about a year earlier. The chief inspector led him through the crowd and indicated something on the ground with a jerk of his chin. Kindaichi looked down and saw a man dressed only in underpants lying there, mostly hidden by deep underbrush. Kindaichi pushed on through the crowd to get closer, but when he did, he had to turn away, fighting down the bile rising in his throat.

The man was dead, and in a terrible state at that. His face, arms and legs had been chewed to shreds, and even the intestines were protruding from gashes in his abdomen. The face in particular had been so terribly mutilated—either intentionally or not—that it was beyond recognition, leaving it a mere lump of unidentifiable meat.

"Who is it?" Kindaichi asked, his voice hoarse.

Todoroki grimaced as he answered, "Well, we can't be sure yet, but we think it's someone we've been looking everywhere to find."

His voice was thick with anger.

"Looking everywhere…" Kindaichi wondered aloud, then with dawning realization, said, "You mean, this is Toyosaburo Iio?"

"Right. As you can see, there's not much of the face left to identify, and his clothes are nowhere to be found, but our information leads us to be pretty confident this is him. And, if we're right about that…" A terrible rage glinted in his bloodshot eyes.

Kindaichi felt the same thing, and his hair stood on end.

"But, in that condition, there's no way to prove who he is, right?"

"Of course there is! Iio had a record. We have his prints on file, and luckily his fingers are still intact."

"Oh, that's—"

Just then, the crime scene doctor walked up after finishing his inspection.

"We'll have to do a full autopsy to be sure, but I'd say he's been dead about two days. He was strangled to death with some kind of rope, it looks like."

"What about his face? Was that the work of wild dogs?" Todoroki asked.

"Well, the dogs helped, but it seems someone deliberately disfigured him too. The murderer must have wanted to hide the identity."

Kindaichi felt another chill and turned away from the corpse.

"Todoroki-san, who discovered the body?"

"Wild dogs. He was buried in the weeds over there, and the dogs dug him up. Someone passing by spotted them eating the corpse."

Todoroki turned back to the doctor.

"Doctor, you said he'd been dead about two days. That would put the murder on the 8th, right?"

"Yes, I'd say probably the evening of the 8th. The autopsy will help us say more certainly, of course."

When they saw the forensics team had replaced the doctor at the corpse's side and were taking the body's fingerprints, Kindaichi and Todoroki turned to leave.

The wind was building, and the grit it carried kept them from raising their faces. Scraps of paper danced through the darkness on the eddying gusts. Heavy drops of rain came falling.

"Todoroki-san, there's something I'd like to talk to you about."

"What is it?"

"Here," Kindaichi said and started to pull something out of his pocket.

But the chief inspector stopped him.

"Let's at least get in the car, first. This weather's no good."

They leapt into the nearby car, narrowly escaping a sudden burst of fierce rain.

"It looks bad out there."

"It's going to be a real downpour tonight."

They sat watching the storm outside for a moment, each lost in his own thoughts. The chief inspector broke the silence.

"So, what did you want to talk about?"

"This. You should give it a read."

Kindaichi held out an envelope. Todoroki raised his eyebrows when he saw the sender's name, but he said nothing as he took out the letter and started to read. After the first couple of lines, though, he jerked in surprise and looked up in wonder at Kindaichi, staring at the younger man, as if trying to glean some meaning from his expression, but soon went back to the letter and read as if consumed.

Here is the gist of what so utterly shocked Todoroki in Chief Inspector Isogawa's letter:

"Kindaichi, here, in brief, is my report on the results of our investigation into Totaro Mishima, the individual you inquired about.

1. Confirmed: Around 1942, a man named Shogo Mishima was deputy head teacher at an Okayama Prefectural secondary school. He and his wife Katsuko had a son named Totaro.

2. Confirmed: Shogo Mishima attended school with Viscount Tsubaki, and there is talk that they lived in the same dormitory.

3. Confirmed: Shogo Mishima died of a stroke in 1943. Katsuko Mishima was killed in an air raid on Okayama City that same year.

4. Confirmed: Prior to their deaths, their only son Totaro died of a war-related illness at military hospital in Hiroshima.

"We are still recovering from the damages of war here, so I cannot claim that our investigation has been perfect. However, I find no room for doubt in any of the above. Therefore, if someone around you is claiming the name Totaro Mishima, he either happens to have the same name as the above man by coincidence or is an impostor. At this stage, I will leave that to your judgement."

"Then, Totaro Mishima is a fake?" Todoroki's face was flushed and swollen in rage. The veins at his temples throbbed like they would burst.

"It seems so. I can't imagine it's a coincidence. He said his father was a schoolmate of the viscount's and taught at a school in Okayama."

Todoroki's eyes were boring holes in Kindaichi's face.

"Kindaichi-san," he said, his voice harsh. "How did you know? How did you know he wasn't who he said he was? This letter says you asked about it…"

"Well, you see…" Kindaichi said, slowly scratching his head, "there was a problem with his accent."

"What?"

"You remember when we ran into him at the hothouse that day? He walked with us and said, 'There's a bredge here, let's use et.' It was the way he said 'bredge' and 'et'. He's been in Tokyo for a while, and his accent has faded. But there's still just a hint in the vowels."

"But the man was born in western Japan. Why wouldn't he have that accent?"

"Well, that's exactly it, Todoroki-san," Kindaichi said, his hand still slowly rubbing at his head. "He said he was from Okayama but his accent is pure Kobe. People from Okayama actually don't have much of an accent, although it's in the west."

His listener's eyes widened.

"Are you sure about that?"

"I am." Kindaichi went on scratching at his mop of hair. "I think you know I have some friends in Okayama, right? They all have the same accent as people in Tokyo. So, then, if this man calling himself Totaro Mishima actually was born and raised in that area, then he should have an accent like someone from Tokyo. But when I heard those words, I asked him if he'd ever lived in the Kobe area. He said he'd never even been there. I knew then that he was lying about something. They say that words are the fingerprint of your home town, but that man had no idea that Kobe and Okayama have different accents."

Todoroki glared in silent rage at Kindaichi, but before he could say anything, a soaking-wet detective came rushing over and gestured through the window.

The storm had arrived in earnest, and the Zojoji temple grounds were hidden behind a veil of sideways rain. The onlookers that had been swarming like ants scattered, and left in the rain were just the detectives and reporters. The photographers' flashes split the storm's darkness like lightning bolts, serving only to accentuate the gloom. An ambulance arrived to take the body away.

The chief inspector gave some kind of hand signal to the detective, then turned back to Kindaichi.

"Well then," he said and took a deep breath. "If that man is not Totaro Mishima, then who is he? Why did he take a fake name and work his way into the Tsubaki household?"

"Todoroki-san, you haven't read Detective Degawa's latest report yet, have you?"

"Degawa? Did he send something else? I suppose I haven't then."

Kindaichi pulled out the report he'd received from Degawa, and said, "This is a copy, so I assume he's sent the original to

286

police headquarters. It must have arrived after you left. Anyway, read it now."

The chief inspector snatched the paper and quickly took to reading.

Degawa's report was quite long, so I will summarize it as best I can for the reader. After Otama, Uetatsu's mistress, ran away from the hot spring inn where she had worked in Kobe, she entered the lowest class brothel in Osaka's Tennoji ward. She worked both as a madame and, despite her considerable age, as a prostitute herself. Degawa was able to track her down, but those details are not pertinent so I shall skip them. When he found her, Otama was crippled by a terrible disease and had been housebound for a long period.

After all this hard work, the facts that Otama revealed were as follows:

The father of Sayoko's child was most likely Haruo, Uetatsu's son. He had left Uetatsu's care when he was just a child and gone to apprentice with a merchant family in Kobe. From that point he only rarely visited his father, in whose house Otama was then living, but she heard that he often went to see Komako, Sayoko's mother.

Komako and Haruo were half-siblings through their father, but they were as far apart in age as parent and child, and Sayoko was roughly of an age with Haruo.

Through Uetatsu, Haruo and Sayoko were technically uncle and niece, but Komako and Haruo had different mothers, and with the difference in age too, it was difficult for them to feel that relationship. At some point, it seems they fell in love.

Sayoko took her life in August 1944, but Haruo had only been drafted in June so her being four months pregnant was not out of line with that time frame.

Otama did not know why Sayoko killed herself.

However, it might well be that when Komako found out that she was pregnant with Haruo's child, she ended up condemning the girl too strongly in her shock. Komako had been an old-fashioned, proper type, so she likely could not share the young couple's lax attitude about their blood relationship. So, she attacked Sayoko, and the girl could not bear it. The result was her suicide. Otama said that was simply the type of woman Komako had been.

Otama had one more reason for believing that Haruo had been Sayoko's lover.

The summer before, after his discharge from the army, he dropped in suddenly to visit Otama when she was still working at the Kobe inn. The first thing he asked was what had become of Sayoko, and when he learned of her suicide, the shock had left him in a wordless daze. When Otama went on to say that the girl had been pregnant, Haruo seemed to nearly go mad.

He had raged about why Sayoko had done it, but of course Otama had been unable to answer. She had not known herself. However, she did suggest that he ask Komako and told him where to find her on Awaji Island. He had written it all down in a notebook, and so she is certain he must have done just that. She never saw Komako or Haruo again, so she doesn't know any more.

That's roughly what Degawa reported, but at the end he added a handwritten section that Todoroki could not resist reading out loud. "After that, since Otama has not seen Haruo again, she's unable to say at all where he is or what he's doing. And, as discussed, he rarely visited Uetatsu so she can't say much about his character. However, she mentioned that due to an injury in the war, Haruo is missing two fingers from his right hand."

That last line buried itself like a poison dart in the chief inspector's chest. "Haruo! The man calling himself Totaro Mishima is actually Uetatsu's son Haruo!"

Kindaichi nodded, his eyes hooded.

The storm was building, and the car itself sometimes creaked senselessly in the wind. The ambulance carrying the body crept slowly out of the grounds. The chief inspector's driver arrived and got into the car, soaked to the bone.

"Sorry for the wait, sir. Where to?"

"Head for Azabu Roppongi," Todoroki ordered, then turned to Kindaichi to confirm.

He only nodded.

"But, listen, Kindaichi-san, why did he do it? Why assume a fake name and trick his way into the Tsubaki house?"

"I don't know that yet. But what really puzzles me is why he chose that man, the son of the viscount's old friend. There's no way Uetatsu's son could know about a viscount's school friends. So, I wonder if the viscount came up with it? If Tsubaki himself gave him the idea?"

"Viscount Tsubaki himself?" Todoroki was taken aback. "But why would he do that? What role did he play in all of this?"

"I don't know, yet. All I do know is, Otama's story might well be the key to everything. There is still something we don't know, some deep, vital secret hidden underneath it all."

With that, Kindaichi fell into silent thought.

CHAPTER 26

Akiko's Flight

When the car carrying Kosuke Kindaichi and Chief Inspector Todoroki left the Zojoji temple grounds, the rain grew even heavier, and the wind so strong that it seemed ready to blow both passers-by and even houses off into the sea. Later, everyone learned that this typhoon of the autumn of 1947 was the worst in decades, and the devastation it left along its path through the southern Kanto region is remembered to this day.

They arrived at the Tsubaki estate before six o'clock, but the heavy storm clouds meant it was as black as midnight. The storm had also knocked out the electricity, so the looming manor house stood in darkness amid the whirling typhoon. The scene was so ominous that the mere sight weighed on Kindaichi's spirit.

Todoroki stood in the rain and pounded on the front door, and soon they saw wavering candlelight appear through the glass. It drew close, and the door opened. Mineko, rather than the maid Otane, stood before them. It might have been an effect of the flickering candles, but Mineko's face once more looked like that of a witch.

Before anyone could say anything, their candles died in the wind.

"Hurry inside. We need to shut the door!" Mineko shouted, and the two men rushed in. The entry was pitch-dark, and as they came in both stumbled over some unseen obstacles, raising an enormous racket.

"Oh, I am sorry about that! I completely forgot," Mineko apologized as she rushed to relight the candles. The light revealed that the entryway was piled with trunks and suitcases.

"What's going on? What is all this?" the chief inspector asked, his eyes filled with suspicion. Kindaichi also looked questioningly at Mineko.

"Oh, well, you see—" she began, but just then, a voice called from the drawing room.

"Mineko-san, what was all that racket?" The slurring voice was Doctor Mega's. He sounded quite drunk.

"It was nothing, never mind. We have guests."

"Dammit, I know we have guests. Who is it?"

"It's the chief inspector and Kindaichi-san," Mineko snapped back, but Mega did not answer.

"Well then," she said, turning to the two men, "please, do come on in. Has something happened?"

"In a sense," answered Todoroki, "but…"

He blinked as they all entered the drawing room, which was lit dimly by an emergency lantern and filled with more piles of trunks and suitcases. Amid them all stood Mega, shirtless, and working hard to pack the boxes with Kazuhiko's help.

"What is going on here? Are you moving out?" Kindaichi asked, shock filling his voice.

"Ah, all this," Doctor Mega said, wiping sweat from his thick neck. "That Akiko, she's decided she can't bear to stay in this house. So, she's run off to the villa over in Kamakura. Now we're all running around trying to catch up."

"Run off… You mean, everyone's leaving for Kamakura?"

"No, not everyone. Just Akiko, old Shino and the maid Otane. I'll be going back and forth between here and there. Poor Akiko gets lonely if I don't show my face every now and again, you know. Ga ha!"

His body glistening with sweat and oil, the old toad croaked an eerie laugh. The sweat-clumped patch of hair on his shiny chest seemed somehow obscene in the gloom.

"But why are you packing so much for just three people?" Kindaichi asked, glancing at the piled-up bags.

"My mother always makes everything into an enormous ordeal," said Mineko. Her voice was still angry, but also somehow apologetic at the same time. Kazuhiko wordlessly carried on with the packing.

"Well, this won't do. I forbid it!" Todoroki burst out, his voice shaking with rage. "I've told everyone they are not to leave this house! I've said it a hundred times. I'll let you off with a caution, but you're to stop this at once!"

"It's a bit late, I reckon. Akiko's already gone."

"Unbelievable!"

"Now then, Chief Inspector, I'm well aware of our position. I know you're all working hard and everything, and this is a bother. I tried to stop her, I did. I talked and talked, but, well... You know how it is. People like her just live outside of the law," said the doctor.

"When did she leave?"

The chief inspector seemed to have his temper under control now.

"Just a couple of hours ago. She wanted to make sure they reached the house before the storm got too bad."

"And you said it was Lady Akiko, Shino-san and...?"

"The maid Otane went with them."

"Where exactly in Kamakura is this house?"

Mineko gave him the address, and as he was writing it down, Totaro Mishima came in carrying more suitcases.

"Doctor Mega, I think these are all—Oh, welcome. I didn't know you were here." When Mishima saw the two men standing in the gloom, he bowed his head in greeting and hurriedly buttoned up his open shirtfront.

"Yes, yes, that's all of them. Anyway, Mishima." Mega stretched his spine and thumped his lower back. "Let's give the packing a rest and have a drink or two. We've got these two gents as guests, and it's just too damned hot to keep working like this."

It was, indeed, hot. The close space trapped the damp, warm air like a sauna, and even those not working were pouring with sweat. The rapidly dropping air pressure was also making it hard to breathe.

"Right, I'll go and get some glasses."

Mishima left, and Doctor Mega said, "I'd best go and wash up a bit, too. Kazuhiko, what about you?"

"All right."

The two left the room.

"Miss, may I use your telephone?" asked the chief inspector.

"Of course, it's right this way."

Mineko went with him, leaving Kindaichi alone. He stared at the piled-up baggage in a kind of daze.

He felt sure that Akiko's sudden departure must also carry some great import. Although he could sympathize with her desire to escape this house and all its troubles, why would she brave the terrible storm? Why did she have to leave today? Even as childlike as she was, could she not wait for the storm to pass? His spirit was filled with tumult every bit the equal of the storm shaking the windows outside.

"Oh, Kindaichi-san, are you all on your own?"

He jumped at the sudden interruption of his thoughts. It was Kikue, standing in the dim lamplight, holding a silver tray. The missing finger on her left hand stood out against the silver in a strangely unsettling way.

"How rude, Kindaichi-san. Why are you staring at me like that?"

"Oh, no, I do beg your pardon. I was just lost in thought."

"Then I hope you'll forgive me. It must have been a shock, me talking to you out of nowhere like that. Where's the chief inspector?"

"He's using the telephone."

"Ah, I see. Then he'll be here soon, I imagine. Sorry, could you slide that table over here, please?"

The silver tray she placed on the table was mounded with sandwiches.

"I bet you haven't eaten, have you? We'll all be joining you, I'm afraid. The dining room's in a worse state than this one! I mean, just look at me!"

She spread out her dress, covered now in an apron, to show him.

"Lady Akiko truly is like a little princess, you know. She never does make anything easy."

"I understand that she decided to leave for Kamakura rather suddenly."

"The decision wasn't sudden at all. She made it four or five days ago. After Shingu-san died, I think it was? Right after that, she started saying she wanted to go, so we've all been shuffling back and forth getting the house ready for her, and it's finally all set up."

"But at any rate, she left today, even with the storm."

"That was strange, I have to admit."

"In what way, exactly?"

She gave Kindaichi a long look before smiling.

"Oh ho ho, I have to be careful. You don't miss a single word, do you? Very well. The plan all along was to leave today. Then along comes this storm, right? Well, at first it wasn't that bad, but the radio was saying it would get much worse. Everyone was really quite worried, and even her ladyship was having second thoughts. When everyone was gathered here and Doctor Mega had his whisky while everyone else drank tea, all of a sudden, her ladyship... She..."

"She what?"

"Well, she screamed. It was such a shock! I just assumed she was making a fuss about nothing like she does."

Hanako and Mineko came in. They were carrying more trays, with cups and plates this time. There was also a platter with salad and finger sausages.

"Well, look at this. A feast!" exclaimed Kindaichi.

"It's no such thing, I'm afraid. You know how it is, these days. Oh, where are my manners. Welcome, Kindaichi-san," Hanako said. She was as quiet and demure as ever, but he could not help but notice that her expression seemed somehow brighter than it ever had when Toshihiko was alive.

"But that we've managed even this much is all thanks to Mishima-san," put in Kikue. "We'd be lost without him. Oh, but..." She suddenly lowered her voice. "Where's the other one? That Doctor Mega?"

Sensing something in her tone, Kindaichi stared into her eyes.

"The doctor is right here!" Mega, still naked from the waist up, sneered as he hobbled in on his bandy legs.

Normally, Kikue would have been quick with a jibe, but for some reason, that day her expression only stiffened and she held her tongue. Mineko and Hanako, having arranged the plates, exchanged glances and simply stood, silent and stiff.

Something had happened! Kindaichi's heart began to pound as his eyes danced between the gross old toad and the pale women in the room.

The doctor looked around, his eyes gleaming. "Bwa ha ha, what is all this? What's got into you all? Come on, let's dig in. And where'd the chief inspector run off to?"

"Todoroki-san is on the telephone."

"Yes, yes, then what about Mishima? Where are those glasses?"

Doctor Mega grumbled as he took up the whisky bottle and refilled his glass from earlier. Hanako filled a cup with tea.

"Please, Kindaichi-san, help yourself."

"Thank you. Pardon my hands."

"Not at all."

Mishima and Kazuhiko then came in.

"Finally, the glasses!" Mega cried. "Kindaichi-san, how about it?"

"No, thank you, I'm fine with t— Oh, well, if you insist, then just one…"

"Mishima, a tipple? What, nothing? Ga ha ha, acting shy for our guests? After you were gulping it down earlier? And what's taking that chief inspector so long?"

On cue, Todoroki walked in, covered in sweat and looking deeply irritated.

"Is something the matter, Chief Inspector?"

"Hmph. They've closed off the Yokosuka line."

"What?"

Everyone stopped and stared at him.

"Seems there's been a landslide, and they still don't know when it'll be back in service."

"Then, what of Lady Akiko?" Hanako said, frowning with worry.

"I'm sure she made it through. What time did you say she left?"

"Just after four o'clock."

"Then she's fine. The line closed just after six. Apparently, a hillside collapsed over by Totsuka."

"What were you planning to do if the trains were running, Todoroki-san?"

"I was going to have someone go and bring her back, of course. We can't have everyone scattered all over at a time like this." He had a disgusted look on his face.

"Now now, Chief Inspector, what's done is done. Akiko isn't going to go running off somewhere. Anyway, here, bottoms up," said the doctor.

Todoroki took the glass Mega offered him and gulped it down on pure reflex. His gaze rested on Totaro Mishima, who stood wolfing down a sandwich. Then, the policeman realized he'd been drinking whisky. He started coughing and hurried to put the glass down. When his choking subsided, he opened his mouth to speak to Mishima, but Kindaichi quickly interrupted.

"Oh, by the way, Kikue-san, getting back to what you were talking about earlier. Why did Lady Akiko scream like that?"

"What?"

Todoroki gaped at Kindaichi, who summarized the events.

"So, I was just hoping to find out what it was that made her shriek as she did. Kikue-san, let's start with what was going on at the time."

She glanced around the room, her face pale.

"I suppose I can do that," she said eventually. "But I honestly don't know what she saw, or why she was suddenly so terribly afraid."

"You say she was frightened of something?"

"Oh, yes, very much. Well, that's what it seemed like to me. How did it look to you, Mineko-san? And you, Lady Hanako?"

"Yes, I had never seen Mother so frightened before." Mineko's tone was sharp, and she stared pointedly at Doctor Mega.

"I see, I see," Kindaichi said, as he began scratching his mop of hair. "Can you tell me exactly what was going on just before she shrieked?"

"Well, Lady Akiko had just decided to give up on leaving today. Then, everyone gathered here for tea at around half past three. She was sitting on that sofa, there…" Kikue pointed to the centre of the room, where two sofas and a couple of armchairs were arranged about a table. "Shino-san was sitting next to her on the sofa. The rest of us were scattered around the room. Then, all of a sudden, Lady Akiko gave a scream. It caught me by surprise, and I turned to her, and she was staring at Doctor Mega as if she'd seen a ghost."

"Oh, really! She wasn't looking at me—"

"Doctor, please. Kikue-san, do go on. What happened then?" asked Kindaichi.

"Well, I have to say I can't be sure what she was looking at, but at the very least she was looking towards Doctor Mega. She was behaving so strangely. I couldn't take my eyes off her. Suddenly, she cried out again and grabbed hold of Shino-san. Then, she pointed at something behind Doctor Mega and started babbling. It sounded like she was saying, 'Shino, Shino, the devil!' I'm sure I'm not the only one who heard that."

"Yes, that's what it sounded like to me, as well," Mineko said quickly.

"I see, I see," said Kindaichi excitedly. "And then?"

"Then, she started moaning like she'd gone mad, and cried out, 'I cannot stay in this house another instant! Shino, take me to Kamakura, right now!' She wouldn't listen to another word against it and took off like she was being chased."

The room fell quiet. Despite the storm raging outside, inside it was silent as the grave.

"So, it seems that somewhere in this room, Lady Akiko saw a devil," said Kindaichi.

"Yes, I think that is what happened."

"And you feel that this devil she saw was Doctor Mega."

"No, well, that is… I can't really say for certain."

Mega let out a snort and seemed about to go into a rant, but Kindaichi was quick to cut him off.

"Just wait a moment. Where were you when this happened, Doctor Mega? It could very well be that whatever Lady Akiko saw had nothing to do with you. If you don't mind, could you go back to where you were at that moment?"

The doctor seemed puzzled but went and stood across the room. "I was standing here with a glass of whisky. Yes, just like this. Shirtless."

"And Lady Akiko was sitting here?"

Kindaichi sat on the sofa Mineko had indicated and looked towards Doctor Mega. He immediately saw that just behind the doctor was a mirror in a mahogany frame, reflecting his greasy back. Of course, he was not the only thing reflected there. If Kindaichi angled his head just a little bit, the whole room to the right of the sofa was revealed.

Kindaichi was somehow relieved.

"May I ask, at that time, was everyone here? No one was missing?"

"Yes, everyone. Even Otane, who's left for Kamakura as well."

"I see. Then, can I ask everyone to return to where they were at that moment? Todoroki-san, you sit in Shino-san's place."

Everyone did as he asked, though they all seemed somewhat perplexed. Mineko and Hanako sat on the sofa opposite Kindaichi, while Kikue took the chair to his right. Kazuhiko stood behind Hanako, and Mishima behind Kindaichi's sofa, with his back to the window.

"Otane-san was standing right there," Kikue said, pointing to a spot a little way in front of Mishima.

Kindaichi once more looked into the mirror from Lady Akiko's seat. However, he was immediately disappointed to find that even the smallest adjustment in line of sight revealed everyone in the room. He could see Hanako's and Mineko's backs, with Kazuhiko right in front of them, and Kikue in profile. Mishima was visible, too, in the middle of the whole scene.

Kindaichi slowly shook his head in disappointment, then stood and walked over to the window. He opened it for a moment, then immediately closed it. The wind was blowing hard enough to tear it from his hands.

He glared into space for a moment, then blurted out, "Oh, fine. Let's settle this!" Turning to the chief inspector, he said, "Todoroki-san, you still have a car out front, right? So…" He took a quick count of the people in the room, "call for two more, please. And we'll need two or three… make that five detectives."

"What are you thinking, Kindaichi-san?"

"We're all going to Kamakura. One of these people is a devil. Lady Akiko saw whoever it was. We have to strike while the iron is hot! We're going to ask her directly!"

Todoroki swept from the room like a gust of wind to use the telephone.

"But, who will watch the house?" Hanako asked in a faltering voice.

"Don't worry, they'll put a detective outside."

No one else said a word. They just sat with stunned faces. For Kindaichi—for everyone, in fact—there was a sense that the coming evening would mark them for the rest of their lives.

The next three hours were a trial of fear and trembling. The three cars raced full speed through the howling gale and rain towards Kamakura. Looking back, it was a miracle that all three reached their destination without crashing.

It was well past ten o'clock in the evening when the car carrying Kindaichi, Todoroki and Mineko reached the villa in northern Kamakura. The whole neighbourhood was in pitch-darkness from the power outage. The doorbell would not ring, so Kindaichi pounded on the front gate. Otane came with a torch to open it, and when she saw him, her eyes widened. Her gaze travelled over the chief inspector, and finally came to rest on Mineko. When she saw the young woman, she began wailing, waving both hands wildly.

"O-Otane-san, what's the matter?" Kindaichi rushed to catch her just as she seemed to collapse to the ground. His mind whirled with terrible premonitions. "Has something happened to Lady Akiko?"

"The devil!"

"What about it?"

"He played his flute… and her ladyship…"

"Her ladyship? What about her? Otane!"

"She's dead! She took the medicine Doctor Mega gave her, and she…"

CHAPTER 27

The Locked Room Reborn

The night of the typhoon ended, and 11th October dawned.

From the morning, the Tsubaki estate in Azabu Roppongi was on high alert. It felt as if the whole area was under martial law. Curious gawkers, brought out by the newspaper reports on the latest tragedy, swarmed around the estate. There were constant rows between police officers and newspaper reporters trying to sneak in through gaps in the typhoon-ravaged garden wall.

Then, around seven that evening, the atmosphere around the manor grew even more tense.

The whole household was returning home, bringing with them the remains of Akiko Tsubaki after the autopsy in Kamakura. When they got word, the police around the estate went into higher gear. And yet, they were all simply fed up with the whole business. This had happened far too often. None of them could bear another such tragedy, and they were determined to restore the good name of the police department by closing this case. Someone would have to do something that evening. But… What?

While the lady's remains were being taken to the back parlour, Kosuke Kindaichi arrived to much commotion. He had left for Tokyo that morning, just after service on the Yokosuka line was restored. Now, his exhausted, bloodshot eyes gleamed with an odd light. He had an idea.

He met with the chief inspector, who pulled him into a corner of the drawing room and whispered fiercely, "Kindaichi-san, there's been another report from Degawa."

"I know. He sent me a copy."

"The reason behind Sayoko's suicide…"

"Yes, that's what I'm thinking, too."

They fell silent and stared at one another. Kindaichi shivered.

This is what Detective Degawa had reported.

After his last message, he had stayed in Kobe, following every possible lead in trying to discover the reason behind Sayoko's suicide.

He found that the day before her death, Sayoko visited a good friend he called M—. She recalled that she only realized later that Sayoko had come to say farewell, but even at the time, she said something that seemed strange. Her words were: "I have fallen into incestuous damnation."

Fallen into incestuous damnation… M— had trouble understanding what she meant with such old-fashioned phrasing. But Sayoko's expression and tone left a powerful impression.

"'Incestuous damnation'… Kindaichi-san, what do you think it means? Do you think it was because she realized her lover Haruo was actually her uncle?"

"No, she knew that from the beginning, didn't she? I usually understand that phrase to mean someone much more closely related than a half-uncle…"

The two fell once more into silent contemplation. Something began to burn in the depths of Todoroki's eyes.

Kindaichi looked away and began slowly scratching his head.

"What about her ladyship's autopsy?"

"They found our good friend potassium cyanide. It had been mixed with a strong sedative Doctor Mega had given her. The damned stuff is everywhere these days. You can't get away from it. Another one of the war's little gifts," Todoroki grumbled angrily. "Kindaichi-san, what do you think? Is it time to have a go at Mishima?"

"Yes, or at least, later tonight. Let's give it just a little longer. Before that, Todoroki-san, what about that room I asked for?"

"They're just getting it ready now. They should be about finished."

A detective came in and whispered something in Todoroki's ear. He nodded and hurried out of the drawing room.

Left behind, Kindaichi sank exhausted onto a sofa. He looked around the room and saw that the trunks and suitcases packed the night before were still piled all around. There was no longer any need to send them on to Kamakura now. All that sweat Doctor Mega and Totaro Mishima had shed packing them had gone to waste. Staring absently at the mounds, Kindaichi thought once more about the events of the night before.

Lady Akiko's final moments had gone so quickly.

At around four in the afternoon, something had frightened her so much that she had taken Shino and Otane from the Tsubaki house to escape to the villa in north Kamakura. The three had reached the villa just before six o'clock, and the sprawling house was already embraced by the storm's darkness. But the power was still on, and that fact came to play a key role in ending Akiko's life.

The fearful woman insisted Shino and Otane stay by her side, and they half carried her into the Western-style bedroom. Shino flipped the light switch on the wall, but rather than turning the lights on, it only filled the dark room with the sounds of that terrible, cursed melody—"The Devil Comes and Plays His Flute".

The effects were absolute and immediate. Outside, a frightful storm raged, while inside Akiko was already filled with abject terror. So, when the pitch-dark room echoed with the blood-curdling notes they had heard so often lately, Akiko's spirit might well have simply flickered out from the shock of it.

Shino and Otane both were frozen in shock themselves for a moment. Shino, though, had already seen this trick, and immediately knew what to do. She felt her way through the room to the lamp on the nightstand and switched it on, revealing the source of that accursed tune.

She pulled a small electric phonograph from under the bed. The evil record was still spinning on the turntable. She stopped it, took the record and threw it to the floor, shattering it into shards, which scattered across the floor like dead leaves. At this point, Akiko fainted into Otane's arms.

If, after that, Shino and Otane had been able to properly give her into the care of doctors, perhaps the coming tragedy could have been prevented.

But the storm still raged outside. Shino feared that no doctor would come in such weather, and indeed she was as concerned as always with appearances.

And so, she brought out some capsules that Doctor Mega had prepared for such occasions and placed one into Akiko's mouth herself. Never did she dream that it would end the poor woman's life. Those capsules all contained cyanide. Akiko died thrashing and convulsing in agony. Shino and Otane, near mad with terror themselves, held her in their arms as she passed.

The storm outside grew ever more fierce.

Now, Kindaichi was wrestling with the question of who had set up that phonograph and put cyanide into the capsules.

Everyone in the household had repeatedly gone out to help prepare the villa since long before Akiko left the Tsubaki house, which meant that they all had plenty of opportunity to set up the record, and likewise anyone could have mixed cyanide into the medicine.

But the thing that truly haunted Kindaichi was what Akiko had seen in this room. She had seen a devil. Who had it been hovering over? Kindaichi looked again around the room, as if waking from a dream. He rose and wandered between the piled trunks and suitcases. He stood in thought before the wood-framed mirror.

Was it Doctor Mega himself who had frightened Lady Akiko so much? Or was it some reflection she had seen in the mirror? If the latter, then what had been reflected there?

Once more, Kindaichi ran his eyes over the room behind him. No, not once. Over and over. He bit his nails, scratched his wild hair and tapped out a complicated rhythm with one slipper-shod foot.

Then, his eyes fastened on one single point. In that instant, his hand and foot both froze, and a great fire seemed to ignite in his staring eyes. His eyes were nailed to the window and its metal security shutter.

"Devil…"

He gasped, and the once-frozen fingers took to working at the wild mop again with heightened vigour and intensity. It was almost like he was trying to tear out his own hair. Finally, finally, Kindaichi felt that he had grasped what Akiko had seen.

Just then, a detective came rushing into the room.

"Oh, Kindaichi-san, they've got the room ready."

"Right, right…" He blinked as though waking from a dream. "Where's the chief inspector?"

"He's waiting there for you. We've gathered everyone."

"All right, then, let's go."

Kindaichi pulled up the hems of his *hakama* trousers and followed the detective down the corridor. His eyes betrayed an excitement greater than any he'd shown since this case had begun. He knew now that this truly terrible case was finally coming to a close. The detective led him to the soundproofed studio where the first in this tragic series of murders had taken place. There, he found all those who had attended the mysterious divination on that seemingly long ago evening. All except, of course, those who had lost their lives: Count Tamamushi, Toshihiko Shingu and Lady Akiko.

They were surrounded by a swarm of plain-clothes police, all of whom glanced around the room anxiously. Their expressions betrayed how frayed their nerves were.

"Is this what you wanted, Kindaichi-san?" Todoroki called out from deep inside the room.

Kindaichi squeezed through the crowd to the door, and looked inside. He saw a space of about eight tatami mats enclosed on three sides by black curtains. The rechargeable emergency lantern hung from the ceiling. Of course, that was just for consistency, as the lights were all on.

Below the lantern stood the round table, surrounded again by chairs. The table bore the same round dish used in the divination. It was filled with fresh white sand, spread smooth across the top. And there, a little distance away stood one of the pair of statues on its stand.

After Kindaichi had taken in the room's layout, he turned to Mineko beside him and asked, "Mineko-san, is this how the room was that night? The night that Count Tamamushi died? Is anything different?"

Mineko, her face pale as a sheet, looked carefully at the layout, then started to nod, but suddenly shook her head.

"Oh, no, something is different."

"What?"

"See, that statue of Fujin on the stand. That evening, only Raijin was here. Uncle Tamamushi was struck with the Raijin statue…"

Kindaichi gave a slight smile.

"Actually, Mineko-san, that evening it was the statue of Fujin in this room. However, the statue was standing outside the lantern light, and they do look so similar that anyone might make that mistake. I mean, nobody was paying that much attention to it in the first place, right?"

Mineko stared at him in confusion. "But someone stole the Fujin statue last year, didn't they?"

"That's right, but isn't it here now? Someone did indeed try to steal the Fujin and Raijin set but dropped both in the garden. You found Raijin relatively quickly, but Fujin was lying somewhere hidden. Then, our murderer found it, and made it part of their plan on that night."

Mineko still stared in confusion, and made as if to say something, but thought better of it and closed her mouth. Kikue, though, did not.

"Well, Kindaichi-san, what is about to happen here? Are you trying to scare the murderer into confessing by recreating the scene from that night?" Her tone was as teasing as ever, but this evening she could not hide a note of tension in her voice. She was a clever person and must have sensed something new in his attitude.

Kindaichi, though, just grinned, and said, "Well, something like that, I suppose."

"Surely our murderer isn't so easily frightened, though?" she said, and as she did she deliberately slid away from Doctor Mega's side, where she had been standing. His eyes glinted with fury.

"Oh, no." Kindaichi continued to grin as he spoke. "I don't really need any confession. What I'm more interested in, actually, is that strange *kaendaiko* that appeared on the sand, the devil's mark as someone called it. That, and how such a violent, bloody murder could have happened in a sealed room. So, I've recreated it here."

"Oh, you're trying to reveal the magician's trick. Is that all?" Mega said, a mocking sneer on his coarse toad features.

Hanako and Kazuhiko both stood grim-faced in silent misery. A little apart from everyone else, Totaro Mishima and Otane looked on in interest. Shino stood with her usual ramrod-straight back and eagle-eyed glare.

"Right! That's it exactly! And just like how every magician's trick turns out to be as simple as child's play, the secret behind this locked room murder is actually quite underwhelming. Yet, at the same time, I wouldn't say it's something just anyone could do," Kindaichi explained as he entered the room. Everyone followed him with their eyes.

He stood between the table and the Fujin statue, turned towards the door and said, with a slightly embarrassed look, "To be honest, part of me wanted to go even further—have everyone sit down, turn out the lights and ask the doctor to perform his divination again. But there is still so much to do this evening that I thought we'd better just get on with it."

With that, Kindaichi reached out to pick up the Fujin statue, then brought it down on the sand like the base was a stamp. He lifted it up, and all gaped in surprise. Just as it had on that evening, the sand now bore that fat flaming teardrop shape, like a *kaendaiko* drum.

Doctor Mega croaked out a laugh.

"So it was child's play, after all that! Now that I think of it, the mark that evening did look like it had been stamped there. Isn't that right, Hanako-san?" he asked the woman on the other side of the room, making a show of ignoring Kikue and Mineko beside him.

"Ah, well, if you say so…"

No one disagreed with the doctor or Hanako.

"Well, that's that, Kindaichi-san," Kikue said with a gulp. "I suppose we know how the mark got there. But that doesn't explain why anyone would kill his lordship or how it was done."

"That's true, yes. That's why the chief inspector and I are going to act it out for you."

"What, me?" Todoroki blinked in surprise.

"Yes, that's right. Don't worry, it's very simple. Just do what I say. Oh, but first…" Kindaichi turned towards the door once more. "I think everyone remembers what happened after the mark appeared in the sand, right? That record started playing. 'The Devil Comes and Plays His Flute'. That was partly a way for the murderer to inspire dread in the victims, but it was also meant to distract everyone's attention away from the mark for a time because they wanted to exchange Fujin with the statue of Raijin that should have been standing there without anyone noticing. So then, where was the Raijin this whole time?"

Kindaichi stepped outside the room and pointed at the large flower vase standing there.

"Does everyone remember how as I entered the room, I put my hat over the top of this vase? Then, the lining got caught on the lip, and we had so much trouble getting it off. Ironically, that evening, the Raijin statue was hiding inside this pot all along!"

Kindaichi looked from face to face as he spoke.

"The culprit used that record to get everyone out of the room, then rushed to the pot to get the Raijin. But no matter how they tried, they couldn't get my sad old hat off the top, so Raijin remained where it was. They were probably afraid they'd tear the lining if they pulled too hard. And, of course, they couldn't afford to work too fiercely, or they'd attract attention, so they must have decided to put off the exchange. Then, once the whole record excitement died down, we finally got my hat free, and the Raijin statue could be retrieved for the exchange. But this time…"

"His lordship Tamamushi was in the way," Kikue said. Her voice was gentle.

"Exactly. Count Tamamushi had been deeply shocked by the mark's appearance, and he stayed behind in the room. Our culprit waited, but he showed no sign of leaving, so they must have given up and gone back to their room for a time, but they knew they had to make the exchange before morning. They waited for the middle of the night, when everyone should have been asleep, and snuck back to this room. The lights must have been out in here. The murderer likely assumed that the count had left, so they took the Raijin statue from its hiding spot and brought it inside."

Kindaichi reached into the vase and took out the Raijin statue. He tiptoed into the room, the statue in his right hand, and said, "Of course, when they came inside, they found the count still here. His lordship had drunk himself to sleep, or perhaps he had just turned the lights off to be alone with his thoughts. At any rate, he noticed someone sneaking in and, being the suspicious type, turned on the lights."

Here, Kindaichi turned to the chief inspector.

"Right, Todoroki-san, you are Count Tamamushi. I am the culprit. Taken by surprise when the lights come on, I stare at Tamamushi. He looks at the culprit, and what I have in my hand. His lordship, being a sharp-eyed and clever man, must have immediately seen through the *kaendaiko* trick. So, he tries to question the culprit, me, but I rush him…"

Kindaichi held up the hems of his *hakama* as he rushed at the chief inspector and pretended to hit him with the statue. He pushed the detective back down onto the sand, and holding his throat with his left hand, pretended to strike Todoroki several times in the face and head with the Raijin statue.

The scene was actually quite comical. The chief inspector, having had no advance warning of this, stared like a deer in headlights, while Kindaichi pursued his role with

311

determination. Still holding him by the throat, he went on: "Their struggle disturbed the sand and sent blood flying. The count's nose had started bleeding, and that actually was much bloodier than any of his actual wounds. Now, Tamamushi must have struggled fiercely atop the sand. He was probably asking the murderer who they really were, and what they were trying to do. Remember, Todoroki-san, you're Count Tamamushi."

The chief inspector took his reminder in stride.

"Oh, right." He began playacting, still lying on the sand. "Who are you? What are you doing?"

"The murderer then whispered something into the count's ear," Kindaichi said, then leaned down towards the chief inspector's face. "I am—" he began, but whispered the rest of his sentence. As he did so, Todoroki's expression suddenly shifted. He threw Kindaichi off and jumped up.

"What?! Kindaichi-san, is that true?!" Todoroki was no longer acting. His face was flushed and twisted in horror, and his eyes bulged out of his head.

Kindaichi, on the other hand, stood calmly brushing the sand off his clothing.

"It is. Or rather, I believe it is. And I believe that Count Tamamushi must have been every bit as shocked that evening as you just were, and likely asked the murderer the very same thing."

Everyone stood in silence.

What had Kindaichi whispered to the chief inspector? And why had it shocked the man so much? The onlookers stood with expressions frozen in place while the air in the room grew tense and anxious. Was that because they couldn't imagine what he had whispered, or because they knew that someone in that room knew exactly what it was?

Finally, it was Kikue who broke the silence. Her tone was still taunting, but the tension was clear now. "Kindaichi-san, just what kind of spell did you put on the chief inspector?"

"Ah!" Kindaichi answered, still staring at Todoroki. "That will have to wait for later. But I think a look at his face should give you an idea of just how bad it was. Remember, it would have been worse for his lordship."

"Kindaichi-san," Mineko said, and her voice was filled with fear. Her eyes were gaping wide, and her pale cheeks were taking on a feverish red flush. "Is it… that? The secret that would drag the Tsubaki name into the mud?"

"Y-yes, I believe it might be." Kindaichi averted his eyes from her fevered gaze and awkwardly cleared his throat. "So, then, that closes the curtain on the first act of that evening's tragedy. Count Tamamushi was gravely wounded. The blood from his nose spattered everywhere and left the room a scene of grisly misery. However, he was not yet dead. No, he was actually not that badly injured."

"But why didn't he call for help?" the doctor croaked in his toad voice.

"That would be the magic spell's fault, right?" clever Kikue pointed out.

"Exactly. There was a good reason he didn't want to call anyone and give the culprit a chance to talk. So, the count made a temporary deal. Or rather, it might be better to say the culprit made a deal with his lordship. They left his lordship behind in the room. Naturally, they exchanged the statues first. Then, the count stayed behind, locked and barred the door, and closed the curtains. Of course, both the door and the curtains must have been closed during the attack. Otherwise, someone would have heard something, and there was blood spatter on the curtains, too. Anyway, the culprit left, and Count Tamamushi

313

stayed behind. He was likely in a great deal of shock, and not yet ready to leave. He needed some time to pull himself together, I imagine. And, of course, with all that blood…"

At this, Kindaichi nodded towards Kikue.

"He probably didn't want to show up at his lady's bedside in such a state. Thus, we have the culprit outside a sealed room with his lordship still inside. Then, the culprit must have had a thought."

With that, Kindaichi hurried out of the room, then shifted the stand that had held the flower vase over in front of the door.

"Now, watch carefully. At the time, the door was closed. It was also locked and barred. Remember that the curtains were closed, too. So, the culprit climbed up on this table and looked in through the *ranma* window."

Kindaichi did just that.

"Then, it must have gone like this. 'Your lordship, your lordship, there was something else I needed to tell you. Come here, let me whisper in your ear.' Now, Chief Inspector, you're still Count Tamamushi."

"Oh, right, um, one moment." Todoroki looked around, then took a nearby chair over to the inside of the door and climbed up onto it. "Like this, Kindaichi-san?"

"Right, exactly. Now, could you open the window?"

Todoroki slid the glass panes closing the vent to each side. Kindaichi looked down at the faces of the onlookers from his vantage point atop the table.

"So, here is how the culprit faces Tamamushi through the *ranma*. As you can see, the opening is quite narrow top to bottom. I can't even get my face through. But there is plenty of space for my arms. And I think you probably all remember that the count was wearing a scarf around his neck. It was perfect.

The culprit leaned in close as if to whisper into the count's ear, then reached both hands in and—"

Kindaichi swallowed audibly.

"It was an easy thing to do. Count Tamamushi was a frail old man, and he had already had quite a shock. He was strangled without a sound. The murderer threw him aside with main force, and in the fall the count must have hit a chair or something and got another wound on the back of his head. And that is how we ended up with the horrible locked room murder."

Kindaichi climbed down from the table. No one spoke a word. Once again, everyone was wrapped up in a ghastly reverie.

It was once more Kikue who finally broke the silence. "But then, what about that other *kaendaiko* mark, the one stamped in blood? Did the murderer make it when they left? Surely not with his lordship right there watching?"

Her question set Kindaichi to scratching his head again, a happy grin on his face.

"Kikue-san, you really are clever. You notice things that other people miss. It was like this. This all was the second act of the tragedy. Now we come to the third act."

Kindaichi returned to the room, picked up the Fujin statue and showed everyone the bottom of the base. Naturally, it was carved with the kaendaiko shape. Kindaichi fidgeted with it, and the bottom part of the base came off in his hand. He was now holding a disk of around three and a half inches across in the palm of his hand.

"I have to admit that I made this myself, but when we found the Fujin statue it was missing a section of the base of around this same thickness. So, in the panic after everyone discovered the murder, the murderer snuck this disk into their pocket. With the door broken down and everyone focused on the corpse, they could secretly stamp the mark in blood on the sand. That marked the tragedy's third act and put the finishing touch on this locked room murder."

Kindaichi seemed quite satisfied with the show, but Kikue was less so.

"But it's all so far-fetched. If the murderer had cut the base short, why go through all the silliness of switching the Fujin and Raijin statues at the divination, then switching them out again afterward? There was no need for all that trouble. Using the disk would have been so much simpler."

This observation made Kindaichi even happier, and he took to scratching and tugging at his wild mop of hair.

"Th-th-that's right! Kikue-san, y-y-you've got it exactly. You truly are a sharp woman!"

He calmed himself and went on, "I really think this particular act was a spontaneous one. The murderer hadn't planned on any of this. They might have wanted the count dead from the start, but at the very least they didn't plan to do it that evening. Their primary goal that evening with the shock of the mark, the panic from the record player, and then that appearance by the fake Viscount Tsubaki was to bring dread to this house. I imagine they would have been satisfied to see certain members feel that horror closing in on them. In a sense, they were just preparing the way. But, like I just described, they ended up committing murder almost by accident. Then, thinking about it after the fact, we have this truly bizarre situation: a grisly, obvious murder in a locked room. The culprit realized how mysterious it must seem, so they decided to inflate that sense of the bizarre even more with the bloody stamp. They went back to their room after the murder and cut the base off in a rush. Then, once you'd discovered the scene and set off the panic, they put their stamp in their pocket and came out as if nothing was up at all. Or, at least, that is how I see it all happening."

"I see, Kindaichi-san." At this, it seemed that even reluctant Kikue was convinced. "Well then! That clears up the locked room murder. All that's left, then, is the murderer's identity, and I suppose you've got that figured out as well, don't you? And they're here, in this room, aren't they?" she said, a cheery smile on her face as she looked around her.

Everyone else, though, grew only paler as the tension in the air seemed to squeeze all the air out of the room.

CHAPTER 28

The *Kaendaiko* Reappears

It was just as Kikue said.

The mystery of the locked room had been resolved, and now the time had come to reveal who had been behind it, and who had gone on to slay Toshihiko Shingu and Akiko Tsubaki. There also remained the matter of the motive behind these terrible crimes.

"Yes, th-th-that's right…" Kosuke Kindaichi began, in answer to Kikue's question, but then fell silent.

Suddenly, he could not help but resent the cheerful smile on her face. He had been doing his best to postpone this moment. Indeed, if he could, he would have abandoned this case altogether. The secrets he was about to reveal were simply too painful, too heart-breaking and terrible. But to shirk his duty would be inexcusable. And, indeed, the conscience of an investigator like him, someone dedicated to the truth, would simply not allow it. There was also the issue, of course, of the troublesome vanity that spurred him ever onward.

His mind made up, Kindaichi opened his mouth and said in a leaden voice: "I am now possessed of a certain conviction. However, I would like to carry out one last test to confirm it before we go further."

"What kind of test?" Todoroki interrupted, his brow furrowed.

"Well, we still haven't established what Lady Akiko saw, and which frightened her into flight."

"But we already tried to figure that out yesterday," Doctor Mega said with a forced chuckle, glaring at Kindaichi.

"That's right. But yesterday's test didn't go far enough. I want to be even more thorough today. At any rate, I think if we can find out what it was that Akiko-san saw yesterday, we will know for sure who the murderer is."

Todoroki stared at Kindaichi hard enough to bore holes through his face. "So, then, should we all head back to the drawing room?"

"Yes, if you would…"

Everyone shuffled out of the studio and made their way to the drawing room. Plain-clothes detectives and uniformed policemen herded them along like sheepdogs. No one could escape. No one tried to.

When they arrived at the drawing room door, Kindaichi stopped short and called out hesitantly, "Mineko-san…"

"Yes?"

"I think it might be best if you, Kazuhiko and Hanako Shingu did not enter this room."

"Why would you say that?" Her eyes widened in surprise. Her face threatened to consume Kindaichi.

"Why? I-it… That is—"

"No, Kindaichi-san," Mineko cut him off. "I am going inside. I need to know. Whatever it is. And I think Kazuhiko and aunt Shingu do, as well. Please, Kindaichi-san." Her tone grew suddenly gentle, and she put a hand on his arm. "I think I can guess how you feel. You don't want us to hear anything upsetting. But I am ready. So is Kazuhiko, and so is aunt Shingu."

Kindaichi made as if to say something else, but she spoke over him once more. "Don't you think I have a right to know, Kindaichi-san? I am your client, after all. I hope you'll forgive me for putting it like this, but I hired you. Though I've not

319

offered anything in return yet." At that, Mineko turned to the Shingus. "Shall we?"

Kindaichi, his head hanging low, followed them into the room.

This little argument meant that he was the last to enter. The sheepdogs were keeping careful watch over their flock. Kindaichi looked around at the gathered people, a troubled expression on his face, and then leaned in to whisper something to Todoroki, who raised his eyebrows, and protested, "But, what if—"

"It's fine. Just have men on the door and outside the windows."

Todoroki gathered his men and waved them out of the room. As they were leaving, Kindaichi grabbed one by the arm and spoke to him in a low voice, then turned to Hanako.

"Excuse me, Lady Hanako, if I may have a moment?"

Hanako went over as asked. The three exchanged a few hushed words before the detective left, then quickly returned, carrying a silver tray bearing a bottle of whisky and a few glasses.

Kindaichi took the tray, pushed the detective out of the room and closed the door behind him. He turned to the crowd, still holding the tray.

"Right then, now we have the room to ourselves. The door is quite thick, so I doubt anyone outside will hear what we have to say."

His voice was thick and hoarse.

"Kindaichi-san, what are you on about? Are you planning on getting us all drunk?" Mega complained.

"Exactly, Doctor Mega, I'd very much like you to have a drink. In fact, I want everyone in the exact state they were in yesterday, when Lady Akiko said she saw the devil."

Kindaichi sat the tray on the centre table and poured some whisky into a glass.

"Go on, help yourself."

"Well, if you insist," the doctor said, looking flustered, and took a glass.

"Kazuhiko-san, Mishima-san, please, don't be shy. It could be the last one you ever have!"

Kazuhiko took a hesitant sip, but immediately set his glass down. Mishima, though, drained his glass in a gulp, then turned to Mega and asked, "How many did I have yesterday, Doctor?"

Mishima was grinning.

"Well, let's see. Five or six, I reckon. I remember I was impressed!"

"Is that all? Well then…" Mishima picked up the bottle and poured and downed five glasses in quick succession. His cheeks soon flushed and sweat beaded his brow.

"Yes, this is about how it felt. Yesterday. When it happened."

Everyone stared at him, now, their eyes full of surprise and not a little fear. Even Mega, glass still gripped in his hand, could not look away from the young man's face.

"Th-that's…" Kindaichi's voice was still choked. "Yes, I think everything is ready now. Now then, if everyone would take their place from yesterday. That's right, Doctor Mega, you were shirtless, weren't you?"

He glared at Kindaichi, but quickly removed his shirt and vest and stood in front of the mirror once more.

Kazuhiko hesitated, then removed his shirt as well. Totaro Mishima walked over by the window and quickly stripped off his top.

Kindaichi closed his eyes and sighed deeply. It was almost a sob.

"Kindaichi-san, what next?"

He stood for a moment in the centre of the room, then walked over and threw himself into the seat Lady Akiko had sat in the day before.

He closed his eyes again, took a deep breath, then opened them. He looked at the mirror behind Doctor Mega and shifted his perspective a couple of times.

From between his lips came another long, sobbing sigh.

"Todoroki-san, come here and look at the mirror. It's showing something reflected in the window behind Mishima. That is what Lady Akiko—"

"That's enough, Kindaichi-san."

Everyone in the room except Kindaichi looked towards the voice that had interrupted him.

It belonged, of course, to Totaro Mishima. Oddly enough, his expression was not only unconcerned, but almost happy. He was as cheerful as if he were getting ready for a picnic.

"It would take forever to have everyone go and look in the mirror. It would be easier if I just showed you all."

He came to the centre of the room and turned so that everyone could see his back. They all recoiled, as if they had fallen under a terrible spell.

The chief inspector gave a high, flute-like cry, and even Mega gaped as if his eyes would fall from their sockets.

There, on Mishima's flushed and sweaty back, marked out in pink was a *kaendaiko*—identical to the one that had been on Toshihiko Shingu's shoulder.

Everyone stared at the mark as if possessed. Hanako and Kazuhiko were pale as paper, and even Kikue was shocked to silence. Shino's face was twisted in loathing. Only Mineko seemed not to understand. She simply looked confused.

Mishima soon turned to face everyone, and now his face was pale with nervous tension. He forced a manic grin, and said, "Do you see, now? The devil's mark that Viscount Tsubaki drew in his notebook was my birthmark. I came to him with this birthmark as proof of my identity."

"Are you saying you're—" Hanako began, but could not finish her sentence. She sat, her mouth gaping, as the sound died in her throat.

Mishima turned his manic grin on her. "Yes, Lady Hanako, I am your husband's bastard son. Kazuhiko, I am your half-brother."

Kazuhiko flushed with humiliation. His whole body tensed.

"Then you killed your own father?" Todoroki said gruffly.

Mishima answered calmly. "Yes, I did, Chief Inspector. Oh, now, wait one moment. Don't call your men yet. That would spoil Kindaichi-san's little plan. Don't worry, I am prepared for my fate. I won't do anything rash, so you can relax."

Kindaichi gestured to Todoroki to hold off, then went and stood at the door himself, more to keep anyone from coming in than to stop Mishima from trying to escape.

"If that was all, then why didn't you tell me sooner? I would have done what I could..." Hanako broke down weeping. For the first time, Mishima's grin wavered.

"Thank you, Lady Hanako. But I'm afraid you don't understand. He... your husband was no man. No human. He was a beast. A monster. He was the most shameless, detestable creature on this earth. He was an animal with a human face."

For a brief moment an expression of hatred that was almost too terrible to behold appeared on his face, but he hid it almost instantly and shrugged his shoulders.

"A ha ha," he laughed deep in his throat. "Kindaichi-san, can I have another whisky?" he asked, but poured another without awaiting the answer.

Mineko had got over the initial shock now, and she stared coldly at Mishima as he drank. Then she spoke, her voice cold as ice. "Mishima-san, say what you like about my uncle. In fact, I agree with everything you just said. But then, why... Why did you kill my mother? My poor, innocent mother? She never—"

Kindaichi ran over and stopped her with a hand on her shoulder.

"Mishima-san!" he said with a sharp, meaningful look.

Mishima glared back at him.

"Let him speak, Kindaichi-san," said Todoroki.

After a moment, Mishima said in a wavering voice, "She wants to know. And… And, just once, I would like to call her… sister."

"Sister?" She was once more taken aback.

"That's right, Mineko. I… I am the child born of Toshihiko Shingu's terrible sin of lust for his own little sister, your mother."

CHAPTER 29

The Devil's Tale

It was I.

I, Haruo Kawamura, who joined the Tsubaki household under the assumed name of Totaro Mishima last year, am setting down this confession to spare anyone around me any greater trouble should anything happen to me.

It is finished.

I have killed my great-uncle and my father and set in motion the death of my mother. She is not yet dead as I write this, but I do not see any way that my plan could fail. So, although she still lives, I do not think it is premature to confess to her murder.

I killed my great-uncle and my father out of unbearable hatred and a need for revenge. I feel no shred of remorse or regret over their deaths. Indeed, I feel only the relief and thrill that anyone would get after accomplishing a task that needed doing.

Yet now, with all my preparations for Mother's death complete, what is this desolate wind that blows through my soul? When I came to this house, I resented and hated my mother every bit as much as I did the other two. And yet…

Perhaps I am writing this confession in some small hope that my plan for Mother's death will fail. Perhaps I hope that someone will find it and stop my plan before it finishes. But no, there is no hope of that.

She must die. Leaving her to live such a life would be an unkindness both to the woman herself and to Mineko.

Oh, Mineko. Poor, poor Mineko.

That's it. I shall write this confession to her. I imagine that learning such horrific truths will scar her for life. But, Mineko, you must endure, and I know that you have the strength to do that.

Now, before I offer my full confession to the terrible things I have done, I must give some explanation of my background.

I was raised as the first son of gardener Tatsugoro Kawamura, known as Uetatsu, in the Sumadera district of Kobe city. The family register shows that I was born to Tatsugoro and his wife Haru.

However, for as long as I can remember, I have known without it ever really being discussed that I was not Tatsugoro's real son. I do not remember when or how I learned it, but I knew that I was adopted from somewhere.

My mother of record, Haru, had died and Tatsugoro had quit his job as a gardener before my first memories. The earliest I can recall, we were living with his young mistress in a place called Itayado in Kobe.

She was only the first of many women that he went through. I believe her name was Okatsu, and I imagine she was the one who told me I was not the man's real son.

However, neither Okatsu nor any of Tatsugoro's later mistresses seemed to know my true parents, and I myself had no knowledge of my true identity until after I was discharged from the army in the summer of 1946.

Of course, Tatsugoro knew. I pleaded with him repeatedly to tell me who my real parents were. Whenever I did, he would always get a strange leer on his face. Now, oh, now, I know the meaning of that look…

"You're better off not knowing, boy," he'd say. One time, "If you knew you'd never be able to live with yourself. You should be grateful you're registered as my son", or words to that effect.

If I persisted, Tatsugoro would get angry enough to throw things at me. He grew to be so frightening that eventually I gave up trying to find out who I was.

I think it goes without saying that he and I shared no familial affection. At the same time, though, I would not say that our relationship was particularly bad, or that we were always quarrelling.

Soon after I graduated from secondary school, I left Tatsugoro's house and took an apprenticeship with a merchant in the centre of Kobe. That was something both Tatsugoro and I wanted. I rarely returned to see my adoptive father, who continued to go through mistresses and gamble his money away. I imagine that he was happy to be rid of me once I came of age.

During my apprenticeship, I took night classes to continue my education. Then, when I was nineteen, I took a position with a trading company on the coastal road. The company was a German affiliate, and I learned to type there.

During those days, my greatest joy was to visit Komako and her daughter Sayoko at their home. They were living in a rear tenement in the Minatogawa Shinkaichi district. I do not remember her husband Gensuke well, so he must have died sometime before. Komako was always at home doing piecework and the like, and Sayoko worked as a hostess at a cinema in Shinkaichi.

In the official family registry, Komako and I were brother and sister. But as she and Sayoko both knew, we were, in fact, no such thing, and there were no bonds of blood between us. But back then, Komako did not know my true parentage.

If she had known, then what happened next never would have been allowed.

As I said, my only joy in those days was to visit Komako and Sayoko at their home. For me, what I felt there was the closest

I could ever come to enjoying the warmth of a loving family, something I'd never had as a child. Both women held some sympathy for my lot in life and welcomed me with kindness whenever I visited.

Then came the summer of my twentieth year. The trading company had a celebration, and the liquor flowed. I had never tried strong drink before, but the others all kept pushing strong spirits on me, and I got terribly drunk. I wandered over to Komako's house.

The heat of summer and the influence of drink meant I was pouring with sweat. When they saw me in that state, Komako and Sayoko set up a washtub in the garden for a cold bath. I was happy to cool down in it, but then… Sayoko shrieked with laughter and said, "Look! What's that strange mark on Haruo's back!"

I, of course, already knew about it. The birthmark usually faded into the skin around it, making it nearly invisible, but after a hot bath, or when I was otherwise hot and sweaty, it stood out clearly. When I was sitting with them later over tea, how could I have known that Komako's dark mood had anything to do with my birthmark?

She knew, though. She knew that the man who had raped her, who had impregnated her with Sayoko, had that same birthmark. Later, I learned that Komako began to suspect the truth of my parentage that day. At some point, she visited Tatsugoro in Itayado to question him about it. He finally relented and told her the truth, it seems, and then, naturally, she started avoiding me. She surely noticed that Sayoko and I were growing closer, that our feelings were deepening, and as they did so, she started to fear me. She grew cold, distant and snappish.

I misunderstood her feelings, and I raged at her.

I thought that she had decided I was an unfit partner for Sayoko because of my unknown parentage. But then, wasn't her daughter in the same position? In fact, I said as much to Komako's face.

Oh, if only she had told me then what she knew!

But no matter how much she tried to keep Sayoko and me apart, there came a time when all her efforts had to end. Sayoko was conscripted to work at the Kawasaki shipyards, and Komako was driven alone from her home when the city was put under forced evacuation.

That was the spring of 1944. Finally, I was free to visit Sayoko as I liked, and eventually we began to live as a couple.

I swear, I will offer any oath that my love for Sayoko was true. And I will swear that Sayoko loved me as well.

She and I had similar backgrounds. She did not know her father. The shadow of that gave depth to her beauty, and even at times of joy, her eyes held a touch of melancholy. That, more than anything, is what captured my heart, and I think she would have said the same of me.

When we did finally step across that final line, it was because I wanted to leave something physical of myself with her, some impression of me that would last once I was inevitably sent off to the army, and she wanted it as well. I was, in fact, conscripted not long after, and when it happened, we promised each other that we would marry if I returned alive.

I will not speak of my time at war. It has nothing to do with my confession.

Then came May 1946. I returned, safely discharged from the army. The first thing I had to do was find out if Sayoko was safe.

I did all I could to find her, eventually even tracking down Tatsugoro's last mistress Otama. That is when I learned that Sayoko was dead. Oh, the shock, the misery of that moment... And soon, that shock and misery transformed into despair and rage beyond words.

Sayoko had taken her own life soon after I left. And she was pregnant when she did. Pregnant with my child. Why did she have to do it? When she held our child in her womb?

Otama did not know. She told me that if anyone did know, it would be Komako, who had become a nun and moved to Awaji. She told me where to find her, and so I went to Awaji.

When I appeared so suddenly like that, Komako's surprise and fear were extraordinary. Her reaction only fuelled my rage. She bent to my demands and revealed everything. Every sordid truth.

There, in that dark retreat in the Awaji countryside, Komako in her nun's habit shared the abominable secret behind my birth, and from that instant I was no longer human. I sold my soul to hell.

Here, then, is Komako's story in brief.

In the summer of 1923, Komako was employed as a maid at Count Tamamushi's villa at the foot of Tsukimiyama hill, outside Kobe city proper. That summer, the count's nephew and niece, Toshihiko and Akiko Shingu, were visiting.

One day, Komako stumbled on brother and sister in the midst of an unforgivable act. And that very same evening, Toshihiko forced himself on Komako. It seems that he believed this would keep her silent about what she had seen.

Toshihiko and Akiko went back to Tokyo early, before the end of that summer, and it was not long before Komako realized she was pregnant. Her father questioned her as to who her partner had been, and finally she revealed who it was.

Naturally, Tatsugoro was not the type to keep such a thing quiet. He went immediately off to Tokyo and laid his case before Count Tamamushi, who offered a pay-out to keep him quiet. Not long after that, the pregnant Komako was married off to her father's apprentice Gensuke.

This means that Komako was not around to know much about the circumstances of how I came to be at Tatsugoro's house. So, she never gave much thought as to who my parents might be.

As I mentioned before, she only realized after that bath. Komako had been forced to scrub Toshihiko's back a few times back in those days at the Tsukimiyama, and she had noticed his odd birthmark then. So, imagine her shock when she saw the same mark on my back that night...

Komako had gone to Tatsugoro the very next day and so learned of my parentage.

In June 1924, Akiko Shingu had given birth to a baby boy in secret at the villa. Count Tamamushi had arranged for the boy to be given over to Tatsugoro as soon as he was born. Neither the count nor his servant Shino said a word about the boy's father, but Tatsugoro knew about Toshihiko and Akiko's shameful secret from his daughter, so he quickly guessed the truth.

Yet, he never told a soul about it, not even his wife Haru. For he had already decided that the secret would set him up for life, and he knew that telling anyone about it would mean the death of his money tree. His fierce guard over the secret, then, had not been out of concern for the good names of the Shingus, but only over his own profit.

Now, imagine Komako's shock on learning this. A boy born of the union between brother and sister was growing close to a young woman who shared his father, a half-sister by a different mother. Oh, despite all she did to stop it, the terrible, unforgivable sin was repeated, generation after generation. When Sayoko learned the terrible truth from her mother, bearing the fruits of that sin in her own womb, she could not live under its weight. Oh, my poor Sayoko!

When I heard this story spill from Komako's mouth in that dark Awaji hut, I went mad. I became a demon, my soul sold to the devil himself. I pledged to get revenge, for Sayoko and for myself.

I think, now, that maybe I should have strangled Komako on the spot. If I had done so, it would have saved much trouble later.

Leaving that aside, that evening I stayed at her hut, then the next morning I left Awaji and headed directly to Tokyo. I began working in the black market, brokering deals and the like, and around that same time when I started looking into the activities of Toshihiko Shingu and Count Tamamushi, I came to know a man by the name of Toyosaburo Iio.

I should probably write about him here. He was a man wholly without a sense of morality. He had no conception of good or evil. I would not say that he was particularly driven towards wickedness, though. He was overall quite amiable, although he was too lazy to be particularly reliable. He was the kind of man who could commit an atrocity like the Tengindo murders and only come to regret it when he saw how great the repercussions were.

Anyway. While I was working as a black-market broker, investigating Toshihiko Shingu, his sister Akiko and Count Tamamushi, I happened to learn that circumstances were so perfect for my plans that it was like someone had arranged them for me. They were all living on the same estate.

When I found that out, I went immediately to meet Viscount Tsubaki. I myself do not particularly understand why I chose him. I didn't know what kind of man he was and certainly had no idea that he would be so useful in helping my plans move forward. All I knew was that I wanted to avoid a rushed frontal assault and hoped to get my revenge through subtle flanking

332

manoeuvres. Perhaps I instinctively realized that Viscount Tsubaki, who had absolutely nothing to do with the secret of my birth yet was now the person closest to my mother, was ideally situated for that.

When I first met him in the drawing room of his great house, my very first reaction was shock at how much he and Toyosaburo Iio resembled each other.

Naturally, if you lined them up side by side, it would be no problem telling them apart. But, seen separately like that, the shape of their faces and the position of their features, and yes, even their somehow worn-out, vague expressions were very similar. At the time, though, I had no thought of using that fact to my advantage.

Since I refused to give him my name at first, the viscount was initially quite suspicious. However, after I told him my story and showed him the birthmark on my back—I made sure to have a few drinks before I did—he was convinced, and terribly shocked. It's likely that the idea of suicide first planted itself in his mind in that instant, even if only subconsciously. That is how deep the look of disgust and despair was that flashed across his face.

Now, having struck my first blow by discussing my parentage, I went on to talk about what had happened after. I told him about my own life, and about Sayoko. When I told him about how our relationship grew, and what happened to her as a result of it, the viscount grew literally as pale as a sheet, and I feared he would faint at any moment.

What truly struck me as strange, though, is that at no point in my story did the viscount offer a single word of resistance, despite the abomination I was describing. As disgusted as he seemed, he never accused me of lying, or claimed the story was too mad to be true. Perhaps he was already half-aware of the unnatural relationship between his wife and her brother.

So, when my story was finished, the viscount simply sat there, a look of pure despair in his eyes.

"And so, what is it you want me to do?" he had asked.

I told him I wanted him to take me into his household. The look of despair turned to one of terror. He asked me what I would do once I was here, and I answered, "I haven't given it much thought. But I don't have anywhere else to go, and it seems like a reasonable request to be allowed to stay where my parents are."

The fear in his eyes only grew greater, unbearably so.

"And... and, if I say no?"

How pitiable he was then. His face was dripping with sweat. His body nearly spasmed with fear. And I was as calm as ever.

"Like I said, I haven't thought about it much, but I suppose my first idea would be to go to a newspaper. I have heard that some pay good money for stories like this..."

I believe that last might have been what truly killed the viscount.

In the end, we agreed that I would move into the estate in the guise of Viscount Tsubaki's assistant, but in exchange, I would not tell a soul anything of my story as long as the man drew breath. I also promised I would make no move against the three in that time. And, as you can see, I have kept my word.

It was, of course, the viscount's idea for me to take the name Totaro Mishima. Since I still had a western Japan accent, he chose the name of the son of a friend from Okayama, now dead.

The misery Viscount Tsubaki experienced from that day forward was painful even for me to watch. It must have truly disgusted the delicate man to live under the same roof as such a wife and brother-in-law. And with the child of their sin right there before his eyes, smiling and laughing! I suppose it was only natural for such a timid, quiet little man to soon find he could not bear to live with it.

It was probably right around then that he started to compose "The Devil Comes and Plays His Flute". The fact of its composition shows that he had already decided to die. For the piece itself clearly indicates the identity of the devil.

Now we come to Viscount Tsubaki's fateful trip of 14th to 17th January. I, of course, knew exactly where he had gone because he had asked me how to find Komako, now living as the nun Myokai. I assumed that, after all his misery, he had decided to check my story.

And then, in a twist of fate, the Tengindo murders happened while he was gone.

I never would have dreamed that Toyosaburo Iio was behind the incident, but then the photo composites started circulating, and when I saw them, I knew at once. In February, I saw a newspaper article saying he had been picked up for questioning as a suspect. I stumbled then on the idea for a nasty little trick.

I sent a tip-off letter to the police claiming that Viscount Tsubaki was the Tengindo murderer.

I'm not sure myself why I did it. It certainly wasn't to rescue Toyosaburo Iio. I hadn't been in contact with him since I moved. He didn't know where I was.

All I can assume is that I was driven to it by the brutal, vicious blood in my veins that I inherited from my father Toshihiko Shingu.

I had been watching that man closely since I moved into this house, and of all his many bad qualities, the one that seemed most defining was his base brutality. The one thing that gave Toshihiko the most pleasure was tormenting those weaker than himself. For example, he was terrified of dogs. If he saw one on the street, he would go dozens of yards out of his way to avoid it. But if he saw a dog on a tight leash, he couldn't help but torment it. I myself once saw Toshihiko appallingly brutalize a poor dog that had been chained up. Even someone who isn't a particular fan of dogs would, on seeing him like that, hope that the chain would break so the dog could savage the man to death.

For me, Viscount Tsubaki at that time was like a dog chained by his own family name. No matter what I did, he could not bite me. I imagine that he knew I had sent the tip-off, but he could say nothing. For I had in my hands an unbeatable trump card.

The viscount spent a while locked up, then finally offered his alibi, and was released. But at the same time, or just before, so was Toyosaburo Iio.

Not long after the viscount vanished, I secretly visited Iio.

He was living in a shantytown hut in some burnt-out ruins near Shinbashi. Despite his living conditions, though, he kept himself neat and dressed elegantly. His neighbours called him "sir", with some admiration. It seemed they did have suspicions about where his money was coming from, but I—having had a few encounters with the man before—knew exactly how he could afford it. It was his exquisite dress and unflappable demeanour that made him such a successful criminal. At heart, nothing really touched his nerves. He could lie without a second thought, and cheat everyone around him without the slightest qualm.

Even Iio, though, seemed somewhat put out when I showed up to see him. When I congratulated him on his narrow escape from the police in the Tengindo case, he gave a thin smile, but I could see the anxiety in his eyes. I left him soon after, satisfied with the day's work.

Later, he confessed to me that I was the only person he'd ever met who he disliked on first sight. He said that it seemed like some dark, shimmering aura was seeping from my body, and it both frightened and attracted him. Iio said that when I showed up, he knew that he was finished.

Leaving all that aside, though, I had no trouble finding the goods. I was well aware of an odd little habit of his. Whenever he got his hands on something important, he always buried it somewhere. He was like a puppy that finds a biscuit and hides it the grass near a rubbish tip. I even knew that his preferred hiding place was in the Zojoji temple grounds.

So, what did Iio do with the goods he'd got from the Tengindo murders? No matter how morally bereft he might be, he wouldn't be in a big hurry to try and move the jewels after all the fuss the murders had raised. I reasoned everything must still be buried somewhere on those temple grounds.

So, I decided to keep tight watch over Zojoji for a time, and it turned out I didn't have to do it for long. Iio came to the temple on the evening of the third day after my visit. It must have really shaken him when I showed up like that, and he got nervous about the goods. He went to dig everything up and move it somewhere else, but that's when I grabbed him. I'd caught him red-handed. Not even Iio, as sly as he was, could talk his way out of that. Still, I was surprised at how quickly he confessed to everything. We made a deal. I would take the stolen goods off his hands, and in return I would send him some money every month. And with that, he was mine.

At the time, I didn't have a clear idea of what I would use him for. One thing I did know was that having such absolute control over a man so closely resembling Viscount Tsubaki would surely be useful someday. That is how I came to have both of them completely within my power.

It was right around then that the viscount disappeared, though. My first thought was that he'd gone somewhere to take his own life, but my greatest fear was that he would leave behind a record of what I was doing before he did. Luckily, there was nothing at the house, but I was still worried he might have it with him. That is why, when his body was found, I volunteered to go with Toshihiko Shingu, Mineko and Kazuhiko to claim the remains.

Once more, I was lucky. There was no note or such in his effects. The closest thing was a notebook in his pocket. It must have been the very limit of his nerves to draw that *kaendaiko* shape and label it "the devil's mark". For him, as shy, delicate and reserved as he was, it must have been simply too much to speak or even write about the terrible story I had told him.

I think it was around that time that a vague plan began to take shape in my mind. Could I use the viscount's suicide and Toyosaburo Iio's resemblance to him in some way? And so, when we came back from Mount Kirigamine and Lady Akiko, my mother, asked me about the body, I very carefully answered that it had looked like Viscount Tsubaki, but also that it somehow didn't.

Dear Mineko, you know better than anyone how suggestible your mother was. The viscount's disappearance had already been terribly frightening for her in a whole other sense, so she was immediately swayed by what my answer implied. After that, I took every opportunity I could to hint that he might still be alive, and soon she was completely consumed by the delusion.

I let the idea gain momentum, until finally I was ready to take the first step of my plan. I doubt there is any need to say it outright, but that was to dress Iio as the viscount and let Akiko see him somewhere. As I said, the two men were not truly identical. If you lined them up together, you would have no trouble telling them apart. However, it had been over six months since the viscount had vanished. I doubted it would be that difficult to trick Akiko, what with his overall resemblance. I tried it out first at the Togeki theatre. I think you know how well it worked.

With that first shock still fresh in everyone's mind, I proceeded with the next step in my plan. As you might have guessed, that was the incident on the night of the divination. However, and let me state this as clearly as I can, I had absolutely no intention of killing Count Tamamushi that evening.

Now I know it seems that I wanted him and my parents dead from the start. The fact is, I can't really say for sure what it was that I wanted. I don't think I was truly set on that course at first. I did, indeed, want my revenge for all the pain they caused. I was determined to make them suffer and ready to be as brutal as needed to make that happen. But in truth, I had not really thought about killing them.

I think it was being in this house that eventually turned my desires towards murder. There was something about the warped atmosphere surrounding Toshihiko Shingu, Akiko Tsubaki and Kimimaru Tamamushi that would have given even someone who didn't know the secrets of their past or their true relationship a sense of something disgusting, something filthy. It was that aura around them that drove Viscount Tsubaki to suicide and me to murder. But I have no desire to try to defend my actions.

Anyway. My plan that night was simply to confront those three with the shape of the *kaendaiko* and the viscount's final melody.

I imagine that Kosuke Kindaichi has figured it all out, but I will write it down here for the record.

Not long before, I had stumbled on the missing Fujin statue in a pile of dead leaves, and I had carved that mark in the base. I had exchanged it with the Raijin statue in the divination room in advance, hiding the Raijin inside a flower vase standing just outside the door.

A close look would quickly reveal the change, but the room was dark, and no one was paying much attention to it anyway. That part went off without a hitch. When the emergency lantern went out, I stamped the sand with the Fujin statue. Then, when the electricity came back on and everyone was thrown into shock by the music, I planned to exchange the statues again.

But of course, Kindaichi's damned hat got caught on the vase's mouth so I couldn't get the statue out. When I tried to force it, the hat seemed ready to tear. And then everyone came back, so I gave up on the switch for the time being.

At the time, I had no idea who Kosuke Kindaichi was, but when I saw him struggling with the vase to get his hat, I broke out in a cold sweat. It set the vase rocking, and I could hear the Raijin statue thumping around in it. Thinking back on it now, I know that he must have noticed something.

At any rate, I knew that I had to switch those statues that evening. I waited until everyone had gone to bed, then snuck to the studio. The door was closed, and the lights were off. I was certain that Tamamushi had gone to bed, so I took the Raijin statue from the vase and opened the door. The curtain inside was closed, and when I ducked through it, suddenly the lights came on and a sharp voice cried out, "Who's there?!"

What a shock! Tamamushi was still there! I froze still as a statue in shock, and so did he.

We stood silently glaring at each other, but when Tamamushi noticed the Raijin statue in my hands, he turned around to look at the Fujin statue behind him. He was a sharp-eyed and clever man, and he must have seen through my *kaendaiko* trick immediately. He lifted up the Fujin to look at its base, so I raised the Raijin and ran at him. My feeling in that moment was the same as when I had been ordered on a desperate charge at the enemy during the war. I was driven by unspeakable hate and resentment.

340

Dear Mineko, you know the state of that room. Tamamushi's wounds were honestly not that serious, but the first blow took him in the face, which set his nose bleeding much more than any of his more serious injuries.

I pushed him down onto the sand and lifted the statue to strike again, but below me the man grunted out a question, asking me who I was. I leaned down close to whisper in his ear exactly who I was. And that is when I defeated him.

Just as Viscount Tsubaki had, Count Tamamushi shrivelled up like a salted slug when he heard the truth. There was no more need for violence at that point. That man, who more than any other valued his name and reputation, would never call for help or tell the police and risk the dirty truth getting out.

And so, we came to an agreement. I would keep the secret of my birth, and he would assure my future.

In that moment, if it had not been for a murderous gleam I saw in the old count's eyes, I might have been satisfied. I might have left that house and the terrible murderous impulse growing within me might have faded. But, when our negotiation was over, I walked to the door. I turned once, to say some meaningless thing, and saw in the old man's eyes a look of pure, violent hatred.

Ah, I thought. *Right now, old Count Tamamushi is filled with an even greater will to kill than I am.* I knew well what kind of man he was. He would, and could, do anything he put his mind to. He would never hesitate to have me killed. And since no one knew the secret of my birth, there would be no reason to suspect him if I did end up murdered. That decided it. And so it was that my murderous impulse, which had thus far been only a vague sense of rage, took on a clear shape.

I left the room, and I heard Tamamushi close and bar the door from the inside, then draw the curtains. I assume that he wanted time to think of an excuse to tell his woman Kikue and the others to explain his wounds.

I got an idea, then moved the vase stand over by the door so I could climb up and look through the *ranma* window.

(Author's note: This next section is more or less the same as Kosuke Kindaichi's explanation, so I will cut it short.)

It should be clear, then, that killing Kimimaru Tamamushi was not on the programme for that night. If I had planned it from the start, then I don't think I would have had Toyosaburo Iio wander around the estate like that.

My somewhat childish idea at the time was to use the *kaen-daiko* mark and the music to create panic in the house, especially in Akiko, and then have her once more see that vision of "Viscount Tsubaki" to cap off the growing terror.

It would have been far too risky to plan a murder with Iio around. He'd have sniffed it out for sure, and if the police caught him, I knew he'd have spilled everything. As it is, I'm sure he suspected me right away when he heard about the murder. That fact alone should convince you that it was spontaneous.

And in fact, so was Toshihiko Shingu's.

I had actually started to plan his death after Count Tamamushi's, and indeed I had already set the stone rolling downhill. I knew that if nothing happened to stop it, it would end in blood. What I did not know, though, was when it would be.

That evening, I came home much earlier than everyone else believed. As was my habit on such occasions, I snuck in through a gap in the garden wall. It helped me avoid the unpleasant gazes of the policemen keeping watch. The path to the servants' entrance leads through a spot offering a distant view into

Lady Akiko's room. By chance, I glanced that way and happened to see Toshihiko Shingu looking warily around as he shut her sliding door. Then the lights in the room went out.

I will refrain from writing down what happened after that, but it is the reason I can call him a monster with such confidence. My heart grew so full of hate it nearly burst.

I watched as the man went on to weasel the ring from my mother's finger, then when he came outside I dragged him into the hothouse. Disgraceful beast that he was, he still went pale and meek when he realized his shameful deeds had been discovered. I forced him to listen to my story, and afterward, as he stood there with that idiot look on his face, I beat him to the ground with the Fujin statue I had hidden there. He fell after a single blow and started crying like a child. I climbed atop him and strangled him in a fury.

Just as with Count Tamamushi, I felt not a shred of remorse after I killed Toshihiko Shingu. Indeed, I felt a sense of relief, as if I'd rid the world of a harmful pest. I almost regret not giving him an even more painful end.

The things that happened later fall outside the scope of my own confession, but one thing that I do feel some remorse for is Komako. If I had known my chance to kill Shingu would come so quickly, there would have been no need to kill her. I sent Toyosaburo Iio to silence her because I feared that if anyone learned my secret too early, I would lose my chance to murder Shingu.

I also took care of Iio. I suppose that someone will eventually find his corpse on the temple grounds and that the police will identify him. I have made the preparations for Mother's death. The stone set rolling so long ago will soon come to rest.

The only one left in this terrible affair is me, and I do wonder what will become of me. Will they catch me and hang me on the gallows? Or will I take my own life first? I do not care either way. I will die soon, one way or the other.

But mark this, Mineko…

You must live. I am sure it will be hard to go on after learning these terrible truths. I think you can endure, though. Kazuhiko, I fear you aren't very strong, but I hope that Lady Hanako will be there to support you. But… I suppose that's not something that a devil would say.

Goodbye, Mineko.

Goodbye, Kazuhiko.

CHAPTER 30

A Farewell on the Devil's Flute

The final confession of Totaro Mishima, or rather Haruo Kawamura, was discovered a few days after everything was finished. There were five people there for the reading of it: Mineko, Kazuhiko, the widowed Hanako, and of course Kosuke Kindaichi and Chief Inspector Todoroki.

There in that drawing room, now so filled with memories, Mineko read it aloud to the others.

Mineko, Kazuhiko and Hanako all endured the gruesome story to its end but could not help exchanging looks of horror and surprise when it reached the part relating Toshihiko Shingu's despicable behaviour just before his death. Hanako was so hurt that she broke into anguished sobs.

Todoroki could not help but sigh.

"Kindaichi-san, did you know about that?"

He sighed, as well.

"I wouldn't say I knew, but… Let's say I had my suspicions. When I heard about Doctor Mega's outburst later that night, well…" Kindaichi stopped and cleared his throat. "No, no, forgive me. We should see this through now. Mineko-san, do you think you can continue?"

"Yes, let's go on." Her strength of will shone in her eyes.

When Mineko had finished reading the long, terrible record, the room fell silent for a good long while. Hanako occasionally broke into tremors and sobbed as memories welled up. Kazuhiko simply sat on the sofa with his face buried in his hands.

Mineko sat down beside him and laid a gentle hand on his shoulder.

"Kazuhiko-san, don't let yourself dwell too much on it. Your father did terrible things, but your mother is a wonderful person. And they say that boys inherit much more from their mothers, you know, while girls inherit more from their fathers. I am glad I am a girl and have more of my father's blood than my mother's. He might have been weak, but he was a proper, kind man. I think you would agree, wouldn't you, Kazuhiko-san?"

He nodded fiercely. His face was still hidden in his hands. Tears dripped from between his fingers to splash on the floor.

"Thank you. Let's put an end to tears. You, too, aunt Hanako. Now, you are all we have."

"Forgive me, Mineko-san."

"Let's get rid of this house as quickly as we can. Then we can all live together somewhere bright and sunny, even if it ends up being some cramped little house, and wash away the dark shadows that have seeped into us."

Mineko then turned to Kindaichi.

"It seems everything is finished now, Kindaichi-san, but there is still one thing I would like to ask you."

"What is it?"

"How did you figure it out? That my mother... and uncle..."

Kindaichi thought for a moment of trying to change the subject, but when he saw the resolute look in her eyes, he could not deny her. The young woman was determined to know everything.

"Well, Mineko-san, it was the book your father put his note in. *Wilhelm Meister's Apprenticeship.*"

"The book? Oh!" She stared in surprise.

"Yes, I think maybe you see now. It includes a story about a brother and sister who unknowingly fall in love and have a

346

child, but the three are then destined for unhappiness. When I thought about the type of man your father was, I realized everything that he said and did in those days had a hidden meaning. So, his recommendation of the book to you must also have meant something. I read it myself and then stumbled on that rather shocking romance. Along with some other clues, I came to believe that Totaro Mishima, that is Haruo Kawamura, was not only a brother to Kazuhiko but to you as well. But I think we have talked enough about that."

"Yes, we have. Thank you, Kindaichi-san."

Strangely enough after learning of these terrible dark secrets, that dark shimmering shadow that had wrapped around her when she first came to visit Kindaichi had vanished.

But what became of Haruo Kawamura, who had lived as Totaro Mishima?

To tell of that, let us return to the ending of Chapter 28, "The *Kaendaiko* Reappears", which I intentionally left unfinished.

After Mishima confessed to his crimes, he turned to Kazuhiko and said, "Kazuhiko, could you open the suitcase at the bottom of that stack? You should find the golden flute in there."

Kazuhiko glanced at Kindaichi and Todoroki for approval, then did as Mishima had asked. He pulled out the golden flute.

Mishima took the flute and removed his glove.

"Kindaichi-san," he said, turning to him, "Why didn't you ask someone, like Kazuhiko here, to play 'The Devil Comes and Plays His Flute' for you? If you had watched someone perform it, then I think you would have seen in an instant who Viscount Tsubaki had meant as the devil. I'll do it now. Watch my fingers closely."

Mishima put his mouth to the flute and played that terrible music.

It was perhaps the ideal accompaniment to close the curtain on this tragedy that had rocked their world to its core.

The gloomy drawing room was filled with a melody dripping with resentment and madness, and as it grew louder and faster, the listeners could not help but feel that it was truly the voice of a demonic spirit, more horrifying than even the blood-drenched corpses that they had seen.

Kindaichi alone found his heart racing for another reason, though. As the music proceeded past its fierce crescendo to the final bars, he saw that Mishima had not needed his missing middle and ring fingers for a single note.

A shock ran through him, as if his brain had been pierced by a red-hot poker.

"The Devil Comes and Plays His Flute" had been written so that it did not need those two fingers of the right hand, and that is how Viscount Tsubaki had shown the world who the devil was.

Just as Kindaichi was about to speak out, Totaro Mishima fell to the ground like a rotted tree, the flute still held to his lips. He had taken his life with the same poison that his partner Toyosaburo Iio had used in the Tengindo murders.

And so, the devil that had swooped down on the Tsubaki house played his flute one final time, then left this world for good.

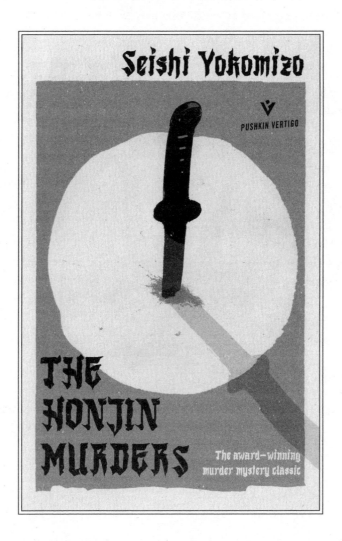

Seishi Yokomizo

A classic Japanese
murder mystery

THE INUGAMI CURSE

PUSHKIN VERTIGO

Seishi Yokomizo

A classic Japanese murder mystery from the author of *The Honjin Murders*

THE
VILLAGE OF
EIGHT GRAVES

PUSHKIN VERTIGO

Seishi Yokomizo

A classic Japanese murder mystery from
the author of *The Honjin Murders*

DEATH ON GOKUMON ISLAND

PUSHKIN VERTIGO